PRUSSIAN BLUE

TOM HYMAN

PRUSSIAN BLUE

VIKING

VIKING
Published by the Penguin Group
Viking Penguin, a division of Penguin Books USA Inc.,
375 Hudson Street, New York, New York 10014, U.S.A.
Penguin Books Ltd, 27 Wrights Lane, London W8 5TZ, England
Penguin Books Australia Ltd, Ringwood, Victoria, Australia
Penguin Books Canada Ltd, 2801 John Street,
Markham, Ontario, Canada L3R 1B4
Penguin Books (N.Z.) Ltd, 182–190 Wairau Road,
Auckland 10, New Zealand

Penguin Books Ltd, Registered Offices:
Harmondsworth, Middlesex, England

First published in 1991 by Viking Penguin,
a division of Penguin Books USA Inc.

10 9 8 7 6 5 4 3 2 1

Publisher's Note: This is a work of fiction. Names, characters, places, and incidents either are the product of the author's imagination or are used fictitiously, and any resemblance to actual persons, living or dead, events, or locales is entirely coincidental.

LIBRARY OF CONGRESS CATALOGING-IN-PUBLICATION DATA
Hyman, Vernon Tom.
    Prussian blue / Tom Hyman.
        p.   cm.
    ISBN 0-670-82996-X
    I. Title.
PS3558.Y49P78   1991
813'.54—dc20   90-50397

Printed in the United States of America
Set in Simoncini Garamond
Designed by Fritz Metsch

TO IAN

CONTENTS

PRUSSIAN BLUE

THE WOMAN IN THE RED BRA

Something woke me.

It was an awful noise, cataclysmic and earthshaking, like a collision of planets or an explosion of the sun.

I opened my eyes and held my breath. I felt disoriented, fearful.

I heard familiar sounds—the buglike buzz of my bedside clock, the rattling hum of the kitchen refrigerator, the intermittent plop of water from a bathroom faucet and the faint background rumble of traffic on Central Park West, fifteen stories below.

A thin, high-pitched electronic squeal from the direction of my study told me that my answering machine was just turning itself off.

I sighed. I was alive and home in my own bed, lying facedown, with my legs entangled in the covers and my hands clutching the brass rails of the headboard. The pillowcase reeked of sweat and perfume.

The apocalyptic thunder that had jolted me from sleep must have been the telephone.

I groaned, lifted my head from the pillow with extreme caution, started to reach for my eyeglasses on the night table and discovered that I couldn't move my right arm.

It was attached to something.

I rotated my eyes gingerly up toward the headboard and saw that my wrist was bound to the brass corner post with a sturdy strip of plastic. I tested my other arm. It moved freely.

I lowered my head back onto the pillow and made a pathetic effort to think. I had no recollection of anyone doing this to me. But then I couldn't remember going to bed, either.

I twisted around onto my side, brought my legs up, swung them onto the floor and pulled myself to a sitting position. I reached my eyeglasses, finally, with my left hand, slipped them clumsily over my ears and focused on the clock's dial. It was 7:32 A.M.

I examined my right wrist. The bracelet of plastic cord that held it lashed to the bedpost was a larger version of those little laddered loops of white plastic you encountered in places like K Mart and Sears, roped through the eyelets of pairs of sneakers. One end of the laddered strip slipped through a little loop on the other end. It was designed so that once the end was pulled through, it couldn't be pulled back. The only way to remove the damned thing was to cut it off.

I tugged at the strip. The headboard jiggled noisily. I squeezed two fingers of my other hand between the plastic and my wrist and tried to stretch it. It started to slice into my skin.

I sat there, feeling so helpless and stupid that it brought tears to my eyes. How could I be caught in such an idiotic predicament?

I looked around me. The murky twilight of the bedroom was broken by a few narrow shafts of sunlight squeezing past the window shades. I stretched around, managed to get my fingers on the night-table lamp and switched it on.

Last night's clothes littered the floor. On the carpet near the bed an uncorked green bottle rested on its side. The area around it was wet and smelled of fermented grape. I bent down, gagged against a sudden throatward welling of nausea, got a grip on the bottle and stood it upright on the night table.

I opened the night-table drawer and rummaged through it. Near the back, under a pile of old credit-card slips and discarded key chains, I found a small sewing kit I had acquired years ago for emergency button repairs. It contained a tiny pair of scissors designed to cut thread.

For some minutes I scissored and squeezed in vain at the plastic cord with this toy implement, cheering myself on with a stream of profanity. Finally, after a ferocious effort, I hacked my way through it.

Freed from the bedpost, I threw the scissors and the kit back into the drawer and banged it shut with the edge of my fist.

I pressed my palms against the sides of my head and closed my eyes. My mouth was dry and I could barely move my jaws. I ached profoundly, especially around the head, the stomach and the groin. I touched an elbow. It was raw and bloody. So was the other one. So were my knees.

I pulled back the blanket and top sheet. Something lay in the middle of the bed. It was wrinkled and crushed flat, like a pressed flower in a book. I had been sleeping on it. I lifted it with a forefinger and examined it more closely.

It was a red bra—a flimsy, small-cupped affair, trimmed with black lace and scented with a musky perfume.

I glanced around the room again. No sign of the bra's wearer. The bathroom door was ajar, and the light was out. Down the hallway the kitchen, study and living room were dark and silent.

I tried to spoon the bra owner's name up out of the opaque stew of my memory, but came up empty. Discouraging. Remembering names was something in which I took some pride. It was one of the special little skills that I fancied separated me from the common journalistic herd.

I thumbed mentally through the alphabet, pausing at each letter to find the one that would trigger that little pulse of recognition in my brain cells. Again nothing. How could I not remember? I could visualize her perfectly in my mind's eye. I could recollect precisely the timbre of her voice, could catalogue her entire repertoire of facial expressions, physical gestures and habits of speech.

I barely knew her, yet I was already feeling withdrawal symptoms from her absence. She had appeared at a large party thrown the week before by *Tomorrow* magazine to celebrate its fifteenth year. We met. She was friendly. I asked her out. Last night was our first date. What the hell was her name? Had I also suffered brain damage during the night?

The telephone rang again.

I swung around and planted my feet on the carpet, careful to avoid the still-damp stain of wine. Maybe she—name still missing—was calling to explain why she had tied me to the bed and disappeared. And to inquire about her bra. I stepped to the window, pushed apart a couple of slats on the blind and peeked out at the day. Beyond the looming penthouse water-tank tower across the street the sky was a dirty gray. Rain was on the way.

The weather. Her name had something to do with weather.

The answering machine in the study clunked once more into action, offering up my recorded message.

Sun, moon, wind, rain. Thunder, lightning, tornado, hurricane. Cyclone. Gale. Gale. Gail Somebody? Gail Storm? Gail Force? Gail Warning?

Gail Snow.

My brain cells were beginning to dry out.

Gail Snow: Twenty-seven and unmarried. An A.B. in history from Stanford. Currently employed as a researcher at *Newsweek*. Her parents lived in Glen Cove, she lived in the Village, 774 West Eleventh Street. Five-six, a hundred twenty pounds, blond hair cut short, small perfect breasts, dimpled cheeks, satiny-smooth skin decorated with a few discrete freckles, and large, unusually transparent blue-gray eyes. And exceptional legs—her best feature, in her own estimation. In my estimation she was exceptional all the way around. She conveyed a careless, almost arrogant, sensuality that transfixed me.

I have to confess, however, that I am easily transfixed. I can find something attractive in almost any woman. And frequently do. Immoderate amounts of my time and money have been spent pursuing females I should never have shown any interest in, in the first place. But we seldom do what we should do in life.

The women with whom I have had serious relationships—and I count five or seven, depending on how strictly one defines "serious"—have all been mistakes, each in her own unique way. My failures haven't discouraged me, but they have made me wonder sometimes why what I like and what might work for me seem to have so little in common.

Little bits of dumb dialogue from the previous evening, not yet swept away out of sight into my unconscious, started surfacing. It seemed that she had asked all the questions, and I had given all the answers. I had rambled on for hours about everything—my past, my profession, my current projects, my opinion of world leaders, the state of civilization and the environment, and my predictions for the future—my own and mankind's. What a fucking bore I must have been. But she had seemed fascinated; had searched my face with those blue-gray eyes as if the wisdom I imparted was transforming her entire outlook on life even as I spoke. Finally, unable to resist the onslaught of wit and insight any longer, she had pulled off her clothes and pulled me down on top of her.

She had told me almost nothing about herself. The facts enumerated a couple of paragraphs back just about cover what I learned of her. My own fault, of course.

I staggered down the hallway toward the study, bracing myself at intervals against the wall.

"John? Hello, John . . . is that you? Are you home? Hello? I guess you're not home. . . . Ahh, this is Whit Atherton, John. Calling you. Can you drop by my office today? I know it's short notice, but it's rather important. . . . It's about, uh, what you're working on. You know, the Carlson . . . the Carlson project. Please call me back when you get this message. . . . Well, thank you . . . that's all, I guess. . . . Yes, that is all. . . . Good-bye."

The answering machine clunked off.

I rubbed my head. S. Whitney Atherton, millionaire, raconteur, intimate of the great and powerful of the earth and chief executive officer of the conglomerate that published my books, reduced to an inarticulate boob by an answering machine. It was possible he had never heard one before. He kept two editorial assistants, one personal secretary and a wife. They normally placed and screened all his calls for him.

What could be so important that Atherton would call me—himself—at seven-thirty in the morning? I had rarely spoken to him. He delegated everything to his office staff and was seldom in town. Or even in the country.

I dragged the desk calendar toward me. I flipped over the pages for Saturday and Sunday and stopped at Monday. A day's work was penciled in. For nine-thirty, I had printed out in large letters the name "Admiral Bobby Conover" and underlined it twice in red with an exclamation mark. It had taken me months of wheedling and cajoling and begging to arrange this meeting. Conover was a former deputy director of plans for the CIA, and a vital source for my book. If Conover felt as garrulous as I hoped, the interview would take up the entire morning. At twelve-thirty I was having lunch with my agent, Matilda Bauer, and a producer who claimed interest in buying the movie rights to my last book. At three o'clock I was catching the shuttle to Washington to talk to an obscure figure in the Pentagon's Special Operations Division who had had some dealings with my subject in the past.

I dialed Atherton's number. No answer.

I hung up and squinted down at the answering machine's message counter. Three other messages, besides Atherton. This surprised me. It meant that the telephone had rung four times on three different occasions during the night and I had not heard it once. I punched the machine's PLAY button and waited for the tape to rewind and play back.

The first message was from a former wife:

"This is Gloria, Johnny. It's late at night, on May the . . . May something. Twelfth? Arturo says the thirteenth. . . . I'm a little high, to tell you the truth. [Laughter.] *Arturo says I'm a lot high. Anyway, this is my message. I hate to bug you again, but if there isn't a check in the mail to me* today, *motherfucker, you'll hear from my* abogado. *That's Mexican for lawyer. I'm calling from San Miguel, so this is costing me* mucho dinero. . . . *Hey, Johnny, you should come visit. Really. We could all get it on together. Think about it. The sex is better down here. Really. They say it's the high altitude. It's like a lungful of grass and poppers at the same time. 'Bye, Johnny. Peace."*

Having fucked and ingested drugs in many climates, Gloria would certainly know.

I had been married to Gloria for one year and divorced from her for fifteen, and she was still collecting alimony from me. She shared a house in Mexico with a changing cast of sixties dropouts. My alimony checks were supporting most of them.

Dear flower child Gloria—almost forty years old and still wondering where the Woodstock Nation went. She had an IQ in the high 150s, and was still reasonably attractive. How was it she could never find gainful employment? Or at least someone else to take care of her?

I anticipated supporting her—or neglecting to support her—for the rest of my life. Some lessons I learned the hard way. It took me a whole year living with Gloria to realize that her emotional and intellectual development had been permanently arrested by Abbie Hoffman and Timothy Leary. Not that I blamed them personally.

Gloria was one of my earlier failures. I seemed prone to fall into high-risk relationships. My second wife, Alicia, claimed that I was attracted to the wrong qualities in women—emotional instability, short-temperedness, cheap flirtatiousness. Mature and sensible women scared me, she said.

Well, that was her opinion. There was probably some validity to it, certainly during the two years we were married, but Alicia was also an impossible snob.

Friends, including Alicia, inevitably cited Tracy Anderson as the chief evidence against me. That was understandable. Tracy was capable of permanently warping anyone's judgment. I could have had a dozen sensible affairs and two great marriages and they wouldn't have begun to counter the impression left by Tracy Anderson. Now there was truly a triumph of romance over reality. Of emotion over common sense. Yet it had lasted, in its own peculiar manner, for many years. It was masochistic and absurd, but what would I have been without it?

The second message on the tape was from Admiral Bobby Conover:

"Listen, old chap, can we make our rendezvous today a tiny bit earlier? Say nine o'clock? I've got a plane to catch at ten-thirty. Come on out to the TWA Ambassador Club at JFK. See you there, then. Cheerio."

I pulled my hair and uttered a high-pitched squeal. Why was he doing this to me? Race out to JFK for an hour of interview? I needed much more than that. No use getting worked up. I'd have to take whatever I could get. Maybe his flight would be delayed a few hours.

The third message was a minute of silence, terminated by a hang-up. I had been getting these lately. My electronics-genius friend Frank Chin advised me that it was probably just some hacker's computer, auto-dialing its way through the phone book in quest of unlisted data banks. I didn't think so. When I turned the volume up all the way, a background murmur of voices and a tinkle of ice cubes against glass were audible. If it was a computer, it was making its calls from a pay phone in a bar.

I glanced back through the bacchanalian shambles of the apartment. Where was Gail Snow? Running around the streets without her bra. Why did she tie me to the bed and leave? I didn't think it was kinkiness. I wasn't even awake when she did it.

Her idea of a prank?

I stumbled toward the bathroom and cracked my already bruised elbow on the doorjamb. I cradled my arm piteously and moaned out loud. I swallowed three extra-strength acetaminophen tablets, gasped my way through a cold shower and shaved with trembling fingers.

Back in the bedroom, I put on fresh underwear and socks. From the top shelf of the closet I pulled down a thin elastic shoulder harness and holster and strapped it around my chest. I had purchased it some years ago from a private detective during my stint as a reporter for *Time* magazine. The detective had used it to secrete a .32 pistol. I used it to hide a microcassette recorder.

I loaded a blank cassette into the device, tested it, then tucked the tiny machine into place in the holster under my arm.

I buttoned a clean blue shirt over the harness, climbed into a pair of corduroy jeans, and snapped a pen into the shirt's pocket. This particular pen contained a remote microphone and voice-activated transmitter for the recorder under my arm. I could take it out, write with it, place it on the table in front of me, or just leave it in my pocket. It would pick up conversation within a range of ten feet.

It was a breach of journalistic ethics to tape subjects without their knowledge, but pad and pencil weren't always reliable— either for reconstructing what someone had said or for purposes of self-defense if someone tried to sue. In any case, I taped all my interviews this way. Even when a subject consented to the use of a recorder, the hidden device served as a useful backup. And for someone like Admiral Conover, whose elaborate syntax and Byzantine thought patterns were sometimes as difficult to decipher as a Wallace Stevens poem, it was absolutely essential.

I pulled a sweater over the shirt and confronted myself in the full-length mirror on the bedroom door. My pallid face and slumped shoulders made me look more like a propped-up corpse than a journalist. Otherwise, considering my forty-three years of age, irregular sleep habits, abuse of alcohol, indifference to exercise, neglect of my appearance, and a diet high in sugar, starch and cinnamon rolls, I looked more youthful and fit than I had any right to expect. My five-foot-eleven-inch frame was tall and broad enough to hide my soft paunch and flagging muscle tone. My dark-framed glasses hid the bags under my eyes, and my thick, sandy hair had yet to show any inclination to either turn gray or fall out.

I was self-conscious about my pallor. My bone-white, melanin-deficient epidermis was a legacy of my ancestors, from Ireland's cloudy northern climate. Gloria, I remembered, had envied its alabaster smoothness, but it secretly embarrassed me.

I returned to the study to find the ten pages of briefing notes I had assembled on Conover. The pages contained a rough biographical sketch—something I always prepared in advance of an interview—and a long list of questions and subjects to be covered. I looked in all the obvious places in the desk and file cabinets, but I couldn't locate the notes. I looked again. Nothing. I made a thorough search of the study, and then the rest of the apartment, but the ten pages refused to show up.

I booted up my word processor and scanned through the files stored on the hard disk. I had a brief biography of Conover on one file, but no questions. Well, of course I already knew that. I didn't normally enter questions for a interview into a computer file, anyway. I wrote the questions out by hand. Only after I had answers to them did I put anything into the computer. I checked my watch. No more time to look around. I'd just have to go without them.

It was no calamity. I had been thinking about what I wanted to ask Conover for several months. I could use the cab ride to JFK to jot down a fresh set of questions.

Something else was missing, I noticed: the locked tray of floppy disks I kept beside the computer. At first I thought I must have moved it, but another look around the study confirmed that it had disappeared.

The tray contained backup copies of the computer operating

program, my word-processing program, a few video games and about thirty disks that I used to make backup copies of my hard-disk files. About eighteen of those disks were full—some of them with valuable information. All my files were protected by a special access code I used, so they couldn't be opened by anyone unless he knew my password.

At least I believed they couldn't be opened.

I dialed Gail Snow's number. I let it ring a dozen times, hoping at least to hear from an answering machine.

I hung up. I thought of calling her at *Newsweek,* but it was too early.

A thin trickle of anxiety began to leak in somewhere around my breastbone. Tying me to the bedpost might be justified as a prank; making off with six months of research on my next book could not.

I glanced again at my watch: 8:25. And Admiral Conover might not wait.

I'd deal with Gail Snow later.

2
THE LONG WORLD'S GENTLEMAN

The Ambassador Club, a special lounge for members only, was tucked discreetly out of sight of the economy-class waiting areas at the top of a stairway off the main concourse of the TWA terminal. Admiral Bobby Conover was there, waiting nervously inside the door. He was sixty-six, but looked to be in his mid-seventies, possibly older. He ushered me past a reception desk manned by two politely bored females in tan uniforms, across the nearly empty lounge and into the club's ultimate inner sanctum, a small, dimly lit private meeting room with a low round table, six leather lounge chairs, a TV and a telephone.

"Bobby Conover," he announced, with a rhetorical flourish. He clasped my hand with an overly vigorous grip, shook it too long and then waggled a finger energetically toward one of the chairs, as if he were accusing it of naughty behavior. "Please," he demanded. "Sit."

I sat.

"I've ordered a Bloody Mary," Conover said, plumping himself down in a chair across the table from me. "You'll join me?"

The admiral had had several already. He was doing his best to hide it, but his flushed face and poorly modulated speech gave him away.

Was he just fortifying himself against the fear of flying? I understood that phobia well. More likely he was a chronic drinker. I understood that one, too. I had become pretty chronic myself of late. I wrinkled my brow to test for traces of headache. A dull throb at the temples still lingered. "It's a little early," I replied. "But . . . Okay. Sure. What the hell. Thank you."

Conover scraped the telephone toward him with a broad sweep of his hand, punched a couple of buttons and shouted a drink order into the mouthpiece in an imperious tone. The world traveler, I thought, at home in airport VIP lounges around the globe. Was that the admiral's own self-image? He looked more like president of the Has-Beens' Club. The Bloody Marys arrived in fat, smoked-glass tumblers with stalks of celery floating upright in them.

"When the king is weak, the barons are strong," Conover began, without preamble. "The president . . . well, you know about our president. Playboy of the western world, and all that. Really in over his head from day one. He was delegating authority all over the lot, just to stay afloat, so Andy naturally moved in and grabbed what he could. Andy's that sort. Loves power the way others love flesh and money."

The admiral stirred his drink with his celery stalk, looking pleased with the way he had expressed himself. "But no director has ever amassed the kind of power Andy has," he continued. "It's rather astonishing, actually, what he's done—the strength of the position he's achieved. And it's become a bad thing. A dangerous thing."

Conover let his hands thud dramatically onto the armrests of his chair. "Really quite a dangerous thing. I've told Andy as much. But he's not ready to face the consequences. He may never be ready to face the consequences. That's the problem, you see."

I had never heard anyone refer to the director of the CIA, Andrew Carlson, as "Andy." He was too remote and intimidating a figure. Had anyone ever called Charles de Gaulle "Chuck"?

I coughed politely into my fist. "Let's just back up a bit here, can we, Admiral? I frankly don't have any idea what you're talking about."

Conover harrumphed impatiently. "Yes, of course. Andy just wanted to see to it that the CIA was never humiliated again. I think that's been at the bottom of everything. Every time the U.S. screws up internationally, what happens? The politicians all piss in their trousers and then blame the Company for the urine stains. After the Bay of Pigs, what does Kennedy do? Does he blame himself and his advisors? Of course he doesn't. He cans Allen Dulles. When Watergate brings down Nixon, what happens? Congress packs our DCI, Helms, off to prison. Then Carter sends Turner over to kick more CIA butt. No fellow admiral he. I damned near got thrown out during Turner's Halloween massacre myself. A nasty affair that was. I hung on for a time, but I was thoroughly disgusted, I can tell you. Thoroughly disgusted. I took early retirement."

Conover puffed up his cheeks and then let the air out of them in a long, theatrical exhalation. "Since then I've enjoyed my retirement. Been very busy, actually, these past years, doing consulting work. For Andy. We go way back, you know. Way back. OSS in Europe. I'm one of the original Old Boys, in fact. Seen it all, done it all. But I suppose you already know that."

I raised an eyebrow. I didn't know whether to be amused or alarmed. Why was the admiral blabbing on like this? I hadn't yet asked him a question. What he was telling me was both useless and inaccurate. Helms did not go to prison. He was fined. And Conover himself was in fact fired by Turner—or forced to take early retirement, which amounted to the same thing. Minor quibbles, I suppose, but it made me suspect that either Conover's memory was deteriorating or he had things to hide.

"You know Dylan?" Conover asked me.

"Bob Dylan?"

"Dylan Thomas." The admiral raised his glass toward the fluorescent light fixture in the ceiling and, in a deep, portentous voice, intoned a couple of lines of poetry:

> " 'I am the long world's gentleman, he said
> And share my bed with Capricorn and Cancer.'

That's me, my boy—the long world's gentleman."

I nodded. The individual sitting across from me just didn't seem much like the great Admiral Bobby Conover I had read about in my collection of clippings. This version appeared too damned ostentatiously peculiar to have ever been a spy, let alone the head of U.S. Naval Intelligence for ten years and a deputy director of the CIA for eight. On top of his obvious drinking problem, there was a slack, openmouthed, bluff and hearty pretentiousness in his demeanor, a studied indolence that seemed intended to suggest a life-style of expensive, privileged dissipation, spent with all the right people in all the right places. His entire persona seemed consciously manufactured, as if he had gotten himself up for a part in a J. M. Barrie play.

His physical appearance and manner of dress, for example: He was florid-faced and overweight, with watery blue eyes, a mane of carefully barbered snow-white hair that curled over his shirt collar, and a white Guardsman's moustache that bushed out extravagantly under the flared nostrils of a red-veined nose. He was turned out in a paisley ascot, an Irish tweed jacket, yellow socks, hand-stitched cordovan loafers, and cavalry-twill trousers that pinched him so tightly around his bulging middle that he seemed to be in the process of dividing into two separate entities, like a gigantic single-celled organism in the early stages of mitosis. He reeked of lime cologne, which, combined with the alcohol on his breath, made him smell like a vodka gimlet.

Beneath the grand manner and the dandyish attire Admiral Conover appeared ramshackle and worn out. He was a rusty old gas-guzzler hiding under a gaudy new paint job. Despite the jaunty colors, you sensed he didn't have a lot of miles left.

I removed the stalk of celery from my glass and let it plop onto the table. I hated celery, and particularly resented its presence in a Bloody Mary. Since the admiral wasn't giving me much time, I was impatient to shake some useful information out of him. But I hesitated to interrupt him. If he had something important to say, I suspected he would probably say it sooner if I didn't further confuse his thought process.

But the admiral suddenly stopped talking. A far-off, distracted glaze came over his eyes, as if he weren't quite sure where he was or why. He looked disoriented, frightened. Was it just the booze, I wondered, or was Conover losing it altogether?

"What's so bad about it?" I prompted, finally. "The power Andrew Carlson has?"

Conover traced a finger along the bottom edge of his moustache to wipe off the accumulated drops of tomato juice. "My dear boy," he replied, his tone a gentle reprimand. "It's too much power. And it's secret power. Power without accountability. I may be a bit of a right-winger myself—I like things orderly and people in their place—but I still believe in Jeffersonian democracy. Andy's tilting the democratic balance, I'm afraid. I blame it on the president. The president just doesn't pay any attention to what's going on around him. Never has, the damned fool. He's let Andy do just as he pleases, and Andy has taken advantage of it. And so here we are."

I heaved a deep inward sigh. "Where is that, Admiral?"

Conover retracted the stalk of celery from the drink thoughtfully and sucked it into his mouth with a loud slurping noise. "In the shit, my boy. In the shit. Andy's something of a hero now. And a Republican hero, at that. Untouchable, you see. Removing him would be bad form. And more than a little tricky."

"Why tricky?"

"Well, he's become something of a Hoover, hasn't he." Conover phrased the question in the British manner—as a statement of fact with which the listener is assumed to be in agreement.

I smiled. I wasn't sure for an instant whether Conover meant J. Edgar Hoover, or was using the English colloquial term for a vacuum cleaner. "You mean he's got something on everyone?"

"Oh, he has," the admiral confided. "He has indeed. And he can be ruthless. I don't know that he'd go to quite the lengths old J. Edgar did to keep his job, but he really doesn't need to. At the moment there's no one at the White House who has the stomach to tangle with him. Certainly not the president. Andy has him by the short and curlies. You've got my say-so on that. And Andy plans to stay. Intelligence is his life. He thinks he can still accomplish big things."

Conover's information was hardly top secret. A regular reader of the *Times* would know at least as much. "Can he?" I asked idly.

The admiral widened his eyes quizzically. "Can he what?"

"Still accomplish big things."

Conover grimaced in confusion. He didn't seem to be following his own conversation. He shrugged my question off and continued his disjointed ramble, jumping from subject to subject like a man negotiating his way across the rocks in a fast-moving stream. He barely paused for breath. He seemed determined to prevent me from getting in any of my questions. "Do you know the story of Dr. Frankenstein?" he asked me suddenly.

I looked at him stupidly. "Dr. Frankenstein?"

"Well, do you?" the admiral persisted.

"Yes, Admiral, I do."

Conover revealed his long, yellowed canines. "Dr. Frankenstein let his genius outstrip his common sense. He created a monster. This is precisely the case with Andy. He has also created a monster. Not a tangible, flesh-and-blood monster, but a monster all the same."

Conover's analogy startled me. "Carlson's in some kind of trouble? But you just said he has the president in his pocket."

The admiral wet his moustache with his tongue and appraised me thoroughly. "His trouble is not with the president."

"What's the monster you're talking about?"

Conover fixed his attention suddenly on his watch, steadying the dial with thumb and forefinger and tilting his head back to bring the numbers within range of his bifocals. "Good Lord! My plane leaves in ten minutes."

"Where are you headed?"

Conover ignored the question. "You *are* writing a book on Andy, aren't you?"

The question caught me off guard. "No. Well, not exactly."

Conover scowled. "Then what on earth *are* you writing?" he demanded.

"It's on the intelligence community as a whole," I lied, feeling ashamed of myself even as I said it. This was the standard response I gave to anybody who insisted on one. I had already told Conover just that in a letter to him some months ago, when I first requested the interview. But Conover was right. The book was indeed on

Andrew Carlson. An unauthorized biography. It was supposed to be a big secret.

The admiral chuckled conspiratorially. "The intelligence community as a whole," he echoed. "That's very droll, Mr. Brady."

"I still have a lot I'd like to ask you about, Admiral," I said, frustrated that the interview was accomplishing so little. "I was hoping for some worthwhile information from you."

Conover pulled himself up ramrod-straight. "Of course, Mr. Brady. And you shall get it." He reached down beside his chair and came up with a small ripstop-nylon carrying case. He unzipped a compartment and extracted an 8½-×-11 manila envelope.

"This is for you," he said, his tone suddenly matter-of-fact. He slid the envelope across the table. "I suggest you find a very safe place for it."

I picked it up. It was not very bulky. I began bending up the brass clasps on the flap.

"Please open it at home," Conover said.

"What's in it?"

"It will explain itself."

"No hints?"

Conover glanced about nervously. "Obviously it has to do with Andy's monster."

I lifted back the flap and pulled out three sheets of paper, stapled together at the corner. The first page, underneath the legend "Night Watch" typed in at the top, contained two columns of names, single-spaced. The second page looked like a map. I didn't get a chance to see the last page. Conover grabbed my wrist and forced the documents back into the envelope.

"I warn you—don't look at it here," he growled.

" 'Night Watch'?" I asked. "What's that?"

"Young man, I have taken a great deal of personal risk to get this to you." Conover wiped vigorously at his mouth and moustache with a napkin, harrumphed noisily into his fist, and rose to his feet. "I thought you were the one man who might be able to help. I thought you knew more than you do. Now I see that you know scarcely anything. I don't understand why they're bothering with you."

"Bothering with me? Who's bothering with me?"

"You'll find out. Soon enough. You would be damned well advised to forget this business entirely."

"What business?" I demanded.

The admiral was in a great hurry to leave. He retrieved an overnight bag from under the table, tucked his carrying case tightly under his arm, and headed for the door. "The business of Carlson and the Night Watch, of course," he mumbled, casting a quick last glance back at me. "Once you're in it—once you know what it is, what it's done, and what it can do—you'll never be able to get out of it. You've got my word on that."

He pushed the door open and glanced out into the lounge beyond, as if there might be someone there he wished to avoid. "Good day. I really must rush."

I picked up the envelope, bent the little brass ears of the clasp back into place over the flap, and followed Conover out the door. "I'll see you to the plane," I offered, stepping quickly to catch up. Conover didn't object.

"Let me help you with your bags."

Conover shook his head firmly. Since leaving the lounge, his mood had shifted dramatically. He was now tense and wary, his rheumy eyes darting furtively from side to side as we hurried along the south boarding concourse. It was comical. Who did the old duffer imagine was after him? The KGB?

A soft female voice whispered from the ceiling that TWA Flight 14 to Chicago was boarding at Gate 21 on the south concourse.

"My flight," Conover gasped, quickening his pace.

I walked faster to keep up. Gate 21 was still some distance away. The pedestrian traffic in the south concourse suddenly thickened and slowed as it funneled toward the bottom of an escalator ramp.

A dark-haired woman with a big white kerchief tied around her head squeezed in front of me and hopped onto the moving steps behind Conover. She seemed agitated, as if she were anxious either to get away from somebody or catch up with somebody. She was thickset and muscular, with heavy cheekbones and an aggressively protruding jaw. Conover's corpulent figure pretty much blocked the moving stairs, but she insisted on squeezing past him. Her suitcase clobbered the admiral sharply in the back of the leg. Conover yelped from the pain and muttered an obscenity at her. She never even looked back. She pushed on farther up the escalator, squirming and shoving her way rapidly past everyone in her path.

I stepped up to close the gap between myself and Conover before somebody else tried to shoehorn into it. Why the hell was I letting myself get swept up in a mad crush to a plane I wasn't even taking, anyway?

Because the admiral had teased me, then left me hanging. I had little hope for the contents of the envelope he had given me. Three pages? What could be on three pages? It could be part of a speech the admiral once made to the Overseas Press Club. It could be anything. And it wouldn't be the first time someone had pulled a trick like that on me. It was the reluctant interviewee's version of "The check is in the mail": *"Everything you want to know is right here in this package. Now excuse me, I really must go. Don't call me, and I won't call you. Have a nice life."*

The top of the escalator bank was coming into view. The down escalator, to our left, was empty. I decided that once I reached the top I'd ride it back down and get back to Manhattan before the whole day was ruined.

Conover, on the step immediately in front of me, suddenly lost his balance and teetered backward on his heels. Instinctively, my hands shot out to catch him. For a few moments I was able to hold him upright, wobbling precariously. But instead of regaining his balance, the admiral threw his arms up, hurled both overnight bag and nylon case into the air, twisted around sideways out of my supporting grasp and toppled against me.

I tried to brace myself, but there was no room to plant my feet at a better angle. I made a desperate grab for the rubber handrails, but before I could get my fingers on them, I was falling backward.

I felt hands push against my neck and the small of my back, and then a muffled shriek as the woman on the escalator step behind me absorbed the accumulating weight of both me and the admiral on top of her.

For several seconds it seemed as if the concentration of people on the escalator steps might act like a resilient bank, giving way and then bouncing back, pushing the figures near the top of the escalator back to an upright position. But the bodies weren't packed tightly enough. Instead, like dominoes, we all began to topple.

I landed hard on my back, my lower body pinned down by Conover and my head resting on the stomach of the woman behind me. I could feel her muscles contracting as she screamed. Everyone seemed to be screaming. I tried to pull my head up, but my legs, caught under Conover's back, were higher than my head, and my hands couldn't reach the rubber guardrails. The escalator was still moving, pulling the whole squirming, hysterical pile of mankind upward.

Since he was the first to fall, the stairs in front of Conover were empty. It took only seconds for the escalator to bring him to the top of the run.

My head finally came up level with my feet as the top steps collapsed flat to continue their endless-belt journey around and underneath. But as Conover's inert form slid off onto the floor above, his forward motion ceased, and I felt a new crush from behind as the mass of squirming passengers began to pile up against me.

I kicked at Conover from underneath, yelling at him to get up. He didn't respond.

Spurred by desperation, I twisted my legs out from under Conover, caught the rubber rail with one hand, and yanked myself to a squatting position. The woman behind me had begun pounding my head and back with her fists. Panic and confusion were growing.

The moving weight of flailing humanity behind me finally pushed me onto the floor behind Conover. I got to my feet, reached down and dragged Conover off to the side, then grabbed one of the woman's gyrating arms and pulled her out of the way as well.

The escalator continued its remorseless ascent, spilling bodies out onto the concourse floor. I grabbed arms and legs and pulled them clear as fast as I could, like someone unloading a tangle of heavy suitcases from a conveyer belt. As others regained their feet, they began helping.

Someone finally stopped the escalator, and the panic immediately abated. One young woman was sitting on the floor, crying hysterically, and a middle-aged man was being helped to a bench by two others. He appeared to have sprained or broken his ankle. Others were laughing and joking. Most quickly gathered their wits and dropped luggage, and continued on to their destinations down the concourse.

Except for Admiral Conover.

I knelt beside him, thought about rolling him over, then thought better of it. I felt for the artery in his neck, to at least assure myself there was a pulse.

I couldn't find one.

A young Hispanic stopped and knelt down to help. I sat back, trembling now. Conover lay absolutely motionless. The Hispanic felt for a pulse, then jumped up and called out to a couple of terminal security guards headed in our direction.

At the same instant two uniformed TWA employees materialized. One of them rolled Conover over on his back, examined him rapidly, and immediately began administering CPR. The other, a woman, called for more help over a mobile telephone.

The CPR effort went on for some time. Three policemen arrived, and more airline personnel. Eventually two white-uniformed medics, toting a stretcher, a resuscitator and a first-aid case, showed up. I stood back, out of the way, not sure what to do. Most of the other victims of the escalator incident had disappeared, and the escalator itself had already been restored to service. Passengers rushed past, eddying around the fallen form of Conover like river water around a rock.

Eventually the medics loaded the admiral onto a stretcher and, with the cops running interference, rushed him back down the concourse. I got one last look at him as they departed. His face was blue and his eyes wide open, frozen in a theatrical parody of pain. He was pretty obviously dead.

I started to walk away, and then remembered the envelope Conover had given me. I had been carrying it in my right hand.

I assumed that I must have dropped it when Conover collapsed on top of me. I walked back over to the escalator bank and looked around. Someone had apparently already picked up Conover's overnight bag and nylon case. The envelope was not in sight. I jumped on the down escalator and then I spotted it, lying innocently on the bottom step of the broad concrete stairway that flanked the escalator bank. A man in a camel's-hair coat was just bending over and picking it up.

By the time I reached the bottom, the man had hurried about a hundred feet down the concourse and ducked into the nearest men's room.

I sprinted after him. He was standing at a sink holding the envelope when I burst through the inner door.

"That belongs to me," I said. I snatched it from his hands before he could react.

He gasped, then froze, staring at me with his mouth open and his hands poised defensively in front of his chest, as if he expected me to attack him.

I felt embarrassed. "Thanks for picking it up," I said. I folded the envelope and tucked it into the big side pocket of my trench coat. "Sorry if I alarmed you."

The instant I put my hand in my pocket, the man bolted past me and out the door. The reaction would have struck me as peculiar had I not lived for so long in New York City. He had every reason to expect that I was about to rob him—probably at gunpoint.

I stood in front of the mirror for a few minutes, leaning on the sink, catching my breath and composing myself. Why hadn't I just asked him for the envelope? He had no doubt picked it up in completely innocent curiosity. But then why had he dashed off to the privacy of the men's room to open it?

I used the urinal, washed my hands, and left.

A bus and a subway ride got me back from the airport. I opened the envelope during the trip and discovered that it was empty.

I closed my eyes. I saw the man running from the men's room. No wonder. He had already removed the contents.

I didn't want to believe it. I slipped my hand inside the envelope several times and felt the sides. It was unmistakably empty. I folded it up again and stuck it back in my pocket.

I reminded myself of my original reaction to the documents when Conover had first given them to me. Despite the admiral's theatrics, I had guessed they were probably worthless. Director Carlson's Frankenstein monster indeed. What the hell was the guy talking about? I wished there were a monster. That was exactly what my book needed. But over six months of dogged research had failed to turn up even a scary gremlin.

The admiral's mental state was unreliable. His remarks and his behavior were paranoid—delusional. He not only thought people were after him, he thought people were after me, as well.

But the admiral wasn't crazy. He was scared. And now he was dead. I had the feeling I was going to regret losing those documents.

3

HOWARD AND FRANK

By noon I was back in Manhattan. I emerged from the subway at Sixth Avenue and Fiftieth Street, and crossed the street to a pay phone, only to find that some barbarian had ripped out the handset, leaving a two-foot length of cable dangling in midair. I glared at the raw strands of color-coded wire protruding from the end of the wound and wondered why I lived in New York City.

I walked over to Rockefeller Plaza and finally found a working phone in the lobby of the RCA building. I dug some quarters out of my pocket and sat down on the small metal bench. In the time it took me to dial one number, two men had already lined up outside my booth. I pulled the glass door shut.

I called my agent, Matilda Bauer, and begged off our lunch date. I described Admiral Conover's spectacular demise on the escalator at the TWA terminal, and pleaded that I was desperately short on sleep. I told her that my publisher, Whitney Atherton, had called and left a message that he was anxious to see me. Had he called her? No, she said. I promised I'd call his office again and find out what was on his mind.

I looked at the two men waiting in front of my booth. They appeared to be together. Both were young, tanned and muscular, with expensive haircuts, expensive pleated slacks, pastel T-shirts, Reebok sneakers, and a self-conscious, out-of-place manner. They looked familiar. I had the vague suspicion that I had seen them earlier, at the TWA terminal. Occasionally they would bend their heads toward each other and talk in low, serious whispers. One of them kept casting an eye in my direction. I had the peculiar sensation that they were talking about me.

But I often harbored vague suspicions and peculiar sensations. Like the late Admiral Conover's, my paranoia threshold was abnormally low. My excuse was professional. It was a journalist's occupational hazard. Miners got black lung, anesthesiologists became drug addicts, journalists went paranoid. Journalists and spies.

They were probably just a couple of gay bodybuilders from the Village.

My call to Whitney Atherton got only as far as his personal secretary. She refused to believe he wanted to see me until she checked with him herself. When she had satisfied herself that I wasn't conning her, we entered into protracted negotiations to settle a time for my appointment. I ended up canceling my trip to Washington so Whit could squeeze me in for five minutes at four-thirty.

Back outside on Rockefeller Plaza, I walked across to the skating rink, rested my arms on the ledge and gazed down. The skating season was over. The ice on the rink had been replaced by a sea of café tables with pink umbrellas. The tables, sparkling with white linen and silverware, were empty save one, occupied by a pair of tourists determined to dine alfresco despite the overcast and the chill breeze.

I looked across the rink. Leaning against the parapet on the far side I saw one of the bodybuilders who had been waiting in line for my phone. His pastel-pink T-shirt was hidden under a cyan windbreaker. He was holding a newspaper down on the ledge and trying to read it in the buffeting wind.

I could still taste the Tabasco sauce from that Bloody Mary with Conover. I needed some breakfast. I looked around for a coffee shop. At the corner of Fifty-third and Fifth I paused and turned my head to follow the movements of a young blond woman in a tightly belted trenchcoat. There, scarcely a hundred feet behind me, was the other bodybuilder.

I turned and resumed my pace. I started to shake all over. Were they tailing me? I decided I'd better find out.

I strolled over to the subway station at Fifth and Fifty-third, walked slowly down the steps, bought a token, went through the turnstiles and out onto the platform, caught an eastbound E train and got off at the next stop, Fifty-third and Lexington.

I waited on the platform there for several minutes, but saw neither of them. I began to feel ridiculous. What had come over me? My paranoia was becoming a clinical condition.

I needed sleep, I decided. I was tired and hung over, and it was affecting my judgment. It wasn't yet one, and I'd already had enough bad luck for three days. I hailed a cab and rode back to my apartment.

In the corridor on my floor, I fumbled for a long time trying to get my front door unlocked. There were three locks, but after I had turned the cylinder in each, the door remained locked. This was a common annoyance for Manhattan residents, whose doors were typically barricaded with a whole row of locks. If you neglected to lock every one of them on leaving, you were likely not to remember which were locked and which weren't when you returned. You could expend a lot of time twisting keys to the right and left in different combinations before you finally got all the locks opened simultaneously. I didn't normally have that problem, because by habit I only locked the bottom one. It made issuing sets of keys to cleaning ladies, girlfriends and out-of-town guests cheaper and simpler. I also figured that if someone tried to break in by picking the locks, he'd have the same problem I was having now.

The door yielded at last. I peeled off my raincoat, hung it in the hall closet, and made straight for the bedroom. It was still in the same disordered mess I had left behind several hours earlier.

The only obvious difference was the presence of the two bodybuilders.

They were standing by the foot of my bed, their hands tucked nonchalantly in the pockets of their windbreakers, regarding me with blank, unsmiling faces. They didn't seem in the least disturbed or surprised that I had walked in on them. They looked as if they had been waiting for me.

The blond one in the cyan windbreaker bared his teeth in a friendless grin, revealing a slight gap between his two top front teeth. "You John Brady?" he asked.

A dreamlike confusion engulfed me. None of this was making any sense. How did they get in? Were they burglarizing the apartment or not?

"You John Brady?" he repeated.

"Who are you?"

The dark-haired one, in a magenta windbreaker, pulled a thin black leather billfold from his pocket, flipped it open and thrust it toward me.

My confusion intensified. "What the hell do you want? What are you doing here?"

"I'm Special Agent Howard Wallace, FBI. This is my partner, Special Agent Frank Littlefield."

I stared wide-eyed at the wallet in his hand. I saw a white ID card with the man's photo on one side and the legend "United States Department of Justice, Federal Bureau of Investigation" across the top.

Wallace snapped the billfold shut with a practiced gesture and slipped it back into his windbreaker. From another pocket he produced a folded sheet of paper and shook it open in front of me. "This is a warrant for your arrest."

I glanced at the sheet of paper, but couldn't bring my eyes to focus on it. "What the hell are you talking about?"

Wallace refolded the document and tucked it neatly back in his pocket. I couldn't read his face. If he was feeling any emotions—malice, glee, fear or anger—they were well hidden. He wore the appearance of aggressive boredom common to customs inspectors and petty bureaucrats. I looked over at his partner and saw an equally stony countenance.

"You guys must be looking for another John Brady," I said, keeping my voice calm. "There were several dozen in the phone book last time I looked."

"You're the one we want," Littlefield said. He sounded very certain.

I took a half-step backward. These two couldn't be genuine, I thought. They had a good act, but they looked about as FBI as two dudes cruising a singles bar.

"You're kidding," I said, not able to think of a smarter rejoinder.

Wallace's lips tightened menacingly. "No sir, we are not kidding."

"Who sent you?" I demanded. "Who's your immediate superior? Give me his name. Let me call him."

They exchanged glances. Wallace cleared his throat. He was in charge. "We showed you our ID. That's all that's required."

"Bullshit," I said. "You can both get the fuck out of here, right now."

"Don't give us any crap, Brady," Littlefield said. "We're just doing our job." He sounded genuinely put out.

I should have been frightened, I suppose, but I wasn't. At least not yet. When you catch intruders on your own territory the first reaction is usually righteous anger. That was mine. Fueled with my usual paranoid conviction that someone was always out to get me for some reason of which I was at best only vaguely aware.

"I'm walking back to the front door," I told them. "I'm opening it. You two are leaving."

I didn't expect them to accept my invitation to depart, but at least if I got to the door I could make a run for it. I made it about three steps into the living room and then froze when I felt Littlefield pressing a revolver against the nape of my neck. "Stay right where you are," he warned.

Both men no longer looked bored. They looked furious.

"Turn around and put your hands on that wall over there," Wallace ordered.

I refused to move. I still didn't believe they were FBI. I was just about to bolt for the door when Wallace grabbed my arm and pushed me toward the wall.

My confusion intensified. If they really were from the FBI, they would soon have to realize that they were making a seriously stupid mistake.

"Both hands on the wall. And plant your feet apart behind you."

I placed my hands against the wall.

"Get those feet back," Wallace commanded.

I hesitated, not sure what was meant. I felt the top of Littlefield's sneaker nudging hard against my instep.

"Back 'em up, dickhead," Wallace warned, letting his exasperation show. "Quick."

I shuffled my feet backward, until I was leaning into the wall at what seemed like a forty-five-degree angle.

"Hold it right there. Don't move."

Wallace's partner began to frisk me, his pistol in one hand, the other running rapidly up and down my legs and torso. His fingers slipped up under my arms and stopped when they hit the bulge under my left armpit.

"He's armed!" Littlefield shouted.

Before I could explain that it was only a tape recorder, Littlefield jammed the gun up hard against the skin just under my ear. Wallace stepped around and in a fluid series of movements ripped open my shirt and yanked the recorder out of the holster. He looked at it in surprise, withdrew the cassette tape, then threw the recorder across the room in disgust. It cracked against the edge of a bookcase, and thudded onto the carpet in a shower of AA batteries.

"Hey, be careful," Littlefield warned his partner. "That's evidence."

"We'd better strip-search him," Wallace replied.

Littlefield pulled me back off the wall by my collar. "Take your clothes off," he ordered.

Still overwhelmed by what was happening, I started to argue. Littlefield grabbed me in a hammerlock from behind and Wallace ripped my shirt and undershirt off, undid my belt and zipper and yanked down my pants and underpants.

With Littlefield holding me, Wallace bunched his big fist and drove it with great force into my stomach. I gasped, choked my breath back to keep from throwing up and let out a groan of pain. I gagged and tried to bend over to relieve the spasms shooting through my gut.

"Okay, let him down."

Littlefield released the hammerlock hold and kicked my legs out from under me, sending me sprawling. My chin caught the floor and nearly knocked me out.

Wallace drew out a notepad and pen from his jacket pocket and started writing in it. "Time of arrest," he said. He looked at his wristwatch. "One-ten P.M., May fourteenth. Place of arrest, suspect's home at one-eighty-two Central Park West, apartment fifteen-C."

Wallace flipped his notebook over to the back cover.

I felt the weight of Littlefield's Reebok pressing into the small of my back while Wallace read from the back of his notebook: "You have the right to remain silent. You have the right to consult a lawyer. If you do not have a lawyer, one will be provided for you. Anything you say may be used against you in a court of law."

Wallace knelt down and slid a document up near my face, along with his pen. "By signing this document," he said, "you indicate that you have understood what I have just read to you. Sign it, please."

I reached my hand out, picked up the pen and signed it. Wallace pulled it away. I tried to sit up.

Littlefield lifted his running shoe from my back and pressed it against my neck. "Move one inch, you son of a bitch," he said. "Go ahead. I'll blow your brains all over the rug."

After a while they let me get dressed. Then Wallace pulled my arms around together behind me. I felt the cold steel of handcuffs clasp one wrist, then the other. Each agent grabbed an elbow and together they started pulling me in the direction of the front door.

"What's this about?" I demanded. "Why are you arresting me?" I was appalled at the sound of my own voice. It was quaking with fear.

Wallace cleared his throat and snuffled noisily. His anger had subsided. "Espionage," he said, recapturing his earlier tone of bored indifference. "Four counts."

4

FEDERAL PLAZA

Rain was falling. Broad puddles shimmered across the scarred
macadam surface of Central Park West and hissed beneath the
car's speeding tires. I gazed out the rear side window at the empty
sidewalks and the dripping green foliage in the park.

My hangover was gone, but fatigue weighed me down like a
lead vest. I had consumed a week's worth of adrenaline in the past
few hours, and I felt depleted to the point of paralysis. My stomach
was sore from Wallace's blow; otherwise I felt dazed, insensate.

Espionage. It was incredible. Ludicrous. The only possible explanation was that they had arrested the wrong man. That would
become clear soon enough. Until that happened, I had to work at
remaining calm.

I had tried to coax some further explanation from the two agents,

Wallace and Littlefield, sitting up front, but they were not in a gregarious mood. Their initial hostility had abated somewhat, but all I could elicit from them were shrugs and grunts and surly stares, so I stopped trying. They appeared to regard me as something not quite human.

I guessed it was now about two o'clock. With my hands cuffed behind my back, I couldn't read my watch. I also couldn't find a comfortable sitting position. I gave up trying, finally, and just leaned against the seat, letting the cuffs cut into my wrists and the small of my back.

The automobile the agents had hustled me into was a late-model white Plymouth Reliant K, with no markings other than a big dent over the wheel well on the driver's side. I wanted to roll down a window to get more air, but I couldn't move my arms.

Aside from the shock of my arrest, there was something alarming in the ease and rapidity with which I seemed to have lost not only my special status as a well-known and more or less respected journalist, but my basic status as a citizen.

For special agents Wallace and Littlefield, up front, I was just another bozo who had gotten a little out of line and had to be dealt with firmly. Part of another's day's work. They had gotten the opportunity to take out a little aggression on me, but that wasn't meant to be personal. For all I knew, they treated all their collars that way. What for me was traumatic, was for them everyday.

Over the noises of the traffic I listened to the droning voice of a female dispatcher on the car's two-way radio, tuned to the local police frequency. Between bursts of static, she was busy dispatching cruisers to various calamities around the city.

Littlefield, riding shotgun, turned the radio down, dug a cassette recorder out of the glove compartment and popped a tape into it. It was a Spanish language lesson.

"*Es verdad . . .*" a rich baritone began, starting a recitation of "it is" phrases. "*Eso no es verdad. . . .*"

Littlefield cleared his throat self-consciously and began repeating the phrases. His accent was flatfooted and tone-deaf.

"*Es malo. . . .*"

"Ess mallo. . . ."

"*Es muy malo. . . .*"

"Ess mooey mallo. . . ."

Bored with his efforts at self-improvement, Littlefield leaned forward and punched the cassette player off. Wallace, the driver, glanced over at his colleague with an amused smirk. The two agents chatted about the new baseball season. Both were Yankee fans.

The Plymouth turned east on Fifty-seventh Street, then south on Second Avenue. The heavy rain slowed up traffic and the trip downtown consumed half an hour. On Duane Street, near City Hall, Wallace steered onto a ramp that wound down to a large underground parking garage. He pulled into a space between two other white Plymouth Reliant Ks—the auto of choice for the federal bureaucracy these days—and switched off the ignition.

The agents walked me to an elevator, and we rode up to the lobby. I knew where I was—Federal Plaza, the Jacob K. Javits Building. Among its tenants was the FBI, which occupied all of the twenty-fifth, twenty-sixth, twenty-seventh and twenty-eighth floors, and portions of several others. The New York field office was large—some twelve hundred full-time employees. About half of them worked in the counterintelligence sections, keeping tabs on the U.N. missions. I knew that because I had been here before. Some of my best sources worked here.

We crossed the lobby, and took another elevator to the twenty-sixth floor. Wallace and Littlefield each grabbed an elbow and escorted me at a fast walk down a series of long corridors. The walls were in need of fresh paint. Wallace muttered something about all the paperwork he'd have to do before the end of the day.

Our journey ended in a ten-foot-square, windowless room with worn brown carpeting, dark yellow walls, a small battered metal desk, and three unmatched office chairs that should have been discarded years ago. Heavy metal handrails were attached to one wall at waist level, like the practice bars in a ballet school. I wondered about their purpose.

Wallace removed my handcuffs and I sat down. Littlefield produced a form from the desk's drawer and filled it out, asking me questions in his flat and irritating tone of voice: Name? Age? Place of birth? and so on. This went on for about fifteen minutes. Wallace stood behind me the entire time, guarding me. Littlefield had trouble with his pen.

Wallace then instructed me to empty my pockets and remove my watch. I piled the items, including my shoulder holster and the pen with the built-in microphone, onto the desk. Littlefield made an inventory of them, and then scooped them into a plastic bag. Wallace let me keep the change I had in my pocket—seventy-eight cents.

These procedures completed, they marched me down the corridor to another room—a white, windowless chamber not much bigger than the first room.

A heavyset male in his mid-forties, with a shiny bald pate, was sitting reading the New York *Post*. He had a large purple hemangioma—a port wine stain—that discolored one side of his neck and part of his cheek. Around him was a clutter of objects—two light-stands, a big camera on a tripod, a stool and a few scattered chairs. In one corner a desk and cabinet were shoved against the wall. He exchanged greetings with the two agents. His name was Roger. They all laughed about something together. It was remarkable how they ignored me. I was simply a part of their work, and otherwise of no interest to them.

"What's his name, Howard?" Roger asked.

"Brady, John T."

"Grady?"

"Brady, with a *B*."

The bald man fished around in a box of letters, found the ones that spelled out my name and arranged them in the slots of a small rectangular frame, like a miniature movie marquee, suspended from the protruding metal arm of a movable stand. Under my name he slid in the date, and some numbers which I supposed identified my case.

Littlefield guided me over to a tall yardstick marked in boldly numbered inches up to 84 and told me to stand beside it. Roger of the port wine stain arranged the marquee in front of my chest, then went around behind his camera and snapped my picture. Littlefield turned me from full face to profile, and Roger snapped another. They then moved me to a metal stool and took a set of close-up head-and-shoulder shots, again full-face and profile.

After the photography session, I was directed to a small counter against the far wall. Roger inked up a big roller from a pad, rolled the ink out carefully onto a shiny metal surface the size of a thin book. He pressed each of my fingers into the ink, then rolled them in the ten squares of a cardboard fingerprint form placed in a frame next to the metal pad. His beefy hands were surprisingly gentle, and I was impressed with the sharpness of the fingerprints that he produced on the card.

He pushed a can of petroleum-based soap—the kind auto mechanics use to clean their hands at the end of the day—and a couple of paper towels in front of me so I could clean off the ink. While I concentrated on doing that, Roger printed out my name and other essentials on the fingerprint card.

The wall immediately around me was heavily defaced with smears from ink-stained fingers—as if many people had tried to clean their hands simply by wiping them off on the wall.

The petty humiliations of each procedure stung me, but I felt docile and helpless, caught in a processing machine that didn't allow me an opportunity to protest what was happening to me. To resist the relentless bureaucratic tide of procedures now would only exacerbate my sense of futility. I forced myself to be patient. I kept reassuring myself that sooner or later someone was going to have a lot of apologizing to do.

Wallace and Littlefield slapped the handcuffs on me again and took me back to the first room.

"You want to make a statement?" Wallace asked.

"I want to call my lawyer."

Wallace pointed to the phone on the desk. Littlefield removed my handcuffs.

I dialed the number and listened to the phone ring. I knew the odds of finding Sam Marks in his office were not good. A secretary finally answered. It was a man, and I didn't know him.

"He's in court today, Mr. Brady. Can he return your call?"

"No, he can't. When will he be back?"

"He'll probably go right home. But he'll check in with me by phone. Can I give him a message?"

"Tell him the FBI has me in custody at Federal Plaza. I need him down here as soon as he can get here. They've arrested me. I don't know why."

"I'll be sure to tell him, Mr. Brady," he replied cheerfully. Like the FBI agents, the assistant also considered my dismal predicament as just another part of the daily routine: *Oh, and some guy*

*named Brady called, Mr. Marks. FBI's holding him at Federal Plaza.
He wouldn't tell me what he wanted. I'm sure it can wait until
tomorrow.*

I hung up the phone. I suddenly wished that I had a wife. Or
a mentally competent parent. Or one close friend. Someone nearby
who would be personally concerned about my situation and would
start doing something about it. Why wasn't there anyone around
I could depend on? Was my life that hollow and lonely? I hadn't
thought so. People were always pestering me to help them. I usually
did. But I wasn't the type to burden others. I hated to appear
needy. To ask a friend for help usually damaged the relationship,
whether you got the help or not. "A friend in need," as Joseph
Heller once put it, "is no friend of mine."

"So you want to make a statement or not?" Wallace said.

"About what? Make a statement about what?"

"For the record."

"I don't even know why the hell I'm here. How can I make a
statement?"

Wallace shrugged. "We've got you on four espionage counts. If
you want to talk about your activities, we'll listen. We're just giving
you the chance to say anything you want to say."

"I don't *have* to say anything," I said.

Wallace yawned. "That's right. You don't *have* to say anything."

That was the best course. I knew that much. Don't say anything
until Sam Marks gets here. "When will I be able to see my lawyer?"

"You have to be arraigned first."

"What do you mean?"

Wallace spelled it out as if he were explaining an everyday fact
of life to a child. "We take you over to the federal courthouse for
a bail hearing. Your lawyer will meet you there. You'll appear
before a magistrate. The magistrate will set your bail."

"When will this happen?"

Wallace ran his tongue thoughtfully around the inside of his
mouth. "Not for a while. You have to go over for an interview
with Pretrial Services first."

"What do they do?"

"Determine your status in the community, your assets, your
family circumstances, and so on. They pass this information on to
the judge. And the U.S. attorney handling your case. He'll be at
the bail hearing, too."

"This is all ridiculous," I said. "It's a misunderstanding. You've arrested the wrong man."

"Tell me about it," Wallace replied, looking bored.

"I just did."

"Yeah. Right."

Why the hell should I wait for Sam Marks? I thought. I'm not guilty of anything. Let them ask me questions. I'm at least as smart as either Wallace or Littlefield. Maybe I can clear the whole mess up myself and get the hell out of here.

"If you have some questions you want me to answer, go ahead and ask them," I said. "I'll do my best."

Wallace became interested in me again. "You will?"

"Yes. I will. Let's get the damned thing straightened out. Right now."

Wallace seemed suspicious of my intentions. "You sure you don't want your lawyer?"

"Just tell me the crimes you think I've committed and the evidence you have. Then ask me your questions."

Wallace looked over at his partner, who was sitting in back of me. I turned to see Littlefield nod his head.

Wallace brought out his handcuffs. "Listen. We're going to have to leave you here for a few minutes. You're still officially in my custody, so I have to secure you. . . ." He handcuffed my right hand to the metal railing on the wall beside me and moved the telephone out of my reach.

The two agents departed, closing the door firmly behind them. I heard them talking in low voices on the other side, and then they walked away.

I looked up at the acoustic-tile ceiling, wondering if it contained bugs or hidden cameras. The premises looked so neglected that I doubted it. It was a waiting room in limbo—forlorn, dilapidated and depressing, with nothing to focus on, nothing to engage or confront. There was no powerful lamp to shine in my eyes, no scratches on the walls, no scrawled confessions or protestations of innocence, no dried blood on the floor, no psychic reverberations of past ordeals. There were only cigarette burns and coffee stains in the brown carpet.

I felt a desperate urge to flee. I glanced at the door, wondering if it was locked. What difference did it make? I was handcuffed to the wall, unable even to reach the telephone on the desk.

I should have been indignant, furious. But being who I was, all I felt was a wretched unease. Was this really a simple bureaucratic fuckup, or were they trying to scare me for some reason? I did know some important sources, and I was occasionally privy to confidential information about subjects and people that might interest them.

If I had known that they were just softening me up as a prelude to squeezing some information out of me, I wouldn't have been worried. I could handle that. The FBI could get heavy-handed, but it wasn't the Gestapo, after all.

But I didn't know. And not to know was to be defenseless. I had spent my whole professional career as a journalist in a crusade against not knowing.

Littlefield and Wallace were gone for some time. I looked at my handcuffed wrists, and the white band of flesh where my wristwatch had been. I felt a sudden welling of anger at being deprived of the time.

Along with not knowing, I hated being forced to wait. God, I truly hated it. Did they know that? I would walk out of a grocery store or a bank before I'd wait in any line more than two people long. I hadn't seen a movie in Manhattan in years for the same reason. Waiting was limbo, purgatory. Waiting was like not knowing. It meant that you had lost control over your life, that you had surrendered your autonomy to others. Waiting was a surrender to powerlessness.

Composure, I whispered to myself. Don't lose it.

The door finally opened again. Wallace came in. I asked him the time. He glanced at his watch. "Four-thirty," he said. "Look, I'm trying to get the U.S. attorney assigned to your case up here to question you himself. Do you have any objections to talking to him now—without your lawyer being present?"

Wallace was being extremely careful not to commit any procedural screwups that might compromise the prosecution's case. This didn't make me feel any better, but I just wanted to get on with it and get out of this place. "No, I have no objections. Where is he?"

"Littlefield's trying to locate him," Wallace said. He sat down at the desk, telephoned Littlefield in another office somewhere and inquired about his progress.

More time passed. Wallace and I stared at each other. I asked him to remove the handcuffs. "When the others get here," he said.

"How long is this going to take?"

Wallace refused to speculate. He looked at his watch. "It's already too late to arraign you."

"Too late?"

"The magistrate's court shuts down at five. We'll have to bring you back in the morning."

I felt a surge of euphoria. I could go home, recover from the events of the day, return in the morning with Sam Marks at my side and finally end this nightmare. "You want me to come back here tomorrow morning?"

Wallace's lips twitched in irritation. "We're not letting you go, if that's what you think. We'll put you in the MCC overnight and get you in the morning. You can see your lawyer then."

"The MCC?"

Wallace snorted unpleasantly. His tolerance was wearing thin. "The Metropolitan Correctional Center, dickhead. It's right across the street—in back of the courthouse."

5

EL CARDOZO

Littlefield returned with two other men. After a brief discussion in the hall, they decided to move the interview to a bigger room.

Another space was located, and when Wallace brought me in, the three others were already seated in a row on the right side of a big conference table. At the far end was a young woman with a steno machine. This room was much larger; it had windows and a fairly recent coat of white paint. The chairs were new and they matched.

Littlefield stood up and pulled out the particular chair they wanted me to sit in—on the left side of the table, facing my inquisitors. Wallace settled himself into the chair at the end nearest the door. I was effectively surrounded. It was hard to escape the feeling that they were ganging up on me. I supposed that Sam

Marks would be furious when I told him that I had agreed to this, but I was intent on showing my innocence.

"This is John Brady," Wallace said, to the man sitting in the middle. "He's agreed to answer your questions without having his attorney present."

The man looked at me. "Is that correct, Mr. Brady?"

"I've agreed to listen to your questions," I replied. "I'll answer them if they make any sense."

Nobody said anything for what seemed like nearly a minute. They were all waiting for the deputy U.S. attorney, engrossed in the study of some documents on the table in front of him, to launch the proceedings. In his own good time he looked up and smiled coldly at me. "I'm Vincent Cardozo," he said. "I'm with the U.S. Attorney's Office. I'll be representing the government in its case against you."

My stomach lurched. I had heard of Vincent Cardozo. He was Mexican, and had briefly been a bullfighter before moving to the United States and taking up the study of law. Despite his promise as a matador, his family—wealthy and socially prominent in Mexico City—had pressured him into retiring after a minor injury during a fight in Spain when he was twenty-two. The New York press, which had done many features on him, had dubbed him "El Cardozo."

He was said to bring the matador's skills to the prosecution of criminals—swiftness, intelligence, agility, bravery and the certain confidence of victory. There was talk that he would be appointed to succeed the present U.S. Attorney for the Southern District when he retired.

El Cardozo was a small, formal-looking individual with a narrow face and a beak of a nose that overshadowed a thin, straight mouth. His skin was dark and smooth, like a fine leather, and decorated with a dark mole on his chin. His hair was jet black and slicked back close to his skull in a style reminiscent of the twenties. He was wearing an expensive double-breasted black suit with a wide chalk stripe and a high-collared white shirt with French cuffs and pearl cuff links. This was no nine-to-five bureaucrat at the Justice Department. El Cardozo looked every bit the performer, the man sure of his talents. He consciously dressed and acted in a way that set him apart from his colleagues.

I seemed to have drawn, by chance or by design, the Justice Department's equivalent of the Grand Inquisitor.

If Cardozo's presence was disturbing, the presence of the man sitting next to him was downright irritating. He sat with his back ramrod-straight and his fingers laced tightly together on the table in front of him, like somebody who was getting bad service in an expensive restaurant and was about to let the maître d' know about it. He had no materials with him, and did not seem ready to play any direct role in the proceedings. He just glared at me with his agate-hard blue eyes. He looked repulsively tidy and fit. His perfectly straight nose, square chin, wide jaw, and steel-gray crew-cut hair gave him the kind of crude handsomeness associated with comic-book heroes. The manly image was marred somewhat by his ears, which were small and cupped and stuck out from his closely sheared temples.

I looked at him. "Who are you?" I demanded.

He stiffened with annoyance at my effrontery.

Cardozo intervened with a tight-lipped but apologetic grin. "I'm sorry. This is Colonel Westerly, Mr. Brady. He's a member of the president's National Security Council intelligence coordinating committee."

I cocked an eyebrow in astonishment. "The president's what? Why is he here?"

"He's monitoring this interview for the Justice Department— and for the president's intelligence coordinating committee," Cardozo replied smoothly. "I must request that you keep his presence here today a confidential matter."

"Confidential or not, is his presence necessary?"

"So I'm told," Cardozo said, looking down at his papers. He apparently didn't much like having him there either.

I was determined not to be intimidated. I nodded meaningfully at Westerly's nondescript gray civilian suit. "Are you on active duty, Colonel?" I asked. "Or are you retired?"

Westerly shot me a contemptuous smirk that was fully as offensive as a shouted insult. "I'm on leave from active service with the United States Marine Corps, sir. I'm on loan to the White House. I've had the privilege of serving my president in a special capacity for the past fourteen months."

Cardozo cleared his throat to direct our attention back to the purpose of the meeting. He opened a two-inch-thick folder in front of him. His fingers were slender and his nails long and manicured. A gold ring set with a ruby glimmered from the pinkie of his right hand. He gazed across the table at me with the impersonal manner of a surgeon about to settle in for some serious cutting.

"Mr. Brady?"

"Yes."

"You're aware of the charges against you?"

"Well, I'm aware that the FBI is making some pretty incredible accusations about me, yes."

Cardozo's eyes scanned my face, looking for evidence of stress. "Simply put, you're accused of passing classified government documents to an agent of a hostile power."

"And I can assure you that that is a complete fantasy." It felt good finally being able to confront my accusers face to face. I was eager to make confetti out of whatever evidence they had assembled.

The government prosecutor patted his straight black hair absently and looked down at the dossier in front of him. Beneath a bony and prominent brow, Cardozo's eyes protruded slightly, possibly from an overactive thyroid. He blinked them slowly and deliberately. He evoked the air of a reptile, I thought—cold, detached, unfeeling. Possibly predatory. "You don't believe you're guilty of any such crime?" he asked.

"Of course not. What classified documents are we talking about? Where did I get them? Who did I pass them to?" I slapped the edge of the table with my fingers. "The charges are patently ridiculous."

Cardozo nodded. He ran a long finger slowly down the lines of the dossier's top page. He paused finally at an item near the bottom.

"Do you know a Mr. René Gervais?" he asked.

I hesitated. It wasn't an innocent question, but I saw no reason to deny I knew the man. "Yes, I do."

"Who is he, please?"

"He's a correspondent for the French news service, Agence France Presse."

Cardozo nodded again, his gaze still fixed on the dossier. He opened the file and flipped through several pages, backtracked several times, then settled on a page. He looked up. "How long have you known him?"

I thought about it. "I first met him—let's see—it was during the Iran crisis, 1979. I was doing my book on the Shah. He was covering the Shah's flight from Iran."

"How well do you know him?"

I could practically see the hooks on this question. René Gervais was apparently in some kind of trouble, and Cardozo hoped to make me look guilty by association. "Not very well at all," I replied.

"You aren't friends?"

"No."

"How would you describe your relationship, then?"

"Professional. We know each other as fellow journalists."

"Do you speak French?"

"A little. René's English is very good."

"René? You call him that, do you?"

El Cardozo was quick. I tried to blunt his insinuation. "Everybody calls him René."

"You see him frequently?"

"No."

"How often, would you say?"

"I really have no idea. I never counted up the number of times."

"Would you say you've seen him a dozen times?"

"I suppose."

"Two dozen?"

"Possibly."

"And talked with him on the telephone?"

"Now and then."

"Did you ever correspond?"

"No."

"You're quite sure?"

"Quite sure."

"When you talk, do you exchange information?"

"Of course. That's what journalists do—exchange information. Information, tips, opinions, gossip . . ."

Cardozo leafed through the documents in front of him. The pile looked to be several hundred pages thick. Most of it, from what I could see, was single-spaced typescript and well thumbed. On some pages I caught glimpses of phrases underlined in red pencil.

It was a common trick of prosecutors to plop a huge dossier down in front of a suspect, to make him think they had more on him than they actually did. I didn't think Cardozo was operating on that level, but how could so much material relate to me? Despite my apprehension, I felt a reporter's intense curiosity to see where the interview was heading.

Cardozo's slender fingers shifted several piles of documents around and unearthed a large black-and-white photograph. He placed it on the table, turned it around and slid it toward me. "Is this René Gervais?"

I looked down. The photo showed a man sitting in a chair in an outdoor café somewhere. The print was grainy, indicating that it had been enlarged. The man's face was caught at three-quarter profile, and was somewhat blurred, but there was no mistaking who it was. The wide eyes, with their expression of perpetual surprise, the unruly mane of hair that curled over ears, forehead and collar, and the ever-present smoldering Gitane stuck in the corner of his mouth, were all uniquely René Gervais.

Across from him at the same outdoor table, pointing a rolled-up newspaper at something out of the camera's field of view, sat yours truly, John Brady.

I glanced up at Cardozo. The man's eyes were trained on me like cocked gun-barrels. "Yes, that's Gervais," I admitted. "And that's me with him, in case you had any doubt." I pushed the photograph back across the table.

"Do you recall the occasion?" Cardozo asked, pushing the photograph back toward me.

I studied it again. I recognized the location. It was a café off Seventh Avenue, south of Sheridan Square. "I guess it was in the West Village, last fall sometime." It was a chilling thought that the FBI had apparently had the French journalist under surveillance for months.

"Do you remember what you talked about?"

I considered the question. I could just say no, I didn't remember, but I was determined to demonstrate my innocence as emphatically as possible. "Gervais wanted my views on the fall election. That was it, primarily. We talked politics. We talked about the dollar and whether it would rise or fall against the franc. I was planning a trip to Paris this summer, and I was interested in how much it was going to cost me. . . . That's all I can remember. . . ."

I let my answer trail off, but Cardozo didn't follow up. Instead he just fixed his languid gaze on me expectantly. An awkward silence ensued. I waited for the next question, but Cardozo just continued to stare. I felt pressed to expand my answer: "I'm sure there were other subjects, but it was over six months ago, after all. . . ."

I stopped. An embarrassing shock of recognition descended on me. Cardozo was employing a technique against me that I often used myself—the expectant pause. Conversations abhor a vacuum, and if a questioner doesn't rush in to fill it, the subject usually does—often to his regret.

I had occasionally caught some startling confessions that way. In this instance, however, Cardozo was going to come up empty. I simply could not remember anything else from that meeting. Cardozo continued to wait, nonetheless, his hands neatly folded in front of him, his expression anticipating further elaboration.

"I think that's all," I said.

Cardozo smiled. "Did you give Mr. Gervais anything at this meeting?"

"Give him anything?"

"That was my question."

"Like what?"

"Did you hand anything over to him? Papers? Documents of any kind?"

"No."

"You're quite sure?"

"I'm quite sure."

Cardozo produced another photograph and slid it across to me. It had been taken on the same occasion as the first one. It showed me handing Gervais what looked like a rolled-up stack of papers.

"What are you giving him here?"

I flushed, suddenly angry and defensive. Cardozo had made it appear that he had caught me in a lie, when no lie had been intended. I studied the print, then pushed it back. "I don't know. It must be a magazine. Or a newspaper."

"It doesn't look like a magazine or a newspaper."

I felt my adrenaline surge. "Maybe it's the menu. Your photographer should have come over to the table and taken a closer look."

"You still claim you gave him no documents?"

"Yes, that's what I claim. I didn't give him any documents."

Cardozo began thumbing through his stack of papers again, searching for something. His manner was maddeningly unruffled and deliberate.

Abruptly I remembered something. There was a document of sorts that I had sometimes in the past lent to Gervais. Each week *Time* magazine circulated a confidential interoffice memo to the top editors that contained reports from the magazine's bureaus on national and international affairs. The report consisted of twenty or so typewritten pages of raw news—unverified information that could not be published in the magazine but provided useful background information for the editors. It was full of the latest Washington gossip and rumors, and invariably made fascinating reading. Its contents were in great demand. The White House, for example, regularly obtained a pirated photocopy—apparently through some spy they had in the Time-Life organization.

From my past employment there, I also had sources inside *Time*, and I regularly received my own pirated copies. Gervais was always asking for a peek at these memos, and I had sometimes let him read them. I couldn't remember whether I had brought one of them on that day or not, but it was possible that that was what the photograph showed me handing across the table. The memos were hardly top-secret stuff, and there was nothing illegal about having the material in one's possession. But I decided not to volunteer any of this information.

Cardozo found what he was looking for. He pulled a stack of stapled-together papers from the pile, looked at each page to verify its contents to himself, then passed it across to me.

"Is this what you gave him?"

I turned the pages around and looked down at them. I expected to see a copy of one of the *Time* interoffice memos, but what I saw instead was a batch of classified government documents. They constituted a series of CIA field reports, gathered from embassies, foreign listening posts and agents in the field. They covered a wide range of matters, from rumors about guerrilla activity in Central America, to troop movements in Ethiopia, to some very sensitive and unflattering information about a number of Third World leaders. They were raw intelligence reports, the kinds of things that probably crossed the DCI's desk every day of the week. They were all labeled TOP SECRET, but I saw nothing earthshaking in them. Indeed, any of the same information might well have appeared in one of those *Time* interoffice memos.

"No, I didn't give these to him."

"You're quite sure?"

"I'm quite sure."

"Have you ever seen these documents before?"

"No. Never."

"Are you familiar with any of the information in them?"

I sifted through the documents again. Oddly, much of the information did seem familiar. I wasn't sure why. Maybe some of the same stuff *had* appeared in those *Time* memos. And the CIA was notorious for constantly marking information TOP SECRET that had already been widely published.

I avoided a direct reply: "As I said, I've never seen these documents before."

El Cardozo offered me a patronizing smile. "I didn't ask you that. I asked you if you were familiar with any of the information in them."

Hell, I decided. This kind of question deserved an outright lie. "No," I said.

"You're quite . . ."

"I'm quite sure."

Cardozo blinked a few times, then separated another stack of papers from the pile and slid them across the several feet of polished tabletop toward me. From the self-satisfied expression on his face, I guessed that the matador was about to demonstrate some more fancy capework.

I looked down at the new stack of typewritten pages. The material here was unmistakably familiar. Marked in red pencil was information almost identical to what I had just read in the "top-secret" reports. It took a few seconds before it dawned on me that I was now reading a transcript of my own research notes, collected for the biography I was doing on Carlson.

It was a stunning moment.

This material could have come from only one place: the files in my computer. I didn't think it possible that anyone could break into my files without my passwords, but someone had, because here they were, decoded and neatly typed, in the hands of the

United States Department of Justice. I took a deep breath. My lips felt dry. I ran my tongue over them.

"You recognize this material, Mr. Brady?"

An image of Gail Snow's lithe and willing, nude body flashed into my head. Was she an undercover FBI agent? It seemed insanely improbable. She had apparently swiped some of my files, but that was only last night. The Justice Department had clearly spent many weeks working up this material.

"Yes. Of course I recognize it. It's my own research. You people stole it from me—somehow."

Cardozo didn't deny it. He merely glanced around the room with an expression of mock innocence on his face.

"I never passed any of the information in my files on to anyone. Not to René Gervais or anyone!" I insisted, in much too emotional a voice. I felt my face burning. "And I collected every goddamned word here entirely legally. Which is more than I can say for you bastards!"

Cardozo blinked slowly. "Do you wish to change any of your statements?" he asked me.

"No, I damn well do not."

Cardozo gave me another of his expectant pauses. I just glared across the table at him.

The U.S. attorney propped an elbow on the table and leaned his chin against his thumb. "If you did not, as you claim, obtain the information in your files from these secret CIA documents, would you tell me where you did obtain it?"

"From my own sources. In the government and elsewhere. Perfectly legally."

"Can you tell me who any of these sources are?"

"No, I cannot."

"How else can I corroborate your statement?"

"That's your problem. A journalist has a constitutional right to keep his sources confidential."

Cardozo took his elbow off the table and lifted the stapled-together collection of CIA documents. "These reports were surrendered to us by René Gervais. He has sworn, under oath, that you gave them to him on the day these photographs were taken. He has also sworn that you fed him similar classified material over a period of several years."

I swallowed, stared at Cardozo for a second, and then laughed. I knew the man wasn't joking, but I had to force out a laugh just to demonstrate the absurdity of the accusation. "That's really quite ridiculous. Why would I do such a thing?"

Cardozo had an answer: "Apparently in exchange for information, Mr. Brady. Mr. Gervais was a spy for several Middle Eastern countries. We assume you knew that. He often had excellent intelligence on the West—intelligence collected from a wide variety of sources in Europe and the United States. Intelligence that you were as eager to have as were Gervais's secret paymasters."

Part of what he said was true. By trading with Gervais, I had often obtained excellent leads and off-the-record information from him. I had never questioned his sources. It was none of my business. He would never have questioned mine.

"I didn't know he was a spy. I swear I had no idea. And in any case, I never gave him anything classified."

Colonel Westerly, who had spent this entire exchange with an expression of terminal boredom on his face, suddenly came to life: "You can tell he's lying, can't you?" he said to Cardozo, his mouth twisted in disgust.

I felt sick. I suddenly wanted this interview session to end. God knows what else Cardozo had in that stack of documents in front of him, but I knew if I stayed here much longer, he'd soon be coming over my horns with his sword for the coup de grace.

"This is enough," I said. "I'm finished. No more."

"What did I tell you?" Colonel Westerly crowed, grinning broadly at Cardozo and the FBI agents.

The U.S. attorney gazed at me with a wistful expression. "I have quite a few more questions," he said.

"Talk to my lawyer in the morning."

Cardozo didn't argue. He restacked his papers in a neat pile and closed the folder back around them. He allowed himself a faintly convivial grin, conveying neither apology nor triumph. "Then we'll see you in the morning, Mr. Brady."

"I can hardly wait."

I stood up, and felt a swelling light-headedness, as if I were about to black out and topple into a void.

Wallace put the handcuffs back on my wrists. He and Littlefield returned me to the underground garage and from there drove me the one block across Foley Square to the Metropolitan Correctional Center, a squat, modern, brown-brick structure tucked in behind the tall gray neoclassical hulk of the United States Courthouse and another building that housed the U.S. Attorney's Office and the U.S. Marshal's Service.

Wallace checked me in at a special station on the second floor of the MCC. Federal prisoners were housed here while on trial.

"Got a safekeeper for you, Harry," he said to a uniformed guard sitting behind a counter surmounted by a wall of bulletproof glass. "I'll pick him up in the morning."

Forms were filled out and signed. Technically I was still in Wallace's custody, and would remain so until after my arraignment. Since Wallace couldn't get me arraigned today, he was turning me over to the Bureau of Prisons for "safekeeping" until tomorrow. This was the common practice. Wallace said I was lucky it wasn't Saturday. Then I'd be in for the whole weekend.

If I made bail, I'd be let go tomorrow. If I didn't, I'd stay in the MCC until my trial was over. That would take months. Even a year—or longer. After the trial I would either be a free man or would be sent to a federal facility somewhere to serve out my sentence.

Wallace took back his handcuffs and a guard sitting in a glassed-in control booth buzzed me through a steel gate. There were a few more formalities. I was given a thin, starchy towel, a small packaged bar of soap, a plastic glass, a tiny tube of toothpaste and a toothbrush. I was told I could keep my street clothes and the loose change I had in my pocket. A guard then escorted me down a long, tile-lined corridor. Surveillance cameras bristled like miniature gun emplacements from every corner and over every doorway. Loud noises echoed around me. A strong ammonia smell hung in the air, interlaced with the subtler, sharper odors of rage and fear.

"You won't be in a regular cell block with the other prisoners," the guard reassured me. "You'll have your own private room for the night." He was black and spoke with a soft, gentle voice. He seemed genuinely eager to put me at my ease. I felt pathetically grateful.

We reached a metal door. The guard unlocked it. On the other side was a room about eight feet deep and six feet wide, with a single metal-frame bed, a toilet with no seat, a sink and a wastebasket.

There was a window. It was recessed into the brick and tile at shoulder height, and covered with a heavy steel grating. I could hear the faint rumble of street traffic through the glass.

"Just like the Holiday Inn," the guard said, grinning broadly. "And a whole lot cheaper. You even gonna get room service. We'll bring you some dinner right now and some breakfast in the morning. You need anything else, we'll be around."

The guard closed the door behind me and locked it. I walked across the tiny cell and stood between the bed and the toilet, feeling very sorry for myself.

6

SAM MARKS

I woke often during the night, each time shocked anew by the sensation of the coarse starched sheets and the narrow bunk and the realization that I was locked in a prison cell. For what seemed like hours I lay awake listening to the unfamiliar and vaguely sinister sounds of the detention center around me in the dark—the occasional disembodied voice, the hollow echo of footsteps, the rumble and whine of the building's machinery.

The malevolent image of the U.S. attorney, El Cardozo, kept coming back to me. Whenever I closed my eyes I saw him as if he were present in the room, tapping that mound of documents—his case against me—with his long, bony forefinger.

Four counts of espionage.

I thought about René Gervais. How well did I really know him, after all? We saw each other only occasionally. I didn't know his friends or his habits. If he was a spy, then he had used me. Even so, I had not passed on to him any secrets vital to the national security.

Or had I?

The longer I dwelled on my situation the more ambiguous it seemed to become. The matter of my innocence, only hours earlier an absolute, started to take on qualifications in my own mind.

There were gray areas.

I had not passed on any secret documents, no matter what Gervais might have told the prosecutors. Of that I was certain, because I had never possessed any such documents. But I might have inadvertently passed on classified information I had obtained from some of my sources. Not in printed form, but in conversation. Unless Gervais honestly didn't remember what information he had obtained from me or in what form, then he was lying to the prosecutors—implicating me in hopes of getting the charges against him dropped or reduced.

My mind groped in vain for answers. All I could do was guess. And I didn't know enough even to make good guesses. The truth cannot be seen in the dark.

Four counts of espionage.

I was a victim of either circumstance or conspiracy. Maybe in the morning, with the help of Sam Marks, I would at least find out which.

The night creaked by with interminable slowness, ticking out each second with the ponderous sluggishness of a wound-down clock. By the time a guard brought breakfast around, I was exhausted.

I did my best with the prison's supply of toiletries to make myself look presentable. It was difficult. My underwear and socks smelled and my shirt was wrinkled.

Wallace and Littlefield both showed up around nine o'clock, handcuffed me and took me to room 311, the magistrate's court, on the third floor of the federal courthouse.

It was a tiny, cramped chamber with a low ceiling—not much like a courtroom at all. There were two small windows, one partly plugged with an air conditioner. Three benches faced the judge's platform, barricaded behind a partition. What space remained in the middle of the room was taken up by a pair of lecterns with microphones—one for the defendant and his lawyer, the other for the prosecutor. Two other benches and several wooden chairs lined the side walls.

The chamber showed signs of heavy use. The carpeting was worn and dirty, and had been taped in several places. The benches had lost much of their finish, and the once-yellow walls behind them had been blackened by the many greasy heads that had rested against them since they were last washed or painted. The darkened area formed an unbroken wavy band around the room, like a charcoal mural of some mountain skyline.

I sat on the bench along the back wall, sandwiched between Wallace and Littlefield. They chatted across me about some kidnaping case the Bureau had just broken the day before.

At nine-thirty Sam Marks burst through the door, swinging his attaché case. He looked impatient and grim. He said hello, identified himself, and asked the agents to remove my handcuffs. They did. I stood up.

"In here," Sam said, pointing to a door just behind us marked COUNSEL'S ROOM. We went in and Sam slammed the door behind us. It was a closet-sized space, barely big enough for four chairs and a table. I sat down.

Sam plonked his attaché case down on the table and snapped it open with two angry flicks of a forefinger.

"Jesus, I'm glad to see you," I whispered.

"I wish I could say the same," he replied, with a big sigh.

Samuel Paul Marks was about my age—a tall, slender reed of a man with thinning brown hair and a quiet, inscrutable façade that hid an aggressive, resourceful, encyclopedic mind. He had made a name for himself as a brilliant legal strategist in the courtroom—an attorney who seemed always to be able to come up with a winning defense for his client, no matter how gloomy the prospects.

Sam wasn't a flashy showman. He didn't thunder or weep, or quote the Bible or indulge in mawkish and hypocritical pleas in behalf of his clients. He relied on his knowledge of the law and the courtroom, and on an extraordinary natural ability to win a jury to his side. He did this with more than charm. He exuded a sense of moral virtue and rectitude so thoroughly attractive and convincing to the members of a jury that they just couldn't resist him. By the end of a trial most jurors had come to so identify themselves with Sam Marks—to want Sam Marks's approval—that they would accept any plausible argument from him on behalf of his client. His client could be a sleazeball of the lowest order, but if Sam Marks said he was innocent, the jury tried hard to believe him. Sam just didn't look like the sort of person who could associate himself, even for strictly professional reasons, with a liar or a criminal.

I had met Sam ten years earlier, at the murder trial of celebrity socialite Brian Boyerson. Marks was defending Boyerson and I was covering the trial for *Esquire* magazine. We became friends, and saw each other occasionally over the years.

I even fixed Sam up with Judy, the woman who was now his wife. They had two children. I had slept with Judy twice before her first date with Sam. She was attractive and terrifically smart, but nothing had clicked between us. In fact, we got on each other's nerves.

After their marriage, my friendship with Sam cooled somewhat. We talked on the phone occasionally, and kept promising to get together, but I hadn't seen him in person for several years. It was partly a clash of life-styles. As soon as he was married, Sam became very much the family man. He might defend murderers and child molesters in court, but in his private life he was relentlessly middle-class. I, on the other hand, was usually divorced and single, and apt to be found in disreputable company.

I suspect Judy also had something to do with the chill in relations. As soon as she was safely married to Sam, I think she saw me as a corrupting influence on her husband. Having slept with me herself—a matter of which Sam was innocent—she just knew too damned much about me. And my social life certainly did not amuse her. It didn't amuse me much these days, either.

But friendships and conflicts aside, there was never a second's doubt in my mind who I would call when I was arrested. As a criminal lawyer, Samuel Paul Marks, of Forest Hills, Queens, and Columbia Law School, was as good as they got.

"How do you feel?" Sam asked.

I managed a small laugh. "Much better, now that you're here."

"I'd have been here sooner," he said. "But I wanted to talk to Cardozo first."

My anxiety began to subside. I was sure Sam would have things straightened out in short order. Perhaps he already had straightened them out. I began to feel embarrassed. "It's a shitty experience, Sam—arrest and incarceration. I don't recommend it. I've been awake all night imagining everything from homosexual rape to a firing squad at dawn."

This didn't get even a grin out of Sam.

"How's Judy?" I asked.

"She's fine."

I rubbed my hands over my face. Sam's manner disturbed me. I didn't sense any confidence. He pulled a stack of papers from his attaché case and dropped them on the table in front of me. He remained standing, one foot resting on a chair.

"Tell me what the hell this is?"

I looked at the pages. They were a transcript of my "interview" with Cardozo.

"What did you think you were doing?" Marks demanded. "Acting as your own attorney?"

"I wanted to find out what they were charging me with."

Marks sighed. "You were a goddamned fool, John, is what you were. Especially against someone like El Cardozo. He's a killer."

"I broke it off when he came after me with his muleta and sword."

"A good thing, too," Sam grumbled. "Another half an hour and he'd have cut off an ear and a testicle and thrown them to the crowd."

I didn't disagree.

"The FBI. Did they Mirandize you?"

"Yes, they Mirandized me. Twice, in fact."

"Did they show you an arrest warrant?"

"Yes. Then they stripped me, punched me, stomped on me, handcuffed me and dragged me down here."

"At what point did they tell you you were under arrest?"

I squinted at Marks incredulously. "Does that make a difference?"

"Yes, it makes a difference. The first thing we need to know is if the arrest was legal. They frequently fuck up on procedure, and when they do, they jeopardize their case. If they picked up evidence at your apartment without a proper search warrant, for example, we can move to have that evidence quashed."

"I don't know if they had a search warrant or not. All I saw was the arrest warrant. I think that's all I saw, anyway." I described how Wallace and Littlefield had ripped the tape recorder from my shoulder holster and roughed me up.

"How are you now? Any bruises that show?"

"I don't think so. Probably not."

"Want me to get a doctor to check you? See if you have internal injuries?"

"No."

"It's your word against theirs, then."

"The hell with it. They'd say I resisted arrest. And they'd be right. Just get me out of here."

Sam sat on the edge of the table. "Okay. Now listen to me. We'll discuss the merits of the case later. Right now we have to worry about one thing. The bail. The magistrate'll be coming in any minute. We're first on the docket this morning. I've talked to Cardozo. He's going to ask for a very high bail."

My guts tightened another turn. "How high?"

Marks scratched the back of his hand. "He was vague about it. Said he hadn't made up his mind, but don't be surprised if it's half a million."

I choked. "Half a million dollars?"

Sam put a hand on my shoulder. "I know, I know. It's ridiculous. But the charges against you are serious. Extremely. Conviction on any one count can carry a life sentence. Treason cases make law-enforcement types angry and scared. Their impulse is to show no mercy."

Sam pulled out a pad and pen and started to scribble some notes. "I'm going to insist that you be released on a PRB," he said. "Personal recognizance bond. You've no previous arrest record, you're an upstanding citizen with roots in the community, and so forth. The Pretrial Services report will certainly be favorable. The magistrate this week is Harriet Waterman. She should go for a PRB, but on this one we have to face the chance that she may not. She might compromise. If Cardozo asks for half a million, and I argue strenuously enough, she should at the very least come down halfway—to two hundred and fifty thousand. That's my guess. That's what you have to be prepared for."

My throat felt as if it had rocks in it. I wiped my palms on my pants legs.

"You'll need collateral," Sam said. "Stocks, bonds, property deeds, that kind of thing. And they'll want at least ten percent in cash before they'll let you out. That might be twenty-five thousand dollars. Can you raise that?"

"I don't know," I mumbled. "I don't have it in the bank." The thought that I might not be able to go free immediately after the bail hearing had never even occurred to me. I was finding it hard to believe.

Wallace stuck his head in the door. "They're ready out here," he said. Marks waved him away.

"Now, this thing has a long way to go," Sam said, poking his case with the end of his forefinger. It was a characteristic of his, I remembered. He had long pianist's fingers, and he liked to poke things with them when he was saying something important. "Don't start imagining the worst yet. After the hearing, we'll find out how strong a case they really have. Maybe it won't even survive a grand jury."

"Imagining the worst? Christ, I can't imagine any worse, Sam."

Marks didn't reply. He busied himself putting papers back into his attaché case.

"You don't think I'm guilty, do you?"

Sam cleared his throat with some difficulty. "Look . . . what can I say? They have a case against you. Come on, let's get this over with."

Marks followed me back into the courtroom. Cardozo was there, standing by the lectern on the right, looking sharp as a swindler in a tight-fitting dark blue double-breasted suit. The cloth hung from his lean frame flawlessly. His red silk tie with blue polka dots was knotted perfectly and the matching handkerchief was precisely folded in his breast pocket. He brushed some lint off his sleeves, revealing French cuffs and gold cuff links.

Someone said, "Please rise." A door by the judge's platform opened and a short, businesslike woman with iron-colored hair and half-frame glasses perched near the end of her nose strode across to the big leather chair behind her bench and settled herself in. Once she was sitting, I could see only her head and neck.

She studied some papers in front of her for a moment, then looked up at Cardozo. "When was the defendant arrested?" she asked.

Cardozo told her.

"Do you swear the statements in the affidavit are true?" she asked.

"I do, Your Honor."

"What is the government's position on bail?"

Cardozo stood very straight. "Your Honor, although the defendant has no previous criminal record, he has been charged with one of the most serious crimes a man can commit—the crime of treason. The evidence the government has collected against him is well documented and persuasive. It will show that the defendant, using a well-developed network of informants and collaborators, has, for a prolonged period of time, been engaged in illegally collecting vital military and diplomatic secrets and passing them on to the agent of a hostile foreign power. The damage this espionage has done to our national security has not yet been fully assessed, but we expect that it will prove to be substantial."

Cardozo, who was standing barely three feet from me, glanced over at me briefly, then turned back to the magistrate. "Few acts can be as damaging to a country and its people as the act of espionage. It is a crime deserving of the severest punishment. If the defendant is found guilty, as we have every confidence he will be, we would expect to ask the government for a life term, without possibility of parole. . . ."

"Come to the point, please, Mr. Cardozo," Judge Waterman said.

El Cardozo reddened slightly at the interruption, then continued: "Considering the seriousness of the charges against the defendant, and considering the defendant's relative affluence, and the likelihood that he would consider fleeing the country rather than facing life in prison, the government requests that the bail be sufficiently high to either prevent his release from government custody or at the very least guarantee his appearance in court. The sum of one million dollars, half to be put up as a cash bond, should satisfy those requirements."

I felt faint. I grabbed the wooden railing in front of me and held it tight.

Judge Waterman peered over her half-frames at Sam Marks: "Counsel?"

Sam hit back angrily: "Your Honor, the government's request is patently ridiculous. Not only does my client have no previous arrest record, he is a prominent and respected citizen, a journalist with an international reputation. His books have been published in many countries and have won awards for their exposures of corruption and wrongdoing. And the government's case, Mr. Cardozo's fantasies to the contrary, is based on the most extraordinary combination of hearsay and slander, and a basic failure of the governmental agencies involved to understand the nature of my client's profession—or indeed, the meaning of a free press in a democracy. The case brought against my client totally misconstrues the legitimate gathering of news as the practice of espionage. My client is an investigative journalist. He sometimes steps on the toes of the big and the powerful, and that may make him a nuisance. It doesn't make him a spy. It looks to me as if the government is trying to silence him. I seriously doubt that a grand jury will return an indictment on this complaint. Under the circumstances, the only fair and reasonable thing to do is to release my client on a PRB. The vindication of his good name is absolutely essential to him both personally and professionally. There is no question of his not making all his court appearances."

Judge Waterman turned her gaze to El Cardozo, who had been listening to Sam's rebuttal with an amused grin. "How does the government respond, Mr. Cardozo?"

"I have only the greatest respect for my colleague here, but I must object to his characterization of the government's case against his client. He has not yet had the opportunity to review all the evidence we have collected. Granted, an enterprising journalist may sometimes gain access to government secrets—the Pentagon Papers case, for example—and exercise his First Amendment rights to make these secrets public in the belief that they serve the greater good of the public's right to know. It's a gray area. Men of goodwill can and do argue either side of this issue. It is also true that a journalist has a right to protect his sources—even if these sources have themselves broken the law by passing classified information to the journalist. But what is not in dispute—in the law or even in the realm of public opinion—is the right of anyone— journalist or great statesman—to secretly pass classified information, however obtained, to the agent of an unfriendly power. This is treason—pure and simple. And the government will prove that Mr. Brady has knowingly engaged in precisely this activity."

The argument continued back and forth. I found I was unable to maintain my attention. My head was nodding. I had to blink my eyes hard to force them open. My legs felt weak and my knees were wobbling. I wanted to sit down.

The courtroom fell silent. Sam Marks and Vincent Cardozo had finished their debate, and the federal magistrate was trying to make her determination on bail. Sam had told me that she was a very decisive woman, so I was surprised that she seemed to be taking such a long time to make up her mind.

She read some papers on her desk, looked up at me several times, read some more, gazed out the window, and then announced her decision.

"This is a difficult judgment for the court to make," she began. "Both sides have presented persuasive arguments to support their recommendations. I feel my decision, therefore, must be a compromise, taking into account the extreme seriousness of the charges against the accused. In any espionage case, there is a greater than ordinary danger of flight to avoid prosecution. Perhaps there's no such danger in this case—the defendant's history would indicate there is not—but still the court feels that there must be bail, and that it should be high enough to make any thought of flight on the part of the defendant very unlikely. I set the amount at half a million dollars. I will require that fifty percent of this be posted in cash. I will also require that the defendant surrender his passport to the court until the disposition of his case."

The magistrate looked at Sam Marks. "Is your client able to post bail?"

"Not at this time, Your Honor."

She explained to me that I would be held at the Metropolitan Correctional Center until I could come up with the bail money— or until my trial was over.

Wallace put the handcuffs back on me and he and Littlefield escorted me back to the MCC. Sam Marks came with us.

7

GETTING OUT

There was a special room in the Metropolitan Correctional Center for prisoners to confer in private with their lawyers. Sam Marks met me there half an hour after my bail hearing. The room was divided by a waist-high wall surmounted with a heavy steel-mesh partition that ran all the way to the ceiling. A shelf ran along each side, and chairs were positioned facing each other at four stations along the barrier. A guard kept watch from the door on the prisoners' side.

When they brought me in, Marks was already sitting at one of the stations on the other side of the barrier, fidgeting with his tie. Another prisoner and his attorney were bent in deep conversation at the far end. Their whispering voices reverberated faintly around the tiled walls.

I slumped into the chair opposite Sam. I had never felt so lost and helpless in my life. "What am I going to do?" I said. "I don't have a quarter of a million dollars in cash. Who the hell does?"

Marks nodded sympathetically. "I'm sorry about that."

"It's not your fault. You argued my side magnificently."

Marks grimaced in disgust. "The prosecutor screwed us. And the judge didn't help. She always splits it down the middle like that. If Cardozo had asked for *two* million, she'd have compromised at *one*."

"You should have asked the court to lend me a million. That way she might have sprung me on recognizance."

Marks grunted at my attempted humor. He pulled a pen from his pocket and snapped open his attaché case. The guard looked over at us. "I'll try to get the bail reduced," he said. "That'll take a few days, though. No way you can raise the money? Relatives?"

"Maybe your relatives, Sam. Not mine. My old man's dead, my mother's living on some savings and Social Security. She's got high blood pressure. I don't even want her to know I've been arrested. I have a sister in Hartford. Her husband's with one of the insurance companies there. They're comfortable, but they don't have a quarter of a million kicking around. They think I'm the rich one."

Marks began nervously punching the button on the end of his pen with his thumb, releasing and retracting the point. "How about some collateral I can convert to cash for you? Stocks, property deeds, that kind of thing?"

I shook my head. "My apartment. That's it. It might be worth half a million by now, but it's a co-op. I don't know if it can be used as collateral or not. And anyway, it's mortgaged to the hilt."

"What about that house in Vermont?"

"Alicia got that with the divorce."

"I thought she was an heiress, or something."

"She is. She's worth fifty million. When her mother dies, she'll be worth a hundred and fifty million."

"Ask her."

"I couldn't stand to give her the pleasure of turning me down."

Marks seemed perplexed. "I don't get it, John. You've had what—two, three best-sellers? What've you done with all the money?"

I looked away. The prisoner down at the end of the barrier, an angry-looking black with a gold earring and dreadlocks, was arguing some point passionately with his attorney. He kept punching the steel mesh in front of him with his fist, his voice raised to a hoarse stage whisper. I knew exactly how he felt.

What the hell *had* I done with all the money? I didn't really know. "It's gone, Sam. Here, there, everywhere. Gone. On living, on travel. On I don't know what. I'm not smart with money. If you asked Alicia she'd say it was because I'm Irish. We're born servants, she'd say, good at drinking, brawling and story-telling. Maybe that's the best answer."

Marks looked shocked, incredulous. "You're not using drugs, are you?"

The question angered me. "No, I'm not, Sam. Look. I make a good living, but my expenses are high. Alicia might be rich, but I pay another ex-wife alimony—five hundred a month. The maintenance charges on my apartment are almost two thousand a month, the mortgage is fifteen hundred. Property, auto and health insurance eats up another five hundred a month. And so on. It adds up. It costs me seven thousand a month just to meet basic expenses. And it takes three, four years to write a book. There are heavy outlays for research. I don't deny myself, but I'm not exactly a big spender, either."

"You're telling me you have no money?" Having no money, to Sam, was probably as serious a crime as espionage.

"Worse, Sam. I'm in debt. Negative cash flow. Right now, I'm down about fifty thousand dollars. And I will be for at least a couple more months, until I collect another installment on my book advance, or get some royalty money. I don't even know how I'm going to pay you. And I hate to think what you're going to charge me."

Marks put his pen down and looked at me sternly. "If you want to get out of here, John, you've got to think of some way to raise bail. This case may take months. I'm sorry. That's the way it is."

I slumped in my chair.

Marks picked up the pen again. "You must have some rich friends who could post bail for you."

I had considered that. I had always thought of myself as such a well-connected individual. I had dined with senators and ambassadors, met royalty, been to the White House, slept with movie stars, palled around with sports celebrities, movie directors and famous writers. I did know a lot of rich and influential people. My Rolodex was very impressive. But it wasn't going to get me out of jail. "None so friendly they'd be willing to put a quarter of a million dollars at risk for me."

"You never know. Ask them."

"I can't think of anybody, Sam."

"Let's come back to it," he suggested. "I want to discuss the case with you." He pulled out of his attaché case the transcript of my encounter with Cardozo the day before and began leafing through it. "Where did this material come from that Cardozo said you gave to Gervais?"

"I don't know."

"You said some of it looked familiar."

"I had some of the same information in my computer. Research notes. Cardozo had those, too. Somehow they got the material. Damned if I know how. They must have downloaded it from the computer, somehow."

"How much is there?"

I thought about it. "I never printed it out. But there must be the equivalent of three hundred single-spaced pages."

"You think they got access to all of it?"

"If they got this, they must have the rest."

"What's in the rest?" Marks pointed down to the transcript. "More stuff like this?"

"Sam, I'm doing a biography of the director of the CIA. Sure it's more stuff like this."

"We'll have to try to prove they obtained this material illegally."

"Why do we have to prove anything? I have every right to that material. I didn't steal it. It's the product of a lot of damned difficult legwork."

A pained look spread across Sam's lean features. "If we can prove they obtained the material illegally, it can't be submitted as evidence. And without it, I doubt a prosecutor could sell this to a grand jury. So, no indictment. You're a free man. With it, I think he can. That means a trial. Let's try to get out of this the easy way, John."

I pressed the heels of my palms against my eyes and yawned so hard I felt my jaw snap. "Somebody is doing this to me. Setting me up. It can't be an accident."

Marks directed me back to the subject of my defense. "Is it possible that you *did* give those CIA documents to Gervais?"

"No, Sam, damn it. No. I never saw them." I explained to Marks the business about the confidential interoffice memos that circulated among the top *Time* magazine editors, and how I still obtained copies of them. "That's the only thing I ever actually gave to Gervais."

"Well, is it possible you *told* him some of the information that was in those CIA reports?"

I sighed. "Yes. That's possible."

"Well, how the hell *did* you get that information if you didn't get it from the CIA documents themselves?"

"I told you, Sam. Legwork. Sources . . ."

"Who, John? Who? I want the who, what, why, where and when. I can't defend you unless I know the whole story."

I shook my head.

"For God's sake," Sam said. "I'm not going to tell anyone, if that's your concern. There is such a thing as lawyer-client privilege, you know."

"Okay. There's a woman works at Langley. We were in graduate school together. She was a political-science major. A real committed public-service type. She did two years in the Peace Corps, then decided . . . I don't know, somehow she ended up working for the CIA. She's a brilliant political analyst, and that's what she does for them. Analyze. She has a real sensitive position. Top clearance. Sees everything. Some of what she sees she doesn't like. She sometimes leaks stuff to me. On a very selective basis, mind you."

"In what form?"

"I can't tell you that."

Marks threw up his hands in defeat. "Well, does her name happen to appear anywhere in those computer files of yours?"

"No. I give all my sources private code names. Any references to her in the files would be only her code name. She's 'Cassandra.' "

"I see. Did the two of you . . . was there ever any romantic involvement?"

Sex embarrassed Sam.

"We slept together a couple of times. Years ago, when we were in graduate school. It's irrelevant."

"You never know. Where do you keep your sources' real names?"

"In my head."

"Nowhere else?"

"No."

"Thank God for that, anyway. You realize that if they caught her she could be charged with serious crimes?"

I was getting exasperated by Sam's attitude. "That's why I protect her identity. I'm an investigative journalist, Sam, remember? I deal with people who risk getting arrested, losing their jobs—and worse—all the time. Where have you been?"

"Defending them."

"Yeah. Sorry."

"How many more sources like her do you have?"

"Dozens."

"Your own spy network?"

"Sure, Sam. But there's a minor difference. Any spying I do is for the public, not a foreign power."

"What about René Gervais?"

"I had no idea he was working for the Libyans or the PLO or whoever the hell he was working for. If I knew, you think I'd have given him anything? Or ever met with him? I'm not stupid."

"You were careless, then. Is that your defense?"

"You can't run background checks on everybody you talk to. You don't have the clearances and you don't have the time. You're always racing the clock or the competition. Gervais's information was reliable, it checked out, and that's what mattered. He was a useful source. And I paid him back in kind."

"You were a useful source to him, you mean."

"Yes."

"Maybe his information checked out too well. Didn't some of it raise your suspicions?"

"Absolutely not. Maybe it should have, but it didn't. I considered him resourceful, a good reporter. I never had any reason to suspect him. None. An enterprising reporter can get that kind of information. I know, because I do it. So I wasn't surprised. Maybe if I'd taken the time to look back over all the bits and pieces he'd ever handed me, I'd have seen some suspicious patterns, but who the hell has time to do that? There just was no reason to doubt him."

Sam scratched his chin. His expression was doleful. "The government has a case against you, John. That's the bottom line. You appear to have passed classified documents to an agent of a foreign government. Even if you didn't do it wittingly, you did do it. Or at least you appear to have done it. And not once, but repeatedly. And we can't make much of a case for you by claiming you were just naive. Especially if Gervais testifies against you."

"Well shit, Sam, he can't do that. He knows I wasn't aware of his involvement with any foreign government."

"He *can* do that. And he probably *will* do that. Most likely he's already made a plea-bargain deal with the federal prosecutors. The more names he gives them, the more points he scores. He may be willing to sacrifice you to get some time off his sentence."

"I know the guy. I can't believe he'd do anything that dishonest."

"Jesus, John, the man is a spy. Being dishonest is what he's all about. And he's already incriminated you. Probably to protect someone else."

"I don't follow that."

"If you didn't give him those CIA documents, then somebody else did. Who?"

"I don't know. A real spy?"

"Bingo."

I tipped my head back and stared at the ceiling. The tight, fluttering sensation in my chest and stomach returned. I wanted to wail, to moan, to cry out in anger and pain.

Marks closed his attaché case. "I've got to go, John. I'll be back this afternoon. It might be a bit late."

"Okay."

"You need anything from your apartment?"

"A change of underwear and shirts. And my shaving kit. If they'll let me have it in here."

"Keys?"

"The super will let you in."

"You want me to call anybody for you?"

I thought about it. "No. I don't want anybody to know."

"It might be in the newspapers."

"Then they can read it in the papers."

"Where do you keep the shares you own on your co-op?"

"The bank has them. I told you, they're mortgaged."

"There still might be enough equity there. Give me the name of the bank. I'll find out."

I gave Marks the information. He wrote it down on a small pad and tucked it in his jacket pocket.

I bit my lip. It was hard for me to remain composed in the face of this grinding government assault on my career and my personal liberty. But there was nothing heroic to be done. I had to sit and wait, and trust my fate to others. The true peril of my situation— the possibility of my actually being found guilty and sentenced to a long term in prison—was still not something I could grasp as real. What I felt was the depressing weight of my powerlessness.

Marks left and the guard took me back to the cell block. The cell I had slept in the night before was no longer mine. Since I had been arraigned, I was now officially in the hands of the U.S. Marshal's Service and the Bureau of Prisons. This entitled me to an orange prison jumpsuit and a new cell. It was the same size as the first cell, but it had a bunk bed in it and a cellmate to share it with.

The cellmate was skinny, young and Hispanic. He was lying on his back on the bottom bunk when I was let in, pounding his fist into his palm, muttering to himself in Spanish. He stopped the pounding long enough to register my presence. His eyes were glassy and his expression somewhere between stunned and crazed. He quickly lost interest in me, and went back to his muttering and pounding. I climbed up onto the top bunk and stretched out on it. The ceiling was barely two feet from my face. I stared at it and fell immediately asleep.

Sam Marks returned at around three o'clock. "It's all set," he said, grinning back at me through the steel-mesh grating.

"What is?"

"Your bail."

I felt a dizzying rush of euphoria. "God, that's great. How did you do it? Did they reduce it?"

Sam snapped open his case and pulled out some papers. "I found someone to put up the money. It's all arranged. Sign these forms and we'll get you out of here. I took your passport from your apartment, by the way. You know you have to surrender it to the court along with the bail bond."

"Who did you find? Who's putting up bail?"

Mark's grin grew wider. "An old friend of yours. Someone who obviously thinks a great deal of you. And happens to have no trouble coming up with a few hundred grand."

"Don't keep me in suspense."

"I would think you'd have guessed—Tracy Anderson."

I went limp.

Marks cocked his head at me questioningly. "What's the problem?"

"Did you call her and ask her?"

"No. I wouldn't have done that without your permission. She called me. My first thought was, Of course! Tracy Anderson. Why didn't John ask me to call her? And there she was, calling on her own. She actually came down to our offices. She created quite a commotion. You'd think they'd be immune to celebrities, but they were like a bunch of star-struck fans. Everybody had to get a look at her."

"How could she have known?"

"I don't know. I didn't even think to ask her. It must have been on the news last night."

"Tracy Anderson doesn't watch the news."

Mark's grin faded. He looked hurt. "You don't seem very damned pleased."

"I'm grateful to you, Sam. Of course."

"What's the problem, then?"

I shook my head. "No problem. I was just trying to stay away from her, that's all."

Sam laughed. "Stay away from her? Wait until I tell that to Judy."

I signed the bail forms. Tracy Anderson had delivered to the court $250,000 in cash, and another $250,000 in T-bills and certificates of deposit. If I failed to show up for my trial, she'd lose it all.

In twenty minutes I had my possessions back, and was standing out in the afternoon sunlight of Foley Square, temporarily a free man. Sam Marks hailed a cab and we rode uptown together.

"What happens now?" I asked.

"Nothing—for a few days. Cardozo will present his case to a grand jury in about a week. Meanwhile, I'll find out how much more he has. If it's just this business with René Gervais, I think we have an excellent chance at a dismissal."

"How long will it take the grand jury to decide?"

"Hard to say. A few days. But don't get your hopes up. They'll probably return an indictment against you. Grand juries are predictably a little in awe of espionage cases. And count on Cardozo to paint a frightening picture for them. You'll be portrayed as the enemy within, burrowing away at the foundations of our great society, threatening the liberty of us all. He'll call in René Gervais, he'll call in witnesses from the FBI, he'll put on a show. And it'll all be done in secret. The grand jury can question witnesses, but basically it's a trial with no defense. All they hear is the prosecution side. Fortunately all they can do is deliver an indictment. You're still innocent in the eyes of the law."

"How nice."

"I almost forgot," Sam said. He reached into his breast pocket and pulled out a small embossed envelope, the kind used for sending out invitations and thank-you notes. "Miss Anderson gave me this to give to you."

I ripped it open impatiently and pulled out the thick square of notepaper:

My Precious Darling Johnny,
What terrible news about you! I'm so pleased to be able to help. In return, you must promise to come to dinner this evening. Seven-thirty. I have someone who wants to meet you. It's important. Don't disappoint me!

I love you, darling,
Tracy

I handed the note to Sam Marks. He read it and handed it back to me. His expression was thoughtful. "Judy and I used to talk about this a lot," he said.

"Talk about what?"

"About you and Tracy. I mean, we both know you pretty well, so we always wondered what it was like."

"Fucking a movie star, you mean?"

Sam's face reddened. "Well, that's putting it pretty crudely. I mean your whole relationship. . . ."

I laughed. "You aren't the first to ask, Sam."

"Okay," Marks said. "I withdraw the question, Your Honor."

"No, I'll answer it. It's the worst thing that ever happened to me."

Marks nodded. "That's interesting. That's what Judy always thought. I find it a little hard to believe, myself."

"So do I, Sam."

THE BUGS

Back safely once more behind the walls of my apartment, I poured myself half a tumblerful of scotch, threw in a few ice cubes and a splash of water and went into the study to check the messages on the answering machine.

There was only one—from Gloria:

"It's me again, Johnny. My lawyer told me that if you don't cable me the money by tomorrow, latest, you're in mucho *big trouble. God, you're so* unreliable. *I know it's a drag, but you do have the money, after all. Why do you put me through this hassle every month? I think you just like to make me suffer. It was your idea to leave me, don't forget that. If it was up to me, we'd still be together. So you have only yourself to blame. . . . Anyway, I'm going to get a job pretty soon, so I won't be so dependent on you. I'm following*

up on a couple of things that I'll tell you about later. . . . Since I've been in Mexico I've really found a lot of answers—about myself, and about life. There's this psychic here I met recently, and she's told me some incredible *things. I mean incredible! I know you think it's all nonsense, but you know what she told me yesterday? She said I was once married to someone named John Brady. She actually knew your name! I swear! Isn't that amazing? She also said she thought you were in some kind of serious trouble. She said there were people out to get you. My God, is that true? I mean I got really upset when she told me that. She was right about so many other things, I began to wonder, maybe something was wrong, and that's why I haven't heard from you. If you're really in trouble, you can always come down here and stay with us, you know. . . . I wish you'd just call me and let me know what's going on. I'm sorry to bug you, but I* really *need the money, Johnny. I mean I really do."*

The machine clunked off. I rewound the tape and checked it again. Just Gloria's monologue. I had expected the tape to be jammed with calls from the wire services, the major newspapers, the networks. My agent. But there was nothing. It puzzled me.

I opened the *Times* and thumbed through it, page by page, carefully checking every item. On page B11 I found Admiral Conover's obituary. The article provided a brief summary of the admiral's career, and listed the cause of death as a stroke.

There was nothing anywhere in the newspaper about my arrest.

Odd. How could they have missed it? Journalist and best-selling author arrested in New York for espionage. It rated the front page, above the fold. But there was nothing. A complete and inexplicable silence.

I sipped the scotch, and pressed the side of the cold tumbler against my cheek. I wasn't sure if I was relieved or disappointed. Or both. On the one hand, I was grateful not to have to cope with a crowd of bloodthirsty fellow journalists trying to beat down my door. But the press was acutely sensitive to its First Amendment rights. Whenever a reporter was arrested or harassed, anywhere, the press could be counted on to launch an instant media blitz, blanketing the airwaves and the news pages with the story. An arrested reporter was to the news media what a murdered cop was to the police. A time to close ranks. A summons to action. What happens to him or her could happen to any of us. Band of brothers. All for one, and one for all—that kind of stuff.

But not this time? Maybe I wasn't considered part of the brother-hood anymore. I didn't work for a newspaper or a network. I wrote books, not news stories. I was an author, a loner with no real allegiances to anybody.

I thought about telephoning some friends on the newspapers to find out what they knew, but of course that would put them onto the story. For the moment anonymity was best.

I rummaged around on the desk, found Gail Snow's telephone number and dialed it. This time I got a recorded message informing me that the number I had reached was no longer in service.

This bothered me. A lot. I had been clinging to the fading hope that I was going to get back together with Gail Snow. And that she would have some reasonably innocent explanation for having tied me to the bed and walked off with my files on Andrew Carlson.

I paced around the apartment, nursing the scotch. The batteries for my microcassette recorder, ripped from my shoulder holster by Wallace when they arrested me, still lay where they had fallen, in front of the bookcase in the living room. I picked them up and put them on the bookshelf. The FBI had returned the shoulder holster, the recorder and the tape that was in it, which contained my interview with Conover. Incredibly, they hadn't even bothered to listen to it.

I walked back to the telephone, called *Newsweek* magazine and asked the switchboard to ring Gail Snow's number.

There was a lengthy pause. Finally: "No one here by that name, sir."

"You sure?"

"Would you like me to connect you with someone in personnel?"

Personnel verified what the operator had just said—no one there by that name.

I dialed information for area code 516.

"What city, please?"

"Glen Cove."

"Yes?"

"Do you have any listings for Snow. S-N-O-W, as in winter."

"First name?"

"Don't know."

Within seconds I heard a computerized voice: "The number is: 246-3187. Please make a note of it: 246-3187."

I dialed the number. An old man answered.

"Is Gail there?"

"Who?"

"Gail. Gail Snow."

"You must have the wrong number, Bud."

"Is this 246-3187?"

"Yes it is, but there's no Gail Snow lives here."

"Are you Mr. Snow?"

"That's right. But there's no Gail Snow here."

"Do you know anyone by that name?"

"Afraid not, Bud. My wife's name was Anna. She's dead now. I have a son, his name is Paul. Lives in Florida. His wife's name is Patty. Had an aunt named Nell, but that's about as close to Gail as anyone in our family ever got. Now there's some Snows that used to live up near Lyme, Connecticut. There might be a Gail there. . . ."

"Thank you."

I called information again to make sure there were no other listings under Snow in Glen Cove. There weren't. I got out a map and tried all the surrounding towns—Glen Head, Great Neck and so on. No more Snows.

I paced around some more, sipping rapidly at the scotch. What the hell was going on? I was damned if this woman was going to disappear on me like this.

I managed to locate by phone a friendly and cooperative staff member at the Wellesley College library. I laid on a long and not entirely untrue story about looking for a lost girlfriend. She checked all the names of Wellesley graduates from 1980 to the present, and called me back to inform me that there was not a single Gail Snow among them.

I thanked her and hung up.

If Gail Snow had lied about her past, then it was also possible that she had lied about her name as well. I was probably looking for somebody who didn't exist.

I unscrewed the mouthpiece of the telephone and knocked the microphone diaphragm out into my hand. I turned it over a few times, examining it, then replaced it and screwed the mouthpiece back into place. The diaphragm looked identical to the one that had originally come with the phone, but I knew it wasn't. I had marked the original with a pair of small scratches on the edge. This one was unscratched, and although it otherwise looked entirely innocent, I knew that as sure as the earth was round and revolved around the sun, the diaphragm had a remote-controlled listening device built into it.

I went into the bedroom and examined the other phone. Same story. Since the bugs were built into the diaphragm, I couldn't remove them without disabling my phones. I would have to buy new ones.

I looked at the back of the television set on the chest opposite my bed. The changed positions of the slots in the screw heads told me that the back cover had been recently removed. So another device was hidden in there. I found a Phillips head screwdriver and removed the back. With a flashlight I was able to locate the bug fairly quickly. They had not bothered to hide it very well, probably because they had assumed I wouldn't open up the set. Most people wouldn't. I removed the small plastic device and replaced the back of the set, once again lining up all the screw heads vertically.

Over the next hour I found three more bugs—one under the toilet tank in the bathroom, another behind the Con Ed gas meter in my kitchen, and a third tucked up inside the frame of my living-room sofa. I suspected there might be more. I'd have to get Frank Chin to bring in his electronic gear and do a sweep for me.

It was almost pointless to bother. The technology of electronic eavesdropping was so advanced that if the FBI wanted to bug me, I would have to live with it. By removing these bugs I was only telling them I knew what they were doing. That meant they'd just replace them with more sophisticated ones. But I had to put up a fight.

Had Gail Snow installed these devices? Or had the FBI simply sent a team of technicians over after my arrest?

I took the screwdriver into my study and removed the metal case that covered the central processing unit of my computer. I swung the desk lamp over the unit and peered inside. Nothing out of the ordinary caught my eye. I got out the computer's wiring diagram from the instruction manual, laid it out alongside the opened case, and made another, more careful search. Eventually I found it. It was so big I had overlooked it.

Residing in what had once been an empty add-on slot between the internal modem and the color-monitor adapter was a bulky, tightly packed sandwich of circuit boards, wires, resistors, capacitors and other exotic gadgetry.

My knowledge of computers was limited, but I knew that what I was looking at was a kind of electronic Trojan horse. I could imagine—guessing from its considerable size and complexity, and the fact that it had leads that tapped it directly into both the power line and the modem's telephone line—what it was capable of doing. Most likely it could switch the computer on from some remote location by sending a signal over the telephone line, and then download the files from my hard disk.

Once they had my material copied and stored in their own computer, they could break the access codes that went with it at their leisure.

I sat down heavily. At least I now knew how Cardozo and the Justice Department had obtained my files on the Carlson book.

The fictitious Gail Snow had not installed this. That was certain. Tying me to the bed had given her time to snoop around the study and swipe my tray of floppy disks, but it hadn't given her time to do major implant surgery on my computer.

How long had the damned thing been in there? Weeks? Months? And what about the other bugs? When was the last time I had checked the telephones and the TV set? Never. That was when. I was paranoid, but I was also careless.

I had been living and working with an invisible audience. My every conversation and thought—spoken or written—was available immediately to the FBI. No wonder Cardozo's dossier on me was so thick.

I replaced the cover on the CPU, booted up the computer and called up the directory containing the files on Andrew Carlson.

I got another shock. The directory was empty.

I reset the computer and tried again. The Carlson directory still showed no files. I gaped at the screen in disbelief. I tried the MS–DOS RECOVER program, which could sometimes recapture files that had run afoul of a bad sector on a disk. It recovered nothing. I looked through all the directories on the disk, hoping the files might have somehow gotten misplaced. Nothing anywhere.

Having copied all my files, the bastards had then decided to erase them from my disk. And they had done this just in the last day or two.

Everything was gone. Six months' worth of effort. I had stored some floppies with some interviews and notes in my safe-deposit box at the bank, but I had neglected to update it for a long time.

I switched the computer off, yanked the power-cord plug from the wall outlet and unsnapped the modem's telephone line.

I drained off the rest of the scotch and plunked the empty glass down onto the desk. I rubbed my hands over my face.

My situation was intolerable. I was not used to being a victim. Everything was in jeopardy—my professional career, my personal well-being—everything.

The enormity of my predicament paralyzed me. I couldn't think, couldn't plan. I wanted to sleep, to make my mind a blank, to forget, to escape.

I picked up the empty scotch glass and threw it across the room, aiming for the window. It missed and hit the wall. Instead of shattering, it dropped with a dull thunk onto the carpet, spewing out the remains of the drink and the ice cubes.

I stared at the wet spot on the wall, tears of frustration welling in my eyes.

The glass had not even dented the plaster.

9

TRACY ANDERSON

I slipped my hand through the strap by the rear window. It was soft black leather. The whole interior of the limousine was soft black leather. The embodiment of privilege and luxury, I thought. The look, smell and feel of it.

Tracy's distinctive perfume permeated the space and enveloped me in recollections of past places, events and conversations that caused me twinges of both nostalgia and regret.

Evening was falling and it was raining. It seemed that it had been raining for days. The world outside the limousine appeared colorless, muted, forlorn—draped in shades of gray. Park Avenue, the stone and concrete walls of the prewar apartment buildings flanking it on either side, the swath of sky overhead—all gray and sad. Even I felt gray and sad.

Oscar, behind the wheel up front, had said barely a word to me. I wondered if the old man remembered me. His real name wasn't Oscar. It was Prosper. He was from Haiti and was at least eighty years old. Tracy Anderson called him Oscar because of some long-since-forgotten joke having to do with the Academy Awards. She was in the habit of renaming all her servants. (She had also renamed herself. Inspired as a teenager by Katharine Hepburn's role as Tracy Lord in *The Philadelphia Story*, she had changed her first name from Trude to Tracy.) And she was something of a tyrant in her dealings with them. But she never fired them. And they seldom left her.

She got her hooks deep into people—servants, agents, friends, fellow actors and lovers alike. She demanded an extraordinary degree of loyalty from those around her, and through various combinations of charm, money, promises, intimidation, flirtatiousness and protestations of helplessness extracted it from them. No matter how rotten her behavior, people stuck with her—the way you'd stick with a troublesome and exasperating member of the family. Because you were emotionally involved.

I was twenty-nine years old when Tracy Anderson first invaded my life.

I was a reporter for *Time* magazine. With the exception of a six-month stint on a small-town newspaper in Connecticut, I had been there since graduating from Boston University, and was getting restless. The job paid well, but promotions were glacial and the atmosphere was political and cutthroat. I felt like an outsider. And I didn't like *Time*'s style of group journalism. In those days you didn't even get a byline. You could write your ass off, and nobody in the outside world would ever know it. Nobody took you seriously as a journalist—even on the magazine itself. Especially on the magazine itself. Like the dozens of other reporters, I was nobody. Anonymous. A creature who provided reams of copy on demand for some unseen editors to chop up and rewrite to fit the spaces left between the cigarette and liquor ads—and often to fit their particular views on the subject.

As a career it was a dead end, unless your goal in life was to be a male-chauvinist bureaucrat. I saw myself in my fifties still filing stories from Southwest Nowhere that some editor on the twenty-fourth floor would either mutilate or kill entirely between his three-martini lunch and late-night closing dalliance with one of the resident female fact-checkers.

Groping around for alternatives, I wrote to a new magazine called *Tomorrow*. It was making a big splash in the city. In the one year of its existence, it had earned a reputation for running controversial stories that other magazines wouldn't touch. It didn't pay well, but it was muckraking and irreverent and it had style. It was also a showcase for new writers. If your work appeared in *Tomorrow*, people talked about it.

I suggested an article on the Swedish actress Tracy Anderson, who had just divorced her French film-director husband and come to this country to make her first American movie. I was already an ardent fan. I had seen all four of her films many times, from the low-budget Swedish romantic comedy shot when she was nineteen to her latest, a widely acclaimed movie about French women collaborators during the Second World War. Miss Anderson, just turned thirty-two, was already a celebrity in Europe, where her jet-set life-style and turbulent marriages had made her a regular feature in the fan magazines and tabloids. But she wasn't yet well known in the United States.

No American magazine had done a major profile of her, and I pressed that point upon *Tomorrow*. Here was a fresh face—an original. A woman of talent, beauty and charisma certain to become a hit with American audiences.

Tomorrow gave me the assignment.

I took two weeks of my vacation from *Time* and a day later arrived at Tracy Anderson's suite in the Pierre Hotel with tape recorder and notebook and sat down to work.

We turned our charm on each other. She was new in town, without many friends, and eager for publicity. I saw her as the potential vehicle for a whole new writing career, a way out of anonymous *Time*-style journalism forever.

But beyond each other's self-interest, we just seemed to get along. We were roughly the same age—she was three years older— we had both been divorced recently and we shared a reasonably similar outlook on life. Our tastes in music, food, literature, politics and even the cinema were in remarkable harmony. Or so it seemed.

Tracy's radiant creamy blond Swedish gorgeousness alone was enough to leave me trembling in awe, but she was also rich, talented, charismatic, vivacious, intelligent, sophisticated and famous. She was a heady experience, even for a *Time* reporter who thought he'd been around. Our interview sessions quickly became daylong affairs. I showed her my New York, took her to my favorite restaurants, my favorite places in the park, introduced her to my friends.

Tracy Anderson undoubtedly thought I was a more important journalist than in fact I was, but it didn't seem to matter to her. I was an American and at the moment she was in love with all things American. She saw the United States as a fresh beginning for her, professionally and personally, and she was flattered by my unquenchable curiosity about her thoughts, her opinions, her life— by my uncritical acceptance of everything about her. She said I made her feel free and pure again, as if she had left all the baggage of gossip and scandal behind her in Europe forever.

So she emptied her heart, sharing intimate details about herself that she had never told anyone before, let alone a journalist writing an article about her.

At the end of eight days of interviewing, after dinner at an Italian restaurant in the Village, drinks at Elaine's and a nightcap in the bar at the Pierre Hotel, we went to bed together.

Going to bed with Tracy Anderson wasn't what I had fantasized. Even today, all these years later, I am tempted to lie and say it was. But in truth it was a disaster.

To begin with, I was terror-stricken. The pressure I felt, the consuming desire to impress her and to outdo myself, was so intense that in retrospect it's a wonder I survived the occasion at all. After an hour or so of futile, humiliating effort, I drifted into a drunken, tormented sleep, promising myself that I would commit suicide the first thing in the morning.

The anguish of my failure was, thank God, short-lived. I woke in the morning to a hangover and feelings of resentful inferiority. I started an argument with Tracy about some trivial matter. She became violently angry and began yelling, punching and slapping. We ended up wrestling on the floor. The struggle turned erotic, and as we groped and squirmed and grabbed and pulled at each other on the bedroom's deep pile carpeting, my self-consciousness evaporated. I developed an erection as hard as a crowbar.

Tracy and I spent most of the next week together in bed. I had never known such sexual bliss. I wallowed in a happy oblivion, forgetting the outside world entirely.

At the end of the second week, I pried myself away from my adorable subject, locked myself in my apartment and wrote the article—a three-thousand-word poetic rhapsody—in one five-hour burst of creative fury, and took it to the magazine the following day.

Tomorrow's editor-in-chief, a tough little rooster of a man named Noel Franklin, a veteran of *Esquire* and *Harper's* magazines, had the unusual habit of reading a new contributor's work immediately, right there at his desk, while the writer waited in a chair across from him. It was great to get such instant, personal attention, but Franklin could be cruel and insensitive. He always said exactly what he thought, and he had a maliciously capricious temper. He had been known to drive writers from his office with a shotgunlike barrage of insults if he didn't like their work.

I showed up on a Thursday, the magazine's closing day. The place was in turmoil, the staff flat out trying to meet all the deadlines, but Franklin insisted on reading the article immediately. Under the blizzard of telephone calls, urgent conferences with the art director, with the managing editor, with the publisher, with the sales manager, with the copy editor and with several staff writers, it took him the entire afternoon to get through it. I passed the time excusing myself frequently for trips to the bathroom. I nearly went berserk from the building tension.

At first I was merely impatient. I was sure Franklin would like the article—that at worst I might be asked to add a bit here, cut a bit there. I was prepared for that. Although I had never written for another magazine, I was a *Time* reporter, after all, a seasoned professional journalist.

But as the afternoon wore on, with Franklin repeatedly picking the article up, glancing at it to find where he had left off, then throwing it down again to deal with some more immediate matter, I began to realize just how important it had become to me that his magazine accept the article—and me. If Franklin didn't like it, I wondered how I was going to prevent myself from feeling devastated. And if the article was rejected, how would I ever explain it to Tracy Anderson?

As I waited, Franklin's pending opinion of the article began to take on ominous dimensions, to loom over me as a decisive moment in my life. I began to sweat and squirm. Several times I suggested that I should leave and come back tomorrow. Franklin wouldn't let me.

Tomorrow's editor-in-chief finally found a couple of consecutive minutes of relative quiet, and finished reading the article. He leafed rapidly through it a second time, as if to confirm to himself that his initial reaction was correct.

He tipped back in his swivel chair and squinted across his desk at me. "You planning a career in journalism?"

I licked my lips and swallowed. "Yeah, I guess so. . . ."

Franklin tossed the twelve pages of typescript onto his desk with a lazy flick of the wrist. "You might look into public relations."

"I beg your pardon?"

The editor scratched the inside of his ear with a forefinger. "What you've turned in to me isn't an article. It's a goddamn three-thousand-word press release. Have you actually been interviewing this broad, or just boffing her?"

It turned out that it was a decisive moment in my life after all. And I knew it even as it was happening.

"I'll revise it," I replied, when I was able to find the controls to my tongue again.

Franklin laughed. "Hey, don't waste your time. Sorry we can't use you." The phone rang and Franklin picked it up, turning his chair away from me.

I struggled to my feet. I was trembling. I felt weak and sick. Tears burned in my eyes. My teeth were clamped so tightly together my jaw muscles twitched. I snatched the article from Franklin's desk, tore it into four quarters, and dropped it in a large wastebasket near the door.

"I'll be back," I said.

Franklin, busy arguing with someone over the phone, paid no attention. I careened out the door, scurried past the elevator banks and galloped down eight flights of fire stairs to the exit.

The next week I reported in sick at *Time*. Tracy called me every day. I was aching to see her, but each day I put her off with a different excuse.

By the end of the week I had completed a new article. The effort had been considerable. It had required a kind of discipline that I had never exercised in anything I had written. I suppressed my personal feelings and inhibitions, and forced myself to approach my subject with a cold-blooded objectivity. When the article was done, it bore no resemblance to my original effort at all. It was five times as long, and it laid Tracy Anderson naked and unlovely before the world, exposing her innermost thoughts on everything from diet and hygiene to sex techniques; repeating her opinions on a wide range of people and subjects, including her agents, her family, her former lovers and husbands, several movie directors, the movie industry as a whole and a number of prominent politicians she knew. Most of those embarrassing secrets about herself she had shared with me were included for good measure.

I even went so far as to cross the boundaries of good taste and break an old journalistic taboo. I included in the piece a description of my own ongoing affair with Tracy.

The article was merciless. But it was accurate, revealing and in its own hard-hearted way, fair. I didn't misquote her, or quote her out of context, and I went to extraordinary lengths to describe her and everything about her in as painfully honest a manner as possible. I strove for meaningful insights, and I found a few. The profile captured the woman's character in a memorable way. And unless you were a psychiatrist or a priest, on intimate confessional terms with humanity's many frailties and failings, it was not, on the whole, a pretty picture of Tracy Anderson.

But it sure was an interesting one.

Noel Franklin was ecstatic. He loved it. He raved about it. He fell off his chair. He called in members of the staff and read parts of it aloud to them. He gave me a bonus, promised me the magazine would make it the feature story for the next issue, and would print every word of it—making it the longest article it had ever run. He begged me to get started on another profile for him immediately— at triple what he had paid me for the Tracy Anderson piece.

I went home grief-stricken. I could not completely understand why I had done what I had done. I knew that when Tracy Anderson read the article it would devastate her. It would probably damage her career. I had betrayed her profoundly. I knew I would never see her again.

And I was desperately, helplessly in love with her.

I have never hated myself as much as I did that night.

When the article appeared, it created a sensation. My description of my affair with Tracy Anderson became something of a national scandal. I was pilloried by pundits, commentators, editorialists and, it seemed, every busybody and crank who had access to the media. Tracy was equally vilified—the perception being that she was as much to blame as I was for the article's embarrassing revelations.

My life changed dramatically. Despite the public lambasting I took—or because of it—I became a celebrity journalist overnight. Suddenly everybody wanted a piece from me—or a piece *of* me. Everybody, at least, except *Time* magazine. It fired me, presumably because I had violated my contract by publishing my work elsewhere without first obtaining *Time*'s permission. The more likely reason was the magazine's acute embarrassment. The management made it clear that they didn't wish to be associated with my exhibitionistic article—or me—in any way.

Time's cowardice hardly mattered. I was prepared to quit anyway. My phone now rang constantly. Talk shows asked me to appear, magazines begged me to write for them, book publishers offered me contracts. Several aspiring actresses even sent me nude photographs of themselves, urging me to write a profile of them, too.

It was astonishing. It was as if at the age of twenty-nine I had suddenly awoken to discover that the world—or at least America's version of it—worked in an entirely different fashion from what I had been taught to believe.

I ducked the celebrity treatment as much as I could manage. Not out of humility—I didn't have much of that in those days— but out of fear. I was afraid of making even more of an ass of myself in public than I had already with the article. I refused TV and radio interviews, refused calls from reporters, and left the hundreds of letters I received in connection with the article unanswered.

When the media hurricane died down, I picked over the offers that had blown in with it, and decided on one. I signed a contract with a publisher for a large advance on a book on the entertainment industry, a subject about which I knew next to nothing.

Tracy Anderson also avoided the media. But three days after the article's appearance, she released a written statement through her agent:

Miss Anderson deplores the shameless manner in which the writer John Brady, a man whom she had trusted with both her affections and her innermost thoughts and feelings, has exploited her to feed his own selfish ambitions. She does not deny that much of what Mr. Brady said in the article is true, but she deplores the insensitive, unfeeling manner in which it was presented. By subjecting her to public ridicule and embarrassment, Mr. Brady has caused Miss Anderson tremendous personal and professional anguish.

That was all. I called her, an abject apology worked out in advance and ready on my tongue, but she was no longer at the Pierre. She had canceled her movie contract and returned to Europe.

I received a letter from her several weeks later, postmarked Stockholm. It was excruciatingly brief:

> Dear Johnny,
> You have broken my heart.
> Tracy.

There was no return address.

In the weeks that followed, I drank a great deal.

I convinced myself that while I had not done a noble thing, I had nevertheless done the smart thing. My relationship with Tracy Anderson, examined objectively, boiled down to a case of who was going to exploit whom first. If the editor at *Tomorrow* had published that early version of my article, I would have been the exploited one. By seducing me so thoroughly, Tracy would have gained herself a free bit of personal promotion in a national magazine. My stock, as the author of such an obvious piece of PR flackery, on the other hand, would have fallen through the floor: A *Time* magazine reporter, reduced to writing celebrity puff pieces? What's this guy's problem?

And Tracy Anderson would then have gone on to another lover. What did a John Brady have to offer her, after all, other than a little helpful publicity? And once she had extracted that from me, she would have discarded me like a soiled Kleenex. I knew her well enough to know that. Tracy Anderson was not only rich, talented and beautiful, she was tough, manipulative and ruthlessly ambitious. The John Bradys of this world don't get to keep lovers like Tracy Anderson.

Thanks to a blunt son of a bitch of an editor named Noel Franklin, I had saved myself by a whisker. I had exploited Tracy first. As a celebrity, she had to expect it. She couldn't have been totally surprised. And she would certainly get over whatever hurt or embarrassment it had caused her. She wasn't the type to brood.

I wasn't sure that *I* would ever get over it, but I had to admit to myself that whatever residual shame and remorse I felt, I had instantly improved my career prospects a hundredfold.

And my involvement with Tracy Anderson, far from becoming the fading bittersweet memory I was resigned to, had barely begun. The best—and the worst—was yet to be.

About three months after the article appeared she called me. She was in London. It was late at night and she was drunk and despondent. She had made a whole new mess of her life since last I had seen her. She had already married again—this time to a well-known English actor—but, predictably, it wasn't working out. He was difficult, he was selfish, he was cruel and he was seeing other women. And probably other men, as well. She realized she didn't love him. She was thinking of leaving him, but was afraid of the scandal.

"I think I'm still in love with you, Johnny."

I thought she was joking. "After that article?"

I heard her wonderful laugh. I had described it in the article: "a calculated but irresistible mixture of mirthful conspiracy and helpless abandon." I marveled at the idea of the sound, bouncing off satellites high in the night sky over the Atlantic, and then slipping down to earth and into my ear three thousand miles away in a mere wink, still preserved in more or less the same unique shape she had given it—and still able to melt my heart.

"The article wasn't the worst thing you did."

"No?"

"The worst thing was that you wouldn't see me. Don't you remember? For a whole week. What could I think? Only that you didn't love me anymore. And then the article. Well, then I was sure that you didn't love me. I thought you hated me. It made me so sad, Johnny."

I felt a rising pressure against my tear ducts. "I'm sorry about the whole thing. I didn't dare see you. I knew the article would hurt you. I felt bad about it, Tracy. But I felt I had to do it. By the time I got up courage to call you, you were gone."

"You didn't hate me, then?"

I hesitated. I felt uneasy about the drift of the conversation. I couldn't recall that the subject of mutual love had ever actually come up during those few torrid days together. Still, we had certainly acted as if we were in love. "No, of course I didn't hate you. I felt ashamed of myself. I still do. I'm really so sorry, Tracy."

Tracy's voice grew suddenly louder, creating the momentary illusion that she had just walked into the room. I heard something clunk against the side of the phone. "It was all a stupid misunderstanding, then, Johnny. . . ."

I said nothing. It wasn't a stupid misunderstanding at all. It was a calculated exploitation. Still, I was happy if she wanted to remember it that way.

"It was a good article, Johnny," she said, her tone decisive. "Hell, it was a great article. I've read it over dozens of times. Sometimes it makes me furious, sometimes it makes me cry." Her voice seemed to slow down, then speed up again. "But I swear it's the only true thing that's ever been written about me. You really understand me. No one had ever understood me before, but you do. A lot of it hurt me—still hurts me—but you taught me so much about myself."

There was a long pause. I thought the connection had broken. Then I heard her innocent, lost-little-girl voice: "The article made me love you even more, Johnny. Can you believe that?"

No, I thought. I couldn't believe that.

"It doesn't mean that I'm a masochist, Johnny. It means that I saw that you were an exception . . . an exceptional person . . ."

"Are you drunk, Tracy?"

A long pause. "Yes, damn it, I'm terribly drunk," she admitted. "I'm in bed and I'm drunk. It's three in the morning here. Terence is out screwing around somewhere. I can't sleep. I'm very unhappy. I think of you all the time. I miss you. I wish we could be together again. I wish you were with me now. I wish you were right here making love to me."

I switched the receiver to my other ear. The plastic was wet from the sweat of my palm.

"Do you love me, Johnny . . . ?"

I didn't reply.

"Johnny?"

"Yes."

"You do love me, don't you?"

I took a deep breath and blurted out what surprised me as the truth: "Yes, I love you."

Another long silence. In my mind's eye I saw her smiling to herself in triumph. Having extracted this admission from me, she let me in on a little secret.

"I'll be in New York next week, Johnny," she said.

I felt my chest constrict.

"We'll be on location there for a month. I'll be at the Pierre. You remember the Pierre? Oh darling, I'm so excited! I want to see you so much! I love you, I love you, I love you!"

It was not a week, but almost two months before she finally arrived in New York. She had probably told me she'd be in town much sooner than she knew she would be to tease me, to whet my appetite, to make me worry. It's hard to be certain. With Tracy, tactics like this were so natural, so second-nature, that she was often not conscious of her own manipulations.

We picked up more or less where we had left off. I couldn't resist Tracy and I didn't pretend to try. I met her plane at the airport on the afternoon of her arrival, and by the early evening we were in her suite at the Pierre—in bed.

After the movie was done, Tracy decided to move back to New York. She filed for divorce from Terence, bought a ten-room co-op in the Dakota on the floor above John Lennon and Yoko Ono, and I moved in with her.

Our first months together were intense. Tracy was between films, and I was just starting research on my book about Hollywood. So we indulged ourselves in each other. We made love, we traveled, we dined out, we went to parties. We made love some more.

I found myself plunged into an environment whose existence I had only imagined from afar. Tracy was an international celebrity, making millions of dollars a year. She was in tremendous demand professionally and socially. The fact that she was—at least for the moment—in love with me was a perpetual source of disbelieving pride and pleasure. Being seen with her regularly in public gave me extraordinary status. My name began appearing in the society pages and the gossip columns.

I knew I was basking in reflected glory, but it was powerful stuff just the same. Suddenly John Brady was one of the beautiful people, seen at the parties and places that mattered, mingling with a crowd I had only read about and seen on talk shows. I wasn't just happy— I was in a state of perpetual, astonished euphoria. My ego swelled and whooshed skyward like a helium-filled balloon.

The social demands and temptations were so numerous that after the first few weeks, we rarely spent much time together alone. An evening at home—without guests, interruptions, telephone calls—quickly became a memory.

The problems began when Tracy started work on her next movie. She was frequently away for weeks at a stretch, and when I did see her—on location, or on one of her brief stops in the city—it seemed always to be in a crowd. Her time was spent with her director, her fellow actors, her agent, people involved in the making of the movie, people from the studio. And this was a world in which I had no real part.

A year passed and I did no work at all. The advance I had received on the book I spent in a reckless effort to keep up with Tracy.

Under financial pressure, I tried to get back to work on the book, but it was difficult. Tracy's absences began to occupy more of my time than she did when we were together. I heard rumors that she was having an affair with her leading man. I confronted her with it—over the telephone—and she denied it hotly.

I didn't believe her.

And my accusation had obviously alienated her.

One of the drawbacks of living with a beautiful celebrity, I discovered, was the fact that every man who saw her wanted her. It was impossible to escape the climate of rivalry. She was a sex symbol, after all. Being attractive to men was part of what she was all about. She could have the pick of most of the world's male population any time she felt like it, and being the narcissist she was, I knew she was bound, sooner or later, to feel like it. Despite her reassurances to the contrary, it was only a matter of time before she would find another male to replace me.

I sensed that that time was near, and I didn't know how to cope with it. My days away from her became a fog of distraction and unfocused jealousy, and my increasingly brief times with her were routinely spoiled by accusations and quarrels. I hated myself for this behavior, knowing that it could only succeed in doing what I was so desperate to prevent—driving her away from me. But I was in the grip of an obsession. I was helpless to act otherwise.

I picked up a copy of *People* magazine at the corner newsstand one morning and saw Tracy's photo on the cover. The cover line read "America's adopted darling: Has she found true love at last?"

I tore through the pages to find the article. The opening spread showed Tracy in the arms of the film's star. And it wasn't a still from the movie. It was snapped as they were coming out of a Beverly Hills restaurant. I glanced down at the text, but it quickly became a blur. I couldn't focus on it. I discarded the magazine in the trash basket and ran back to the Dakota.

Between bouts of rage and despair, I packed up my belongings and moved back to my own apartment.

With the perspective of a few months behind me, I came to the conclusion that, on the whole, our relationship had been a wash. She had evened the score. I no longer needed to feel guilty about that article I had written for *Tomorrow* magazine.

And the time I had spent with her had an unexpected side benefit. Through Tracy I had gained an insider's access to the people who ran Hollywood's film industry. I was able to transform my book on the film community from a routine piece of journalism into a genuine behind-the-scenes exposé of the business side of moviemaking. The book, *The Dream Makers*, was a big success, and my career, thanks once again to Tracy, took another leap upward.

I had also met many beautiful women through Tracy. When the acute pain of her rejection had subsided to a dull throb, I began dating some of them. One, a novelist and screenwriter named Alicia Shelborn, I married a year later. Alicia came from a very intellectual WASP family from Massachusetts. Her father was a prominent scientist, her mother taught at Harvard, and her older brother published a computer magazine. Alicia was pretty, smart, witty and a roaring snob.

Our marriage lasted two years. Although it was on the rocks before it was six months old, it was Tracy Anderson who finally sank it.

Whenever she was lonely or feeling unhappy or just wanted advice, Tracy would telephone me. It didn't matter if she was in New York or Beverly Hills, in France or Singapore, whether it was two in the afternoon or four in the morning—when she needed me, she called me. It all went back to that damned article I had written. Despite the thousands of dollars she spent yearly on shrinks, business managers and agents, and despite her many husbands and lovers, she still thought she needed me. I was the only one who "truly understood her."

Tracy frequently made a nuisance of herself, but the attention still flattered me. I still had some power over her, after all, and I guess I enjoyed that.

But Tracy's renewed attentions drove Alicia quietly crazy. She demanded I break off my association with the woman completely. I might have done so on my own, but not in response to an ultimatum from Alicia. I tried hard to persuade her that Tracy was no threat, but she never believed it.

And she was right not to believe it.

After Alicia's departure, I began seeing Tracy Anderson more often. It was always spur-of-the-moment, and it was always in answer to a summons from her, not me. Sometimes we slept together, sometimes we didn't. Mostly Tracy just wanted a friend to talk to—sympathetic company upon which to unburden herself.

At heart, Tracy Anderson was selfish and greedy, forever insecure, forever unable to extract enough love and devotion from those around her. I had lost my burning desire for her, but I was too involved in her life to turn my back on her. And despite the demands she sometimes made on my time and patience, I knew I owed her a great deal.

Once her lover, I became her confidant. I don't know which relationship was the more difficult or depleted me more emotionally.

After the failure of her fourth marriage, and a string of bad movies, Tracy became hooked on drugs and hit bottom.

Along with a small retinue of doctors, agents, personal assistants, secretaries, maids and faithful friends, I saw her through a bad year and a half, and she recovered. I always expected she would. She was a lot tougher than most people thought. She had an almost vampirelike way of feeding off the energy of others, of draining away their resources, their lifeblood, to revitalize herself. She always bounced back, sometimes stronger than ever. But those around her sometimes didn't.

During those same eighteen months it fell to Tracy's secretary of many years, a woman named Laura Hartz, to bear the heaviest burden of Tracy's descent. Laura was a lesbian, and her devotion to Tracy bordered on that of a slave. Tracy had always tended to exploit that devotion, but during the drug crisis, she exploited it cruelly by letting the relationship turn sexual. When she was cured, she turned against Laura, blaming the poor woman for causing her problems.

Laura, always a fragile ego, couldn't tolerate Tracy's rejection. She killed herself.

The hours I spent with Tracy on the phone trying to reassure her that what Laura had done wasn't her fault I still recall with some embarrassment. It *was* Tracy's fault.

I became so deeply mired in Tracy's life—deeper than any of her husbands or lovers had ever been—that I knew I could never escape from her entirely. I had tried. But she always lured me back, one way or another.

Now she had bailed me out of prison.

And despite all I thought I knew about Tracy Anderson at that moment, despite all that we had experienced together and all that she had confessed to me, I had yet to learn any of the truly important secrets in her life.

10

THE GUEST

At Central Park West and Seventy-second Street, Oscar brought the limousine to a stately standstill in front of the Dakota's main entrance, an arched passageway cut through the building into an interior courtyard beyond. The passageway itself was blocked by another limousine, this one with government license plates and plainclothes bodyguards with dark glasses and earplug phones standing guard on either side of it.

There were two doormen on duty in the tiny office in the passageway wall, and another bodyguard inside with them. They not only called ahead to Tracy's apartment to verify that I was expected, they made me produce identification.

I asked the man in plainclothes who the celebrity was. The bodyguard, his arms folded over his chest, studied me briefly to see if I represented any kind of threat, then decided that I didn't exist.

Tracy met me at the door. She was dressed in a floor-length white gown, a costume that had more or less become her trademark over the years, but she had foregone the usual dazzling strands of pearls and breathtaking slice of cleavage. Her platinum-blond hair, which normally she let cascade down her shoulders, was pulled back severely and coiled into a tight bun at the back of her neck, toning down her sexuality considerably.

She slipped her arms around me and squeezed energetically, planting kisses on my neck and engulfing me in an intoxicating nimbus of expensive perfumes and shampoos.

"It's wonderful to see you, darling," she said. She sounded as if she meant it.

I stammered out more or less the same thing in reply. It had been nearly a year since we had last encountered one another. She was forty-six now, and despite a wanton, reckless life, she still looked remarkably young and beautiful.

But something was clearly askew. Her round, sonorous voice sounded sharper than usual, and her gestures carried an overtone of agitation I had never observed in her before, even during the depths of her drug addiction. Her gray-blue eyes, once clear and innocent as a child's, shifted away from me in a furtive, distracted manner, and her mouth was tense. She seemed uncertain and preoccupied—almost distraught, as if she had just emerged from a violent argument with someone.

She linked an arm through mine and guided me out of the foyer and through the front hall into the apartment's enormous living room.

"I'm the one who's supposed to get in trouble, Johnny, not you," she said, squeezing my arm against her side. "What on earth have you done?"

"Nothing, believe it or not. Absolutely nothing."

"You're the most guilty-looking innocent person I've ever seen. Why were you arrested, then?"

"The government seems to think I'm giving away secrets to its enemies."

"Are you?"

"Of course not."

"Why wasn't your arrest in the *Times*?"

I laughed. "Leave it to you to worry about publicity."

"But darling—not even the split page. I was shocked."

" 'Split page'? Where did you pick that up? Are you having an affair with a newspaper publisher?"

"Don't be nasty, Johnny." She did a little pirouette and flung an arm out, as if introducing a stage act. "My new TV series. I play a divorced WASP mother of three who's decided to return to a career in newspaper journalism. She's being pursued romantically by two politicians who also happen to be running against each other for mayor. One's Hispanic and unhappily married, the other's Jewish and afraid he's gay. How do you like that for high concept? Tuesday nights on CBS this fall. We started taping a couple of weeks ago."

"What's it called?"

"*Late Edition*. I think it sounds too common. People will think it's the eleven o'clock news. They'll change it, I hope."

"You're too good to be doing television."

Tracy sighed, and I knew instantly that I shouldn't have reminded her of the declining status of her career.

"In a moment of weakness—and greed—I let my agent talk me into it. I haven't seen a decent movie script in years, Johnny. I was getting desperate to do something. Frankly, I hate it. The rehearsal schedule is sadistic and the show is mediocre. No, not mediocre. Asinine. With any luck it won't make it past the first sweeps."

Tracy rarely spoke so contemptuously about anything, especially anything to do with her profession. We talked for another minute or two about nothing important, trying to repair some of the damage of a year of mutual neglect.

Then she took my arm again and walked me into the library, a cozy book-lined study toward the rear of the apartment.

I had once read somewhere—or somebody had told me—that as books decompose they emit a chemical gas that stimulates the libido. Library stacks, like close dancing and moonlight walks, are supposed to be a powerful aphrodisiac. It may be true, because I had vivid memories of this room. Tracy and I had several times made love here on the floor—once in reckless and idiotic abandon during the middle of a cocktail party she gave me for the publication of my book on the Shah.

"Someone's here who wants to meet you," Tracy said, her voice suddenly formal.

I looked across the dimly lit room and understood the reason for the presence of the government limousine and the bodyguards out front.

In the burgundy leather high-backed chair near the room's fireplace sat a middle-aged man with wire-rimmed glasses and a large, bald head. He stood up slowly as we entered. He was tall—at least six foot two—and barrel-chested. His clothes were expensive and European in cut, and defiantly out-of-date—a double-breasted blue serge suit with a pinstripe and peaked lapels, and a pale pink dress shirt with a high collar and no breast pocket.

In his buttonhole he wore a pin that on closer scrutiny proved to be the French Croix de Guerre. The man's eyes—sharp and watchful as a ferret's—suggested an individual of uncommon intelligence, even brilliance. The rest of his face hinted at baser qualities. His nose was blunt, with a high, fleshy bridge, tough and cruel as a Roman centurion's. His mouth—wide, with thick, moist lips that never seemed to close entirely—was that of a man with unsated appetites.

I had seen this face so many times—in newspaper and magazine photos and on television—and I had thought about him so often, that meeting him suddenly and unexpectedly in person was a jolt.

"Andrew, this is John Brady."

He thrust his hand out toward me with an aggressive, almost threatening energy. We shook. His hand was surprisingly long-fingered and smooth. But his grip was tight and his palm was dry.

"Johnny, this is Andrew Carlson."

I felt completely off balance. I knew that Tracy Anderson was acquainted with the director of the CIA. A remark she had once made about him in a long-since-forgotten conversation was what had originally put the idea in my head to do a book about him someday. I had written him many letters, talked to him on the telephone several times, and had tried for the better part of a year to meet him and interview him for the book—without success. He had made it clear from the beginning that he had no intention of cooperating on the project, and in fact had begun immediately putting as many obstacles in my way as he could—primarily by scaring off many of my best potential sources.

Tracy flicked an elegant wrist in the direction of the tea cart under the window. "Help yourselves to drinks, gentlemen. Dinner is in an hour."

She turned and departed, closing the library door sharply behind her. I noticed that she had avoided looking at Carlson the entire time she was in the room with us, even when she introduced us.

The CIA director settled back in his chair and picked up his drink. It looked like sherry. I mixed a scotch and soda for myself at the tea cart and, feeling too wary and on edge to sit down, I took up a position by the fireplace, one arm braced on the mantel in what I hoped passed for a casual stance.

Carlson swirled his glass lazily and studied me with a predator's gaze. I was determined that he speak first, so I resisted the urge to make small talk. I just stood and met his stare. We eyed each other for several moments, mentally circling one another like wrestlers looking for the best point of attack.

I felt thoroughly intimidated. I fought the feeling, but I couldn't seem to beat it down. As something of an egalitarian and a wise guy as well as a cynic, I took pride in being hard to impress. I'd met, interviewed, dined with, argued with and even had a couple of shoving matches with many of the world's movers and shakers, not to mention the merely famous. I knew them to be just as unendearingly and pathetically human as the rest of us. More so, since their prominence tended to magnify their flaws along with their talents.

But Carlson was exceptional. His simple presence exuded an almost palpable aura of raw and possibly dangerous force that made one instinctively want to placate him.

I could recall similar sensations in the pit of my gut only once before. Some years ago I was accosted in a restaurant by a Mafia *pezzo novanta* who disagreed with something I had written about him. I don't remember a word he said, but I can still picture the man's rage as he screamed at me across two tables of astonished diners. I can still see his face turning mottled purple, his jaws gnashing, his knuckles whitening and the veins in his forehead pulsing. Knowing what the guy was capable of, I shook like an old barn in an earthquake. It was all I could do to keep from whimpering aloud in front of my date.

That was intimidation. But Carlson was having nearly the same effect on me and he hadn't yet even opened his mouth.

Part of the awe I felt stemmed from what I already knew about him. And what I didn't know. He wielded enormous influence in the administration, and yet he operated entirely out of the public view. Nobody, not even the members of the congressional oversight committee, was certain of his position on anything, or knew what the hell he was up to most of the time. He was the enigma at the center of power, the secret that sat in the middle and knew.

As DCI for eight years, he had built a reputation as the toughest, smartest and most successful director the CIA had ever had.

How he had managed to earn this reputation wasn't clear. At least not to me. Carlson was not an innovator. He had done little to reorganize or streamline the agency during his tenure, other than to consolidate his own authority. He had avoided any major intelligence embarrassments, and that counted for something. He had kept his president out of trouble, and that counted for a lot. But these negative achievements didn't add up to his extraordinary reputation. And who knew the truth? What the CIA did remained secret, so the success or failure of its director was more a matter of impression than fact. And Carlson knew his public relations. He was a master at manipulating both the media and the Congress to his advantage. After seven years on the job, he was hailed from almost every corner as America's great master spy.

Whoever one queried in government or the press, the answer was always a variation on the same theme: Carlson was the best. He might not always play by the book, but he got results. Carlson was a winner. When pressed for evidence of his successes, few could think of any. But they knew, they had faith. Carlson had restored the CIA's reputation around the world, and brought pride back to American intelligence. Carlson could do no wrong.

I didn't believe it. The man's image was too clean, too perfect, too free of warts and blemishes to be trusted. Too good to be true, as the old cliché had it. And no one had ever taken a close look at him.

I had a working hypothesis: I thought of Carlson as another J. Edgar Hoover, an imperfect man hiding behind a self-made myth. I hadn't gotten very far with the thesis at this point, but I had faith that it would ultimately prove accurate.

With the active lack of cooperation of Carlson and the federal bureaucracy, it had taken me damned near six months of dogged detective work just to flesh out the barest chronology of his life.

There were a lot of dark, unexplored corners, and exploring them was turning out to be the most difficult task I had ever undertaken. But the more I uncovered, the deeper became my conviction that Andrew Carlson had things to hide.

He was born in 1920, in a tough neighborhood in south Chicago. His parents were immigrant Swedes with no money, no culture and not much affection for each other. His mother ran off when he was eight, and his father, who used to beat him regularly, was killed in a brawl at a southside bar when Andrew was sixteen.

Carlson and his two younger sisters went to live with an aunt in Grand Rapids, Michigan, but Andrew stayed only a year. At seventeen, in the midst of the Great Depression, he struck out on his own.

According to his government biography, he scraped by for a couple of years with menial jobs, and then, always the brilliant student, got himself a full scholarship to the University of Michigan. He graduated with honors in 1941 and enlisted in the army shortly after Pearl Harbor.

His brilliance was an established fact, but much of his biography was not. I had discovered that although Carlson did spend time at the University of Michigan, he didn't have a scholarship and he never graduated. He was expelled in his junior year for some disciplinary offense that I had yet to uncover.

Carlson also had an arrest record in Grand Rapids. Nothing serious—one petty theft, one assault, and one disorderly conduct. But it was enough to establish a pattern of antisocial behavior. I thought it possible that Carlson might even have made his living off crime during this period—and even put himself through those three years of college with money made illegally.

Provocative stuff, but it was also ancient history. People change, and Carlson, like many successful types who emerge from a tough childhood, might have been expected to overcome or outgrow his early mistakes.

Carlson's career in the army was unexceptional. After training, he was sent first to Africa, where he saw no fighting, then to England, where he was assigned to U.S. Army Intelligence. In 1943 he became an officer. Six months later, he was promoted from lieutenant to captain. Then "Wild Bill" Donovan found him and persuaded him to transfer from the army to Donovan's fledgling

American intelligence network—the Office of Strategic Services.

Carlson blossomed in the OSS. He was parachuted into Occupied France in 1944 to help establish communications with the French underground. By all accounts, he did a superb job. When General Leclerc led his column of tanks into a liberated Paris, Andrew Carlson was there to greet him, it was said, with a bottle of vintage champagne and an envelope containing the order of battle for all of Hitler's troops on the Western Front.

Carlson remained in Europe, operating behind German lines right up until the end of the conflict. He emerged from the war a hero, and became, in the years immediately after, something of an legend, second only to his OSS boss, Wild Bill Donovan, as one of America's master spies.

Ah, the legend.

Like the story of the time Carlson was caught by the Gestapo in Paris. Knowing they had an American spy on their hands, the Nazis quickly spirited him east, toward Berlin, in the back of an armored truck, to be interrogated by top officers of the Abwehr.

Along the way, Carlson overpowered his guard, strangled him with his bare hands, shot the driver and front-seat passenger of the truck with the guard's pistol, and escaped back to Paris, where he remained underground until the city was liberated.

The story had a number of implausibilities, but no one had ever publicly challenged it, even though Carlson was its only source and there was no one alive to either corroborate or disprove it. This was also the case with other storied exploits of his during the war.

After the war Carlson worked for several years under Allen Dulles in the CIA, the newly formed successor to the OSS. His chief accomplishment during that interlude was the digging of a tunnel from West Berlin under East Berlin's main telephone exchange, where the CIA was able to tap into all the military and diplomatic telephone traffic coming in or out of the Communist part of the divided city.

I had interviewed two former CIA men, however, who swore emphatically that Carlson was not responsible for this exploit. They claimed that another agent had conceived and directed the entire operation. When that agent was killed, Carlson found a way to jump in and grab the credit for his work, they claimed.

In the early sixties, just before the Bay of Pigs fiasco cost Allen Dulles his job as DCI and left the CIA's image badly tarnished, Carlson apparently left the agency and turned his talents to business. Within a decade he had become a multimillionaire—primarily, according to the official accounts, by speculating in foreign real estate.

Carlson earned a reputation during those years for being ruthlessly competitive, always operating close to the legal and ethical edge. He was constantly up to his ears in litigation, and finally, in the early seventies, he moved out of real estate and, with some friends from his OSS days, went into the international arms business, selling weapons to Third World countries.

In the late seventies, he became active in Republican party politics. There was talk about his running for senator in New York, but it quickly became obvious that Andrew Carlson, for all his spy-hero luster and vaunted leadership abilities, made a lousy politician. He had a low tolerance for people who didn't see things his way. He was frequently blunt and insulting, and when he spoke in public he tended to mumble a lot. He didn't "project well," the media advisors advised him, so Carlson decided that if he was to have a future in politics it would have to be behind the scenes.

And behind the scenes he operated magnificently. With his conservative business contacts, he became the main fund-raiser for the Republican nominee in 1980, and when the electorate swept his man into office, Carlson ultimately landed the job for which he had been lobbying the president for many months—director of the CIA.

Carlson quickly established his control over the agency, firing potential rivals and troublemakers, promoting old friends and potential allies. After eight years, he was thoroughly entrenched and showed no signs of wanting to quit—ever. He seemed determined to make DCI a lifetime appointment.

Shades of old J. Edgar.

I won the battle of the silent stares. Eyeing me over the tops of his metal-rimmed glasses, Carlson finally spoke: "I hear you're in some trouble."

His voice had a harsh quality. It was gruff and throaty, and he had a tendency to slur his words. He could be articulate, but conversation seemed to require an effort he didn't like to make. He gave the impression that he considered words to be puny, untrustworthy things, to be marshaled and deployed as needed, but not to be counted on.

"I guess I am," I answered. "How did you hear of it?"

Carlson didn't bother to reply to that. "I may be able to help you," he said.

"Really? How?"

Was he suddenly going to cooperate with me on his biography? Not likely. As soon as I had recovered from the shock of seeing him in Tracy Anderson's library, I had suspected his presence had something to do with my arrest. How much it had to do with it I could never have guessed.

"I'll get the FBI to drop the case," he said.

It took me a few seconds to recover and respond. "How would you do that, exactly?"

Carlson grinned and said nothing. It was beneath his dignity to divulge the details. He played with his sherry glass, twisting the stem rapidly between thumb and forefinger and tapping the rim speculatively, as if he were contemplating heaving it across the room. The man fidgeted a lot, I noticed. His hands were constantly groping for something to occupy them, and he shuffled his feet back and forth across the carpet in front of his chair. He was as impatient as a caged animal. He wanted to be on the prowl, I imagined, doing something interesting, making life miserable for his enemies somewhere.

"I suppose you'd expect something in return," I said.

Carlson laughed. It was a rumbling, indolent guffaw, half genuine, half forced, and completely unfriendly. He finished the dregs of the sherry, smacked his lips and deposited the glass back in its coaster on the table beside him. "You're right," he said. "Something in return."

"You want me to guess?" I said. "Or are you going to tell me?"

One of my defenses against nervousness, unfortunately, is to act like a smart-ass. It's always pained me to be deferential to anybody, especially when I know that that's what they expect. But I was also getting angry, even before I had heard his offer. It was bound to be something I wouldn't like. And it was.

"You'll have to drop your book about me," Carlson replied.

I felt blood rush to my face. I took a deep breath and tried to keep my outrage from exploding all over the room. From his point of view, after all, the offer made good sense.

"I really can't do that, Mr. Carlson."

The director appeared genuinely surprised. "Why not?"

"Well, because it's blackmail, for openers. This is what I do for a living. Dropping the book would just about ruin me. I have a reputation and a career riding on it. If I knuckled under to every potential subject who tried to control what I said about them in print, I'd be out of business. I've already invested months of my time in research, and thanks to you, things are going very slowly."

Carlson seemed to hear nothing I said. "Is it the money that worries you?" he asked. "You've taken a sizable advance, I understand."

"And if I don't produce the book, I'll have to return it."

"There are other books you can do."

"But why should I let you decide that for me?"

"To stay out of jail."

I looked down at my drink, momentarily at a loss for a reply. At the back of my mind I could hear the voice of my second wife, Alicia: *Andrew has made an excellent point, John. Don't you think?*

"Why are you so adamant about stopping this book?" I countered. "You're a public figure. You've been written about and you'll be written about some more. You can't stop that. And why should you? Do you have that much to hide?"

The director laughed again, and this time it wasn't forced. He was genuinely amused. "I don't object to being written about," he said. "I honestly don't. But I'm not crazy, either."

"What do you mean?"

All through this exchange Carlson studied me with a rude persistence, his eyes tracking me with the intensity of a cat trying to corner its prey. It was unnerving as hell.

"When you sent me that letter about doing my biography I didn't dismiss it out of hand," he said. "Not at all. I gave it some thought. I checked you out, looked at your track record. Here's what I found: Your first book, *The Dream Makers*—you misrepresented yourself and your intentions in order to get inside the film industry. Several of the people who helped you later lost their jobs because of the book. A producer—the one you accused of dishonesty—committed suicide the day the book came out. A couple of directors and the head of one of the studios sued you. As I recall, the cases were settled out of court. Your publisher paid them off. Your next work, on the Shah of Iran, was one hell of a hatchet job on everyone involved—him, his family, his friends, his government ministers, and every American leader who ever had anything to do with him. And you never once interviewed the man you were writing about. . . ."

"The Shah was already dead," I interrupted.

Carlson plunged on: "Then your third book, about the Long Island socialite convicted of killing his wife. What did you call it? *The Blue-Blood Murder*? You ingratiated yourself with this individual, swore to him you believed he was innocent. You got him and his lawyers to give you access to everything they did and said during the trial. They should have known better, of course. And after a jury found him guilty, you kept up the pretense. You even wrote him in prison, commiserated with him, told him how unfair the verdict was—all the while pumping him for more information to flesh out your book. The poor bastard never guessed that on top of his murder conviction his close collaborator and confidant was going to knife him in the back. You never let him know that you were going to portray him as a monster. And he didn't find out until the book was published." Carlson shook his head. "I'd say you were damned lucky he was locked up at the time."

"That's not an accurate summary of my books or my behavior," I replied stiffly. "I can refute everything you've said."

The director swirled his glass of sherry. "No, no. It's accurate enough. You're not a journalist, you're a character assassin. Every book you've written, you've betrayed the trust of your subjects and destroyed their reputation and honor in print. You had some nerve thinking I'd be stupid enough to let you do that to me."

"I wrote the truth about them, that's all. They destroyed themselves."

Carlson's mouth fell open. "What truth? You selected the facts that fit your bias, padded your libel with secondhand and thirdhand testimony, made up dialogue, did whatever the hell you wanted. You made yourself a lot of money at the expense of other people's reputations. I don't know what you call it, but I call it goddamn despicable."

I closed my eyes. Carlson was verbally bashing my head in, and I couldn't summon the wit to defend myself. I realized I'd better back off. "Okay," I said. "You don't think I'm the man to do your life story."

The director emptied his glass and walked over to the tea cart to pour himself a refill. He ambled back to his chair and dropped down heavily, as if exhausted by the effort of his denunciation of me.

I was burning up. I felt depressed and angry. His blunt broadside had wounded me deeply, and I was having a hard time not showing it. I ached to justify myself, to argue him to the death, but there was just enough truth in his accusations to make the effort pointless. A discussion of journalistic ethics and freedom of speech wasn't in the cards that night.

"Think about my offer," Carlson said, acting suddenly good-humored, as if the exchange about my moral character hadn't even occurred. He even managed a crooked little grin. "Drop the book, and I'll see that the government drops the charges."

"I've already thought about it. I won't do it. I can't."

"Think about it some more, then."

"All right, I'll think about it some more."

I excused myself and went to the bathroom. When I returned to the library a couple of minutes later, Carlson was gone. Tracy was standing by the fireplace, her hands folded demurely in front of her, looking unexpectedly relaxed and serene.

"Andrew had to leave," she said. "So it'll be just the two of us."

PRUSSIAN BLUE

It wasn't just the two of us, though.

About fifteen minutes after Andrew Carlson's departure, a woman named Shelly Wells appeared, to pick up some tapes and transcripts.

Shelly was a ghostwriter Tracy's agent had found to help Tracy write her autobiography, a project that she had been pursuing in fits and starts for over a decade. I had purposely kept my distance from the subject. Tracy had already fired two earlier collaborators, and would likely go through several more before she was done.

Shelly was considerably more presentable than Tracy's previous ghosts. The first one was a cadaverous male poet with a drinking problem, whom Tracy was trying to rehabilitate. The second one was a female former staff writer for a fashion magazine, whose life was even more disorganized than Tracy's.

This collaborator seemed close to normal. She was about five-three, thirtysomething, and turned out in a tight-fitting black denim jumpsuit with a lot of accordion pockets and big, suggestive zippers located in interesting places. Large silver hoops dangled from her ears, and a designer scarf was snugged cutely around her neck. Whenever she moved, the collection of metal bracelets on her arms caused her to jingle like a wind chime in a light breeze.

She was probably Jewish but looked Oriental. Her hair, cut in a short bob, was glossy black. Her nose was small with almost no bridge, and her upper eyelids showed a slight epicanthic fold in the inner corners, giving her large brown eyes a pleasing almond shape.

Her rear end was emphatically un-Oriental. It strained against its denim confines with a callipygian exuberance that was hard to ignore.

Tracy persuaded Shelly to stay for dinner, and seemed suddenly eager to turn the evening into a festive occasion—to celebrate, as she dramatically overstated it, my "release from federal prison."

I was thankful for Tracy's mood change. With so much weighing on my mind, I had been dreading the thought of suffering through dinner with her alone.

When she had me all to herself she tended to get drunk and maudlin, and to burden me with variations on what I had come to call her "big three" sob stories—her fear of loneliness, her terror of old age, and her inconsolable regret in having had no children.

For years I had subjected myself to these outpourings with an uncomplaining stoicism, sometimes for entire evenings at a stretch, and she had grown accustomed to this, even dependent on it. Her uncharacteristically enduring affection for me had more to do with all the hours of hand-holding I had put in than any of my other wonderful qualities. I had always been willing to listen to her, and to sympathize with her. And I didn't require anything from her in return. She prized that. Like all narcissists, she demanded to be spoiled, to have all attention focused on her. When it wasn't, she felt belittled, abandoned. Even angry.

Tracy tended to wear people out, throw them away, and then change her mind and reclaim them. She had recycled me several times. That was why we didn't see each other much anymore. I found the process too exhausting.

The dinner got off to a slow start. Shelly Wells fidgeted with her bracelets and talked compulsively, nervous and unsure of herself in Tracy's presence. Tracy still seemed determined to have a good time, but she was having difficulty putting herself in a carefree frame of mind.

My frame of mind, knocked flat by the events of the past forty-eight hours, I had decided could be improved only by getting roaring drunk.

The three of us brought our drinks to the table and sat down to wait for the first course to appear. Tracy filled our wineglasses with an expensive white Bordeaux. Shelly tasted the wine and launched into a long, connoisseurlike riff about its character, bouquet and aroma. I drank off the remains of my scotch and water and took a hearty slug of the Bordeaux. I observed aloud that the Bordeaux was liquid in form and around 12 percent alcohol by volume—crucial characteristics of a good wine.

Shelly gave me a hurt look. Tracy assured her that I wasn't really the Philistine I appeared.

The dining room had been recently redone, at stupendous cost, by some society decorator who had upholstered the entire room, ceiling and doors included, in a padded cloth patterned with long wavy bands of rich purples and burgundies, like the end papers inside a leather-bound book. The effect was gaudy and suffocating. Tracy asked us for our opinions. Shelly, ever eager to please, said that she thought it was "refreshing and imaginative." I said that it made the room feel like a giant bordello sofa.

Tracy replied I wouldn't know a bordello sofa from a hay rake, but admitted she didn't like the decor, either. The decorator, it seemed, was a friend and she didn't want to offend him. He had AIDS, she said. She would redo the room after he died.

Tracy's taste was usually quite good—certainly much better than mine—but friends, like the decorator, sometimes compromised her judgment. She was a soft touch for any fellow artist. A hangover, perhaps, from her own days as a struggling actress.

That extraordinary painting in the entry hall, for example. It had been done by a former lover, a Czech painter named Jan Vaček. Vaček's entire life had been a relentless catalogue of misfortune—his mother, father and three sisters had been murdered by the Nazis in the Holocaust, his two wives had both died in freak accidents and his only child was run over by a bus in downtown Prague. Vaček himself suffered from chronic blinding headaches, acute asthma and a rare skin disorder that caused him extreme discomfort. He spent time in and out of an insane asylum in Paris, and eventually, according to Tracy, he killed himself.

The painting, entitled *Prussian Blue*, was an astonishing work. At first sight, the four-by-eight-foot canvas appeared to be nothing more than a big streaky blob of bluish-black oil paint. But as you studied it, and saw it at different times of the day and in different states of mind, it started to reveal itself, to come to life in disturbing ways.

Images began to form on the shadowy surface. At first the painting appeared to be a surrealistic depiction of a celebration of some kind, a festive occasion with musical instruments, laughing faces and dancing feet. But eventually you began to see other things. Blurred pornographic impressions of sexual organs, leering faces and orgiastic couplings emerged and then just as mysteriously faded. New images replaced them—the facial expressions became ones of greed and hate, sorrow and bitterness, anger and fear. Hunched and tormented shapes leaped out at you, their features twisted in extremes of agony. Scenes of births, deaths, fights, tortures and violent rapes seemed to coalesce briefly, like a subliminal image, and then evanesce. It was a Thematic Apperception Test of the sensibilities, a Rorschach of corruption, degeneracy, evil, suffering and terror. The longer you looked at it, the more it got to you.

And you could never be sure whether what you were seeing was really there, or just a figment of your own subconscious fears and imaginings. The painting seemed to reflect back at you your own state of mind and expose your hidden anxieties, teeming with all their memories and fears, desires and shames.

Others saw entirely different qualities and images in the painting than I did. And some things that I had seen I had seen only once and could never find again.

The artist had apparently constructed the work by painting in layer upon layer of overlapping and ingeniously juxtaposed scenes, building an impasto of the darkest thoughts and deeds of the human mind, and veiling them skillfully, until they merged together in a deep, shimmering, blue-black well of paint.

It was the work of a tortured, misanthropic genius, and difficult to regard for long stretches. At least for me. It even seemed conceivable to me that the painting could drive someone mad.

Tracy had admitted that the work often disturbed her, even triggered attacks of melancholy, but she felt such a powerful debt to the artist's sufferings that she insisted on displaying it prominently. It was the kind of thing she tended to do to prove to others—and herself—that she was a "serious" person.

I had seen a few of Vaček's works elsewhere. He had a peculiar fondness for the artists' color Prussian blue. And not only for applying it to canvas. He had committed suicide by ingesting a large amount of the pigment, which, in the variety he preferred, consists primarily of the poisonous compound ferric ferrocyanide.

The dinner, which finally started to appear during our third bottle of white Bordeaux, was some kind of chicken-and-rice concoction. It smelled and tasted strange. Being no more of a gourmet than I was a wine connoisseur, I shoveled it down without comment. Shelly pushed hers around on her plate, like a child hoping to make it go away, and jabbered about some strict new diet she was on. The dinner was being prepared and served by a very tiny and forlorn-looking Guatemalan woman Tracy had found God knows where a few weeks before. The woman—or girl, because she looked about fourteen—was named Juanita. Everything about her, from her furtive manner and complete lack of English, to her black, oversized maid's dress, tucked up and pinned in a big fold in the back, spelled "illegal alien."

Tracy's previous cook, a Haitian who was a true culinary artist, had been hired away by the wife of the producer of Tracy's last film. Tracy did about fifteen minutes on this, vowing some terrible revenge on the woman for stealing her help.

As we talked, Tracy's eyes were following the Guatemalan cook, critically monitoring every move she made. Under the heat of Tracy's gaze, the girl, who could not have been more than four and a half feet tall, was scurrying frantically about, straining her short arms across the table to serve the courses and clear the dishes. Tracy barked at her every time she put a foot wrong, which was frequently.

I felt sorry for her. "Give the poor girl a chance," I said. "You're overwhelming her. Look at her, she's scared to death."

Tracy flushed with anger at my interference, but she changed the subject. "I hope your meeting with Andrew was worthwhile, darling."

I ignored the question and asked one of my own. "How long have you known him?"

Tracy sipped her wine and pretended to think about it. "I'm not sure. For quite a long time."

"Where did you meet him?"

"In Europe. Years ago. At a party. He was a businessman then. Very rich, very well connected politically. I was just starting out as an actress. It was a long time ago. I was eighteen."

Shelly chimed in with a cheerful correction: "I think you were actually nineteen then, Tracy."

Tracy cast a glance across the table at Shelly that could have caused frostbite. "Was I," she replied, very evenly.

"You and Carlson have been friends all these years?"

"Acquaintances. Is that so unusual?"

I gulped down some wine. "I was pretty damned amazed to find him here tonight."

"It's really very simple, Johnny. He called me and asked me to do this for him. He said he thought he could help you, but he needed a place to meet you in private. Not to breathe a word to anyone, and all that stuff."

"Was it his idea for you to put up my bail?"

Tracy looked hurt by the suggestion. "That's incredibly ungrateful of you, darling."

"I'm grateful, Tracy. But how did you know I was in jail? Carlson must have told you. And he must have asked you if you could put up the money."

"Yes, he did. Are you satisfied?"

I slumped down in my chair with a disappointed frown. "It's important I know that."

"What's important is that you're out of jail," Tracy declared, refilling our wineglasses. "And Andrew's promised to make the whole nightmare go away. You should be all smiles, darling. What's wrong?"

"I can't let him do this to me. It's insulting."

Tracy sighed with annoyance. "You don't have to write a book about him. Frankly, I think it would be dull, dull, dull. There are thousands of better subjects. Really, Johnny. Don't be such a bore."

Tracy had little patience for other people's difficulties. It wasn't that she was insensitive. Just the opposite. Other people's problems upset her, and she was usually as upset as she could stand to be just from elbowing her way through her own messy life. I think she felt that if her friends were going to burden her with their personal worries, they wouldn't have any time or energy left to help her cope with hers.

"It's a matter of principle," I replied. "It's one of the few I have left, and Carlson's not going to take it away from me."

Shelly offered some hesitant murmurs of journalistic solidarity with me, but Tracy sneered: "You're just being stubborn and silly, darling. Andrew's asked you a perfectly reasonable favor in return, and you won't compromise even a tiny little bit?"

I emptied my wineglass.

"Andrew won't cooperate with you on the book, anyway," Tracy persisted. "So how will you ever put it together?"

"I've done it before. In a way, it's an advantage. I don't feel obligated to the subject. I'm free to write what I want."

"How much have you written?" Shelly asked.

"About half," I lied.

"What are you going to do, then, darling? Go back to prison?"

"Fight it out in court. This is America. I'm innocent."

"Andrew said they had a strong case against you."

"Did he? How the hell would he know?"

"Well, darling, he *is* a spy, after all."

With that exit line, Tracy left the table and went into the kitchen. We heard her bossing Juanita around in Spanish. Tracy was an accomplished linguist. Aside from having mastered an accentless, colloquial English, she also spoke fluent French, German and Italian. And, of course, Swedish. Tracy usually had me wrapped in such a whirlwind of sex and emotions that I tended to forget how educated and intelligent an individual she actually was.

Tracy returned with a bottle of champagne and glasses, muttering under her breath. "We're skipping the coffee," she announced. "My new cook doesn't know how to make it. Can you imagine? Where she comes from that's all they grow."

"That's Colombia, not Guatemala," I said.

"They grow coffee in Guatemala, too," Tracy retorted. Her

accomplishments didn't extend to geography or economics. She didn't really know what grew anywhere, but she hated to be corrected.

Tracy yanked the wire basket off the bottle, twisted the cork out until it was ready to pop, then aimed it at me. The cork exploded out of the neck, missing my ear by a couple of inches, bounced off the wall behind me and rolled under the table. Shelly gasped. She didn't know that this was an established ritual between us, dating from a night many years ago, when Tracy accidentally gave me a black eye with a cork from a hundred-dollar bottle of Dom Pérignon.

Bubbly foam spilled to the tablecloth before Tracy managed to maneuver the bottle over one of the champagne glasses.

"She has two children," Tracy continued. "As well as a mother, father and three brothers—all of whom she expects me to bring into this country."

"Two kids? How the hell old is she?"

"I have no idea, darling. And don't you touch her. She'll get pregnant if you so much as sneeze on her."

As tyrannical as Tracy could be with her help, I also knew that she would end up bringing all of Juanita's family into the country. She had an extravagantly generous heart. Hadn't she just loaned me half a million? I proposed a toast to Juanita and her family: "May they prosper and multiply—at Tracy Anderson's expense."

A few more giddy toasts were made, and then, à propos of nothing I can remember—maybe as a joke—Tracy confessed aloud that she was considering getting married again. She did not want to be alone on her fiftieth birthday, which, she reminded us, was only four years off. I made some dumb remark about feeling sorry for the victim of this decision, whoever he might be. She called me an unfeeling bastard and threw a silver napkin holder at me. This time she hit me. The holder glanced off the top of my head and rolled across the carpet and out into the hallway. We all burst out laughing.

We moved into the living room. I stuck two more bottles of champagne in the ice bucket and took it with us.

Our conversation grew warmer and more disjointed. I don't remember all the details, but increasingly sex became the main topic. With Tracy, that was to be expected. She viewed the world through the prism of sex, and a few drinks were certain to bring the subject to her lips.

And tonight she seemed in a particularly reckless mood. She told some lurid Hollywood stories. I had heard them all before, but Shelly had not, and Tracy was turning her ears scarlet with them.

By midnight we were all feeling quite merry and uninhibited. We had reached that point between sobriety and inebriation where we were laughing at everything.

I remember Shelly beside me on the sofa, then sitting on my lap. We were having an inane but deadly serious conversation about kissing technique.

Then Tracy was sitting on the sofa with us. She was saying things like didn't I think Shelly was sexy, and didn't Shelly think I was. Tracy had a lot of control when she was drunk, and I guessed from her concentrated expression that she had some definite goal in mind for the evening.

Shelly lost her balance from her sitting position on my knees. Or pretended to. Her head slid back away from me and landed in Tracy's lap. Tracy held her there, brushed her hair away from her face and bent forward and kissed her on the lips. My arm was around Shelly's thighs. I felt her muscles tighten, then relax, as if to say, "Oh the hell with it, why not?" I moved my hand between Shelly's thighs and stroked the cloth of her jumpsuit gently, almost apologetically, with my fingers. Near the top it was very warm.

It grew remarkably silent in the room. My blood was rushing to my extremities so fast I felt as if I were being inflated. My pulse hammered against my temples. I felt slightly dizzy.

Shelly broke the mood by suddenly squirming free and excusing herself for a trip to the bathroom.

Tracy tugged gently on the hair at the back of my neck. She wet my ear with her tongue, then blew on it. "I'm in a reckless mood, darling. How about you?"

"Reckless how?"

"Just reckless. You know my moods better than anyone. I want to do something I'll regret in the morning."

I felt a pleasant fluttering anxiety in the pit of my stomach. I was about to be challenged.

"Let's take her to bed with us," Tracy whispered.

I thought about it. I was in a pretty self-indulgent mood myself. Why not get lost in something exciting? I emptied my champagne glass. I was already sorry I had drunk so much, but I wanted to drink more.

"She's very willing," Tracy said.

"You think so?"

"Oh, yes."

"You scare me sometimes, you know that?"

Tracy let her hand wander teasingly down my stomach. "What's the matter, darling? No sense of adventure?"

I shrugged.

Tracy giggled. "You're such a Catholic, Johnny. You're afraid of sin."

"Anarchy. That's what I'm afraid of."

"You're just afraid you might enjoy yourself too much."

By the time Shelly returned from the bathroom the erotic mood had been broken. Shelly saw this as her last good chance to escape and started murmuring that she really had to go home. Tracy insisted that she stay.

The next thing I knew we were all three in Tracy's bedroom, rolling around on her king-size bed.

A lot had happened in this bedroom. Between Tracy and myself, and between Tracy and God knew who else. Her sex life had always been busy. Unfortunately, I had never been able to tolerate that very well. I suffered mightily as a result—jealous rages, sleepless nights, self-destructive behavior. The whole nine yards of romantic suffering. I had let her break my heart so many times because I wanted something from her she could never give me—fidelity and constancy. Of course if she had given me those things, she wouldn't have been Tracy Anderson and I wouldn't have wanted her. I seemed condemned to fall in love only with women who would always withhold something, always betray me in some profound way.

If nothing else, it helped keep my Irish Catholic virtue alive. Women like Tracy never gave you a chance to be much of a bastard yourself. You could never keep up with them.

Tracy had always been sexually adventurous, but there was more to her adventures than the simple satisfaction of her carnal lusts. Sex did truly seem to obsess her. Like a good narcissist, she demanded attention and love in all its forms and in large amounts.

Her career was built on a sexual idealization, her life defined by it. She was too talented an actress to be considered merely a sex goddess, but it was an unmistakable component of her fame. She recognized that, and the power it gave her over others fascinated her. She was always striving for ways to perfect and enhance that power, and in the process she had experimented widely.

Tracy had only to crook her finger and the lovers came running. She reveled in this sexual dominion, and it was a component of her fear of growing old that, along with her beauty, she would also lose that power. She dreaded the day she could no longer attract another human being sexually the way most of us fear death.

Her sexual obsession extended even to pornography, especially pornographic films. She had watched dozens—maybe hundreds—of them.

Her reactions to these films were complicated. On the one hand, she considered them contemptible—a crude, offensive exploitation of sex that went beyond the bounds of good taste and morality. They represented an abuse and debasement of the magic and mystery of that very element that had given her a special status in the world. She saw pornographic films as an attack on her personally.

On the other hand, they intrigued her—even made her jealous. This was a branch of the movie industry, after all, a form of entertainment relying on sex for its popularity, and she felt vaguely threatened by it.

Watching a porno tape with her was not an especially arousing experience. Instead of enjoying them, she critiqued them: "Oh God, will you look at that! What an unbelievable slut! How can she do that and ever show herself in public? . . . Look at that beast—all tattoos and the brain of a slug. Even his cock looks stupid. . . . How can she stand to touch him?" And so on.

But she had her favorites, too. Not among the men. They didn't especially interest her. She assumed that it was unexceptional for a man to do this kind of thing. But the women both fascinated and disturbed her. She was surprised how beautiful many of them were. She wondered about their motivations, their private sex lives, how much money they made, how intelligent they were and if they got a thrill out of this ultimate form of exhibitionism.

Somewhere Tracy managed to meet one of the better-known porno-film actresses. Her professional name was Liana Vine, and for about a year she appeared at nearly every party and dinner Tracy threw. I remembered her well. She was a gorgeous chestnut-haired woman with a perfect figure and an angelic face that could break anyone's heart. She was one of the few porno stars who had any acting talent, and Tracy's attention filled her head with thoughts of becoming "legit."

It was funny to see her at a party of New York and West Coast sophisticates. Although many of the women could barely bring themselves to make eye contact with her, the men crowded around her like a pack of randy dogs. She reveled in the attention. It didn't bother her at all that she was there primarily for her shock value. I took to referring to her as the "conversation piece."

Tracy picked Liana's brain endlessly for details about the porno industry, a subject that Liana loved to talk about. Tracy probably crawled into bed with her, too. It was the only way she could completely satisfy her curiosity about the woman.

Liana Vine and I never got along. I felt no attraction to her, and she knew it. Her great looks and vaunted fucking skills just could not disguise the greed and opportunism that seemed to ooze from her with every word and gesture.

She also whined a lot.

She eventually became a nuisance for Tracy. She began borrowing money from her, and showing up at the apartment at all hours, usually high on drugs and in the company of some sleazy companions she wished to impress. Liana also began exploiting her connection with Tracy to get interviews at studios and agencies.

Tracy was finally persuaded to end their association when she caught Liana in bed in her Malibu beach house with a man Tracy was dating. Tracy broke Liana's nose with a hairbrush. Liana sued her, and Tracy settled out of court for a quarter of a million dollars. The supermarket tabloids had a field day. Liana retired from porno films, married a Brazilian socialite and moved to Rio.

Shelly didn't offer much resistance. After some prolonged and intense kissing and caressing, she was out of her jumpsuit, giggling with embarrassment and whimpering and writhing with pleasure from the effects of four hands and two tongues exploring her everywhere.

She was voluptuous, and her skin had a silky, unmarked perfection that impressed Tracy immensely.

While Tracy and I were undressing each other, Shelly fell asleep. Tracy shook her angrily. Shelly just groaned and rolled over.

"Too much to drink," I said.

Tracy stroked Shelly's hair thoughtfully. "Probably just as well," she said. "She'd only have upstaged me."

I muttered something about that not being possible.

"Are you disappointed?" Tracy asked.

I shook my head. I realized what the point of this was for Tracy. She wanted to enjoy it, but she also wanted it to be a demonstration of her sexual power—proof that she could arrange thrills, harness sexual chemistries, beyond the range of others. The chemistry of a threesome naturally tends to be more determinedly bawdy than a combination of two. A third body raises the erotic temperature and creates a kind of competition. There's this feeling that you're there for the sex and you might not get this chance again, so you don't hold back. In Tracy's mind, Shelly and I were supposed to come away from the experience dazzled by the new erotic heights we had attained in Tracy's presence.

We sat silently for a few moments. Tracy reached across the bed, took my hand and pressed it against her breasts. "I think I'm losing interest in sex, anyway," she said.

This threatened to be the beginning of another lament about growing old. I didn't say anything.

"Darling, I haven't slept with anybody in six months."

"What's the matter?"

"I'm afraid to go to bed with anybody I haven't already been to bed with."

"Well, that still leaves a pretty good-sized crowd to pick from, doesn't it?"

It was an unfortunate remark, and I immediately regretted saying it.

Tracy bolted from the sofa and fled down the hall in the direction of the back bedroom. I didn't follow her. It was a well-worn tactic. In the middle of a disagreement, she would jump up suddenly and run off, expecting you to come running after, calling out apologies and begging forgiveness. She had pulled it on me a good dozen times over the years, always successfully. Often it was in a restaurant, or at a party, but sometimes it was in more surprising places. Once she jumped off a chair lift in Gstaad, Switzerland, during an argument we were having about the merits of the hotel we were staying in. She just raised the bar and pushed right off, dropping straight down about ten feet. She picked herself up and skied off down the lift line. Like a fool I jumped after her, and nearly killed myself.

She had subjected other men to the same treatment, I had learned. Childish games, but they worked. She kept you off balance, worried, constantly placating, constantly on the chase. Men might leave her, but no man ever grew complacent around Tracy Anderson.

And, in a way, she was getting the best of me once again. Because instead of just going home, as I should have, I lingered in the bedroom, wondering if she was going to reappear, or if I should venture down to the back of the apartment to see if she was all right.

I threw a comforter over Shelly and put my underwear back on. I filled my champagne glass with the remains of the bottle on the nightstand, and took it out into the living room. I stared down at the streetlights and the traffic along Central Park West for about five minutes, replaying in my head what Carlson had said to me in the library several hours ago. I regretted not having been armed with my microphone pen and shoulder-holster cassette recorder.

Finally I went back to the bedroom. Tracy had draped a nightgown over a small boudoir chair by the bathroom door. The shower was running. I stood there, thinking for a moment, then decided to wait for her. I sat on the bed and sipped the champagne. Shelly slept innocently on.

Tracy stepped out of the bathroom, wrapped in a large blue towel. She wasn't the least surprised to see me sitting on the bed.

"I'm sorry I insulted you," I said. "I was joking."

She shook her head. She didn't want to think about that. She sauntered over to me, swaying her hips in an exaggerated Marilyn Monroe parody. She raised the bottom edge of the towel suggestively and moved in closer, slipping a still-wet leg between my knees. "Remember Sabrina?" she said.

I nodded.

"That was exciting, wasn't it? The three of us, like that. She really turned us on, didn't she? Do you ever think about that night?"

"Occasionally."

She took my glass of champagne and sipped from it. "I wonder what happened to her? We ought to get her back and do it again."

I laughed. "We did. Don't you remember? And it didn't work out."

Tracy sighed. "It wasn't my fault. It was something the two of you were doing. I got very jealous all of a sudden."

I put my hands on her waist. She straddled my leg and then lowered herself onto it. I felt the weight of her thighs and moist heat penetrating through my pants leg. "It wasn't a good idea, anyway," I said. "Trying for a repeat performance. Like tonight. It was fun once, and we should have left it at that."

Tracy frowned. "I know. I'm greedy. But that first time was heaven. I've been getting very nostalgic lately, Johnny. We used to have wonderfully sexy times together, darling. What happened? Why did we stop?"

"You wanted to have wonderfully sexy times with other people besides me, I guess."

"And you didn't?"

"No. Not until you were no longer available."

"That makes me feel very sad."

We had had conversations like this before. Tracy was always trying to rewrite her past, so all her memories would be pleasant ones. She got up from the bed and disappeared into the bathroom. She was gone some time. When she returned, she was wearing a long white transparent negligee. She had been crying.

She sat back down on the bed and looked up at me with a wistful frown. "I was so selfish when I was younger," she said. "So arrogant. I wanted everything. And believed I deserved it."

"Well, you got everything. Now what?"

She smiled. "I want it all over again."

Tracy leaned into me and wrapped her arms around my neck. I put my arms around her waist and kissed her lightly on the neck and then on the lips. She smelled of scented soap and champagne. She felt familiar, almost comforting.

"Do you think she'll wake up?" Tracy asked, looking over at Shelly, tucked out of sight under the comforter.

"I doubt it. Do you care if she does?"

"No."

Tracy fell back on the bed and pulled me down on top of her.

"Let's pretend it's ten years ago, Johnny," she whispered. "Let's make love the way we did then. When we were so much in love."

I woke up to find that the lights were still on. Tracy was lying on her back, under the comforter, with me on one side of her and Shelly on the other. Both women were fast asleep. Tracy, in fact, was snoring slightly.

I sat up. It was three o'clock in the morning.

I ached everywhere. I was caught in that terrible passage between being drunk and being hung over. I took a cold shower. When I returned Tracy and Shelly remained exactly as I had left them. I rounded up the empty champagne bottles and glasses and took them out to the kitchen.

I wondered if we really all wanted to find each other in the same bed in the morning. I decided we didn't.

I gathered up Shelly's clothes, draped them over my shoulder, then picked Shelly up—all one hundred nude pounds of her— and staggered into the guest bedroom with her. Her bracelets rattled noisily when one of her arms brushed the door frame.

I deposited her on the bed as softly as I could. She stirred slightly, squeezed her eyes against the light and rolled over. I slipped the bedclothes out from underneath her, covered her up with them and turned out the light.

I contemplated going home. It was only a few blocks away. But I doubted I had the strength to make it. I went back to Tracy's bedroom and crawled back into bed with her.

I closed my eyes and felt the room start to spin. In seconds it had spun me into unconsciousness.

12

SHELLY WELLS COMPLAINS

I awoke sometime around dawn, my head pounding from the champagne. I pushed the covers down and quietly slipped out. In Tracy's bathroom I found a bottle of aspirin, but couldn't find a glass. I knocked three pills out into my hand and swallowed them, washing them down with a couple of handfuls of water from the sink. Between the bedroom and the bath, there was a large dressing room. Looking in the closets there for a robe to wear, I found an old one of mine. It was a navy-blue terry cloth, with red piping. I remembered that Tracy hadn't liked it, and had bought one for me that I didn't like. I was surprised that it hadn't been thrown out after all this time. No doubt other men had worn it since.

I slipped the robe on, went into Tracy's small study off the library and shut the door. Shelly had been working with Tracy on her book in here, and all the available flat surfaces were covered with pages of marked-up manuscript. I moved a tape recorder to make room for myself on a chair, and dialed Sam Marks's home phone number.

He sounded wide awake. I described to him the offer that Carlson had made to me the evening before: "If I give up my book about him, he'll get the government to drop its case against me. What do you think I should do?"

Marks didn't need long to reflect. "Are you kidding? Take it before he changes his mind."

"Just like that?"

"Doing his biography mean that much to you?"

"I've put in close to a year of work on it. It could be an important book."

"Important for whom?"

"Me."

"You told me a while ago you weren't getting anywhere on it."

"There are always difficulties, Sam. Besides, I owe the publisher"—I took a deep breath before I said this, because I had never said it aloud—"two hundred and fifty thousand dollars. That's money already received and spent. When I turn the thing in, I get another two-fifty."

Marks was silent for a moment. Then: "Can't you do some other book for them?"

"Half-million-dollar nonfiction projects are not exactly littering the sidewalks. And most of the good biographies have already been done—several times."

"How about Tracy Anderson?"

"Sam . . ."

"I'm just kidding."

"You never kid. Anyway, I've already exploited her as much as I'm entitled to."

"Well, you'll have to go elsewhere for literary advice, but from a legal point of view, I'd say Carlson's just offered you a Get Out of Jail Free card."

"How can I trust him? How do I even know he can do what he says he can?"

"He can do it, all right. And what have you got to lose? You can always hold the threat of the book over him if he doesn't produce."

"Jesus Christ, he's blackmailing me, Sam."

"Let's call it a quid pro quo."

"Hanging a legal tag on it doesn't make it smell any better."

"It does if you're a lawyer. Look at it from his side. He's protecting his own interests. Nothing wrong with that."

"What if I don't take his offer?"

"I'll tell you. The grand jury will almost certainly indict. So unless I can get enough evidence suppressed to convince a judge to throw the case out, we go to trial. I think we'll win, John. I absolutely do. Their case against you is narrow—constructed largely from a single incident. But there are no guarantees. A lot will depend on the kind of jury we get."

"Why?"

I heard Sam sigh. I think he interpreted the way I always questioned everything as some kind of thickheadedness on my part.

"For one thing, journalism is not in high repute these days. The last couple of years it's been taking a beating on libel and invasion-of-privacy cases. Fortunately we can usually get a fairly liberal and sophisticated jury in Manhattan. That'll help."

"So we could lose, then."

"All I'm saying is any trial is a risk. And even if you win, you still lose. It's going to cost you a lot. You won't have any publisher paying your legal bills. It'll be out of your own pocket."

"How much out of my pocket?"

There was a short pause at the other end while Sam worked out in his head the best way to break it to me.

"It'll be time-consuming, John. This is a big case. The feds will haul out the heavy artillery. They won't want to lose an espionage case. They'll unload on us. There'll be motions, countermotions, delays, discovery proceedings—it'll drag on. I'll need a team—two or three other lawyers full time on this. And logistical support. A lot of it. We'll have to farm out stuff—depositions, case research, that kind of thing. A trial like this is major warfare. So even giving you as much of a break as I possibly can with my own time . . . well, I hate to say it, but I know we're looking at six figures."

I swallowed hard. "How high in the six figures?"

"At least one and a half, but it could go higher. Maybe two. If, God forbid, we lose on any of the counts, there'll be appeals, and the whole process will drag on. It'll put you in a deep hole. It'll take up a lot of your time, too. You won't be able to do much work on the Carlson book—or any other book, for that matter—while the trial's going on. You have to ask yourself, can you afford it?"

I massaged my aching temples with thumb and middle finger. "Yeah, I certainly do have to ask myself that."

"Look, John, I think you just lucked out. Take advantage of it. Forget Carlson. Who cares about him? He's not worth risking jail. Do a book about lawyers, for chrissakes—they always sell."

"Maybe I could do a book about my espionage trial."

Marks saw no irony in that. "I'm sure there are plenty of other possibilities around," he replied.

"I'll have to think about it, Sam."

"Okay. Let me know as soon as you've decided. We'll have to pin Carlson's offer down right away, before he changes his mind—exactly how he'll approach the prosecutor, at what point in the pretrial phase, and what the specifics of the deal will be."

"Okay, Sam."

I hung up the phone and fell back against the chair cushion. To Marks it was a foregone conclusion that I'd accept the offer. Sam was a realist, a pragmatist. What else could I have expected him to say?

I went back out into the kitchen and made myself some coffee and toasted an English muffin. By the time I had eaten, the clock on the kitchen wall said six-thirty. Still too early to call either my agent or my publisher.

The hell with it, I had to talk to somebody. I took my coffee with me back into the study and dialed Matilda Bauer's home number. Her gravelly voice came on the line at about the eighth ring.

"Sorry to wake you, Matilda. It's John Brady."

She yawned. "What's the matter, dear?"

I blurted out the whole mess to her. It took me a few minutes, because she didn't even know about my arrest. She listened in patient silence.

Matilda was from Wyoming. She stood just under five feet, weighed about eighty-five pounds, and was sixty-four years old. She drank whiskey neat, smoked unfiltered Lucky Strikes, kept a loaded .38 Smith & Wesson revolver in her desk—with which, according to legend, she had once threatened a publisher—and had outlived three husbands. She was a formidable force in the publishing world.

She was also my guardian angel. I couldn't imagine doing what I did for a living without having her to run interference for me, to make excuses for me, to stand up for me, to give me advice, to protect my professional reputation, and to reprimand me on those frequent occasions when I behaved like a jerk. There was no one else in the world I could complain to, confide in and joke with the way I could with Matilda. I felt some remorse that I hadn't called her earlier.

"You'd better take Carlson's offer, Johnny."

"Why?"

"Because yesterday, when I guess you were still in jail, Whit Atherton called me. He wants to drop the Carlson book."

So that was what the great man wanted to see me about. "What's his explanation?"

"He suddenly thinks the subject's too controversial. Might trigger an avalanche of lawsuits. Or the CIA might try to block publication."

"That's it?"

"He more or less offered you a blank check if you'd do something else for the house. Anything else. He offered to supply another idea himself if you didn't have one."

"That's not exactly in character for him, is it?"

"No, it isn't. I told him I was going to march over there and punch him in his fat, upper-class lip. I screamed bloody murder at him. I threatened him with everything I could think of. But you know Atherton. He's stubborn. If he says he won't do something, he'll apologize a thousand times, but he still won't do it. I said we'll keep his advance and take the proposal somewhere else. And of course we will, if that's what you decide. There's half a dozen houses will pay as much as Whit, anyway. But you'd better think about it."

I thanked her.

She rebuked me gently. "If you're in trouble, Johnny, I expect you to let me know."

I promised to keep her up to date.

I checked the small ceramic clock on Tracy's desk. Almost seven A.M. The maid would be in at eight, and Tracy's secretary, Dolores, at nine. I didn't know what time Shelly would wake up, but I didn't expect it to be early.

Tracy herself, if she still kept the same habits, would wake around ten, have breakfast in bed, give secretaries, cooks and maids their marching orders for the day, call her agent and give him hell for something or other, take a leisurely bath, and appear upright and clothed at around eleven A.M.

I had forgotten about Juanita, the new cook. She poked her head into the study, eyeing me uncertainly. I smiled reassuringly, wondering how much of last night's sex and violence she had overheard. She whispered *"Buenos días"* in a feathery little voice and then disappeared again. I got up and closed the study door.

A bad hangover must be the key to clear thinking. I hit upon that revelation at a few minutes after seven, when I realized how utterly stupid I was not to have seen immediately that Andrew Carlson was the man responsible for my arrest.

It must have been Carlson, not the FBI, who had bugged my computer and stolen my files. Only he could have matched up the information they contained with similar information in some genuine secret documents. He must have planted those documents with René Gervais, the French journalist, and bribed or blackmailed him into claiming that I had given them to him. Then Carlson had turned over copies of the secret documents, along with excerpts from my computer files, to the FBI.

The FBI looked into it, established that Gervais was free-lancing as a spy and that I knew him, and then photographed me giving him something at that Greenwich Village café.

Presto—an open-and-shut case of treason against yours truly.

And then Carlson comes to my rescue with the magic solution to my problems. Of course. He had stage-managed the entire drama—every detail, every scene. I wondered if he would have visited me in prison if I had refused to accept the bail money from Tracy. Carlson seemed to know more about me than I did about him, and I had spent months researching his life.

I could understand the man's refusing to cooperate with me on the biography. I could even understand his scaring off those who might talk to me. And I could even imagine him going so far as gathering information against me and confronting me with it in order to dissuade me from writing the book.

But this. Jesus. It was brutal. Diabolic. He had threatened my publisher, stolen my research, cooked up a case of espionage against me and then handed me over to the FBI.

And I end up facing the possibility of spending the rest of my life in a federal prison.

All to stop me from writing that book. His reaction was way out of proportion to the threat. It was breathtaking. Either Carlson was mad, or he had a lot more to hide than I had ever imagined.

I tried to recall from my now-vanished accumulation of research anything significant about him that I might have overlooked— some pattern, some area of special vulnerability, some hint of major criminality.

There was nothing. I had been through this same exercise before. On the parts of Carlson's career that counted—his activities in the OSS during World War II, his dealings as an arms merchant in the early seventies, his record at the CIA—I had been unable to collect any information. They all remained big, gaping black holes.

Every source I had approached to help me fill in those black holes Carlson had managed to silence in advance. I had had more doors slammed in my face on this project than an encyclopedia salesman.

I had been counting heavily on Admiral Conover to reverse the trend and fill in details for me in all those blank areas. The admiral was now past filling in anything but his own grave.

I thought of the admiral's talk about Frankenstein's monster. And that envelope he had given me, with the three pages in it.

I had passed several hours of my time in jail with my eyes closed, trying to recall some details from those pages. Since I had actually looked at two of the three sheets of paper for a few seconds, I thought that if I concentrated hard enough, I might be able to still find some lingering traces of those images somewhere in my memory and bring them back into my consciousness. But it just didn't work. My memory was good, but it wasn't photographic. All I could recall from the first page were those three words typed across the top: "The Night Watch." And I remembered that the second page had contained a map of some kind.

I knew a psychiatrist who claimed that she could get patients to recall almost anything under hypnosis. The New York Police Department had used her a couple of times to break cases. I considered calling her. It was a desperate idea, but I was haunted by the loss of those pages. I had begun to think that I had failed Admiral Conover in some very profound way.

I found a telephone book in the bottom shelf of a wall cabinet near Tracy's desk at the back of the study, buried under a pile of magazines and cassettes. I spilled several cassettes onto the floor pulling it out.

While putting them back, I noticed a crumpled piece of paper lying behind the wastebasket in the corner. I picked it up and dropped it in the basket. Then I pulled it out again, smoothed it against the carpet and looked at it. In my jealous days, going through Tracy's things when she wasn't around had been a major furtive ritual. It was a form of masochism, I realized, because I was just looking for something that was going to make me angry or upset. And finding nothing didn't really allay my fears or suspicions. It just made me look harder the next time. Love is temporary insanity.

This piece of stationery had the beginnings of a handwritten letter on it:

Dear Andrew,
I have been agonizing about my situation for a long time. I can't let it continue. You have been promising me an answer for years. I have to conclude that you just do not intend to help me. I don't know why. I have done many important things for you

I heard someone coming. I stood up and slipped the unfinished letter into my pocket.

Shelly Wells walked in. Seeing me, she flushed with embarrassment. "I thought you'd still be in bed," she said.

"Couldn't sleep. How do you feel?"

"Awful. Don't I look it?"

Her jumpsuit was wrinkled, and her eyes a little red and heavy-lidded, but otherwise she looked presentable. Attractive, in fact.

"No. Champagne must agree with you."

Shelly lowered herself carefully onto the sofa. "I look like hell. And so do you, for that matter."

"Want some breakfast?"

"I'll throw up."

"Coffee?"

"No thanks. Did I do anything I should be ashamed of?"

"You don't remember?" I teased.

"Who took my clothes off?"

"You did. We helped."

"How did I end up in the guest room?"

"You fell asleep. I carried you."

"You couldn't have. You were too drunk."

"I managed."

"What did I miss?"

"You really want to hear?"

"No. I guess I don't." Shelly scowled. "I need a cigarette."

I passed her the carved jade box sitting on the table near me. "I didn't think you smoked."

Shelly extracted a long filter-tip from the box and examined it with a mixture of curiosity and disgust. "I quit two years ago. But I'm taking it up again. Right now. Hand me the matches."

I found matches on the table and threw them across to her. Shelly lit the cigarette, took a deep drag and blew the smoke toward me. "The two of you got me drunk and ganged up on me."

"Nothing terrible happened to you. In fact, you seemed to be having a pretty good time."

Shelly pulled the cigarette from her lips and coughed. "That makes me even madder. All I got out of the evening was frustration and a hangover. You got me *too* drunk."

"Next time we'll get it right."

Shelly crushed out the barely smoked cigarette in the ashtray with a vigorous twist of her thumb. "She drives me crazy. She manipulates me so shamelessly. I mean she was practically offering me up like a dessert course last night, for the two of you to enjoy. And I was ready and willing. Anything to please. I felt so defenseless. How does she get me into it? I don't want to be part of that woman's sex life. I'm not her slave. I keep thinking I should abandon this whole damned project."

"Why don't you?"

"I need the money. And every time I get mad at something she does, she always apologizes profusely. Can I ever forgive her, and all that. She always seems so genuinely contrite, I give in. Of course she's such a consummate actress it's hard to know. Anyway, I always buy it. I hate myself."

"Tracy likes you. But she does get a little bossy. You have to learn to live with it."

Shelly's shoulders slumped. "I'm too submissive a person as it is. It's amazing how much she's taken over my life already. She thinks nothing of calling me at four in the morning if she's up and has a stray thought she thinks should be included in her book. If I make any plans she's sure to disrupt them. And she drills me relentlessly about every detail of my daily existence. Then tells me exactly what I should do about everything. And gets furious if I don't. . . . At first I was flattered, but now I see she just wants to control me. She's a tyrant. How the hell did you cope with her—when the two of you were . . . whatever you were?"

"I didn't. I fell in love with her and made the mistake of letting her know it. I used to think she was never really happy on any given day unless she could find some new way to put my devotion to the test. My atrophied sense of self-preservation finally took over. I ran for my life."

"That's funny. She told me that you left her because you didn't like her friends."

"It was only her boyfriends I didn't like."

Shelly smiled. "Are you still in love with her?"

"Yes and no. I've tried to keep my distance of late. But at some point in your life I guess you have to recognize that, whether you intended it that way or not, you've accumulated certain friendships and obligations. Tracy's been a big part of my life. Bigger than my two former wives combined. I don't know how big a part I've been of her life, but she still holds on to me. So we have an attachment of sorts. It's often antagonistic, but it'll probably survive."

"Are you in love with anybody else?"

An image of Gail Snow took brief shape in my head. "No, not since Monday. How about you?"

Shelly looked at me as if she were trying to guess my shirt size. "I think I'm ready to chance some coffee now," she said.

We went out to the kitchen and I turned the heat on under the pot I had made earlier. We leaned against the counter.

"Has the subject of Andrew Carlson ever come up in your sessions with Tracy?"

"He's the one you were arguing about last night?"

"Yes. He was here before you arrived."

Shelly thought about it. "She's mentioned him a few times."

"Do you remember what she said?"

"No, I don't. But I don't think she's ever had an affair with him, if that's what you're after."

"I don't know what I'm after. Carlson has gone to great lengths to stop me from writing a book about him. I'd like to know why."

Shelly shrugged. "I don't think I can help you. Sorry."

"Can I look through your transcripts? There might be something there that would mean something to me."

Shelly folded her arms across her chest. "All my notes and taped conversations? Be reasonable. I can't show you those. Not without Tracy's permission."

"All I want is a quick look. What harm can it do?"

"I really don't think I should."

The coffee started to boil again. I turned off the burner and filled two cups.

"Besides," she continued, building herself a defense. "There's hundreds of pages. And tapes I haven't even transcribed yet. You'd never get through it all. It's a jumble, a nightmare. Tracy pops tapes into a machine and records whatever the hell comes into her head and mails them to me. Or drops them into my bag when I show up for an interview. There's no order, no sequence, no consistency. It takes me hours of excruciating labor just to arrange the details and the anecdotes and the gossip and the half-remembered facts and the contradictory information into some kind of synthesis and chronology. I spend most of my time cutting and pasting. Thank God for word processors."

I carried the coffee to the kitchen table and pulled out two chairs. "You're making excuses. I'm not a literary critic. I'm looking for evidence of something that might help me out of the mess I'm in."

Shelly sat down across from me. "I'll tell you what I can remember about Carlson. She met him in Europe quite a few years ago. I mean when she was only about eighteen. He helped her with her career—put her in touch with some producers, or directors, or well-known actors. Maybe he gave her some money—supported her for a while. She says she never slept with him, although you can't trust her on that. She frequently contradicts herself on who she's slept with and who she hasn't. Sometimes I think she doesn't remember. I can tell you this much, if you don't already know it—she's fucked some pretty important people. And I don't mean movie stars."

"Who do you mean?"

"Important political figures. Royalty. Heads of state. People like that."

"Does Carlson figure in any of this?"

"I don't know. But she does seem to have some quarrel going on with him about something. She's talked to him a few times on the phone recently when I was here, and she's made a few disparaging comments about him. It looks to me as if she's pressuring him about something—that there's something that she expects him to do for her but he won't—or can't—do it. But it could be something completely trivial. With Tracy, you never know."

"Do you think she's seemed more anxious than usual lately?"

"Yes. She has. Anxious and preoccupied. I've been having a hard time getting her to do any work on the book the last couple of weeks. But that's happened before. She rides an emotional roller coaster—one day up, one day down." Shelly paused, remembering something. "By the way, what's so special about April the fourth?"

I laughed. "That's Tracy's mystery holiday. How did you find out about it?"

"I showed up to do some taping—this was about six weeks ago—and Tracy wouldn't let me in. It was kind of bizarre. 'It's April fourth,' she said. 'I never see anybody on April fourth.' No explanation. She slammed the door on me. I asked her secretary about it. It's true. She goes into a complete retreat every April fourth. Sees no one, does nothing. Nobody knows why. Do you?"

"No. She won't talk about it. I guess it must have some family significance. Maybe someone close died on that day. But I really don't know."

Shelly bit her lip thoughtfully. "I tried to ask her later. She got quite nasty with me. Maybe I picked a bad day. Tracy's a bit manic-depressive, anyway."

I steered the conversation back to the present. "What could Tracy want from Carlson? What could he possibly do for her?"

"You know them both better than I do."

"The answer may be in your transcripts," I persisted. "Let me take just one quick look at them."

"No. Anyway, the answer's not there—whatever the answer is. I promise you."

I didn't press the matter any further. "Am I in it?"

"Read the book and find out."

"I'm afraid she'll finally get back at me for that article."

"She should, but don't worry, you'll come out sounding far better than you deserve. She thinks you're wonderful. 'I adore Johnny,' she keeps telling me. 'I just adore Johnny. He's so understanding. Wait until you meet him. You'll love him.' I didn't know she expected me to take that literally."

"You should have stayed awake last night."

Shelly embraced her coffee cup with both hands. "I have a confession," she said. "I *was* awake. I got nervous and panicked about what was happening. The only way I could think of to handle the situation without getting Tracy angry was to pretend to fall asleep. Finally, I did go to sleep. But I heard most of what went on between the two of you. It was all I could do to keep still, believe me."

I tasted the coffee. It was burned. "Serves you right."

Shelly watched the steam rising from her cup. "I know. I was a coward. But I'm not quite ready for bisexuality yet. Tracy's beautiful, but I still prefer men."

"So does she, most of the time. But she likes to turn everybody on—just to see if she can do it."

"And she can," Shelly said. "I'm honestly not normally attracted to women. But in a way she does turn me on. I think it's because of what I know about her sex life. Maybe I'm living it vicariously through her—hearing about it all the time when we do interview sessions. Let's face it—it's hard not to think about sex with Tracy around. I think a lot of women would be sexually attracted to her. Certainly nobody else could have lured me into last night's little ménage à trois but her. She made the idea seem really exciting. And okay, somehow. If a big celebrity like Tracy Anderson thinks it's a good idea, why shouldn't I?" Shelly shook her head remorsefully. "Of course that's my problem. I have absolutely no will of my own. I'm the original Miss Eager-to-Please. I can be persuaded to do just about anything."

"Come on. You're exaggerating. You seem pretty tough-minded and independent to me."

The compliment pleased her, but she debated it: "You're confusing tough with defensive. If you want tough, take Tracy. Now there's tough. Men don't walk over her, they genuflect. They kiss the hem of her gown. Tracy always gets what she wants. She insists upon it. Me, I never do. My whole life is about not getting my way. You think I'd be doing this 'as-told-to' book if I were tough? No way. But me, I have to go out and find the one project that demands the total subjugation of my will and personality to somebody else. . . ."

I laughed. "That's ridiculous. It's Tracy's story, and you're the professional who's come in to translate it into readable, salable English. There's nothing wrong with that. You just distance yourself."

"But I should be doing an unauthorized biography of her. I can already see how censored and one-sided her version of her life is going to be." Shelly slumped down in her chair. "But I don't have the guts. I'm just not tough enough."

Shelly bit her lip again. She looked so vulnerable and sad all of a sudden I wanted to embrace her. We drank our coffee in an awkward silence.

"I need some aspirin." Shelly took her cup to the sink and rinsed it out. "If it had just been you . . ." she said, on her way out of the kitchen.

I thought she said, "I'll make love with you anytime," but she was already all the way out into the hallway, and she had reduced her voice to a whisper, so I couldn't be sure.

13

THE COURT-TENNIS PLAYER

Back at my apartment there was a single message on my machine. "Mr. Brady," a woman's voice said. "Could you please call Mr. Grayson Steckler at your convenience. His number is 444-5768. Thank you."

Grayson Steckler? Who the hell was Grayson Steckler?

I dialed the number. It turned out to be a law firm—Steckler and Wycoff, 30 Rockefeller Plaza.

"Mr. Steckler's office."

"Is he in? John Brady calling."

"Yes, Mr. Brady. He's expecting to see you this morning at ten."

"I didn't know I had an appointment."

"Would another time be more convenient?"

"Do you know what he wants to see me about?"

"I'm afraid not, Mr. Brady."

It was nine o'clock now. "Okay. Ten is fine."

"Good. He's at the New York Racquet and Tennis Club, Mr. Brady. He plays there every morning. It's at Park Avenue and Fiftieth Street."

Grayson Steckler greeted me at the top of the stairwell on the second floor of the club. He was in tennis whites, with a towel around his neck and a racquet under his arm. He was not at all the aging, bald, cadaverous, wire-rim-spectacled WASP fuddy-duddy I had anticipated. He was a muscular giant, standing well over six feet and weighing well over two hundred pounds, with most of the weight in his shoulders, chest, biceps and thighs. His hair was thinning but still sandy colored. His skin was tanned, his face smooth, his eyes sharp. Only the wrinkles on his neck and the liver spots on the back of his hands betrayed his age, which was probably early to mid-sixties.

Sweat dripped from his forehead. He made a quick pass across his face with the towel and then shook my hand, squeezing it hard. "John Brady, isn't it? Thanks for taking the time."

"Sure."

Steckler waved a hand around behind him. "We can talk in here," he said. He led me into a narrow gallery that ran alongside one of the club's indoor courts. The gallery was like a hallway, with several windowlike openings cut into one side. Stretched over the openings was a sturdy rope netting. I heard the echoing squeak of sneakers and the hollow *thock* of racquet on ball even before we reached the first opening.

"Court tennis," Steckler announced, gesturing with an upward thrust of his jaw toward the activity on the other side of the netting. "Do you know the game?"

The question struck me as faintly patronizing, but I didn't take offense. Steckler was old enough, rich enough, and no doubt successful and well connected enough to act a little patronizing if he felt like it.

"Not intimately," I replied.

Steckler chuckled. "Not many people do. It's an ancient game, the original French *jeu de paume*. The English call it real tennis. Steeped in tradition. Hell, it's drowned in tradition. Hardly anybody plays it anymore. It's an exquisite anachronism, perpetuated by the idle rich to keep them out of mischief. But it's a hell of a good game, even so. It's to lawn tennis what chess is to checkers. Watch."

I turned my attention toward the court. On the other side of the veil of netting four middle-aged men in tennis whites were playing what appeared to me to be a demented confusion of regular tennis and racquetball. Their racquets were wooden and the frames appeared to be bent at a slight, but clearly cockeyed, angle to the handles. A standard tennis net was strung across the court, but it sagged noticeably, as if no one had bothered to winch it taut. The playing area was surfaced with slate-gray stone or cement, and instead of the usual white lines delineating the forecourts, backcourts and out-of-bounds areas, this surface was divided by painted lines into numbered segments about a yard wide running parallel to the net. On one side, the lines mysteriously terminated halfway back from the net.

There was no out-of-bounds territory at all. Thirty-foot tall gray walls, with windowlike openings cut into them at irregular intervals, enclosed the floor's playing area on every side. About seven feet up along both end walls and one of the side walls, the vertical surface abruptly sloped back to form a shallow roof for several feet, then once again became vertical. The remaining side wall contained neither openings nor setbacks, but at one corner of it a buttresslike protrusion stuck out into the playing area.

"The walls are in play," Steckler explained, tucking his racket back under his elbow. "All the way up to those lines." He pointed to the horizontal red stripes high up on the walls.

I watched one of the doubles partners serve the ball. He tossed it up and hit it, not over the net toward his opponents, as I expected, but against the side wall. It rolled along the sloping roof and then dropped down into the opponents' court, where one of the players had positioned himself. He hit the ball hard as it came up on the bounce. It sailed across the court and into the netting directly in front of me. I ducked instinctively. I thought the ball had been hit way out of bounds, but Steckler's sudden hand-clapping and the muted cheer from the far court indicated that their side had instead just scored a point.

"The *dedans* is a winning opening," Steckler explained cryptically. "The gallery on the left on the hazard side and the grille are the other winning openings. The other galleries and the tambour are hazards."

"Greek to me. Do all court-tennis courts look like this one?"

"More or less. Its original inspiration was supposedly a medieval courtyard, you see. The game originated in France something like a thousand years ago, probably in some monastery cloisters. The French kings eventually brought the sport to their châteaux, and here we are—walls with their odd gallery openings, the grille, the sloping penthouse roof, and even the tambour, which as you can see resembles a buttress."

As we watched the match, Steckler rambled on charmingly about hazards and chases, embellishing his explanation of the game with anecdotes about its royal connections. It seemed to have played a major role in European history. Louis X died of a heart attack after a strenuous match in Vincennes, in 1316. Henry I of Castile, in 1217, and Philip I of Spain, in 1506, met similar ends. James I of Scotland could have avoided assassination in 1437, but a court-yard drain he tried to escape down had been blocked to prevent the loss of tennis balls. In 1498 Charles VIII of France died of a concussion when he cracked his noggin on the stone lintel of a doorway leaving a tennis match in Amboise. And so on.

Steckler paused in his monologue and laughed. "That's what happens when you get to be an old fart. You start dispensing history and advice, whether anybody wants it or not. I didn't ask you here to give you a lecture on court tennis."

"Well, I don't object to getting one, anyway."

Steckler dismissed my polite flattery with an impatient wave of his hand. "I want to ask you about Admiral Conover."

I felt the hair on the back of my neck tingle. "What about him?"

"I understand that you were with him when he died," Steckler said, regarding me attentively.

That hadn't been reported anywhere. "How did you know?"

"What killed him, do you think?"

He wasn't getting away with that. "I asked you how you knew I was with him."

Steckler showed me a cold grin. "I was told he was meeting you."

"Did you know him?"

"Yes. Quite well. We were in the OSS together. Yugoslavia. We kept in touch. We sometimes had business dealings."

"What kind of business?"

"Confidential, I'm afraid."

"I see."

"I should explain that I'm a legal consultant to a number of agencies in the federal government—especially in the intelligence community. I advise on legal matters and sometimes represent the government in court. If Conover's death involved foul play my clients would naturally be concerned."

"Naturally. The obit in the *Times* said it was a stroke." Steckler must know that, I thought. Why is he asking me?

Steckler swung his racket out from under his elbow and fixed his gaze on the strings. "But of course you were right there on the spot. Did you see anything unusual?"

I shrugged. "No. He was on the escalator in front of me, then suddenly he toppled over. No one shot him or stabbed him or poured poison down his throat. He looked unhealthy, anyway. I wasn't that surprised. I'll take the *Times*'s word for it."

The tennis ball hit the netting directly in front of Steckler's face. He barely flinched. "Every time somebody dies who used to be in intelligence," he said, "there are always rumors and speculation that he might have been killed. You can understand why. But you're right. He wasn't in good health. He had high blood pressure and a bad heart."

Steckler turned his attention back to the game, tapping the edge of his racket thoughtfully against the wooden ledge in front of him. Whatever it was that he was after, he was taking his sweet time getting to it. I waited silently, letting the moment develop, careful not to step on anything Steckler might decide to say.

"Did he give you anything?" he asked me, his eyes still trained on the court.

Well, there it was. I pretended that I hadn't heard him. I needed a few seconds to decide on an answer. This annoyed him, but he repeated the question: "When you were with him, did he give you anything?"

"Like what?" I asked.

"I don't know. A tape. A document."

"He gave me an envelope with some pages in it."

Steckler's eyebrows rode up his leathery forehead expectantly. "Yes?"

"That's all."

"What were they?"

"I'm not sure. I'm trying to find out."

That was the truth, as far as it went. I saw no point in admitting that someone had swiped them from me before I had a chance to look at them.

"Do you have these documents with you?"

"No."

"Perhaps if I saw them I could tell you something useful." He said this too casually, I thought.

"I'll keep your offer in mind."

Steckler nodded. I watched his face carefully. He showed no visible reaction. That was unusual. People who register no emotion when you tell them something that should surprise them are either psychotic or very skilled in disguising their reactions. Steckler was apparently very skilled.

"You're writing a book about Carlson, I understand."

"I was."

"What do you mean?"

I instinctively didn't trust Steckler, but there was nothing to be lost in telling him what had happened to me. I suspected he already knew, anyway. And if I was to have any chance of getting anything useful from him in return, I'd have to be reasonably forthcoming myself. I zipped through the story—my arrest, the charges of espionage against me, the offer Carlson made me, and my suspicions that Carlson had arranged the whole thing just to scare me off.

"Am I crazy to think that?" I asked him, trying to look earnest.

Steckler kept his eyes on the game. "You're crazy to try to dig into Carlson's past," he said, his voice almost devoid of intonation.

"Why? What is he hiding?"

Steckler ignored the question. Instead, he pointed out at one of the players on the court. "See Josh out there," he said. "He's my age, and he beat Jimmy Bostwick yesterday. Jimmy's fifty-two and was world champion in the seventies."

Steckler's company was beginning to feel oppressive. "World champion?" I echoed. "How many people play this game? Twenty?"

To his credit, Steckler found this amusing. He laughed boisterously and actually slapped me on the back. "A couple of thousand, I should imagine," he answered. "Hell, there are only seven courts in the whole United States, and two of them are right here."

I jammed my hands into my pants pocket and balled them into fists. "What is he hiding?" I repeated. "Do you know?"

Steckler put his arm around my shoulder and steered me toward the door. "I'm going to change and take a shower," he said. "Wait downstairs. I'll be along in fifteen minutes."

I spent the fifteen minutes in the downstairs lobby of the club, twitching nervously in an overstuffed chair and checking my watch.

Steckler reappeared, dressed in his street clothes. I expected to see him in a corporate lawyer's pinstripe, but instead he was wearing a corduroy shooting jacket—one of those four-hundred-dollar affairs from Hunting World with a leather patch over the right shoulder—a pair of baggy chinos and running sneakers. A white golfer's cap was perched on his head at a jaunty angle.

"Let's take a walk," he said.

We took off up Park Avenue, crossed Fifty-ninth and entered Central Park by the Plaza Hotel at Fifth Avenue. Steckler barreled along comfortably at about ten miles an hour. He asked me about myself. With rasping breath, I managed to blurt out the essentials. It happened that he had read a book of mine—the one on the Shah of Iran.

"You missed a few things," he said. "But I remember thinking when I was reading it, 'How the hell did this son of a bitch get this material?' You may not be a spy, Brady, but you have the talents of a damned good one. Resourceful and persistent. You seem to have an instinct for knowing where to look for what you need, and that's worth a lot. Until I read that book of yours, I never realized how much a spy and a journalist had in common."

Steckler didn't get back to the subject of Carlson until we had reached the southeastern edge of the Sheep Meadow, the huge expanse of open lawn in the center of the park. It was relatively deserted at this hour, save for a gang of kids playing catch with a Frisbee and a few strollers.

"First," he said, "let me give you some advice. Take Carlson's offer and forget about the book. If you go against the man, you'll lose. He'll grind you into the dirt. You already have a pretty good idea of what he's capable of. Journalists tend to take themselves too seriously. Don't get it into your head that it's up to you to save the Republic. Don't be a hero. Do a book on somebody else and live happily ever after."

I didn't reply.

Steckler laughed finally. "Not going to take my advice, I see."

"I don't know yet. I'm trying to sort it out."

We stopped at a refreshment stand and Steckler bought hot dogs and soft drinks for both of us. "I love hot dogs," he said. "My wife won't have them in the house, though. So I have to sneak them on the side."

I doubted that. He wasn't the timid sort. If Grayson Steckler wanted a hot dog, anywhere, anytime, he'd get one—even if it meant shooting the animal and processing the innards himself. He was trying to be folksy with me.

"If Carlson's hiding something big," I said, trying to tease some more information out of him, "it's going to be awful hard for me to turn my back on it."

"Even if it means prison?"

I shrugged.

"Who's your lawyer?"

"Sam Marks."

Steckler nodded appreciatively. "Good choice. And what's his advice?"

"Take Carlson's offer."

"Anybody else suggest differently?"

"Not so far."

"Well, you're a stubborn son of a bitch, Brady, I'll say that. Think it through. If Carlson set you up—and I agree with you that he probably did—he won't quit if you wriggle free once, you know. He'll hunt you down. You have to understand what and who you're up against."

"Tell me about it."

Steckler crumpled up his hot-dog wrapper in his big hands and tossed it into a waste barrel. He took a deep breath. "Andrew Carlson and I trained together in Virginia in 1943 before we were sent to Europe. I didn't like him, right from the start. It was clear to me that he was a clever, unprincipled opportunist. A man never to be trusted. Some things happened at camp that I won't go into, but suffice it to say that had it not been for the confused and bumbling state of the OSS in those first months of operation, and the wartime pressure we were under to get into action, Carlson would have washed out of the program. Instead, he was rushed through training, and parachuted into France, behind German lines. He became the chief secret liaison between the Allied forces and the French Resistance. It was a hell of an important job—difficult, sensitive and dangerous. Carlson survived—I'll give him credit for that—but it was at the expense of a lot of others."

Steckler threw his soft-drink can in the trash container and we continued walking.

"He had only been in place a few months when the Gestapo caught him, in Paris. You've no doubt read about his legendary escape from the Gestapo. Well, the funny thing about that escape was that during that same week the Gestapo and the Vichy police rounded up hundreds of members of the underground, all over Occupied France, including Jean Moulin, their leader. It was no coincidence, I can tell you. Carlson knew the names and the locations. He gave them to the Gestapo. No doubt they tortured him, but he was no hero. He went on collaborating. His escape was phony. It was staged. I can't prove it, but I know it. Nobody ever got away from the Gestapo. And if they did, they sure as hell wouldn't have gone back to business as usual. They'd have gotten the hell out of Occupied territory as fast as they could. But Carlson stayed on in Paris right up through to the liberation."

"No one suspected him, then?"

"Sure they did. But he was clever. The French Resistance was a deeply divided force—the Communists and their sympathizers on one side, the Gaullists and other democrats on the other. When the two sides weren't fighting the Nazis, they were busy betraying each other. Carlson played the two sides off against each other. Anything that seemed to point to him, he was able to deflect onto either the Communists or the loyalists—or the Vichy French. He played a dangerous game, but he pulled it off and came out of the war a hero."

"Is that what he's worried about? That I'll find out that he collaborated with the Nazis during the war?"

"That's part of it," Steckler replied. "After the war he joined the CIA, but Allen Dulles didn't like him. Eventually he either fired him or forced him out. I don't know if there were specific reasons or not. I was never in the CIA myself, so my information is secondhand. After the war I went to law school."

We walked in silence for a time, Steckler maintaining his killing pace, me struggling to stay abreast.

"Carlson dabbled in real estate for a while," he continued.

"Later he got into the arms trade. Our military had a huge inventory of surplus weapons and was delighted to unload them on middlemen like Carlson, who could turn around and sell them abroad. Carlson made millions, I understand, and in the process formed some pretty unsavory business relationships."

"Like what?"

"Like Georges Dasserres, for one. He's a *pied-noir*. French Algerian. A rich monarchist—a supporter of General Salan and the plot to overthrow the French government in 1961. He was also behind one of the assassination attempts on General de Gaulle. Dasserres is an arms merchant, basically, but he's also involved in the drug trade. He's a common criminal, in fact, but protected by his wealth and his connections. Carlson met Dasserres during the war, and there's evidence that they've remained close ever since. Carlson has been very careful to keep this friendship a secret. What they might be up to together is anyone's guess. I don't claim to know myself."

We came out of the park at the Seventy-second Street exit. I was sweating profusely, the champagne hangover leaking through my pores like bilge water. Steckler, hands on his hips, appraised me critically. "You're not in very good shape, Brady."

"You mean physically, or situationally?"

Steckler laughed. "Both, I guess. You know those documents that Conover gave you. They could strengthen the espionage charges against you."

This made my scalp prickle. "How's that?"

"Highly classified information."

"How do you know that?"

"It's about the Night Watch, isn't it?"

I thought to choose my words carefully. "That's possible."

"That's a top-secret CIA operation."

"Why did Conover give them to me, then?"

"Good question. He may have been trying to entrap you."

"Why would he do that?"

"Well, he's an old buddy of Carlson's. It may have been part of Carlson's plot to nail you on espionage charges."

"What should I do?"

"I'd burn those documents. Pretend you never saw them."

"Maybe they're not CIA documents?"

"You're being awfully coy, Brady. If you want my help, show me the documents. I'll tell you what you've got."

"Are you cleared for top secret?"

Steckler didn't bat an eye. "Yes, I am."

"Who can I check that with?"

Steckler put his hands on his hips.

"My problem with you," I said, "is that you have no motive for helping me. I don't know who the hell you are, or whose interests you represent. For all I know you could be a spy yourself."

Steckler chuckled. He put an arm over my shoulder and pulled me along with him up Fifth Avenue. "I'll tell you the truth, Brady. I want to get those documents you have out of circulation. Fast. If they got into the wrong hands, they could cause a lot of harm. Not just to the people involved, but for the whole damned country. I'm quite serious. Now, if the FBI's charges against you are false, as you say they are, then the last thing you want is to be caught with these papers in your possession."

"What's your interest in this?"

"I represent the president's interests. That's very confidential, by the way."

"So if I just went home and destroyed these documents, that would be fine with you."

"Yes."

"You don't care to see them yourself?"

"Only to remove any doubt from your mind as to their identity."

"This Night Watch operation. You know all about it?"

"Pretty much."

"I see. Well, I'll have to think about all of this."

"I hope I've helped you," he said.

"You could probably help me a lot more," I countered.

He didn't deny it. He stood on the sidewalk a moment, squinting into the afternoon sun. I waited.

"I tell you what," he said. "I'll put you in touch with somebody who can help you resolve this dilemma. You tell him I sent you, I'm sure he'll talk to you. He'll check you out with me first. I'll tell him that you're okay. His name is Colonel Westerly. His number is 202-555-1234. It's unlisted."

Surprise. This must be the same obnoxious Colonel Westerly

who had sat in on El Cardozo's interview with me. I wondered if Steckler knew that. "Who is he?" I asked, hoping I looked innocent.

"He's a special assistant to the White House National Security Advisor," Steckler replied, in a low voice.

"I'll think about it."

Steckler's eyes narrowed and his mouth tightened. "Whatever you decide, do one thing for me, will you?"

"What's that?"

"If you decide not to take Carlson's offer, let me know. That's important."

I was puzzled. Why did Steckler care? "Okay. I guess I can do that."

We shook hands and I turned and started back across the park to my apartment.

"Brady?"

I turned. Steckler, still at the same spot on the sidewalk, was waving me back. When I reached him, he put a heavy hand on my shoulder and pulled my face in close to his. "Is your apartment bugged?"

"Yes, it is."

"Don't call him from there, then."

"I didn't plan to."

Steckler patted my shoulder hard, then removed his hand. "Good boy. You remember the name and number?"

"Colonel Westerly, 202-555-1234."

"Good. One more thing. Don't write it down anywhere. You understand?"

"I have a good memory."

Steckler grinned. "Good luck, Brady."

I walked across the park, the muscles in my calves begging for mercy from Steckler's forced march.

The man's information about Carlson was interesting, but highly suspect. Carlson may have exaggerated his heroics during the war—or even have invented them—but it was awfully hard to believe he had been a collaborator. The Gestapo had plenty of collaborators among the French. They didn't need to capture them from the OSS. Whatever Carlson might be hiding, I didn't think that was it.

And why did Steckler tell me so many derogatory things about the director? And why hadn't I asked him about that?

What was happening to me? Since my arrest I seemed to have lost my edge as an interviewer.

Everyone was getting the better of me these days.

14

THE COLONELS

I came out of the park by the Museum of Natural History at Eighty-first Street and headed down Central Park West. Between Seventy-seventh and Seventy-sixth, I stopped.

I could see the awning over the front door of my building, a block farther south. Underneath it, and spilling out around it, was a crowd of about forty or fifty people.

My first impulse was to quicken my step, thoughts of fire, burglary and sudden death flashing through my brain. Half a block away, at Seventy-sixth, I stopped again.

No fire trucks, no police cars, no ambulances.

Worse.

The press.

A huge, deadly swarm of them had alighted on my doorstep:

camera crews, reporters, sound people. Remote units—vans bristling with microwave-dish uplinks—were parked across the street. I could pick out a few familiar faces in the crowd. Everyone was just standing around—chatting, joking, laughing. Whatever they were there for, it either hadn't yet happened or wasn't yet over.

I turned quickly and walked west along Seventy-sixth Street, to get out of sight. I felt jolted, unnerved. They were waiting for me.

I stood on the sidewalk, staring up at the windows of the neat, renovated brownstones that lined Seventy-sixth Street, and agonized for a few minutes. Those people out there in front of my building were my colleagues. I was one of them. Some were my friends. They were on my side.

I felt a dizzy thrill at the idea of suddenly becoming the object of such intense attention—to be embraced by the hot glare of the TV lights, the dozens of extended hands with tape recorders, the loud, insistent jumble of shouted questions.

I walked back to the corner and took another look down toward my apartment building, the adrenaline of the anticipated moment already beginning to pump. I owed it to them—and to myself as a journalist—to go down there and lay the whole thing out for them.

On the other hand: like hell I did.

I turned and hurried back along Seventy-sixth Street to Columbus Avenue. I bought a newspaper, got change in quarters from three singles, and rushed to the pay phone on the corner.

I called the national desk at the Associated Press. After eighteen rings, someone who thought he had better things to do answered it.

"Yeah?"

"Excuse me, but I understand you may be looking for John Brady?"

"Who?"

"John Brady. You know. The spy."

"Oh. Yeah. You know where he is?"

"Yes, I do. He's staying with a woman on West Eleventh Street. Seven-seventy-four West Eleventh Street."

"What's the name there?"

"Snow. Gail Snow."

"Apartment?"

"Third floor, rear."

"Phone?"

"I don't know that. But I know he's there. I saw him not two minutes ago."

"How do you know what he looks like?"

This guy was quick. "Hey, I've known John Brady for years, all right?"

"What's *your* name?"

I hung up, called in similar messages to the three networks, the local bureaus of half a dozen big newspapers, *The New York Times, Time* and *Newsweek.*

My quarters spent, I strolled up Columbus Avenue to a Mexican restaurant and slowly drank two very cold bottles of Carta Blanca and ate a bowl of tortilla chips.

When I returned to my apartment building, half an hour later, the sidewalk in front of the door was deserted. Even the big vans were gone.

I couldn't help smiling.

John, the day doorman, was understandably upset. The news was all over the building now that I had been arrested as a spy. He pretended not to see me as I walked into the lobby.

I grabbed him by the arm when he tried to slip out of sight. "It's not at all what you think, John," I whispered confidingly. "I'm working undercover for the FBI. We're trying to smoke out some real spies."

John was from Lithuania, and believed deeply in political conspiracy, so I knew I was sowing on fertile ground. He nodded uncertainly. He wanted to believe me.

I glanced around the lobby. It was empty. "Don't tell anyone I told you this. Especially the press. We could all be in big trouble."

His expression remained dubious.

"I'm confiding in you because I need a favor."

John's forehead wrinkled in discomfort. "I don't know. . . ."

I pulled out my wallet, took out fifty dollars, and feeling like a private eye in an old, bad movie, slapped it into his palm. He glanced anxiously down at the bills, as if I had just placed a live frog in his hands. But he was beginning to be persuaded.

"Anyone who asks," I said. "Tell them I've left the building. I packed my bags and left last night. You don't know where I've gone. Standing instructions until you hear otherwise. Okay?"

The fifty bucks disappeared somewhere on John's person as if by sleight of hand. He started to say something, but I gestured warningly toward the front door. A tenant was coming in.

He threw out his hands in a gesture of helplessness.

"I knew I could count on you," I said. I hurried toward the elevator bank at the back of the lobby.

Someone in uniform emerged from the mail room, strode over to me, and planted himself squarely in front of me. The expression on his face was peculiar—he looked both angry and relieved. At first I feared he was a cop.

It took me a few seconds to realize he was the colonel Steckler had just told me to call—the same irritatingly self-important individual who had sat beside the Justice Department's Cardozo during my FBI interrogation downtown. Like Clark Kent, he had shed his drab civilian business suit to become, if not Superman, the closest plausible substitute—an officer in the United States Marine Corps, complete with boards, brass fixtures and a heavily decorated chest.

"I'm Colonel Westerly," he said, grabbing my arm. "We must talk at once."

I pulled my arm free and punched the elevator button. Both cars were busy, so I was forced to stand there with him hovering at my side.

"This is important," he said, drawing out the word "important," as if I might not understand anything three syllables long.

I punched the button again and looked up at the floor indicators. One said 5, the other 6. I took a deep breath.

One of the elevators finally arrived. A white-haired woman with a lit cigarette in her mouth, gin on her breath, and a yapping Pekinese dog in her arms strode off the elevator in a swirl of blue smoke and pitched smack into the colonel, spilling cigarette ashes onto his uniform.

She toppled backward on her spiked heels. The colonel caught her by the shoulders and stood her upright. "You're not supposed to smoke in elevators, ma'am," he reminded her.

The old lady jerked free of his grip, and stared at his dazzling uniform with openmouthed incredulity. She turned to me for an explanation. "Who the fuck is this?" she demanded. "The surgeon general?"

Westerly and I rode up in the elevator in silence. The old lady had almost restored my good humor.

I unlocked the door and let Westerly into the apartment.

It had been thoroughly ransacked.

I walked through the rooms, shaking my head and muttering under my breath. Colonel Westerly followed me.

The damage looked worse than it was, but it was still bad enough. Every drawer had been opened and the contents scattered about, every book had been knocked from its shelf, and every item of clothing had been examined and thrown on the floor. The kitchen appeared relatively untouched, but it was clear that the contents of the refrigerator and all the cupboards and cabinets had been gone through.

A few items were damaged. The mattress and the box spring of my bed had suffered the most. The tops of both had been completely sliced open on three sides and peeled back, like animal skins, revealing a mass of cloth-wrapped springs and loose ticking. Nothing, so far as I could tell, was missing. All the obvious items of fenceable value—computer, TV, VCR, stereo set—were still there. But they had all been opened up.

It seemed reasonable to assume that the intruders had been looking for Conover's documents.

"I guess I should hire a cleaning lady," I said. "I just can't seem to keep the place tidy."

Westerly removed his hat and tucked it under his arm.

I restored an overturned chair to an upright position and replaced the cushion. "Have a seat, Colonel. It's been a tough day. I'm going to pour myself a drink. Can I get you one?"

The colonel shook his head. He stared at the shambles around him with the ill-at-ease look of somebody caught in a bad neighborhood.

I went to the kitchen, mixed a scotch and water, and returned. Westerly was still standing, shifting his weight from foot to foot.

I flung myself down on the sofa, slapped both feet up onto the coffee table, and looked at my guest. "Funny you should show up. I was just going to call you."

The colonel came right to the point. "Those documents that Admiral Conover gave you," he said, peeking at his wristwatch. "I would like to have them, please."

I tasted my scotch. After an awkward silence, he repeated his request.

I ignored it. "Do you have a first name, Colonel? Or is it actually just 'Colonel'?"

"What?"

"I was wondering if your name was Colonel Colonel Westerly. You know, like Major Major Major? You remember him? In *Catch-22*?"

Westerly squinted at me, as if committing my features to memory. "Herbert," he replied, evenly. "Colonel Herbert Westerly."

"Do your friends call you Herb?"

His squint intensified.

"Do you have any friends? How about a wife? Kids? Where did you grow up?"

"Those documents are classified at the highest level," he announced. His tone suggested that I should be awestruck by this revelation.

"How do *you* know?" I countered. "Have you seen them?"

"Where are they?"

I certainly wasn't going to admit to Westerly that I had lost them without seeing them myself. "It looks like you're too late, Colonel," I said, sweeping a hand around the room. "Someone got here before you."

"Where are they?"

"You already asked me that. Why don't you sit down? You're making me nervous. You look like a bellhop waiting for his tip."

Westerly expelled his breath in an angry snort, and forced himself down into a chair across from me. He was having a hard time holding on to his composure. "Those documents have to be recovered," he said, his voice hardening to a threat.

"Who asked you to recover them?"

"Not asked," he corrected. "Ordered. I've been ordered to recover them."

"Okay. Who ordered you, then?"

"That's not your concern. Where are they?"

I made the ice cubes in my glass rattle loudly. "They're in my study. Bottom desk drawer on the left. Want to take a look?"

"Go get them."

I walked into my study, banged a desk drawer open and shut

a few times, and then returned to the living room. "They're not there," I reported. "Whoever broke in must have stolen them. Sorry about that. I sure would have liked to have been able to turn them over to you. You look like a guy I could trust."

I could hear some of Westerly's knuckles popping. "You're lying," he said. "You wouldn't leave those documents in such an unsafe place."

I hunched my shoulders and threw out my arms in a Steve Martin shrug.

"Those documents are the property of the government," the colonel said, making an effort to sound reasonable. "They are extremely sensitive. If they fell into the hands of our enemies, they could cause irreparable damage to this country. They must be recovered."

It occurred to me that Westerly himself was probably responsible for the chaotic jumble of my apartment. If he had not actually done the break-in and search himself, then someone had done it for him. When they didn't find the documents, he decided to lie in wait for me in the mail room.

"Maybe we're not thinking about the same papers, Colonel. Could you describe specifically the ones you're looking for?"

"The ones given to you by Admiral Conover."

"Well, he gave me quite a few. Which ones in particular did you have in mind?"

"All of them."

"You can't describe them for me? I'd hate to give you the wrong ones by mistake. If you could just give me a hint about their contents . . ."

The colonel's face was getting red, but he remained calm. "I appeal to your patriotism—if you have any. Don't do yourself and your country grave harm out of some misguided notion that you can profit from having them in your possession. You can't. These documents have no value to you. You can't sell them. You can't even understand them. Give them back and the whole matter will be forgotten."

"What whole matter is that?"

"You won't be prosecuted for having them in your possession."

"That's funny as hell, Colonel."

"Where are they?"

"In a safe place."

"Where?"

"I really can't tell you, I'm afraid. Sorry."

Westerly regarded the round flat top crown of his officer's cap, parked precisely in his lap so that the visor pointed exactly away from him. He ran a thumb along the creased edge, as if testing its sharpness. His expression was grim—resigned but determined. "I expected I might have a tough time persuading you," he admitted.

"Persuade? You couldn't persuade a whore to let you kiss her ass for a thousand dollars. Why don't you go home now, and leave me alone."

"You're in deep trouble," he warned, trying to sound sincere. "If you continue to hold these documents, you'll be putting yourself in personal danger."

I took a drink and thought about the situation. I couldn't get over the extraordinary fact that Colonel Westerly had actually appeared in person, in uniform, to try to scare those documents out of me. I didn't think he was doing it out of simple recklessness or stupidity. Then what was motivating him? Desperation?

"I just can't help you, Colonel. Sorry."

Westerly got up slowly and put on his cap. He adjusted it carefully, one hand gripping the visor, the other pressed against the headband above the back of his neck. When he was satisfied that it was sitting exactly horizontal on his head, he took a big gulp of air, and delivered a karate chop against the side of my neck.

I went flying sideways over the sofa and landed on my face, gasping for breath. My neck felt broken. When I was able to turn over and look up, I found myself staring into the barrel of an automatic pistol.

Behind the fear, my insides boiled with a profound and murderous fury. If I lived, I would get this guy someday.

Westerly flipped back the safety catch and pointed the weapon directly at my head. He was standing barely four feet from me, so the open hole of the barrel loomed a foot from my eyes. I tried not to react, but my gut started tripping with spasms.

"You don't understand," he said, his voice low. "I *have* to have those documents. Things are getting out of hand. They're kicking ass and taking names, now. There's no more time for games."

"Please put the gun down, Colonel," I said. My voice was trembling. It sounded like I was begging him. I guess I was.

"I'm giving you one minute," he said. "Produce those documents, or I swear to God . . . I swear to God I'll put a bullet right through your fucking brain."

"That's crazy talk, Colonel. What'll you gain . . . ?"

He cut me off. "You're worse than a Communist. You're a damned traitor! At least they have ideals and they know how to fight for them. But you don't stand for anything. You don't stand for shit! You'd sell your country down the river for your own personal gain. You're disgusting. You stink. I'd be doing America a favor by blowing you away."

As Colonel Westerly unburdened himself, his arm began to shake, making the pistol barrel vibrate in front of me. The thought lodged in my mind that Westerly was getting himself so worked up that he might shoot me accidentally.

I watched his trigger finger, wondering how much more pressure was needed to trip the hammer. My breathing kept shutting off. I thought about ducking quickly to one side, or diving for him, but I didn't trust myself to move at all. My muscles ached for action, but my limbs were frozen. I despised myself for the fear I knew I was showing him.

I raised my hands placatingly. I was so soaked with sweat I began to feel a chill. I rubbed my neck. He had hit me just under the ear. It throbbed with pain.

"Get them," he commanded. "Get them right now."

"Okay. Take it easy. I've hidden them out in the back hall. In the fire stairs."

"Let's go get them."

He marched me to my front door, looked out the keyhole to check that the corridor was empty, then opened the door and pushed me out in front of him, jabbing the pistol sharply into the small of my back.

The door to the emergency stairwell was down the other end of the hall from my apartment door. I opened it and Westerly pushed through behind me.

"It's right here," I said, pointing to the rolled-up length of three-inch canvas fire hose hanging from its bracket on the wall next to the door. "Inside the hose."

"Get it."

I unscrewed the heavy brass nozzle from the end of the hose, reached a finger and thumb inside and extracted a rolled-up 8½-×-11 manila envelope. I offered it to Westerly.

He shook his head. "Open it up."

I flattened out the envelope, peeled the Scotch tape off the flap, undid the clasps and pulled out six sheets of paper. Westerly snatched them from me.

The light wasn't very good in the stairwell, and he had to bring the pages up close to his face to see them.

I picked up the foot-long brass nozzle. I contemplated bashing the colonel over the head with it and dumping him over the stairwell railing for a fifteen-story plunge to the basement floor. Instead, I calmly screwed the nozzle back into place on the hose coupling.

Westerly put the pages back in the envelope, folded it, and stuffed it inside his tunic.

He parked his pistol in its holster and secured the flap. He grinned at me. "Sorry I had to get tough, but you left me no choice."

"Everybody makes mistakes," I said, grinning back.

"No hard feelings?" he asked.

"You can't win them all," I said.

Westerly agreed. If it was a cliché, he was apt to agree with it. That was the way he was programmed. It was in his software. The time-worn, the tried-and-true—that was the colonel's métier.

With the precious documents now tucked under his jacket, the colonel decided to walk down the fourteen flights of the fire stairs rather than risk the elevator.

I retreated to my apartment, rubbing my neck and gritting my teeth. I locked the door, wedging the long steel bar of the Fox lock into place to barricade it against any further invasions.

I sank down into the sofa, rested my head against the back cushion, and stared at the ceiling. I congratulated myself for my clever advance planning, but now I had to worry about what I was going to do when Colonel Westerly took a good look at those pages. Underneath a phony cover sheet on which I had typed the words "Night Watch" was part of a report I had filed for *Time* magazine many years ago—on spy fiction.

The telephone rang. I let it ring. I listened to my answering message, and then the caller's voice: a reporter from *Newsweek*. As soon as she hung up, the phone rang again. A reporter from *Newsday*. A minute later, someone from NBC News. That was followed by an offer from ABC to appear on *Good Morning America*.

I forced myself up from the sofa and moved toward the study. The phone started ringing again. I looked at my message counter. The tape was full. It had probably been full for some time. I disconnected the telephone, found a pad and pencil on my desk, turned the answering machine back on and stood by it patiently while it unburdened itself.

My lawyer, Sam Marks, had called to inform me that a grand jury would begin hearing evidence in my case next week. The sessions were secret, but I could count on them returning an indictment against me. "They almost always do, John. So don't be upset when it happens. At this point, it's little more than a formality."

Upset? Shit, why should I be upset to be indicted by a grand jury for espionage?

Tracy Anderson had called to let me know she was furious that I had left this morning without saying good-bye. She wanted to see me again this evening. No, she *demanded* to see me again this evening.

The rest were from the press. They consumed the entire half-hour capacity of the answering machine's tape, and were still going strong when the machine stopped recording them.

I spent some time straightening up the apartment.

Back in my study, I replaced the doctored diaphragm in the handset and plugged the telephone in again. It rang immediately. Reluctantly, I picked it up.

I was relieved to hear the voice of my electronics-genius friend, Frank Chin: "Johnny, your phone is bugged."

"How did you guess?"

"Trade secret. Can you drop over? I got something I want you to see."

Frank was always eager to show off his latest gadget. "I'm pretty busy right now, Frank."

Chin insisted. "No. You come over. It's important. Half an hour."

He hung up. I stared at the receiver, completely baffled. Frank Chin was a strange individual, but he wasn't the type to exaggerate. If anything, he was the most understated human being I had ever known. If he said something was important, it was probably a matter of life and death.

Curiosity was my master, anyway.

Frank Chin worked out of a large loft in SoHo, a neighborhood of old factory buildings and warehouses in the southwest corner of Manhattan just below Houston Street.

Frank's place of business was situated over an art gallery down a side street that had yet to feel the brunt of the chic uptown money that had forced out the painters and sculptors and converted the area into a gentrified enclave of fern bars and overdecorated lofts.

I walked up two flights of a creaking, dimly lit stairwell, and pressed the buzzer next to a massive reinforced-steel door. I looked up over the door and saw, behind a small grille, the lens of a television camera trained on me.

After a short interval, the huge door rumbled open to reveal what looked like the remains of a Radio Shack franchise immediately after a tornado. An immense tangle of electronic gear extended across almost the entire breadth and depth of the old warehouse loft.

"Over here, Johnny. Watch your step."

I stepped, hopped and did contortions around boxes, wires, cables, circuit boards, dismembered computer parts and mounds of exotic paraphernalia I couldn't begin to put a name to. At the back of the loft, in front of a big window, was Frank Chin, bent over the barrel of what looked like a giant space-age ray gun mounted inside a small satellite antenna dish.

Seated in a metal swivel chair nearby, his legs crossed and a cigarette cupped in his hand, was a deeply tanned, sturdily built middle-aged man with curly steel-gray hair and a wary glint in his dark eyes. He looked to be either Arab or Israeli. One side of his head was badly scarred from the neck up to the ear, which was fused into a small, irregularly shaped bump about a third the size of his other ear. His throat was also marked with two dime-sized scars that looked like old bullet wounds.

Frank often entertained mysterious visitors on confidential business, so I wasn't surprised when he didn't introduce us.

"Watch this, Johnny," Frank said. He scurried behind a portable control panel connected to the gun, and to a stack of amplifiers and a pair of large speakers. He checked the various ganglia of wires to make sure everything was plugged in where it belonged, pressed a few buttons, flipped a few switches and turned a few knobs.

"See the window on that building over there," he said, pointing across at a big brick factory on the next block.

"Which one?"

"The one with the blue venetian blinds. Sixth floor."

"Okay."

"I aim this laser toward it, like so . . ." He adjusted the barrel of the gun using a telescopic sight attached to its side until he was satisfied that he had it pointed directly at the window.

"Then I give it the juice . . ."

He flipped one more switch. A barely audible hum, like an FM radio, filled the room.

I heard a peculiar sound over the speakers, like something blowing bubbles underwater. Frank fiddled with the controls and gradually out of the jumble of noises a man's voice emerged, at first burbly and indistinct, then clear enough to make out the words:

". . . Sure. He gave me cash. What the fuck you think, I'm handling plastic these days? Visa? MasterCard? Yeah. He had it in a safe. Nah, you know—a wall safe . . . The fucker peeled off twenty yards, just like that. Tucked it in my shirt pocket. He likes to make grand gestures—'We want the same amount and quality every week,' he says. 'Every Friday night.' . . . Yeah . . . I made out like that wasn't going to be so easy. . . . This guy's a real freak, man. Him and his wife both. I mean they're into everything—dope, orgies, weird S & M stuff, bondage—you fuckin name it, they do it. He asked me if I knew where they could rent a couple of dwarfs for one of their parties. Yeah. He wanted a couple—boy and girl—to perform for them. . . . Yeah. Dwarfs, yeah. I go, 'Try the circus, man. I only handle drugs.' Can you believe it? Some people are fuckin degenerate, man, what can I say?" [Loud laughter.]

Frank switched the laser off and turned first to me and then to his other guest, a wide conspiratorial grin on his face. The other guest looked bored. "A little slice of the Big Apple," Frank declared, patting the barrel of the laser with a hand. "This was state-of-the-art a few years ago. Nobody had this but the CIA. Now I've got it. You point it at a window, and it picks up voice vibrations off the glass and amplifies them. Technology is beautiful, what can I say?"

Frank Chin had grown up in Chinatown, just a few blocks from here. His father and mother owned a tiny restaurant, and the family lived upstairs—father, mother, grandmother and six kids, all in three rooms.

Frank went to MIT on a full scholarship, and eventually ended up working for the navy, developing their sonar and radar programs. Some years later the National Security Agency hired him away and put him to work developing their spy satellites.

He went back into civilian life about ten years ago, set himself up as an electronic consultant and soon had a thriving business, employing dozens of specialists. He hated it, so he sold it, becoming rich in the process. After that, he patented a few electronic inventions and became even richer.

Now in his sixties, with four ex-wives and many children and grandchildren, he was supposed to be retired and living on an estate he owned in Hawaii.

But Frank Chin was bent in a funny way. The only thing in life that really interested him was electronics—and especially electronic eavesdropping. At heart I guess he was just an incurable voyeur. So he set up this shop in SoHo as a hobby. He still serviced a few select clients—the CIA, the FBI, and some others he never talked about—but much of the time he just tinkered around. I met him when I was doing some research on electronic surveillance for one of my books. In the years since, I had sought him out occasionally for his special knowledge.

Although second-generation Chinese, he was no stereotype. None of this nervous-chuckling-Chinaman stuff with Frank Chin. He spoke cultured, accentless English, and had the calm, almost phlegmatic manner of a New England Yankee.

I guess I saw some of myself in Frank. We were each in our own way eavesdroppers, invaders of privacy. Me, with my hidden recorder and my endless nosy questions, he, with his exotic devices, prying into the private affairs of others, finding satisfaction in the accumulation of secret knowledge.

Frank opened a bottle of beer for me and then turned to the other visitor, still sitting quietly and smoking his cigarette. The man nodded at him.

"So," Frank said, turning back to me. "I leave you two alone, okay?" He immediately scurried off to the far end of the loft, where he busied himself with another pile of electronic gear.

Surprised, I glanced sidelong at the man in the chair. He was appraising me with an almost rude stare, holding his gaze on me much longer than was polite.

He had been collecting the ashes of his cigarette in his hand. Now he extinguished the cigarette against the sole of his shoe, collected the remains, ground them up between his fingers and dropped them through the neck of the empty bottle of beer at his feet. Here was a man accustomed to keeping evidence of his presence to a minimum.

"Wolf Zimmer," he said, with a pronounced accent.

"I beg your pardon?"

"Colonel Wolf Zimmer," he repeated, thrusting out his right hand.

I stepped over to his chair and we shook. His grip was light. The insides of his forefinger and middle finger were stained dark yellow from nicotine. His little finger was missing.

"John Brady," I replied.

"I know."

"Who are you?" I asked.

"Israeli intelligence," he answered, his hard black eyes still measuring me.

15

WOLF ZIMMER

"Mossad?"

Colonel Wolf Zimmer dipped his head in a brisk nod. His movements were sharp, almost birdlike in their alert quickness. We looked at each other.

"So?" I prodded.

"I think maybe I can help you." He said it as if he had just decided it.

"Do I need your help?"

He grinned at me. His teeth were crooked on the bottom. Many of his molars were gold. "Maybe you already know the answer."

"Are you talking about my arrest?"

"Yes, of course."

"How can you help me?"

"Information. Maybe other ways."

"Why should you want to help me?"

"Because maybe in return you can help me."

His speech was studded with *maybe*s. It was just a conversational tic, but it indicated a man who attached a lot of conditions to things. I took a taste of the beer. It was warm. "That's hard to imagine, but go ahead, I'm listening."

"You want to know something about Andrew Carlson, am I correct?"

"I did. But maybe I don't anymore." Now I was doing it.

Zimmer lit another cigarette. He shook the match back and forth lazily, touched the extinguished tip with his fingers, then tucked the match in the side pocket of his suit jacket. "He's offered you a deal. That's what I know. Do you plan to take it?"

"You know quite a lot, Mr. Zimmer."

Zimmer grinned, showing a mouthful of gold molars. "My professional business is to know quite a lot."

"Do you also know what the deal is he's offering me?"

Zimmer exposed more gold. He enjoyed being tested. "He'll get the spy charges against you stopped if you stop your book."

"Doesn't give me much choice, does it?"

Zimmer watched the smoke from his cigarette curl toward the loft's high ceiling. "You'll know the answer to that when I tell you what I know."

"What do you expect from me in return?"

Zimmer looked me over again. He seemed to be trying to assess my overall mental and physical condition, like a buyer at a horse auction. "I'm hoping we can have a valuable exchange of information."

"I know nothing of value to the Israelis."

"Maybe not now. Later you might."

"Later? What do you mean?"

"I'm willing to make an investment in you."

"Look. If I did have secrets to trade, I don't think I'd want to give my government a *real* espionage case against me by trading them to the Mossad. Now or later."

Zimmer nodded sympathetically. "I understand. That's no problem. You don't have to promise me anything."

I didn't know how to reply. I paced over to the window and

stared out, looking at nothing. With every passing hour I seemed to be sinking deeper into some kind of conflict whose dimensions I could not see, or even guess at. The more I found out, it seemed, the less I knew. And now Colonel Zimmer proposed to deepen my confusion further. Did he also want those documents of Conover's?

I turned from the window and faced him. He was still watching me, his expression unreadable.

"Tell me what you want to tell me, then," I said.

Zimmer tapped the ash of his cigarette onto the new little pile of ashes he was collecting in his hand. The business with the ashes distracted me. I wanted to find him an ashtray.

"You've heard of the Night Watch?" he asked.

"I've heard the phrase a few times."

"You know what it means?"

"I know that there are rumors around that Carlson has farmed out a certain amount of intelligence work to free-lancers—often old OSS buddies. I thought the Night Watch might be a reference to that. But that's only my guess."

Zimmer studied the mound of ashes in his palm as if they might have a secret of their own to reveal. "It goes very much beyond that," he said. "In the years since he became head of your Central Intelligence Agency, Andrew Carlson has put together his own private espionage network—a worldwide empire of covert operations completely beyond the reach of any country's laws."

I pretended not to be impressed. "How big a network?"

"Very big. Bigger than the Mossad. Bigger than the intelligence services of most countries. He has many hundreds of operatives. Some are on a permanent contract basis, but most are part-time or one-time. The operation is answerable primarily to him. There is a shadowy hierarchy, but Carlson is the overall boss. It's a complete clandestine organization, set up like an international business. It has secret branches all over the world. It's highly compartmentalized, so no one knows the details of its structure or its operations—except for Carlson and a few people close to him."

I didn't believe it. "How could anybody hide anything involving so many people?"

Zimmer shrugged. "More of us are finding out about it every day. Today it's your turn."

"What's the point of it? What the hell would he need it for? What would he do with it?"

Zimmer flashed his gold teeth again. "Don't you see? It explains his great success. He found the perfect way to get around your press, your congressional oversight committees and the restrictions you imposed on the CIA by your new laws. The Night Watch gives Carlson a completely free hand to accomplish whatever he wants without worrying about the methods. Your president made it possible. He is a lazy and a complacent man. Excuse me, I hope you didn't vote for him. He's never cared what Carlson did as long as he got results. And the Night Watch is good at that. It gets results. It can do the dirty work the CIA can't."

"For instance?"

"For instance?" Zimmer straightened up in the chair. "Okay. You remember those three American hostages released in Lebanon last winter?"

"Yeah. Around Christmas."

Zimmer nodded. "Abdul Simbel's group held them. They had five originally, but two died on them. One they tortured to death because they thought he was a CIA spy. The other died of medical complications. He had a heart condition, and they neglected it until it was too late. One of those three surviving hostages actually was a CIA spy, and Carlson was afraid that Simbel would eventually find out and torture him to death as well. So it preyed on Carlson's mind. He wanted to do something, take some direct action to get them freed. So he put together a team from the Night Watch. They carried out a quick little operation that got the hostages released."

"What did they do?"

The colonel's face darkened. "Treated Abdul Simbel to some Old Testament justice. They grabbed a sister and a brother of Simbel's off the streets of Beirut. They killed the brother, cut off his head, stuffed his genitals into his mouth, and delivered the head to Simbel's hideout with a little note promising to deliver the head of his sister the following day if the three remaining Americans were not freed, unharmed, immediately." Zimmer paused for dramatic effect. "Simbel's group released the hostages within hours—'as a goodwill gesture to the American people.' "

I experienced a sharp twinge of nausea. "That qualifies as dirty work," I admitted.

Zimmer grinned. "I could tell you many stories. Not all are as colorful—or as successful—as that, but many of them involve assassinations—which your CIA can no longer indulge in."

"How does Carlson finance this?"

The colonel went through his cigarette-crushing routine again. "That's the beauty of his creation. The Night Watch is not only beyond any government's control, it's also self-sufficient. No, better than self-sufficient. Andrew Carlson has converted espionage into a capitalist enterprise, where profit and loss count for as much as ideology. The Night Watch makes money. A lot of money. Nothing else explains how it could have grown so big so fast—or how the men at the top could all have become so rich."

"Where does the money come from? He obviously can't sell stock or hold fund-raisers. The kind of operation you're describing would need millions."

"The arms trade," Zimmer replied. "Carlson was in this business for years. So he's just continued it, but on a grander scale. He keeps several licensed arms merchants under secret contract. They buy and sell for him. Let's say the United States has ten thousand obsolete M-1 rifles it wants to dump. One of these businessmen buys the rifles for five dollars each, then turns around and sells them to Iran or Iraq or a country in Africa or South America for five, ten times that amount. The businessman takes his percentage for making the deal, and the rest goes into one of the Night Watch's secret bank accounts. All of it invisible, tax-free. The Night Watch also raises money by extortion. Marcos of the Philippines, for instance. It extorted millions from him when he was in power. How? Simply by threatening to sell weapons to the Communist insurgents. His regime collapsed anyway, of course. There's a limit to the corruption any country can withstand."

Zimmer lit another cigarette. "Carlson's now adding drugs to his enterprises," he said, sucking a lungful of tobacco smoke into his mouth. "He's cutting himself in on the new cocaine markets opening up in Spain and the rest of Europe."

"How do you know all this?"

Zimmer hesitated, as if he was not sure how he should answer me. "We have a source in his organization," he replied finally.

Could I believe what this man was telling me? "So this is what Carlson is afraid I'll stumble onto if I persist with my book?"

"I think so."

I rubbed my neck, more confused than ever. "If it's true, Carlson would certainly want to keep it secret. But why have you told me?"

"Because something has to be done. The Night Watch is starting to hurt us."

"I don't follow you."

"Andrew Carlson enjoys extraordinary personal power. In many ways, he is the most powerful man on earth. I am completely serious when I say this. No government, no individual in the world is safe from him if he decides to move against them. I know, because it is happening to Israel now."

"I still don't understand."

"In the past we have sometimes collaborated with Carlson's network. They have been helpful to us with the PLO, for example. But things have recently changed. The Night Watch is now working for our enemies in the Mideast. We are extremely alarmed about this."

I studied the label of my empty beer bottle. "If you've been collaborating with such an organization, it seems to me you're probably getting what you deserve."

The colonel laughed. "Yes, you may be right. I suppose maybe we are. But in our profession you always try to keep the devil on your side. Otherwise he plays against you. And it's very hard to beat the devil."

"I don't envy the world you live in, Zimmer."

The remark annoyed him. The ash from his cigarette missed his hand and fell to the floor. With the edge of his shoe he scraped it into the cracks between the boards. "You remind me what it is about journalists that makes me dislike them," he replied. "You adopt a stance of moral superiority that you never earn. You want to know all the world's ugly secrets but you don't want to accept any responsibility for them."

"We expose them. That does some good—sometimes."

"And sometimes a lot of harm."

I watched Zimmer crush out another butt.

"So," he said, with a sigh of finality. "I have told you a great deal. What do you intend to do with it?"

"Absolutely nothing."

The colonel's thick eyebrows danced upward in surprise. "Why is that?"

"Even if everything you say is true, I have no realistic choice but to accept Carlson's offer and get as far away from the whole mess as I can. He's framed me. I have no other way out."

Zimmer exposed his gold molars again. "That would be the sensible thing to do, but you won't do it."

"I won't?"

"No. When you see that what I have told you is true, you'll pursue it. You're a journalist. A good one, I understand. I may not like journalists, but I understand what drives them. Competition. Ego. Vanity. The Night Watch is the story of the decade, Mr. Brady. Perhaps the century. You'll never get another opportunity like this. If you don't take it, someone else will grab it. You know that. And along with it, he or she will also grab the glory—the prizes, the fame, the money. You won't let that happen. If you don't pursue this, you negate your whole life. Everything you claim to stand for. Am I wrong?"

"I didn't say I didn't want to pursue it. I said I can't."

Zimmer waved a hand dismissingly. "You'd make a good spy, Brady. You lie very well. And that's a difficult thing to do."

"I'm not aware that I'm lying."

"Of course you are. Why else would you be spending time with Grayson Steckler if you weren't pursuing the story?"

"He asked to see me. Just as you did."

"Are you trying to say you don't know who he is?"

"He's a partner in the firm of Steckler and Wycoff, a fund-raiser for the Republican party, a good friend of the president's, a political conservative, and one of the world's last remaining court-tennis players. Have I left anything out?"

"Yes," the colonel answered. "The most important thing. Steckler is part of the Night Watch. Second in command, in fact, after Carlson."

This stunned me. "That's hard to believe. He gave me the distinct impression that he disliked and distrusted Carlson. He claimed Carlson was a Nazi collaborator during the war."

Zimmer sneered. "That's nonsense. Did he ask you whether or not you intended to take up Carlson's offer?"

"Yes."

"Did he ask you about the documents Admiral Conover gave you?"

Was there anything Zimmer didn't know? "Yes, he did."

"So. He was feeling you out. Maybe for Carlson, but maybe just for himself. He has as much to hide as Carlson, after all."

"Why are you telling me all this? Just to persuade me to stay on the story? What does the Mossad want to do? Destroy the Night Watch or just turn them around to work for you again?"

Colonel Zimmer didn't answer me.

"What do you expect from me?" I persisted. "You think I'm going to expose it, somehow? An enterprise that the Mossad itself is afraid of? An outfit that, according to you, can make any government on earth tremble?"

"Not at all. I have told you this only so that you can appreciate your situation. You'll pursue the story. One way or another. That much I know. All I ask from you is that you keep me informed of your progress."

"That's all? And what'll you do in return?"

"To begin with, I'll try to keep you alive."

I stared at Zimmer. "You think my life is in danger?"

"For certain."

The colonel's laconic nonchalance was beginning to grate. "Why the hell haven't they tried to kill me by now?"

"Don't be so impatient. They almost did—a week ago. The day you met Admiral Conover. The woman who stuck him on the escalator would have got you, too, if she'd known you had those documents."

"Stuck him? Nobody stuck anything in Conover."

"Yes. Helga did. The suitcase is her specialty. She bumps you in the leg with it in a crowd. She squeezes a trigger on the case's handle. A needle shoots out from the bottom front edge and jabs you in the back of the leg. Seconds later you die of a stroke or a heart attack, depending on the poison she's chosen. There are drugs now that will mimic a wide range of natural deaths, and they leave no trace in the blood. This is what happened to Admiral Conover."

I remembered the woman in the white kerchief shoving past us on the escalator. She had bumped into Conover with her suitcase. "You saw all that?"

"Not me personally. One of our agents. We were following

Conover. He had been Carlson's number-two man for years. But Steckler forced him out in a power struggle. We think Conover may have been trying to get revenge against Steckler. Or he may even have been trying to get back at the whole network, Carlson included. We don't know."

"That's why he gave me those documents?"

"No doubt."

I felt ill. I walked back over to the window and braced my hands against the sill and gazed out at the rooftops of SoHo.

"Something's going on inside the network," I heard Zimmer say. "At the top. A shake-up, a power struggle, something. We need to know exactly what. The security of my country is at stake."

"You said you had a source inside the network. Why can't he get this information for you?"

"I don't know. Maybe we don't trust that source anymore. And, anyway, at the moment you have better access."

I turned around. "I do?"

"Of course."

"To whom?"

"Tracy Anderson."

"What does she have to do with it?"

"She knows a lot, that woman. I think you can get her to tell you how much she knows."

"Christ almighty," I muttered.

"You want a bodyguard?"

"A bodyguard?"

"I could provide one."

"No, I don't want a damned bodyguard. You're just looking for an excuse to follow me around."

A trace of embarrassment flickered across Zimmer's face. "You have a weapon, then?" he asked.

"You mean a gun?"

"A gun, yes," he repeated impatiently. "A gun. A pistol."

"No."

He withdrew a small automatic from his side jacket pocket and held it out toward me. It looked ugly and menacing. "Take this one."

"I wouldn't know how to use it. And besides, it's against the law in New York to carry a pistol without a permit."

The colonel was amused by my reaction. "When I was growing

up on the kibbutz," he said. "I read an English story, *Alice in Wonderland*. You've heard of it? Well, that's you now. You're Alice, and you've just fallen down that rabbit hole. And so here you are. What made sense in your everyday life doesn't make sense on this side. Here everything is different—upside down, backwards. Different. You won't survive long if you don't recognize that."

"Why are you trying to scare me?"

"I'm trying to warn you. To alert you. If it scares you, too, that's good. Maybe you'll do something about it."

"Well, I don't want the pistol—or your protection. Thanks anyway."

Zimmer shrugged. He tucked the weapon back into his jacket. "Think about it." His tone was bored, as if he had suddenly tired of the whole discussion. "If you change your mind . . ." He reached into another pocket and produced a folded piece of paper. He got up from his chair for the first time since my arrival, walked over and handed the paper to me. "You can always reach someone at this number who will get word to me. We'll be in touch."

He walked off across the loft toward Frank Chin's bathroom. He had a slight limp.

I stood by the window, my head spinning. Frank reappeared. "Everything going okay?" he asked.

16

A RIDE IN THE PARK

From the distance of a block, the front entrance to my apartment building looked quiet, but that was deceiving. I had thrown them off for a time, but the press corps had now established a permanent ambush around the building, with remote mobile vans and cars with press plates taking up most of the nearby parking spaces. It was a real stakeout.

The moment I walked into the lobby, they would swarm out of the vans and cars and bushes and be all over me before I could reach the elevators.

I turned in to Seventy-sixth Street. I could get inside the building by using the basement service entrance in the back if there was anyone inside to unlock it for me.

A black limousine was parked on the street, directly opposite the gate leading down to the service entrance. As I walked past, the driver's door opened and the chauffeur stepped out and called my name in a low voice.

I stopped.

He came around the back end of the limousine and opened the rear door by the curb. I half expected to see Conover's supposed assassin, Helga, emerge with her white kerchief and suitcase.

The driver gestured for me to get in. "The director wants to talk to you," he said.

I hesitated, then stepped over to the opened door and bent down. In the dim glow of the interior courtesy lights, I saw the silhouette of Andrew Carlson's head and the shadowy image of his face. He was alone in the back.

I climbed in and sat on the jump seat facing him. The chauffeur closed the door and went back around and slipped in behind the wheel. I glanced behind me, through the bulletproof glass partition that separated the front seat from the director's private domain in the rear. Sitting next to the driver was a bodyguard. An Uzi submachine gun rested on his lap.

The director pressed the intercom button on the armrest under his left hand. "Take us around the park, Tony."

The driver started the limo's big engine, turned out onto Central Park West and drove down to Seventy-second Street, where he swung left into the park drive, a three-lane roadway that snakes through Central Park in a long, meandering loop.

"I had a speaking engagement in New York today," Carlson said very matter-of-factly.

"And you just dropped by to see how I was getting on."

Carlson muttered something about how long he had been waiting, then offered me a drink from the small bar built into the island console between the jump seats. I accepted a scotch and water. He emptied a can of tomato juice into a small glass, added some crushed ice and Tabasco sauce, and stirred it with a plastic swizzle stick. Was tomato juice the preferred beverage of OSS veterans, I wondered? Admiral Conover had been belting back Bloody Marys out at JFK the day he died.

Neither of us spoke for several minutes. The ponderous, armor-plated government limousine growled along in the right lane at a sedate pace, edging out into the faster traffic occasionally to get

around the horse-drawn carriages that tended to clog the south
end of the park drive, hauling tourists to and from the square in
front of the Plaza Hotel. Out the car's rear window I saw the
dazzling façade of lights from the tall buildings along Central Park
South.

"I need your decision," Carlson said, breaking the silence.
"There isn't any more time. If you want my help, I have to know
now. Tonight."

I needed some answers of my own, first. "Did you arrange for
my arrest?" I asked.

Carlson claimed that he had not.

"I mean did you set me up for it with the FBI—plant that secret
material with René Gervais, then pressure him to implicate me."

He repeated his denial: "No, I didn't do that."

Why was I bothering to ask him? Carlson was a gifted liar with
many years of practice. He had effectively evaded, obstructed,
confused, manipulated and misled every investigative and oversight
committee the Congress had ever fielded against him. And no
journalist had ever successfully pried anything out of him that he
hadn't already decided he wanted made public. Indeed, if Wolf
Zimmer knew what he was talking about, Carlson had created and
kept hidden his own private international army of assassins and
spooks.

Secrecy, subterfuge and deception were Carlson's stock-in-trade.
They were part of what made him the powerful figure he was.
Even if I already knew the answers to the questions I was throwing
at him, he could probably talk me out of them. Still, simple professional self-respect demanded that I try.

"Who did do it, then?"

Carlson stifled a yawn. "I really have no idea."

"Somebody set me up. You seem to be the only one with both
the motive and the means."

"I have no information that anyone has set you up. I'm taking
advantage of your situation. You need some help. I'm in a position
to give it—in return for a relatively small favor."

"Why are you so determined to stop me doing this book?"

"We've been through all that, Brady."

"What are you hiding that can be so important?"

"We all have things to hide. I have a right to protect my privacy."

"On personal things, sure."

"This is personal," Carlson replied.

I wasn't ready to quit yet: "You know the truth has a way of surfacing eventually, no matter the pains you take to suppress it. History can't be cheated forever."

I could feel Carlson's scornful look. "I understand why it suits you to believe that, but I can promise you that what you say is not so. Some secrets do keep, my friend—and they are usually the important secrets. Despite the efforts of people like you to hunt them down."

The limo was cruising westward through the northernmost reaches of the park, near Harlem Meer. It was as dark and heavily wooded here as a forest. There were few lit pathways and they were deserted. No sane individual ventured into this area after nightfall.

The instrument console on the seat beside the director buzzed. Carlson pulled one of the pair of telephone handsets from its cradle and cushioned it carefully against his ear. He talked for some time, mumbling into the handset in a low voice. I caught only an occasional disconnected word or phrase.

Someone was giving him some information and asking him for a decision.

It was an arresting image: this powerful government official, the most powerful in the world, if I was to believe Zimmer, issuing secret directives in the middle of the night from a darkened limousine—orders that might compromise some foreign leader, topple some regime, or even spell capture or death to some agents out there in some precarious Third World posting.

Carlson cradled the phone finally and apologized for the interruption.

"I realize that giving up this book creates some hardship for you," he said. "I've thought about it, and I'm willing to offer you help on an alternative subject, if you're interested."

"You have one in mind?"

"No, I don't."

So much for that, I thought.

"I need your decision," he reminded me. "If you want the charges dropped, it has to be done now."

"You already know my answer," I said. "I don't have any choice.

I can't possibly proceed on this book if I have to face going to trial for treason."

The director tasted his tomato juice. He didn't seem to think my acceptance was wholehearted enough. "Don't think you can back out on this after the charges are dropped," he warned me. "They can always be reinstated."

"That sounds like an admission that you've been calling the shots on my arrest from the start."

The irritation in his voice got stronger. "You journalists think there's a conspiracy under every rock. And if you can't find one, you invent one."

"What guarantee do I have you'll follow through on your promise?"

"None."

"My lawyer will want something—"

"Fuck your lawyer," he cut in. "It will just happen. The government will drop its case on my recommendation."

"On what grounds?"

"A trial would compromise secrets vital to the national security."

"How about something simple like lack of evidence?" I tried. "And how about a public apology from the FBI for screwing up my life?"

Carlson grunted. "The only basis on which the Director of Central Intelligence can recommend dropping a case is national security. Period. Anything else is up to the Justice Department."

"When'll it happen?"

"A few days. A week at the most."

Another silence. I ached to confront him both with Steckler's claim that he had been a collaborator during the war, and with Zimmer's incredible revelations about his private covert-action group, the Night Watch. But that would have been dangerously counterproductive. It might appear to him that I was still pursuing the book—and, worse, actually getting somewhere.

I decided instead to put some of the information in someone's else's mouth—someone I would have loved to get into trouble.

"A Colonel Westerly showed up in my apartment yesterday," I said. "You know who he is?"

"I know him." There was no measurable hint of tension in Carlson's voice. "What did he want?"

"He wanted the documents that Conover gave me. He threatened me with a gun."

"Did he?" the director replied, meaning so what?

"Is he working for you?"

"No. Did he say he was?"

"He said the government. I assumed he must be working for you. Because he said the documents were about a very hush-hush CIA operation called the Night Watch, and that I must give them up to him immediately or I would find myself in the very deepest of shit."

In the dim interior of the limousine, I could only see the director's head in silhouette, but I could feel his eyes on me, intent now beyond mere curiosity.

"What did you tell him?"

I rattled the ice in my scotch and water and took a deep breath. "I told him I lost the documents."

"Did he believe you?"

"Probably not."

So far Carlson had given away absolutely nothing.

"You don't seem very concerned about those documents," I said.

"I'm not."

"How come?"

Carlson laughed. "Because I have them. You dropped them by the escalator and one of my men recovered them."

I sank down in the seat, humiliated. That took care of that little mystery.

"What was in them? No harm in telling me that now, is there?"

"There could be."

Red traffic lights ahead brought the limousine to a stop. I looked out to see that we were back at the West Seventy-second Street exit. We had made a complete circuit of the park.

I shook the ice in my glass. "The irony of this whole business is that I probably would have given up on the damned book eventually anyway, since I was getting so little worthwhile material."

I don't know what effect I expected my statement to have, but what happened next certainly went beyond it.

The traffic light changed to green and the limousine began to pick up speed as it passed the exit. The car behind us turned out into the left lane and accelerated fast, until it was abreast of us.

Our driver slowed, and the car beside us slowed, as if it had changed its mind about passing. It was a nondescript American make—black, with dark tinted-glass side windows that shielded its occupants from view.

Our limousine's sudden deceleration brought another car up, almost touching our rear bumper. It squealed as it braked to avoid a collision. Instead of falling back, it quickly recovered and moved right back onto our tail.

I turned around to see what was happening in front of us. Just ahead to our right was the entrance to the parking lot for Tavern on the Green. Through the windshield I could see the bright floodlights over the parking area, and behind them, the gentle glitter of the hundreds of white Christmas-tree lights the tavern owners had strung in the trees around the restaurant.

A car roared out of the parking lot and onto the park drive, and swerved sharply into the lane ahead of us.

The bodyguard riding shotgun up front grabbed his Uzi from his lap and yelled something to the driver.

With one hand hitting the horn, Tony, the driver, swerved sharply to the right, taking the limousine off the drive and up onto the sidewalk that ran parallel to it. A pair of startled joggers managed to jump clear. Tony hit the brakes, and the vehicle screeched and shuddered to a halt. My face slammed against the glass partition before I could get a hand up to cushion the blow. Blood began to flow from my nose down my upper lip. I squeezed my nose shut between my fingers.

Out on the drive, a cacophony of squealing tires and blasting horns swelled and just as quickly died. Miraculously, there were no collisions.

Our driver jammed the shift wand into reverse, then back into forward, spinning the tires in gravel. He cranked the steering wheel hard to the left, and bounced back out onto the drive. All the lanes here were one-way southbound. He pushed the gas pedal right to the fire wall and headed north.

The limo's big truck engine rose to the challenge with a trembling roar. The rapid acceleration caught me off guard again, and I flew backward off the jump seat and crashed into the communications console that divided the rear seat. I rolled over and landed in a more or less sitting position next to the director.

The driver jockeyed the limo northward, hugging the near lane, horn blaring. Approaching traffic swerved wildly past us on the right.

A fork loomed immediately ahead. The driver cut right, and sped eastward, toward Bethesda Fountain. A few hundred feet along, he cranked the wheel sharply left and bumped the limo up onto one of the park's footpaths, headed north again.

The footpath was paved, but it was barely six feet wide. It was used occasionally by park maintenance vehicles and police patrol cars, but at speeds in the vicinity of five miles an hour. The limo seemed to be hitting a hundred. Tree trunks and park lights whipped past in a kaleidoscopic blur.

We lost two of the cars that had boxed us in by the tavern, but a third vehicle managed to stay with us. His headlights were bouncing on the path behind us, and they seemed to be getting closer.

I glanced over at Carlson. His lap was soaked with tomato juice. He was trying to reposition one of the telephone handsets I had jarred loose back in its cradle in the communications console. He looked remarkably composed.

My scotch and water had hit the glass partition and spilled on the carpet. I released the pressure on my nose. The blood flowed over my fingers. I pinched my nose again between thumb and forefinger and tried to tilt my head back, but it was all I could do to hang on and remain upright as we rocketed through the woods.

Carlson was gripping one of the telephone handsets now, talking to somebody in an angry voice. His words were drowned out by the thunderous racket of the limousine's machinery and the air whistling by outside.

The driver executed a fast, skidding turn, shot up a steep incline and brought the vehicle out onto the big open field called the Great Lawn, just south of the park reservoir.

The Delacorte Theater zoomed by on our right as Tony gunned the vehicle straight out across the immense spread of grass in the general direction of Fifth Avenue and the Metropolitan Museum of Art.

I wondered if he knew the park well enough to know where he

was going, or if he was just improvising. The heavy limo seemed to be losing speed on the soft grass. The small sedan continued to close the gap. It looked to be only about four or five car lengths from our rear bumper.

I heard three or four sharp cracks against the rear trunk and window. It sounded as if someone were pelting us with large rocks. Carlson's hand caught the back of my neck and pushed me onto the floor. The director then dropped down sideways across the rear seat, his stomach draped over the console. He was still talking on the telephone.

The driver began cranking the steering wheel back and forth, hard right, hard left, sending the vehicle into a cumbersome zigzag motion. I grabbed the pedestal leg of the jump seat with both hands and pressed my cheek against the carpeting.

An explosion near the left side of the limousine nearly flipped us over. The flash and blast momentarily numbed my senses. I shut my eyes and tightened my grip on the leg.

I heard a throaty, chattering *brpppp, brrrppp* by the door near my head, as the bodyguard put his Uzi into action.

As quickly as it had begun, it stopped. Everything grew quiet again. The limo was still moving, but under control and on a smooth surface.

I sat up, shook my head, and slowly pulled myself back up onto the jump seat I had been clutching from below. We were back on the park drive, heading through the narrow strip of woods between the reservoir and Fifth Avenue. Carlson was still talking on the phone. He looked over at me. "You all right?"

I felt my nose and nodded.

Carlson replaced the phone and pressed a button that wound down the glass partition between us and the front seat. He complimented Tony and the other man in front with a few gruff words of praise.

From the brief exchanges that followed, I learned that our bodyguard, whose nickname was Squint, had shot out both front tires of the car pursuing us, leaving it stranded somewhere on the Great Lawn.

Tony turned right into the drive exit at Ninetieth and Fifth and stopped to wait for the light.

"Better get out right here," Carlson told me.

That seemed like an excellent idea to me.

"This didn't happen," Carlson said as I opened the door. "You weren't in this car with me and this didn't happen. You understand?"

I nodded, stepped out and closed the door. The bulletproofing made it noticeably heavier than normal. It clicked neatly shut with the precision of a bank vault door. The light turned green and the limousine edged out onto Fifth Avenue and headed south toward midtown.

I stood for a moment, still dazed, gazing stupidly at the long wall of apartment buildings that faced the park from the east side of the avenue. My teeth were chattering as if from the cold and my knees felt rubbery. My shirtfront was streaked with blood from my nose, and my ears were still ringing from the blast that had almost toppled the limousine. What the hell was it? A bazooka? A mortar? A tank missile?

I walked down Fifth for a few blocks to regain some composure.

Half an hour later I was in a bar on Third Avenue—the kind of place where someone with a bloody shirtfront didn't look especially out of place.

I sat at the bar and ordered a corned beef on rye and a beer. The Mets game was on the television. Ojeda was pitching. They were playing the Phillies. The season was already well under way and I realized that I had completely lost track of it. Somebody hit a three-run home run for Philadelphia and everyone at the bar groaned.

I went to a phone booth in the back and called Teddy Kovacs, New York bureau chief for the Jerusalem *Post*.

"I met somebody today who says he's in the Mossad," I told him. "Wolf Zimmer. Ever hear of him?"

"Wolf Zimmer?" Kovacs thought for a moment. "Nah. But that doesn't mean anything. The Mossad doesn't publish any lists of its employees."

"This guy acts like he's high up."

"Describe him," Kovacs said.

I did. I saved the scarred ear and neck until last.

Kovacs made a low whistle. "He's high up, all right. Number-two man. His real name is Isaac something. A Polish name. That's where he's from. Cracow, I believe. Lost all his family in the Holocaust."

"Can he be trusted? What do you think?"

Kovacs laughed. "Trusted? Hey, Johnny, he's a spy."

"That's an answer, I guess. What happened to the side of his face?"

"A mine exploded near him during the Six-Day War. This guy was born a fighter. He was a terrorist when he was only fourteen. He was in the Irgun, or so the legend has it. I've never met the man. Few people have. He's pretty invisible. What the hell were you doing with him?"

"Can't tell you that, Teddy."

"Too bad. I could use a good story tonight."

"Someday . . ."

"I hear you were arrested, by the way. . . ."

"Someday, Teddy. Not now." I hung up quickly.

I returned to the bar and watched the rest of the Mets game. I desperately needed a dose of oblivion. I drank ten bottles of Guinness and ate about four pounds of peanuts. I had an ugly argument with some pinhead about the relative merits of Davey Johnson as a baseball manager. At the point where the pinhead was threatening to kick my ass all the way down Broadway and put it on the Staten Island Ferry, his wife or girlfriend or sister showed up and dragged him off. She actually grabbed him by the ear and pulled him out of the bar twisting on it. I had never seen anyone do that. I don't remember a thing about the game.

Much later I called an old girlfriend named Paula who lived a few blocks away and suggested I might drop by.

"It's midnight, Johnny. Kind of short notice for a date."

"It's not a date, Paula, for God's sake," I argued. "It's just for a . . . you know . . ."

She laughed. "Just for a friendly fuck?"

"That's the word. . . . I'm up for it."

"It sounds as if passing out is all you'll be up for."

She was right about that. I never made it past the sofa in her living room.

17

THE DIRECTOR CONFESSES

I spent the morning hung over, and the afternoon running up Paula's phone bill, calling sources. I didn't know what I was looking for, and that didn't help my quest. Just some little bits and pieces from somebody about something—about René Gervais, about Grayson Steckler, about Conover's death, about the car chase through Central Park. Those few I could get to talk to me at all told me nothing. Never did I feel more incompetent as a journalist. And if I kept drinking like this, I'd need a liver transplant and an emergency membership in AA before the month was out.

By midafternoon I'd decided it was time to chance a return to my apartment.

I was surprised to see Carlson's limousine parked once again on Seventy-sixth Street, near the service entrance to my building.

Tony, his driver, was leaning against the hood, arms crossed, dark glasses glinting in the sunlight. He saw me opening the gate and hurried over.

"If you think you're going to get me in that damned tank of yours again, you're crazy," I said, as he caught up to me. "One brush with death a week is all I can work into my schedule."

Tony pulled off his glasses. His eyes were red and puffy. He hadn't been getting much sleep lately, either.

"The director wants to see you," he said. "Immediately. He sent me to pick you up."

"Where is he?"

Tony wouldn't say. He took my elbow and escorted me toward the car. "We have to hurry," he said.

As Tony opened the back door for me, I balked, suspecting a trap of some kind.

Tony got impatient. "For chrissake, Brady, get in the car."

I climbed in, feeling like a jerk. "My paranoia count is way up these days," I mumbled. Tony slammed the door.

I sat alone in the back, marveling at the unusual number of chauffeured limousines I was riding around in these days. Tony took the Sixty-seventh Street transverse through the park, raced through red lights and midday traffic across the East Side and braked to a tire-squealing stop at the main entrance of New York Hospital, on Sixty-eighth and York.

Tony's voice came at me over the car's intercom. It sounded reedy and small. "I have to stay with the limo," he said. "He's in room 515. He's waiting for you. Go on up. They'll let you right through."

"What happened to him?"

Tony turned off the intercom.

I hurried into the hospital and up to the fifth floor. The door of room 515 was closed and two men in plainclothes were posted outside, looking rather prominently out of place with their dark suits, sunglasses and two-way radios. I wondered who employed them. Were they CIA? Or were they Carlson's own personal bodyguard—part of the Night Watch?

"I'm John Brady," I said. "I'm here to see Director Carlson."

They didn't take my word for it. While one checked my New York State driver's license and a couple of credit cards, the other frisked me. Satisfied at last that I was indeed John Brady and unarmed, he opened the door and gestured for me to go on in.

It was a private room—or had been converted into one. There were four beds, and none of them was occupied. Carlson was slumped in a wheelchair by the window.

I walked over and sat on the edge of the bed nearest him. He brought his head up when he heard the bed squeak.

He stared at me for a moment, blinking slowly. "Sedatives," he mumbled. "Make you sleepy."

I nodded. An IV tube was bandaged to the director's wrist, an oxygen tube protruded from his nostrils, and a heart monitor was taped to his chest. He looked waxen and translucent, like a corpse drained of blood. He fumbled in his lap until he found his eyeglasses. He unfolded them and slowly hooked the wire temples over his ears.

"What happened to you?"

He gritted his teeth. "Poisoned."

"What is it?"

"Doctors don't know."

"I'm sorry. Is the worst over?"

Carlson shook his head feebly. "Don't think so."

"At least you're out of bed. That's progress. . . ."

"Wouldn't let them keep me in bed," he said. "Feels worse."

I nodded. I felt out of place and helpless. "You wanted to see me?"

The director inhaled slowly. It required effort and seemed to cause him pain. "I might not make it," he said, his words tumbling out behind his expelled breath. He touched his forehead with his palm. His entire head was a sheen of perspiration. "Clever bastard, Steckler."

"Steckler did it?"

"Most likely."

"Was he behind the attack on the limo?"

"Oh yes."

"He's trying to kill you?"

Carlson nodded.

"Why?"

The director didn't reply. I waited, giving him a chance to recover his energy. I gazed around the room. It was stark and lonely. No flowers, no cards. His wife was dead. I knew he had a daughter somewhere, but I didn't know anything about her. He motioned for the pitcher of water on the stand by the bed. I filled a plastic cup and gave it to him. He drank it greedily. I took the cup from him and returned it to the stand.

"I'm not here," he said.

"What?"

"Officially. No one knows about this. You understand."

"I understand."

"I may not be able to help you," he said. "With your case. I may not have time."

That hadn't even occurred to me. "Don't concern yourself about it now."

"I got you into this," he said.

True, I thought. He did. I wanted a drink of water myself. The room felt hot and dry and smelled of some unpleasant chemical.

"We made a deal," he continued when he had recovered his breath.

"Then you can't die on me now," I replied.

My remark hardly cheered him up. He looked directly into my eyes. There was sudden intensity in his gaze, but it was hard to characterize it. His expression was neither hostile nor warm. It was questioning. At one moment it seemed to penetrate deeply, to be appraising me, to be struggling to attain some deeper understanding of my character. At another moment I feared that it was no more than the gaze of a man who in his present condition might not even be able to remember who was in the room with him.

"You get picked," he said, finally.

Before I could get him to explain the remark, we were interrupted by a nurse. A big, no-nonsense Jamaican woman, she bustled in, humming to herself, took his temperature and pulse and checked the plastic bag of IV solution and the various tubes attached to him. She was a private nurse, hired by Carlson. He didn't trust anybody, not even the hospital staff.

"You ready fo' bed yet, Mr. Carlson?" she asked, in a booming singsong.

He shook his head, without looking at her. He was simply tolerating her presence, waiting for her to finish and leave.

She fussed around him for a little while longer. She adjusted his pillows, mopped his brow with a cold washcloth and asked him if he wanted anything. She kept throwing evil glances my way, presumably for taxing his strength. "He's a very sick man," she warned me at one point. "Don't you be rilin' him up any, you hear me?"

She left finally, threatening to put him in bed when she came back.

The nurse's interruption seemed to have done Carlson some good. His voice was stronger and he began speaking in longer sentences.

"I'm going to keep my bargain with you," he said. "Even if I don't get through this." He pointed at the water pitcher again and I poured him another cupful.

"There's some documents I've put aside," he said. "You can take them to whoever succeeds me at the agency. The documents will persuade him to do what I was going to do—invoke national security to get your case dropped."

"Where are they?"

Carlson didn't reply. It seemed rude to press him, so I forced myself to be patient.

"I made a mistake," he said, handing me the empty cup. He pressed his lips together in a rueful frown. "You're the last human being on earth I ever thought I'd confess anything to, but . . ." He lost his train of thought for a moment, then picked it up again somewhere further along the track. "I need your help."

He studied me for my reaction. I guess he got one, because he managed a faint grin. "Pretty damned funny, huh?"

I waited for him to elaborate. For a long time he remained silent, his face bent toward his lap. I didn't know if he was in pain, if he was thinking, or if he was dozing off.

He raised his head again, finally. "You know about the Night Watch?"

I hesitated. I had the peculiar notion that Carlson was actually staging this illness just to trick me into confessing the extent of my knowledge about him. "I know a little," I admitted.

"Who told you?"

It seemed pointless to keep it from him. "Colonel Zimmer told me."

Carlson's face tightened. He seemed genuinely startled. "How did you find him?"

"He found me."

Carlson growled. It came out as a feeble, coughlike wheeze. "He's an Israeli son of a bitch," he muttered. "What did he tell you?"

"He said he and the Night Watch used to collaborate on occasion. But now you're helping his enemies. He doesn't know why, and he's worried."

"What did he expect you to do about it?"

"I don't know. He said he was investing in my future. Telling me these things in hopes I might one day repay him with some useful information."

"He's smart, Brady. That's a smart thing for him to do. That's what I'd do in his situation. But he's a son of a bitch. You can't trust him. Take my word for it."

"I guess I don't have to."

Carlson repeated his warning: "Just don't trust him."

"Why *have* you turned against him?"

"I haven't. Steckler has."

"How does that work?"

"Steckler is trying to take over," he said.

"Take over what?"

"Everything. The whole network. He wants it."

"Why?"

"He wants to make money out of it. Wants to sell our services to the highest bidder."

"You don't?"

The question angered Carlson. "Of course not," he rasped. "The Night Watch has always served the higher interests of our country. I wouldn't have it any other way. Steckler wants to prostitute it, turn it into a goddamned rent-a-spy service—an assassination bureau. He knows he can do that only over my dead body. Literally."

Carlson fixed his stare on one of the beds across the room. "I started it eight years ago, when I became DCI," he said. "It wasn't a network then. Just an expedient, a quick solution. I had to find a way around the damned federal bureaucracy, or nothing would ever get accomplished. This was it. I farmed out a job here and there to old friends from the OSS days. People like Conover and Steckler. All under the table. It worked well. We did it the way we did it in the OSS. There was no bureaucracy to account to, no Congress to worry about. All that mattered was results. It was the perfect solution . . . for everything. That's why it grew so fast."

"You controlled it all yourself?"

"At first. It started as just a list of names I had put together over the years . . . dependable people who could be counted on to carry out tough assignments." Carlson folded his hands together and looked down at his lap. "Now it's taken on a life of its own. Too many people. Too many deals. Too many conflicts."

Often the director's voice faded so much that I could barely hear him. I leaned forward from the bed until our heads were no more than a foot apart. "I started hiring people on long-term contracts," he said. "Not just operations people, but management types . . . to run the operations I could no longer devote enough time to. That meant expense accounts, office space, equipment. It all got too big. Became a damned bureaucracy of its own— personnel, planes, property, weapons, warehouses. Some were dishonest, disloyal. Projects dragged on forever. Efficiency dropped. Vested interests developed. And conflicts. I couldn't trust anybody anymore, and I couldn't keep watch on everybody. . . ."

Carlson coughed. He found a towel on the armrest of the wheelchair and wiped the sweat from his head and face with it. I sensed he was overtaxing himself, but I didn't want him to stop. I pressed a hand absently against my ribs, where I used to hide my tape recorder, and wished again that I had it with me.

"I decided I had to kill the whole thing," he continued. "Before it got completely out of my control. . . . That was a year ago. . . . But I waited too long. It was already too big. It didn't want to die. Steckler saw his chance. He rallied support by promising to keep the enterprise going, to expand it. And promising to make everybody rich in the bargain."

We sat in silence. Carlson drank water and mopped his face. His eyes watered and he seemed to be burning up from fever, but there were goose bumps on his arms, and his skin was the color of gray putty. His breathing was labored, and several times he seemed about to black out.

"You want to rest?" I asked. "You want a nurse? A doctor?"

Carlson shook his head. "More important we finish this."

"You look pretty ill. What are the doctors doing?"

"Chemical analysis. They're trying to identify the poison. Find an antidote."

"Are they getting anywhere?"

"Doubt it. Compound's probably East German. Or Czech."

"If it was going to kill you, wouldn't it have done it by now?"

"Dosage may have been off. Dart may not have penetrated enough."

"Dart?"

The director pointed to a tiny red spot on the side of his neck, just under his ear. It looked like nothing—a tick bite.

"When did it happen?"

"This morning. When I was stepping out of the limousine. I knew right away, so I got here quickly."

I thought about Zimmer and his *Alice in Wonderland* analogy. I also thought of his offer of a bodyguard and a pistol. If Conover and Carlson, both veteran spies, couldn't protect themselves, what chance did I have?

"He's a psychopath," Carlson said.

"Who is?"

"Steckler. A brilliant psychopath. I suspected that, years ago, in France. I should never have let him in. My worst mistake."

"Zimmer told me Steckler killed Admiral Conover. Did he?"

"Yes."

"A woman did it?"

"Sure. Helga. Zimmer tell you? Women are ideal."

"Why?"

"No one ever suspects them. There aren't many, but . . . Helga's good."

"What about Colonel Westerly? Is he in the Night Watch?"

Carlson sighed. "Yes."

"Whose side is he on? Yours or Steckler's?"

"The winner's side," Carlson replied. "Whoever wins, that's whose side he's on. He wouldn't matter—if it weren't for Steckler. Steckler likes to use men like him."

"What about Tracy Anderson?"

Carlson didn't answer me. He wiped his nose with the back of his hand, then removed his glasses and pinched the bridge between his thumb and forefinger. He seemed to be weeping.

I felt embarrassed. I stood up from the bed and stepped over to the window. I shoved my hands in my pants pockets and stared out through the half-open slits in the venetian blinds. The room felt airless, claustrophobic. There was no way to open the window. Four stories below was the hospital courtyard, with cars parked bumper to bumper along the driveway that curved under the entrance pavilion. A group of people were leaving, pushing a young woman in a wheelchair. She had a newborn baby in her arms, and everyone was excited and happy.

"I met her when she was only eighteen," I heard Carlson say. "My God, she was beautiful then. It was hard not to be in love with her . . . but it was much harder if you were."

I told him that I understood what he meant.

"She was always a difficult woman. And she wouldn't have me. I was too old for her, I guess. . . . But then, I never did have luck with women. My wife, well . . ." His thoughts trailed off. He looked away, then directly up at me. "But even so, Tracy's given me more than any woman I've ever known."

What Carlson meant by that remark I couldn't fathom. I guessed he was referring to the little spy favors Tracy had done for him.

"Does she know about the Night Watch?"

Carlson just shrugged. "She's an old friend."

"She does know, then. Is that what you're saying?"

Carlson closed his eyes and let his head fall against the pillows propped behind his back. "There's too much to tell you. Not enough time."

"What about me?" I asked him. "Am I in any danger?"

"You don't have anything Steckler wants."

"He thinks I have those documents Conover gave me. He doesn't know you got them back. He wants them."

The director just shook his head. He didn't want to hear about it.

"What the hell's in those documents?" I demanded. "Why does Steckler want them?"

"He wants the map, that's all."

"Map of what?"

"The bunker. He wants the files. . . ."

"What are you talking about?"

When Carlson opened his eyes, they were full of fear. "If I don't make it," he muttered. "My daughter, Mara . . . she'll help you."

"Help me?"

"Destroy Steckler."

The director's mind was drifting. Giving me the material to beat my spy rap was one thing—and he hadn't yet remembered to do that. But enlisting me to destroy his enemies was wishful thinking at its most delirious, even for a man who was critically ill and grasping at straws. I humored him, anyway: "How are we going to do that?"

A flash of anger lit the director's face. "There's a way. My daughter knows where the documents are. Just don't let Steckler . . . There's too much power. . . . Steckler will use it for his own ends. You can stop him. You can expose him."

"Where's your daughter?"

"She's coming . . . later."

"Should I wait here for her?"

The director didn't answer. He leaned back against the pillows and closed his eyes again. "Mara," he murmured. "She's . . . She's the best thing that ever came into my life. The best thing . . . I ever did."

I wondered if he was confusing his daughter with Tracy Anderson. Or if he now imagined he was talking to someone else. A discouraging thought. "Your daughter?"

Carlson nodded. "Take care of her," he said. "She's a beautiful woman. She needs someone to take care of her."

I sat with the director for a few minutes more, but he was finished talking. He drifted off to sleep and the Jamaican nurse returned. I helped her move him onto one of the beds. Then she insisted I leave the room and let him sleep.

I gave him three hours.

I walked over to First Avenue, bought a couple of yellow legal pads and a couple of pens from a stationery store, took them to a nearby coffee shop and spent the time busily scribbling down everything I could remember that Carlson had told me while it was still clear in my mind. I also made a list of the questions that I needed to ask him.

When I returned to the hospital it was just past eight o'clock in the evening and Andrew Carlson was dead.

BREAKING AND ENTERING

I walked the city streets for several hours, guts churning, head pounding.

The enveloping spring evening mocked me. A soft, sweet breeze swept the air. Looking up between the canyon walls of Sixth Avenue, I imagined for a moment I could even see stars in the purple twilight sky.

I felt singled out and isolated. Events of the past few days had now wrenched my life so completely out of its normal context that I had become like an animal out of its cage, furtive and uncertain, confused about what was happening, afraid of what was going to happen.

By the time I had returned to his hospital room, Carlson had already been removed. Gone too were his bodyguards and the private nurse. The staff at the fifth-floor nurse's station was somewhat vague about the details. Presumably his body had gone to a morgue for an autopsy, but there seemed to be some uncertainty about this, and, in any case, everyone was much too busy to sit still for my questions.

But they were all quite sure about one thing—Carlson's daughter had never put in an appearance. Only his bodyguards, his nurse and several members of the hospital staff had been in that room with him after I had left. Had there been any calls from his daughter? The switchboard confirmed that there had not been any. Any messages or flowers from her? Apparently not. I looked in the two wastebaskets in his room, but they were empty. Everything had been cleaned up. I tried to find the individual who had tidied up the room and changed the bed, but the nurses got tired of me and told me to leave—I was interfering with their work. I left a message for Mara Carlson at the nurses' station and with the hospital switchboard, assuming that she would have to show up eventually to claim his remains.

It was maddening—Carlson telling me his daughter would be my salvation and then dying without even letting me know where I might find her. Here I had spent months looking into the man's past, and I didn't even know his daughter's name.

I stopped by the window of the Swissair office on Fifth Avenue and looked at the posters of Alpine villages and ski resorts. Get on a plane, I thought. Just pack a bag, go to JFK, buy a ticket and get on a plane. To somewhere far away. And never come back.

I couldn't even do that. The federal court was holding my passport.

A tall, skinny man in his thirties was looking in a shop window across the avenue. He was wearing chinos, a leather flight jacket and a baseball cap. He had been with me ever since I had left the hospital. Who did he belong to? The FBI? Steckler? Or Zimmer? Twice I had tried to shake him. No luck.

I should go home, I thought.

But I was afraid to go home.

I was caught in a stampede of incomprehensible events, pushing me toward some unforeseen end. I had to turn around and hold my ground, somehow—start defending myself, start fighting back.

But how?

*   *   *

Shelly Wells lived in a loft building on West Fourteenth Street, between Eighth and Ninth avenues, a run-down block of Manhattan real estate between the neighborhoods of the West Village and Chelsea. The building was a decrepit structure six stories high, its front façade disfigured by a rusting fire escape.

It was just dark when I arrived. I stepped into the narrow outer lobby and studied the wall directory. There were about a dozen listings. Most of them, like B & B Sales and Zebra Stripe Importers, were commercial. Shelly's loft—6A, on the top floor front—was listed under the name of Holliman. There was no 6B, so I assumed she—and Holliman—had the entire floor to themselves.

The door buzzer panel was old and did not include an intercom system. I located the button for 6A and leaned on it for about a minute. No response. I had already called Shelly's telephone number. She wasn't home.

The only places I had ever broken into in the past had been people's offices, in search of papers and documents they were hiding. I hadn't done it often—only when I knew the payoff would be worth the risk. It isn't covered in the criminology texts, but breaking the law can give you a wicked thrill, especially if you indulge in it only occasionally. And I had always planned the break-ins so carefully that there had never been much chance of my getting caught.

Tonight, though, I'd have to improvise.

I picked up a torn sheet of newspaper from the sidewalk and folded it into a tight wedge about an inch wide and a quarter of an inch thick. I rang the buzzer for 6A. Nothing. I tried two more, and finally got lucky with 3B. When the buzzer sounded, releasing the lock mechanism, I pushed the door open, quickly set the folded rectangle of newsprint down on the sill in the space between the door and the jamb on the hinged side, then let the door swing shut again. The wedge of paper kept it from closing completely and reengaging the lock.

I hurried across the street and waited in the shadows. In a few moments the man whose buzzer I had pushed came downstairs, looked around the lobby, then opened the door and checked the sidewalk around the building. Seeing no one, he went back upstairs. Pressing door buzzers was a common prank in the city.

I let five minutes go by, then recrossed the street, pushed open the door, removed the wad of newspaper from behind it and walked through the lobby. It was narrow and dimly lit, and sported an incongruous combination of worn linoleum tiles on the floor, shoulder-height gray marble cladding on the walls, and peeling green paint on everything else.

The elevator at the back was an ancient model, requiring an operator. I slid the doors shut, grabbed the worn brass handle of the clutch, and eased it gently to the right, which I hoped was up. The car stuttered and banged, the cables groaned and squeaked, and the whole ramshackle mechanism labored upward with a shuddering, ominous hum. I managed to bring it to a stop about a foot below the level of the sixth floor, and climbed out into a small vestibule.

There were two doors opposite the elevator—one to Shelly's loft and another that led to the roof.

The door to the roof was unlocked, as required by the New York City fire code. I went up the stairs, stepping around some empty beer cans and plastic wrappers, yanked open the door at the top, and walked out onto a large, flat, dirty, tar-coated rooftop, enclosed by a three-foot-high brick parapet.

I walked to the front of the roof and looked down. It was about a ten-foot drop from the edge of the parapet to the top landing of the fire escape. I climbed over the parapet, eased myself down by my hands as far as I could, then let go. The old iron grating sagged and squealed alarmingly under my weight as I landed on it. I crouched in the shadows against the side of the building, expecting windows to be thrown open and faces to be staring up at me any second.

The heavy traffic on the street below must have drowned me out. Nobody investigated.

The last obstacle proved the easiest. The window off the fire escape into 6A was already open. I pushed it up and slipped inside.

Some light from the street illuminated the room. It seemed filled with odd shapes. I raised the window shade as high as it would go and stood there by the outside wall, waiting for my eyes to grow more accustomed to the light.

Gradually a big room, about thirty feet deep and twenty feet wide, materialized in the gloom. I saw a floor lamp near me on my right and switched it on.

A long workbench ran across the wall to my left. It was cluttered with patterns, pincushions, tapes and scissors, lengths of cloth, a sewing machine, and other paraphernalia of the trade. Rolled-up bolts of cloth were stacked in one corner, and more cloth was piled on top of a pair of old filing cabinets. Most of the remaining space was taken up by a couple of dressmaker's dummies and a whole crowd of mannequins—sinuous, boneless, anorexic plaster-of-Paris female shapes with wide eyes, nippleless little breasts, bald heads and bald pudenda—just what the human race might actually look in ten thousand years or so, if it survived that long.

Either Shelly was sharing space with a fashion designer, or I had broken into the wrong loft.

A couple of the mannequins were partially clothed. Someone with a cute sense of humor had created a tableau by taking one dummy apart at the waist and positioning the top half upright on the floor, with its arms embracing its lower half around the buttocks and its face pressed into its own crotch.

A wide corridor ran from the back of the big room past a kitchen and a bath into a spacious living area, divided by several artfully deployed folding screens into a bedroom, a sitting room and a workspace.

The work area was tidy and small. There was a modern teak desk with a speakerphone and a word processor on it, and a comfortable swivel chair. I turned on the lamp over the desk and picked up an opened electric bill from Con Edison on the desk and was relieved to see that it was addressed to Shelly Wells.

Hugging the desk was a tall white three-drawer filing cabinet. I tugged at the top drawer. Unlocked. So were the other two.

I went back out front to the window I had come in through and looked down at the street. A man was loitering in a dark doorway not far from the corner. I closed the window, pulled down the shade and turned off the floor lamp.

Except for the small pool of illumination by Shelly's desk in the back, the loft was now plunged in deep shadow. Anyone looking up from the street would see no light in the front windows.

Shelly was quite organized. The two top drawers contained Pendaflex files arranged alphabetically by subject matter: CAREER EXPERIENCES, CELEBRITY ANECDOTES, CHILDHOOD, DIRECTORS, EARLY ENEMIES, EARLY FRIENDS, FAMOUS ENEMIES, FAMOUS FRIENDS, FEARS, FIRST LOVES, IMPORTANT INFLUENCES, LIKES AND DISLIKES, LOVERS, MARRIAGES, MOVIES, OPINIONS, PARENTS, PEOPLE ANECDOTES, SCHOOL, SEXUAL ANECDOTES, WEAKNESSES, WORK ANECDOTES and so on.

The folders in each file contained a mixed bag of newspaper clippings, magazine articles, and transcripts of recordings of either direct one-on-one interviews with Tracy, or transcripts of Tracy talking alone—sometimes in answer to written suggestions from Shelly about topics that needed to be addressed, sometimes just Tracy in free-form recollection.

In their raw, unedited form, the transcripts read like a Barbara Walters interview that had gotten out of hand. What Tracy lacked in wisdom and insight into the human condition, she more than made up for with breathtaking anecdotes and devastating character portrayals. And she seemed to possess something close to total recall. There were several thousand pages of typescript. I despaired of getting through them all.

I pulled the chair up to the desk and wasted some time perusing the folders marked LOVERS, MARRIAGES and SEXUAL ANECDOTES. I was looking for myself, of course. I clenched my jaw every time I caught sight of my name on a page.

Tracy embarrassed me with her praise:

> *Tracy: Johnny's wonderful. He's been one of the few true friends in my life. . . . He's somebody I could always turn to for help and good advice. . . . He's so patient, so understanding. He's helped me through so many crises. . . .*
>
> *Shelly: What about that article he wrote about you? That was pretty mean, wasn't it? Weren't you hurt by that?*
>
> *Tracy: Oh, I suppose I was at first, but then I realized that what he had done must have been very difficult for him. He had his own reputation as a journalist to worry about, after all. He couldn't just do a puff piece. And he was terribly in love with me. It must have been painful for him to be so truthful. But that's what I loved about him, you see. He didn't lower his standards just to flatter me.*

Strange. I had never thought of it in that light.

Shelly: You don't think he exploited you for his own ends?

Tracy: Well, if he did, he earned it. He made the effort to understand me. So I know that he loved the real Tracy Anderson. That meant a lot to me. . . . Although it was sometimes a burden, too. Sometimes I wished he knew me less well—that I was more of a mystery to him. Oh, I confided everything in Johnny. Well, almost everything. He was my lover-confessor. Other men pleased me, or entertained me, or impressed me, but Johnny . . . he was someone I really needed.

Shelly: But did your relationship with him ever really amount to that much? I mean, it wasn't really a grand passion, was it?

Tracy: Yes, it was too! . . . Well, I don't know, maybe it wasn't. Whatever the hell is a grand passion, anyway? We had our share of violent scenes, that's for sure. Half the time I think I probably just drove him crazy. He always thought I was running away from him, I guess.

Shelly: What do you mean?

Tracy: Oh, Shelly, I'm such a completely superficial human being at heart. So narcissistic. Johnny was always on me about it, making me feel guilty. I didn't want to hear that. All I ever want from a man is praise. I'm embarrassed to admit it, but it's true.

Shelly: Did the fact that you were a famous celebrity and he was a nobody ever cause problems between you?

Tracy: Well, I wouldn't say he was a nobody, Shelly. He's a well-known journalist, after all.

Thanks, Tracy.

Shelly: Relatively speaking, of course. Few people are as famous as you are, after all. And he certainly wasn't very well known when you first met him.

Tracy, sighing loudly: I don't think there's any point in going into this.

I should have quit while I was ahead. Further on, I encountered this:

When it came to sex, Johnny was terribly innocent. His Catholic upbringing, I suppose. I don't know what he did in bed with those two women he was married to, but if he'd told me he was a virgin I'd have believed him. I teased him about it. It made him furious. Missionary Position Johnny, I used to call him. That later got ab-

breviated to MPJ. "Come on, MPJ," I'd say. "Get your tongue down there and do something creative." [Laughter]

I put the pages down. It was an edifying experience, getting a taste of what I had been dishing out to others for years.

Secrets. There were no end to secrets. It was really sad, when you thought about it. What you most needed and wanted to know in life—how your behavior was viewed by others—was the last thing you ever found out.

The truth was always in hiding.

I fared better than many of her other lovers, anyway. Her first husband, Sven, to whom she was married for six months when she was seventeen, seemed to prefer punching her black and blue to having sex with her. Her second husband, Stanley the Hollywood matinee idol, drank to excess and had a penchant for underage girls. Her fourth, the famous British Shakespearean actor Terence, liked to do things like service other men while dressed in a French maid's cap and apron. And then there was the photographer she met on location in Italy who took her home to meet his wife. She had an affair with both of them that went on for some months. She went into such elaborate detail about some of her adventures that I squirmed in discomfort reading them.

Despite the role of lover-confessor she had conferred on me, I was astonished how much there was about Tracy that I still didn't know.

I wondered if she weren't inventing some of the steamier stuff— either to turn herself on, or to turn her collaborator on, or both. Tracy loved to invent stories just to amuse herself. I began to appreciate the cumulative effect all this erotica must be having on poor Shelly. It practically amounted to a new form of sexual abuse.

I tore myself away from the sex-and-games anecdotes and began a methodical search for references to Andrew Carlson.

I plowed through the material in the top filing cabinet without finding a single reference to him. That took a couple of hours. I got up to stretch my legs and use the bathroom. I glanced at my watch. Just past eleven P.M. The building was deathly still. And creepy. I wondered if Shelly was the only tenant who lived here. I went out front and peeked around the drawn shade again. A man was still standing in the shadows of the doorway by the corner.

Most of the storefront display lights across the street had gone out, so all I could see of him were the tops of his shoes and the red arc of light made by his cigarette as he brought it to his mouth.

I walked back through the gloomy reaches of the studio, feeling thoroughly spooked. Several times I thought I saw one of the mannequins move.

I had two more file drawers to go through. The bottom drawer contained mostly just the cassette tapes from which the files had been transcribed, but it was likely that Shelly would return before I finished. I drank a glass of water at the kitchen sink, then returned to attack the second drawer.

The folder marked ENEMIES was the thinnest in the files. Tracy's view of the world and other people was remarkably benign, I thought. She told revealing stories, but she rarely said anything really hostile or mean. She wasn't out to even any scores with anybody. She didn't need to. Tracy had managed to get her way in life. She was never frustrated, jealous or envious. People did what she wanted them to do or she replaced them with people who would. She could afford to look on the world with an indulgent smile. It had always bowed to her demands, acceded to her wishes, danced for her pleasure. Or so it seemed.

Andrew Carlson made an appearance at last, in WORK ANECDOTES:

> *Tracy: I met him at a party in Montparnasse, in some rich artist's atelier. There were a lot of writers, painters and actors there, and patrons—or potential patrons. That was the purpose of the gathering, I guess. To raise money for something or somebody. I was there for decoration. I was only eighteen and desperately looking for work as an actress. I don't even remember who invited me. Anyway, Andrew sort of stuck out, because he was an American, and obviously not an artist. He was a friend of the man who lived there, a French painter who I understood had been something of a hero in the Resistance during the war. . . . Andrew impressed me, I remember, because he seemed to know everybody and everything. We talked. He got me to pour out a lot about myself. He took me out to dinner a few times and we more or less became friends. He loaned me money, and helped me get work as an actress. I was indebted to him.*
>
> *Shelly: Did you sleep with him?*
>
> *Tracy: No. I was willing to, just out of sheer gratitude, but it really*

never came to that. . . . He wanted something else from me, it turned out.

Shelly: Something other than sex?

Tracy: He wanted information. He knew a lot of foreign dignitaries—ambassadors, ministers, heads of state. He asked me if I was willing to "be nice" to certain people that he wanted to influence or impress. In return he paid me money—quite a lot by my standards then. He also introduced me to several directors and producers he knew. Eventually I started getting acting parts. My first one . . .

Shelly: Just clarify for me . . . what did "being nice" to these men entail, usually?

Tracy: Oh, you know—being available. To be seen on their arm. Dinner, theater . . . and so on.

Shelly: You slept with them?

Tracy: Sometimes . . . usually . . . yes. . . . You're shocked, aren't you?

Shelly: Well, maybe a little. Can you remember anyone in particular?

Tracy: Oh, I don't know. It was so long ago.

Shelly: How long did you do this for him?

Tracy: For a year or two. Then my career took off, and that was that. Occasionally I would do him another favor here and there, just out of gratitude more than anything else. But I guess I sort of enjoyed it, too. I know it sounds like I was just a whore, but it took a lot of skill, sometimes. I got a perverse kind of satisfaction out of doing it well—manipulating a man so perfectly that he would never know he had been manipulated. I think I learned more about acting from these little favors I did for Andrew than I did in the theater.

Shelly: When's the last time you did one of these quote unquote favors for him?

Tracy (after a long pause): I think we ought to move on to something else. I have a rehearsal in an hour, and I don't want to include any of this material in the book, anyway.

Shelly: Really? Why not? It's fascinating. I think it's all very exciting.

Tracy: There's enough excitement in my life without going into this. I think we'll just leave it out.

Shelly: Well, think about it. Maybe you'll change your mind.

Tracy: We'll leave it out.

Several times in later sessions Shelly brought Tracy back to this subject of the favors she did for Carlson, but each time Tracy was emphatic that she didn't want anything about it in the book. Once they had a short argument about it, and Tracy put her foot down: "It's my book, Shelly, goddamn it, and it'll say what I want it to say!"

There was nothing more about Carlson in the transcripts. I replaced all the folders in the second drawer of the file cabinet.

Carlson had apparently once used Tracy as a spy. Whether he had used her for his own private purposes—to improve his bargaining position in an arms sale, say—or for the CIA was not clear. What was clear was that Tracy didn't want to talk about it.

Was Carlson still using Tracy in the Night Watch network? Zimmer seemed to think so. But what worthwhile services could she provide these days? And why would she take the risk? What motivation could she still have? Not money, certainly. Thrills? With Tracy that was entirely possible.

I opened the bottom drawer of the file cabinet. It was stacked, front to back, with audiocassettes, many dozens of them. I pulled out a couple and looked at them. Both were neatly labeled: T.A. INTERVIEWS, with the dates of the interviews and dates the tapes were transcribed penciled beneath. The other cassettes were similarly marked, sometimes with brief subject tags included. The latest interviews were about three months old.

The tapes that Tracy had recorded by herself were stacked in their own neat piles on the left side of the drawer. These were marked by Tracy with a date and some notations on the subjects covered.

A back portion of the drawer, separated from the front by a metal file divider, was also piled with cassette tapes. I pulled out a handful. The only notations on them were dates. I assumed at first that they involved other projects, but looking at more of them I noticed that the dates overlapped with the dates of Tracy's tapes in front. They were probably tapes she hadn't yet gotten around to transcribing, but I was curious about them.

A portable cassette recorder was sitting on the top of the file cabinet. I pulled it down and popped one of the tapes into it.

The first few minutes contained silence, punctuated by the sound of a door closing a few times. Suddenly there were voices—too far from the microphone to be intelligible—and music. This went on for some time. Then more closing of doors. The music and voices would swell sometimes for a few seconds, and then a door would click shut, indicating that the sounds were coming from another room.

About five minutes into the tape a woman spoke:

"The bastard. You see how he had his hands all over her."

Another woman's voice: *"It doesn't mean anything. He's crazy about you."*

"He should be. . . ."

"Why?"

"What I do for him, sweetie, would make a porno star blush."

Giggles.

"Really . . . Tell me more."

"I'm not drunk enough yet."

"I am. Drunk and horny."

"Let's do some coke."

"You have some?"

"In my purse."

A long pause.

"God, that's a rush. Where do you get it?"

"Carl gets it."

"I hear Carl's got a big cock."

More giggles. *"Who did you hear that from?"*

"Never mind."

"Your husband's is bigger."

A shriek, followed by laughter.

"I'm just kidding, Laura."

The two women gossiped for another minute or so and then rejoined the party.

The next few minutes of tape were filled with occasional bursts of noise, snippets of unintelligible conversation, and the distant flushing of a toilet.

It was a bedroom somewhere, during a party. The microphone was sound-activated, turning on every time someone entered the room, and turning off when they left.

I fast-forwarded the tape for a minute, then let it play again. Party noises were still audible in the background. Then the door closed and shut them out.

"Lock it, for God's sake," a male voice said.

A very fast and energetic no-frills fuck ensued. The microphone must have been hidden right under the bed, because the sound of the innerspring mattress groaning under the pounding was so loud that it drowned out everything else. It had started almost immediately, so whoever they were, they hadn't taken time to shed any clothes. It ended about four minutes after it had begun, in a decrescendo of mattress-squeaking and an explosion of masculine sighs. The woman remained silent, as if she hadn't enjoyed herself very much.

After a long pause, the man spoke:

"You're the most desirable woman in the world."

The woman laughed.

I had the sudden feeling you get when you start a descent from a high floor in a fast elevator. Weightlessness. I jumped up, stopped the tape, rewound it a bit and listened to the laugh again.

It belonged, unmistakably, to Tracy Anderson.

"What are you laughing at?" the man asked.

"You sound so earnest."

"I mean it."

A big Tracy sigh. *"Of course you do."*

"We'll get married," he said.

"No we won't."

"I'll get a divorce."

Tracy laughed. *"Really? When?"*

"Soon."

"Wouldn't that hurt your political ambitions?"

"It could. I'll take the chance."

"Aren't you brave," she teased.

He laughed. *"Politicians and film stars are the rage now. We'd make a hell of a team."*

"It's much too late for that. We have our own lives."

"At least I want to see you more often."

"That's difficult for me. Rehearsals take up all my time."

"It's not exactly convenient for me, either."

"I know."

"Look, Tracy. You've got to help me with Carlson."

"That's what you really want from me, isn't it?"

"You know that's not true."

"Why should I help you?"

"Why? Look at what he's done to you, for chrissake!"

"That's my problem."

"You're not doing much about it."

"You wouldn't really know what I'm doing about it."

"What's that mean?"

"Nothing. Never mind."

"Think about it."

"All right. I'll think about it."

"I'll call you in a few days."

The door opened and closed and the room became silent. I switched the tape off.

I don't know what shocked me the most—that Shelly had bugged Tracy's bedroom, or that Tracy was having an affair with someone I knew nothing about.

His voice sounded familiar.

I listened to the tape again. I knew Tracy's speech patterns and inflections by heart. She had two distinct tones for sincerity—her real one, which was surprisingly flat and clipped; and the stage one, which sounded slightly little-girlish and demure. She was using both here. I listened to the conversation a third time. It sounded as if Tracy were having an affair with someone she didn't care for at all. That was not like her. She followed her emotions the way a blind man follows his dog—very closely.

The rest of that cassette was blank. I listened to several others. The tapes contained mainly telephone conversations. There were at least six phones in Tracy's apartment, but she used the one by her bed for most of her calls.

I fast-forwarded my way through dozens of conversations—long, often angry ones with her agent on the Coast, who wasn't getting her the parts she wanted; long chatty ones with a variety of friends, especially a well-known novelist who spent hours bending her ear with jet-set gossip. Since the bug was under the bed and not in the phone, the microphone picked up only Tracy's end of the conversations, rendering most of them meaningless.

I counted the cassettes of the bugged conversations. Twenty in all. The dates covered were noted on the labels. They were all quite recent, covering the previous five weeks. The party-and-sex tape was thirty days old.

The latest one was just three days old. One short conversation on it caught my attention:

"He wants control, it's as simple as that. . . . You know I can do it, Andrew, and you know my price. . . . You've made those promises before. . . . I insist you deliver the proof first. . . . I'm sorry, not this time. . . . Find another way, then. . . . No, I'm not afraid of him. . . . You would do well to keep that in mind. . . . No more dangerous a game than you're playing. . . . Yes. Good-bye."

I rummaged quickly through Shelly's desk drawers. The top one contained pens, pencils, erasers and a stack of yellow legal pads; the second one boxes of canary, green and orange copy paper. The third drawer was stuffed with personal bric-a-brac—wadded Kleenex tissues, a small box of greeting cards, a makeup kit, a compact with a broken mirror, a box of fresh mints, two bottles of hand lotion, three unmatched earrings and a bracelet.

The bottom drawer contained correspondence, bills and bank statements. I looked at the bank statements. They were neatly arranged by month. The latest one, for April, showed a balance of almost $50,000.

That was a lot of cash for a youngish working female living in a loft on West Fourteenth Street to keep in a non-interest-bearing checking account.

The statements showed that for the past ten months she had been depositing the sum of $5,000 in her account at the beginning of every month.

It could be an inheritance, of course. A trust fund. Even alimony. But eleven months ago, her balance was $123.56, and the month before that, $657.98. Those were all the statements in the drawer.

Was somebody paying Shelly for information about Tracy? Or was she just rich and kinky?

I tucked everything back and closed the drawer. It was two-thirty in the morning. I was tired and hungry.

I went out to the front room again and checked the street. Still someone there. I wanted to confront Shelly, but it was beginning to look as if she weren't coming home.

I had just about made up my mind to leave when I heard the building's elevator motor kick into gear and start laboring upward.

I went to the door and looked out the peephole. The elevator stopped and Shelly got out. She was alone.

I was glad of that.

SHELLY WELLS CONFESSES

I turned on the overhead light and walked back to the corridor near the kitchen.

Shelly unlocked the door and stepped in, blinking up suspiciously at the light she couldn't remember leaving on.

"Stephanie? Are you here?"

I stepped out into the studio. "No, she's not. I am."

Shelly jumped. Her mouth dropped open.

"Don't scream. I'll explain everything."

Shelly's frightened eyes were riveted on me. She threw her purse into a chair and raised her hands in a karate stance, ready to fend me off if I planned to attack.

"What are you doing here?" she gasped. "What are you *doing*?"

"Research."

She went a little berserk. She ran past me down the corridor into the living area in the back, and saw that I'd been making myself comfortable back there.

"I'm calling 911!" she screamed.

"Take it easy, will you? Look, I feel like a creep, invading your place like this, but I have reasons. . . ."

Shelly circled the back room in a kind of aimless distress, looking for more signs of my depredations, calling me a son of a bitch repeatedly. Suddenly she lunged at me. I expected a hard chop to the neck from the edge of her hand, but instead she began pummeling me with her fists. I tried to dodge out of the way, but she kept rushing at me, swinging wildly and cursing, her karate training now completely out the window.

I grabbed her arms and pinned them behind her.

"Leave me alone, you fucking son of a bitch! I'll kill you!"

I could smell traces of alcohol on her breath.

"If you'll shut up and relax, I'll tell you what I'm doing here, and then I'll leave."

She eventually calmed down. She pulled away from me, and went over and dropped down on her bed. She was still breathing hard. "Well? I'm listening."

"I apologize for this. Honestly. I don't blame you if you're furious. But I had to see Tracy's transcripts. Immediately. I couldn't wait. You weren't here, so I let myself in."

"*Let* yourself in? You *broke* in! I'm calling the police."

"Why are you bugging Tracy's bedroom?"

"You have no right to break in here!"

"I know. Answer my question."

"Don't threaten me, you bastard."

"Somebody's paying you a lot of money to do it. Who?"

"I'm calling the police." She marched over to the telephone and snatched the receiver from the cradle. I waited to see if she'd go through with it. She dialed something.

I pulled a tape cassette out of my pocket and wagged it at her. "Hang up the phone and let's talk about these tapes."

Shelly called me several more unpleasant names, then hung up and retreated to the bed. She pressed the heels of her palms hard against her cheeks, fighting back anger and tears. "Why are you doing this to me? Jesus Christ!"

"Who's paying you?"

"It's for a magazine!"

"How's that?"

"A French magazine offered me a lot of money to do a profile of her. I couldn't refuse."

"Fifty thousand dollars?"

"Yes, damn it. Fifty thousand dollars. Is there anything of mine you haven't looked at?"

"That's a lot of money for a magazine piece. What's the name of the magazine?"

"It's not a magazine. It's a syndicate. They buy stories and syndicate them in European magazines. That's why they pay so much."

"Oh, a syndicate. Does it have a name?"

"None of your business."

"Why did you have to bug her bedroom? You've got reams of good material from your interviews."

Shelly found a box of tissues in her night table, removed a couple and dabbed at her eyes. "I tried to write one from the interviews," she muttered. "The syndicate wanted something spicier."

I felt plenty of sympathy for that problem. "Whose idea was it to plant the bug under her bed?"

Shelly snuffled and wiped her nose with the tissues. "The man from the syndicate. He loaned me the stuff and showed me how to use it."

"Where did you hide the tape recorder?"

"In Tracy's study. On the bottom shelf of one of the cabinets. I'm in there working most days, so it's easy to change the cassettes."

"Did this guy from the syndicate ever ask to hear the tapes themselves?"

Shelly looked up at me, surprised that I had asked. "Yes. A couple of times he did listen to them."

"What did he think?"

Shelly shook her head. She balled the tissues up and threw them at a wastebasket and missed. "He was unhappy about the phone calls."

"What do you mean?"

"That I was only getting Tracy's end. He wanted me to put another bug inside the phone—to pick up the other end of the conversation. I thought that was going too far. I refused."

I sat down in her desk chair. "What was this guy's name?"

"Giacometti. Antonio Giacometti."

"Italian?"

"Obviously."

"What did he look like? Can you describe him?"

"Fuck you. I've told you too much already. Go home." She got up from the bed and went into the kitchen alcove and took out a bottle of Perrier water. She unscrewed the cap and drank from the bottle.

"Was he short and stocky, with curly gray hair? Did he have a lot of gold teeth and smoke a lot?"

Shelly leaned against the refrigerator, eyeing me with contempt.

"Are you sure his accent was Italian?"

"I'm not sure of anything. Now leave me alone."

"Did he also happen to have a badly scarred left ear?"

Shelly plunked the bottle down on the counter. "Yes. Yes. Yes! So what? Is he paying you to write an article, too?"

"He doesn't work for a magazine syndicate, Shelly. He works for Israeli intelligence. He's a colonel in the Mossad. He's conned you into spying for him."

"I don't believe you."

I dug the phone number Zimmer had given me out of my wallet. "Call this number and ask him. He also answers to the name Wolf Zimmer."

Shelly shook her head.

"You want me to call him?"

Shelly walked back over to the bed and dropped onto it. She looked stricken. She banged her fists against the mattress. "Shit, shit, shit! Nothing ever works out for me. Nothing."

I walked over to the bed. "Look. I'm sorry. I can understand. You were deceived by a very clever man."

"Are you going to tell Tracy?"

"No."

"What are you going to do? Turn me in?"

"I'm not going to do anything. Except ask for a favor."

"What kind of favor?"

"I want to hear future tapes myself—before you give them to Zimmer."

"You bastard. Now that you know about it, you think I'm going to continue this?"

"Just for a while longer. It's important."

"Forget it. You're not going to trap me in a situation like that. I'm yanking the mike out from under the bed tomorrow."

I threw up my hands. "Okay, forget it."

Shelly seemed somewhat mollified. "What possible interest could the Mossad have in Tracy Anderson, anyway?"

"It's a long story."

"Tell it to me, anyway."

I told her. I don't know how much she believed—especially about Andrew Carlson's mysterious death—but at least she became a little more sympathetic to my plight. In fact, after a while we got quite cozy and opened a bottle of wine.

We sat on her bed. Shelly kicked off her shoes and tucked her legs under her. "Now tell me something else," she said.

"Sure. What?"

"What motivates you?"

"That's a real long story."

"Just tell me the part about why you're so obsessed with knowing everybody's dirty little secrets."

"It's not an obsession. It's how I make my living."

"It's an obsession. You didn't break into my apartment tonight just to make a living. You did it to satisfy an obsession."

I started to get angry. "I'm a journalist, for chrissakes, Shelly. My business is looking into other people's business."

Shelly got angrier. She picked up one of the shoes she'd kicked off and threw it at me. It missed. "You're so perverse, Brady," she said. "Really, you are. You make me furious. What did Tracy ever see in you, I wonder?"

I picked up the shoe—a small black leather pump with a three-inch heel—and tossed it back at her. It hit her left breast. Some wine spilled from her glass. She sighed sadly and rested the glass on the nightstand.

"All right," I said, feeling contrite. "It's a sensitive subject."

"I'll say."

"People always hide the keys to their character. Find a person's most closely guarded secret, and you'll know who they are."

"So people have weaknesses. So what?"

"People hide the things that best explain who they really are. I don't know why, but they do. That's why they don't communicate.

That's why marriages break up, why people kill other people, why nations go to war. Everybody is afraid to be honest. They want people to think something other than the truth about them. So they hide themselves behind a veneer of hypocrisy and pretense. They poison themselves and the air around them with secrets. That's deadly. Get the secrets out of your system, personal or institutional—it doesn't matter—and you'll be healthy. Keep them inside, and they'll eventually eat your guts out."

Shelly retrieved her wineglass. "You're still avoiding my question. What's your secret? Why are you so keen to know other people's business? It sounds like a way to get even with the world. Learn-your-enemy's-weaknesses kind of thing."

I flopped back onto the bed and shut my eyes. "If you want me to talk about my family past, I'll admit I hate to talk about it."

"Why?"

"It embarrasses me. They embarrass me."

"So embarrass yourself. It'll do you good."

I sighed, sat up and drank some wine. "It seemed that everyone in my family hid the one thing that it was most important to know about them. We were all a sorry bunch of repressed Irish Catholics, afraid of sin and afraid of what the neighbors might think. I grew up surrounded by secrets. I'll admit it must have shaped my view of the world."

"What kind of secrets?"

"The usual kind. Department of Common Human Frailties. When I was ten years old I discovered that my mother was having an affair with the man who owned the grocery store where we shopped. It had been going on for years. And no one knew. My father didn't know. Maybe she told the priest at confession, but I doubt it. The grocer—he had a wife and four children—died of a heart attack while waiting on a customer. My mother was grief-stricken, but couldn't tell anyone about it, couldn't talk about the most important love in her life and what it had meant to her. To this day she won't admit to having that affair. For the sake of the family, for the sake of the church, and so on. Well, that's her privilege, of course. I'm glad she did it, because my old man wasn't worth a damn. But it was too bad that she had to keep it a secret. What little joy she got out of life she had to keep hidden.

"Once I knew about the affair, my mother suddenly made sense to me. I understood her behavior, her moods, her actions, her words, everything. For the first time in my life, she became a sympathetic human being. So many things that had been a mystery to me in the relationship between my mother and father suddenly made sense. To understand my mother, you had to know her secret.

"My father had a secret, too, of sorts. He was a drunk. A good old-fashioned Irish drunk. He spent more time in bars than he did at home, getting bombed and shooting his mouth off until someone shut it for him. My whole memory of him is a kaleidoscope of scenes of him coming into the house late at night in a variety of drunken states—drunk and weeping, drunk and mean, drunk and beaten up, too drunk to stand, drunk and sick, and so on and so forth, ad nauseam.

"In those days alcoholism wasn't considered a disease. It was a social problem. We had to pretend it didn't exist. My mother went to extraordinary lengths to hide his behavior from the neighbors and from his employers. Even so, people knew, of course. He lost jobs, he lost friends. He kept us poor. The tragedy was he spent his life trying to keep up this absurd front that didn't allow him to admit to anyone that he had a serious addiction to alcohol and needed help. So to understand my father, you had to know his secret.

"I could go on, right through the whole damned family. One of my mother's brothers was a priest. He was also a homosexual. This was widely suspected—I mean the guy had a flagrantly limp wrist—but of course it could never be openly discussed or admitted. He spent his career skirting the edges of disgrace and scandal. Twice the church had to move him to a new parish. I always wondered why people whispered about Uncle John. When I finally knew his secret, then I understood Uncle John. He was another victim of society's hypocrisy. He had no choice but to take refuge in secrecy.

"So I guess I grew up with the idea that understanding someone meant uncovering his secrets. It's a primitive notion, I suppose, but if you want a motivation for my choice of careers, I guess it's in there somewhere."

Shelly refilled our glasses. She wore a pleased expression, as if I had just given her a gift that she particularly coveted. "Other families are different," she said, trading confidences. "In ours, you couldn't keep a secret. My mother was such an awful gossip, she'd tell everybody everything. She once caught my father fooling around with a woman from his office. They were necking in a car somewhere, I think. Well, she just about put an ad in the paper. By the end of the day, everybody on our block knew about it. She was incredible. She could embarrass a saint."

"Speaking of necking in a car," I asked, "is Tracy having an affair with some politician?"

Shelly rubbed her chin and thought about it. "I don't know. Despite her flamboyant reputation, she's really quite discreet about her love life these days. I'd even say secretive."

I got up. "Can I play one of the tapes for you?"

Shelly made a cute face. "How sweet of you to ask."

I played the tape with the raunchy females sniffing coke and Tracy's quickie with her mysterious lover.

"You have any idea who that guy is?" I asked her.

"None. But it's certainly a turn-on listening to it."

I laughed. "You want to hear it again?"

Around five in the morning Shelly suddenly got up, removed her collection of bracelets, her jumpsuit, and the expensive set of silk bra and panties she was wearing and crawled under the covers of the bed while I was still sitting on it. I got up to leave.

"Where are you going?"

"Home."

"I thought you said it wasn't safe there?"

"I'll take my chances."

"It's too late." She patted the comforter. "Sleep here."

"With you?"

"Who do you think with?"

"What about your roommate?"

"You want to sleep with her, too?"

I smiled. "Touché."

"Stephanie just works here. She won't be in until ten."

"I don't think I should."

Shelly reached out from under the covers, grabbed my belt and yanked me back toward the bed. "Why not, you bastard? You've screwed me every other way."

I undressed and slipped in beside her. She cuddled up against me and fell asleep almost instantly. I stroked her and nudged her

a little, but she didn't respond. I tried tickling her. Still nothing.
This time she wasn't pretending.

Touché again.

I lay awake beside her, staring at the ceiling of her loft. I was
exhausted, but too wired to sleep.

The ghosts of Admiral Conover and Andrew Carlson floated in
the dark over my head. I pictured the legendary assassin, Helga—
white-kerchiefed and deadly—waiting for me somewhere out there
in the night with her suitcase.

I kept hearing the voice of the man on the tape. *You've got to
help me with Carlson,* he had said.

Around six o'clock in the morning, it finally came to me whose
voice it was.

I slipped quietly out of Shelly's small bed, got dressed and left.
Shelly barely stirred.

I walked east along Fourteenth Street, looking behind me to see
if someone was still tailing me. I didn't see anyone. The street at
this hour was deserted, save for the derelicts, who seemed to
occupy every dark doorway recess, dug in against the world behind
their rag-and-cardboard fortresses. Ahead of me, at the far eastern
end of Fourteenth Street, where it met the East River, the sky was
getting light.

At Eighth Avenue I turned north and walked all the way to
Central Park West and Seventy-second Street, a distance of three
miles.

It took me an hour, but I had a lot to think about.

20

TRACY CONFESSES

I sneaked quickly past the doorman's little office in the wall of the courtyard entrance. It was just past seven A.M. Whoever was on duty must have been asleep, because no one came out to challenge me.

At Tracy's apartment I rang the bell and waited. Eventually the tiny Guatemalan cook opened the door, smiled up at my familiar gringo face and greeted me in English with a carefully pronounced "Good night."

"It was a great one, thanks. Is Señora Anderson in?"

Juanita nodded and opened the door. She whispered something to me in Spanish that probably meant Tracy was still in bed and shouldn't be disturbed. Her standing instructions. I nodded and smiled knowingly and started for Tracy's bedroom. Juanita clapped a hand to her mouth and scooted off in the direction of the kitchen.

I knocked on Tracy's door. In my long dawn march uptown, I had persuaded myself that if I accosted Tracy while she was still half asleep, I might get something useful out of her before she had time to get her defenses up. In any case, I couldn't afford to wait.

She didn't answer.

I knocked louder.

Tracy's muffled voice came back through the door. "What *is* it, for God's sake?"

"It's me, John Brady."

A long pause while this sank in. "What do you want?"

"We have to talk, Tracy."

"I'm sleeping."

"Get up."

No reply.

"We have to talk right now."

"I can't, Johnny. . . . I'll call you later."

I rattled the doorknob. "Get up or I'll come and get you up."

"Don't come in!" she commanded.

"Get up, then."

"Just wait a minute, goddammit!"

I heard her stumbling around, cursing under her breath. Eventually she opened the door. She stepped through quickly and shut it behind her with a firm defiance, daring me to ask if there was anyone else in the bedroom with her.

There was a time, not so long ago, when such a situation would have made me break out all over in a rash. The hardest lesson for me to learn in all the years I had known her was that I could never expect to have Tracy to myself, not even for brief periods. It didn't matter what she said or promised; being with Tracy Anderson meant sharing her, competing with others for her attention. Whoever was in her bed was now going to learn the same lesson, if he didn't already know it.

Tracy had thrown on a peach-colored silk dressing gown. Her platinum hair was disheveled and her skin pallid. Her eyes were puffy with sleep and seemed not to be focusing well. The lines at the corners and across her forehead were as sharp as if someone had etched them. It was the first time I had ever seen her look her age.

She pushed past me as if I weren't there. I followed her into the library. She paused in the middle of the room and spun around to confront me, her hands on her hips, her head tilted slightly to the side, her chin out. It was a little piece of stage business from one of her movies that she had made into a permanent part of her gestural repertoire, like an old keyboard exercise. I had seen her use it often.

"What the hell do you *want,* Johnny?"

"Andrew Carlson is dead. I thought you should know."

The statement didn't register completely. Tracy stared at me blankly. "Andrew? What's the matter with him?"

"Aside from being dead, nothing."

She rubbed her arm and looked down at the floor with a perplexed scowl, as if she were suddenly lost.

"He told me he was poisoned," I said.

Tracy managed to focus on my face. Her disbelief dissolved into fright. "How could he tell you if he was dead?"

"I was with him while he was dying. In New York Hospital."

She shifted her gaze away, and glanced anxiously around the library, as if there might be something quick and deadly lurking in one of the bookshelves. She collapsed onto one of the sofas, covered her face with her hands, and bent forward and pressed them against her knees, as if she were in pain.

"He told me that Grayson Steckler was responsible. You know who Grayson Steckler is, don't you?"

Tracy remained rigid and silent, her face hidden in her hands. I couldn't tell whether she was paralyzed with shock or merely trying to collect her thoughts. I sat on the sofa across from her and waited.

She looked up at me, wiping her eyes with the corner of her gown's sleeve and sniffling. "He deserved it," she muttered, her voice nasal.

"Deserved it? Why?"

"Don't you have any idea? Look what he did to you."

"Do you know where his daughter lives?"

"No."

"Don't you know her?"

"No. I never met her. Andrew never talked about her."

"She's supposed to help me."

"How?"

"Carlson promised me some documents. She knows where they are."

"Which documents?"

"Ones I'll need to get the spy charges dropped."

"Don't count on it."

"No?"

"No. Andrew Carlson doesn't keep promises. Don't go looking for anything."

"Why not?"

Tracy didn't reply.

"What did you do for Carlson all these years? Why did you ever get involved with him?"

She hugged herself. "Get me a glass of wine, will you, darling?"

"I have to know, Tracy."

"I just can't tell you, Johnny."

"I may be able to help you."

"I doubt it."

"Give me the chance."

"Please leave me alone, Johnny."

She folded her arms across her chest and began rocking back and forth, a picture of acute misery and defeat. I asked her if she was ill. She refused to talk to me. She curled up on the sofa and closed her eyes.

I went out into the kitchen and asked Juanita to make us some breakfast.

I paced nervously around the apartment, wondering how I was going to get Tracy to talk. Juanita brought croissants, orange juice and coffee into the library on trays.

I ate hungrily. On Tracy's tray Juanita had placed a plastic cup with half a dozen pills in it. Tracy roused herself from the sofa and swallowed the pills with her orange juice.

"What are those?"

"Vitamin C," she muttered.

"What were you taking last night?"

"None of your business."

"Whatever you say." I wasn't her keeper anymore.

"I'm tired and hung over, Johnny. I'm going back to bed." She made no move to get up from the sofa.

"Carlson told me that you've been working for him for years. Since you were eighteen."

Tracy tasted her coffee and made a face. "That's ridiculous. Andrew would never tell you that."

"He did, though. And why not? He knew he was dying."

"He still wouldn't tell you. It was probably Shelly. I can tell from your face. You seduced it out of her. You really are a rat, Johnny."

"Tell me what's going on."

Tracy drank the rest of her orange juice. "I was never part of it. Not really."

"You worked for him. What's the difference?"

"I'm very tired."

"What's Steckler up to? And Colonel Westerly. Tell me about them."

"How do you know them?"

"They both think I have some documents from Admiral Conover that contain important information about the Night Watch."

"You don't?"

"No. I lost them."

Tracy smiled sarcastically. "How careless of you, darling."

"It's the truth. I lost them before I even read them."

"And now you want to go looking for more?" She got up from the sofa. "I'm going to get dressed," she announced.

She disappeared into her bedroom. I heard the front door close. Her overnight guest was sneaking out. I paced around, and then sat in the library, fighting off sleep. I watched one of the row of buttons on the phone on the table beside me blink on and off. Tracy had three lines, and she was busy using one of them. Was she trying to verify Carlson's death, I wondered? I resisted the impulse to eavesdrop. I could hear her side of the conversations later, from Shelly's bug under the bed.

I turned on a radio and listened to the news. Nothing about the demise of the director of the CIA.

Tracy emerged from the bedroom an hour later looking substantially improved, but still tense and guarded. She opened a bottle of white wine and brought it into the library. She filled two glasses, but I left mine on the serving cart.

Tracy carried hers across to the other sofa and drank it down as if it were water. "Andrew is missing," she admitted. "But no one has told me he's dead."

"Goddammit, Tracy, *I* told you he's dead," I replied, tapping my chest. "And I'm an eyewitness."

She nodded thoughtfully. She refilled her glass and deposited it carefully on the table in front of her. She seemed composed, but her hands were shaking.

"I made a terrible mistake, Johnny. A long time ago. It didn't seem terrible then. But how was I to know where my life was going to take me?"

"What was the mistake?"

She reached for her glass, then changed her mind and leaned back against the sofa cushions. She didn't seem ready to answer that question yet. She stared into the middle distance, her face a bleak mask of defeat.

"I've done very few favors for Andrew," she said, answering an earlier question. "Very few. Most of them were many years ago, when no one knew who I was. Recently I've done hardly any."

"Favors? Is that what he called them?"

"That's what I call them."

"Tell me about them."

Tracy focused on the mound of ashes in the library fireplace. "Very well," she said. "I once killed someone."

"Are you trying to shock me? I don't believe it."

"It's true, Johnny. He was an Arab arms merchant. He was also a spy. He had done something terrible, I forget what. Maybe I never knew. Andrew said he had to be killed. This was in London. Fifteen years ago. He was staying at the Connaught. All I had to do was prick his skin with this tiny needle after he had fallen asleep. It was hidden inside the setting of an antique gold ring Andrew had given me. The stone flipped back on a little hinge, and there was the needle, tipped with some exotic poison. Shades of the Borgias. I got myself through the dreadful business by pretending that it was all just a stage drama, not real life. And it was so devastatingly simple. He just never woke up. The papers the next day said he had died of a stroke. He had a wife and five children. I was sick about it for months. Sick and terrified both. I was sure I would be found out and arrested and sent to prison. But there wasn't even an investigation. No one ever knew how he really died. Except Andrew, of course. And me."

"Who was he?"

She mentioned a name I had never heard. "I've never gone back inside that hotel since. I couldn't."

"Is that the worst thing you ever did for him?"

Tracy glared at me.

I shrugged. "Are you sure only Carlson knew?"

"He always kept his little missions very compartmentalized. No one knew what anyone else was doing. Or even who else was under contract. Only Andrew, and a very few others at the top who helped him manage things. Like Admiral Conover."

"And Steckler and Westerly?"

"I don't know. I suppose they know a great deal."

"You know damned well they do."

Tracy didn't reply.

"Why did you do this?"

"Because once you start, they won't let you stop."

"Why did you start, then?"

"Because I was young and silly and ambitious. I let myself get into Andrew's debt. Andrew rescued me from the streets. He knew people. He helped me launch my acting career. I was pathetically grateful and eager to return the favors. At least at first I was. And the truth is I also found it exciting. You know me, darling. I never could resist a thrill."

"Did he pay you?"

"Yes. But once my acting career was going, I didn't need the money. And I didn't need the risk, either. But when I told Andrew I wanted to stop, he just patted my shoulder and smiled. A few months later, he asked me for 'just one more favor.' It went on like that for years. 'Just one more favor.' He used me less—sometimes a whole year or two might go by—but he wouldn't let me go completely."

"Why? Did he threaten you?"

"Nothing so crude as that. That wasn't his style. He would merely mention what might happen to me if some of our enemies ever found out what I was doing. That man I killed, for example. Andrew would say that he was worried that the man's government—or his family—might be on the verge of finding out. That he needed to take some particular action to prevent it. And if I did him this one last favor, he would certainly see to it that they didn't find out. He never had to say he might tip them off himself.

I knew he could, and that was enough. Instead he flattered me, offered me large sums of money, insisted that this would be the last time, and so on."

I sat down heavily in a chair across the room. I felt miserably humbled. Did I know Tracy Anderson at all? I eyed the full glass of wine still sitting on the tray, but resisted the impulse to drink it.

"About two years ago, he asked me to do something very risky for him," she continued. "I told him I'd do it on only one condition. I didn't want money. I wanted an important favor from him in return. A personal favor. One I was sure he could do. He promised me he would. He's promised me many times since. But he's never done it."

"What was the favor?"

"I wanted him to find someone for me."

"Who?"

Tracy shifted her position uncomfortably. "It's a long story, darling. . . . And I don't tell it well."

I waited.

Tracy picked up her glass delicately by the stem and began slowly swirling the wine around inside. She watched the liquid catch shimmering flecks of light from the window as it rotated. When it stopped moving, she swirled the glass again. Such a thoughtful mood was so out of character for her that I held my breath, waiting for her to speak.

"I was only eighteen when I met Andrew," she said. "And I was such a naive child. Really hopeless. I had run away from home the year before, married that unspeakable creature whose name to this day I can't say aloud, and then had to run away from him. You know all that, darling. I told you all that years ago. And I probably told you how I stole the money to fly to Paris. I didn't have any idea what I was going to do when I got there. I had never been anywhere. Once an aunt took me to Mallorca for a week in the winter when I was eleven. That was it. Growing up in rural Sweden is like growing up in the Midwest here. Worse, really, because Swedes are so fearful, so turned inward. Their idea of the perfect life is one in which nothing ever happens. Peaceful, they call it. To me it was premature burial. . . . Paris was a dreamscape, someplace impossibly glamorous. I thought that all I had to do was get there and then I, too, would start leading an exciting, glamorous life."

Tracy drank some wine. "God, it's banal, isn't it, Johnny? My rags-to-riches saga. But the truth usually is banal. Anyway, in Paris I left my past behind forever. I was determined to become an actress. I turned up a few bit parts, playing strange unintelligible roles in Beckett-like little dramas that no one came to see. Eventually I ran out of money and attached myself to this middle-aged Czech expatriate painter I had met in a café. His name was Jan Vaček. I was so innocent and impressionable in those days that even the name made me weak in the knees. Anything exotic was a thrill! And Jan was certainly exotic. I posed for him. Then I moved in with him. After a few weeks I couldn't stand him. He had an ugly temper and the manners of a peasant—but he was food and shelter until I could find something better. . . . Am I boring you, darling?"

"One thing you've never done is bore me. But you told me about Vaček. He did the painting in the hallway. He went mad, ate paint and killed himself."

Tracy twisted her mouth in a frown of distress. "No. That's not what happened."

"That's what you told me."

"There's more I didn't tell you." Tracy produced a tissue from a pocket somewhere and blew her nose. "One day Andrew Carlson appeared at Jan's loft. He was an old friend, a patron of the arts, Jan told me. He occasionally bought some of Jan's work. I saw Andrew there frequently after that. He was always very kind to me, and when my relationship with Jan began to unravel, I confided to Andrew that I was unhappy. I wanted to leave but I didn't know how I could manage it. I had no job, no money and no place to live.

"Andrew solved those little problems for me. He took me out to dinner, then brought me to his townhouse on the Ile St. Louis. There was a view of the Seine from every window. It was the most beautiful place I had ever seen. I was awestruck. He invited me to stay there until I got myself settled. I expected him to make a pass at me, but he never did. I would no doubt have slept with him. Not that the idea appealed to me—he was so much older.

That seems pretty amusing now, doesn't it? Me with qualms about sleeping with a man in his forties."

Tracy put the wineglass down and stretched out on the sofa. She began massaging her brow with her fingers. "I stayed at his house for months. Andrew was away on business trips most of the time, so I had the whole place to myself. God, did I throw some parties there. I didn't even realize until years later that Andrew actually lived out in the suburbs—with a wife and family! Or that his various foreign real estate deals then were really just a cover for his espionage activities.

"I didn't even know until much later that Jan was working for him. He had been running very dangerous missions in and out of Czechoslovakia for years. It involved his artwork in some way—documents or information were concealed in drawings he did—something like that, I never knew the details. But no wonder the man was such a wreck emotionally. The stress must have been terrible."

"Why did he do it?"

"Jan was a patriot. And he was indebted to Andrew for rescuing him years earlier. Andrew collected the debt by turning Jan into a spy."

"Is that why Vaček killed himself? The stress?"

"No. He was murdered. By Czech intelligence. They got on to him somehow. Caught him in his loft in Paris. They tortured him—forced oil paint down his throat. Either the paint poisoned him or he suffocated."

"You knew this and you still did work for Carlson?"

"I *didn't* know. The truth was hushed up—by Andrew himself, with the collaboration of some very high French officials. If I had known what had happened, I would never have worked for Andrew. I would never have dared. Andrew lied to me. He told me Jan had killed himself. I believed him. He made up the story about the cyanide in the Prussian blue paint. He even gave me that painting in the hallway. He told me Jan wanted me to have it. That wasn't true, either, but I believed it, and I suppose that's why I kept the painting. When I found out the truth, years later, I kept the painting for other reasons—to remind me of Jan's anonymous martyrdom. And the whole cruel, immoral futility of Andrew's profession."

"How did Carlson approach you about working for him?"

"He never did—directly. After I had been living there for a while, he asked me if I'd do a favor for him. A senator from Washington was coming to Paris for a couple of weeks on some fact-finding mission. Andrew wanted to have a little reception for him and some other people, and asked me if I would be willing to be the senator's 'date' when he was in town. He loved beautiful women, Andrew said, and he was sure he'd be mad about me. He showed me a picture of him from a news magazine. He was about thirty-five, and quite handsome. And quite married, too, although I didn't even know that then."

"What was his name?"

"I don't want to tell you that, Johnny."

"Does it matter?"

"Yes. It matters."

"What happened?"

"Darling, I was so naive in those days I didn't even realize that what Andrew was really doing was arranging to get this man laid. Well, it couldn't have been much easier. I was absolutely crazy about him from the moment I saw him. We screwed our brains out the whole two weeks. I had never even had an orgasm before that. Now I was having ten a day. I was wildly in love with him. . . . Then he just disappeared—went back home to his wife."

Tracy lowered her hands from her face and let them fall to her sides. "Andrew was extremely pleased with my performance. It seemed I had won the senator over to whatever it was that Andrew wanted from him. But I was absolutely traumatized. I thought he was in love with me. I wanted to marry him. His leaving me like that just about killed me."

Tracy drained her wineglass and refilled it. "I know it's only nine in the morning, darling, but I don't think I can tell you all this sober. Please have a drink. I hate having someone sober around when I'm drunk. Especially you."

I went out into the kitchen and retrieved a cold beer from the refrigerator. When I came back Tracy was lying exactly as I had left her, staring up at the ceiling, waiting to continue her tale. All her style and artifice as an actress seemed to have deserted her. Or she had purposely shed it. Gone were the extravagant hand gestures, the wide-ranging voice inflections, the perfectly studied facial expressions. She seemed contrite, remorseful—as if she were a criminal and I was taking her confession.

"A few weeks after he left, I discovered I was pregnant." Tracy paused, biting her lip to keep back tears. "This made me . . . quite hysterical. I couldn't think of anything or anybody except this damned senator. I wrote him letters he never replied to. I called his office and left messages that he never returned. I got his phone number and called his home. That's how I discovered he had a wife. . . . I wanted to die."

Tracy lay very still, her gaze concentrated inward, on the distant past.

"I told Andrew," she continued. "He seemed sympathetic. He said he was sorry he had gotten me into this and would do whatever he could to help me get over it. I had to forget the senator, he said. He was a notorious womanizer—not the kind of man a young woman like myself should fall in love with. Andrew offered to pay for an abortion, if that was what I wanted. Well, it wasn't what I wanted. I wanted to have the child."

Tracy took a deep breath and stared down at her lap. "She was a girl," she whispered, fighting to keep her voice steady. "She was born on April fourth. A beautiful, perfect little girl. I named her Juliette. . . . Andrew persuaded me that I shouldn't keep her. He arranged an adoption. They came to the hospital when she was a week old and took her away. I had already started nursing her. I remember how sore my breasts were that night and the next day. The milk drying up. God, how empty the world seemed. . . . I never saw my beautiful little girl again."

Tracy swung her hand out and hit her wineglass. It rolled onto the floor and spilled onto the carpet. She dissolved into tears. She sprang up from the sofa and ran from the room. I heard the bedroom door slam. A gloomy stillness descended over the apartment.

I picked the glass up from the floor and mopped up the spilled liquid with a towel from the guest bathroom.

I pulled open one of the library windows, leaned against the sill and watched the activity in Central Park for a while. It was a warm, breezy, sunny spring day, the kind that stirred the heart with deep yearnings. I felt a sudden attack of maudlin sentimentality coming on. I closed the window and paced aimlessly through the apartment's big rooms.

Around noon Tracy emerged from the bedroom. She had changed back into a dressing gown, and she looked drowsy. I suspected she had taken a large dose of tranquilizers.

She read my thoughts. "I'm sorry, Johnny, I need something to get through this. Otherwise I just don't even want to get through it."

She retreated toward the bedroom. This time I followed her. She sat on the bed and I sat beside her. She leaned against me and I put an arm around her. Now that her secret was out, she wanted to talk about it.

"There was no doubt whose baby it was," she said. "I hadn't slept with anyone else during those weeks I was with him. And for a long time after. I wanted to tell the senator about the baby, but Andrew absolutely forbade it.

"I got my revenge, eventually. We met again, years later, at a big party. There was talk about him running for president. The party was a fund-raiser for him, in fact.

"I was a celebrity by then myself. My looks had changed. He didn't even remember that I was the girl he had screwed and abandoned in Paris. Well, darling, I made good and sure that this time things went differently. He was no longer the notorious skirt-chaser of old, but I got him in bed without a great deal of trouble. I had him dancing through hoops in short order. I strung him along, broke dates with him, treated him like dirt. And he loved it, how he loved it. He wanted to marry me. He said he'd leave his wife, do anything. I told him to leave his wife first, then I'd think about it. Of course he wouldn't have dreamed of it. It would have ruined his political career—the only thing that mattered to him then. I made sure that his wife found out about us, though, and that almost did ruin him. But he persuaded her not to make a fuss, not to divorce him. They're married still. And he's still in love with me. He calls me frequently. I even let him see me and make love to me sometimes—just often enough so that he remembers what he's missing. The bastard."

"Did you ever tell him about the baby?"

"Yes. Eventually I did. I wanted him to help me find her."

"Would he?"

"No. He was horrified. All he saw was another potential political scandal. He said Andrew was the only one who could help me. But I had already tried to get Andrew's help, and he was stalling me. He claimed he didn't know who had her. He said he did the adoption through a lawyer in Marseilles. He wouldn't give me the lawyer's name. He claimed he had died years ago. In any case, Andrew always fell back on the argument that when I signed the papers I gave up all my legal rights to the child."

"Including the right to know the identity of her adoptive parents."

"Yes."

"A pretty good argument."

Tracy didn't reply. She stood up and pulled off her dressing gown. Underneath she was wearing the top of a pair of men's silk pajamas. She usually wore men's pajamas when she was depressed. God knows why. She had worn them in one of her more successful movies, a sex comedy called *Tops and Bottoms*, so maybe they made her feel happier and more secure.

"I'm very tired, darling. I want to get into bed."

I stood up. She got into the bed, propped her head on a couple of big pillows, and pulled the covers up. I sat back down on the edge of the bed.

"Maybe I'd have made a terrible mother," Tracy said. "I was awfully young and selfish. And I wanted my career. . . ."

I knew the rest. Three abortions. The doctor telling her that her uterus was so badly scarred she'd never bear children. She tried, anyway. Sometime in her mid-thirties she stopped using birth control completely—with anyone she slept with, including me. Few of us knew it, I guess. I didn't. But the doctor was right. She never became pregnant again. In recent years she had started talking about adopting some children, but she never seemed to get past the talking stage. Now I knew why. But her confession infuriated me. Because she had never told me before. And because it so perfectly exposed those flaws in her character that I had always found so tough to accept.

"You're still selfish, Tracy," I said. "You gave away your child for someone else to bring up. Now that they've done all the work, you'd like her back, to see how she's turned out. To see if she's as attractive, intelligent and successful as you are. Your daughter is probably better off never knowing. What good could it do her? You're her mother only biologically. You gave birth to her, but that's all. And even that was unintentional and unwanted. You gave her nothing. Yet now you expect something from her—instant motherhood in your declining years. It's not attractive, Tracy."

My harsh words seemed to shrivel her. "You're wrong," she replied in her little-girl voice of hurt innocence. "I have a great deal to give her. Love and security, to begin with."

I had no patience for this. "Just tell me why through all of this you continued to work for Carlson? His threats must have finally worn thin over the years. Especially after you became so well known."

"Yes, of course they did. But becoming a public figure made it even easier for him to keep me in line. All he had to do was threaten to expose my past." Tracy closed her eyes. "Anyway, it was the way Andrew operated. Threats and promises. Threats to expose me, promises to find Juliette. He had to control everyone around him, control them absolutely. He didn't believe in anything else. Just control. That was always his key. It's why he was so powerful. He could bring down just about anybody. If not with a gun, then with public exposure. . . . It took me a long time before I understood how power-crazy Andrew was."

"Tell me about Grayson Steckler."

Tracy shook her head.

"Whose side are you on? Carlson's or Steckler's?"

"Neither."

"You've been plotting with both of them, playing one off against the other. Why?"

Tracy wouldn't answer.

"Did Steckler kill Carlson?"

"No. I don't think so. No, I'm sure he didn't."

"Was Steckler just here?"

"Yes."

"What's your relationship with him?"

Tracy opened her eyes and sat up. "I don't care for him."

"Really? Why are you sleeping with the man, then?"

Tracy shook her head. "No more questions." Her voice was fading.

"You're still leaving a lot unanswered."

"You can't have all my secrets, darling."

I got up from the bed. Tracy reached out for my arm. "Do you still love me, Johnny?"

She had probably asked me that thousands of times over the years. I had always said yes, whether I felt it or not. "Of course I love you."

She squeezed my arm hard. "Do you forgive me . . . for all the dumb, selfish things I've done?"

"I don't need to forgive you. But, yes, I do."

"Do you regret all the time you've spent with me?"

"No. Of course I don't."

Tracy settled back against the pillow and closed her eyes again. "I wish we could start all over again," she said. "You and me. I really wish we could do that."

I didn't say anything. I had a perfunctory "Me, too" resting on the tip of my tongue, but I swallowed it.

"Find her for me, Johnny."

"Find her?"

"My daughter. My Juliette. I know you can find her. You're good at that." Her voice drifted. "People tell you things. You could find her if you tried. I really want to see her. I have so much to give her."

I kissed Tracy's hand, then disentangled my own from her grasp. I left the bedroom quietly and let myself out.

21

INTRUDER

By the time I reached the door to my apartment I was so starved for sleep my knees wobbled and my eyes blurred. I fumbled like a drunk with my keys, trying to match them to the right locks. The door yielded eventually, and I was relieved to find that for a change no one had pillaged the premises.

My answering-machine tape was full to overloaded with messages again—from agent, publisher, lawyer and the press. Especially the press.

I turned down the volume of the study phone, then went to the bedroom and turned that one down as well. I realized that I had still neglected to buy new amplifier diaphragms so I could replace the bugged ones in my phones.

I stretched out on the bed, fully clothed, and fell instantly asleep.

I dreamed of prison. It was a place like Devil's Island—remote, windswept, surrounded by ocean. I was sitting on a high bluff, gazing down at the waves smashing against the rocks, wishing for a way to escape. People were hiding in the dense bushes just behind me. I could hear their feet snapping twigs as they tried to sneak closer. I knew what they were up to. They planned to jump out at me and push me off the cliff.

I woke up sweating, my shirt and pants twisted around me. The bedroom was dark. I rolled over to look at the bedside clock: eight-thirty. The dream had felt so real I could still hear the snapping of twigs.

I groaned and rubbed my face. I felt more exhausted than ever. The snapping noise continued. I listened. It was more like a scratching of metal. I sat up and tried to fix the location of the sound. It was coming from the general direction of the entrance foyer.

Someone was working on the door's locks.

I jumped up and headed down the corridor toward the front. My brain felt scrambled. I couldn't think what to do. I cursed myself for not dropping the chain across the door, but I never used it. Too late now. I blinked my eyes and bit my tongue, trying to force myself fully awake in a hurry.

Whoever was out there was making quick progress. I heard the Fox lock squeak as the cylinder rotated and pushed the steel bar out from its wedged position against the door. I couldn't remember if I'd locked any of the other locks or not.

I needed a weapon. There was a softball bat in the hall closet, but that was too close to the front door to risk going for it.

I ran into the kitchen, flicked on the light switch and yanked a large cutting knife from its slot at the end of the counter. It had a floppy ten-inch blade that hadn't been sharpened in recent memory. I threw it down and picked up a small paring knife with a serrated edge. I turned off the light and pressed myself out of sight against the wall inside the kitchen doorway. I could hear my heart lurching dangerously against my ribs. I took a deep breath and expelled it slowly, trying to calm myself.

The hinges on the front door squealed slowly as the door opened. My fingers were trembling so much I almost dropped the knife.

The hall light came on. The front door closed with a click. I heard the Fox lock slide back into position and then footsteps move softly over the rug toward the living room. The hall light went off. I stood stock-still, hands trembling, and listened.

There was no conversation. I hoped that meant only one intruder.

Why hadn't I accepted Zimmer's offer of a pistol? A small kitchen knife wasn't much of a weapon, especially in hands like mine. I doubted I had the quickness, the strength, the skill or the determination to use it effectively.

A long time passed. The dog in the apartment next door started yapping. My fingers gripping the knife began to feel numb. The kitchen window blinds were up, and light from the city streets bathed the narrow room in a sullen orange glow. A lamp flicked on in the window directly across the way. A woman looked out briefly, then pulled the blinds closed. I switched the knife to the other hand and craned my head around to look out into the hallway. A light was on in my living room. No sounds. Whoever it was, he certainly wasn't ransacking the place. Or doing much of anything.

Except waiting for me to come home.

If I ran for the front door, I might manage to get the Fox lock's steel bar removed and the door open before the intruder could reach the foyer.

But then I would have to run the full length of a long apartment-building corridor before reaching the door to the fire stairs—a distance of at least a hundred feet. That would take four or five seconds. Then fourteen flights of stairs. If he didn't get a shot at me in the corridor, he had an excellent chance of catching me in the stairwell.

But how else could I get away?

There was the phone in the kitchen, but it was so still in the apartment that I couldn't use it without being overheard.

I couldn't think of anything else to do.

I waited.

I heard my bathroom toilet flush, then water splashing from the sink faucets. The son of a bitch was certainly making himself at home.

The more I thought about the knife in my hand, the more defenseless I felt. It was too small, too easy to drop or have twisted from my grasp. And too damned difficult to use. Even if I managed to drive it all the way in on the first stab, it wasn't certain—or even likely—that that would immobilize him. And if he was carrying a gun, the knife was next to worthless. Even if I succeeded in catching him off guard, he'd still have plenty of time to shoot me. And even if he was unarmed, I risked a wrestling match in which I might end up being stabbed myself.

I needed a better weapon—something to swing or throw. Something that with a little luck would instantly disarm, immobilize, knock senseless.

I ran through a mental inventory of the contents of the kitchen cupboards. The most promising weapon, I decided, was a cast-iron skillet. It was heavy, and it had a long wooden handle. Groping in the dark, I extracted the skillet from the bottom shelf of the cabinet where it was stored. It took me an agonizingly long time to do it without making any noise, but when I finally had the skillet's sturdy handle in my hands, I felt my odds had improved.

Then I backed against the knife I had laid on the counter and knocked it onto the floor. It struck the tile with a clatter that seemed to echo through the apartment like the report of a shotgun.

I flattened myself against the wall by the doorway. The hall light came on, and footsteps moved quickly down the hall toward the kitchen.

This was as good an ambush as I was going to get. I raised the skillet over my head with both hands and held my breath.

My target materialized at the threshold, paused, and then crossed through the doorway. I brought the skillet down as hard as my arms could swing it. It struck home with a sonorous bong, sending sharp vibrations shooting up both my arms.

In my panic I had struck a fraction of a second too soon. The skillet hit only a glancing blow off the top of the forehead.

Still, the effect was impressive. The intruder toppled backward into the hallway and struck the hardwood floor with a solid thud.

Gripping the skillet for a follow-up blow, I swung around and through the doorway.

My victim lay motionless, mouth open, eyes closed.

What I saw stunned me so profoundly I had to fight off a wave of lightheadedness to keep from tumbling to the floor myself. I dropped the skillet and bent down and felt for a pulse in the neck, whispering prayers under my breath.

I found a pulse. Thank you, Lord.

I flicked the kitchen light back on, poured cold water on a dish towel and rushed back and applied it to the rapidly swelling spot where my skillet had landed.

I slipped a pillow from the living-room couch under her head, folded the wet towel across her brow and massaged her wrists. I leaned close to her mouth. I could feel her breath, light but steady. I watched her eyes, praying for them to open soon. My mind flew in twenty directions at once. How long should I wait? She might have a serious concussion. Should I call someone now? An ambulance? A doctor? There was a doctor in the building, I remembered. I decided I'd call him if she didn't regain consciousness in a couple of minutes.

Fortunately she came around fairly quickly.

When she was able to sit up, I helped her into the bedroom, laid her on the bed, filled an ice bag and gave it to her to hold against her head.

"It'll help keep the swelling down."

"You crazy bastard," she groaned. "Why didn't you just answer the doorbell, like a normal human being?"

I was so relieved to hear her speak that I just grinned at her like a fool. "I was asleep. I didn't hear it. Why did you break in?"

"I didn't break in. You gave me a set of keys, remember?"

"I didn't expect you'd ever be using them again."

She closed her eyes and rolled her head gingerly from side to side. "Christ, it hurts."

"Thank God you're all right."

"You could have killed me."

I had been thinking the same thing. "And you should have called me."

She removed the ice bag and palpated the bump with her fingers. "I did, you birdbrain. All afternoon. Your answering machine is all screwed up."

"I mean days ago. You should have called me days ago."

She lowered the ice bag back onto her forehead and winced. "I know. I'm sorry."

"I thought you were an intruder. I've had a few lately."

She balled a fist and punched me lightly on the nose. I caught her hand and kissed it.

"You deserved a bop on the head," I said. "Tying me to the bed and stealing all my book research. What the hell were you up to?"

"I said I was sorry."

"I tried to find you. I mean I really tried. I spent hours at it. And I had other things to worry about. Why did you just disappear like that?"

Gail Snow exhaled with a long, quavering sigh.

"You want some painkiller before you make a full confession? You'll probably develop a hell of a headache."

"I already have."

I went to the bathroom and returned with a bottle of aspirin, a bottle of acetaminophen, a bottle of ibuprofen and a glass of water. On my way back, I noticed that she had brought with her a large black canvas travel bag. It was sitting by a chair in the living room. I arranged the plastic bottles for her on the night table and sat on the bed beside her. I was so happy to see her again I was almost in tears.

She struggled with the aspirin bottle, then handed it to me. "You're good at breaking things open," she said.

I opened the bottle and removed three pills for her.

"I only want two."

"Take three."

She swallowed all three. Despite the purplish lump mushrooming from the center of her forehead, she looked absolutely beautiful.

"You brought an overnight bag. Does that mean you plan to stay?"

She didn't answer me.

"Why all the lies?" I asked. "What kind of weird game were you playing with me?"

"What do you mean?"

"Everything you told me about yourself. None of it was true."

Gail let her head drop back onto the pillow. "Oh, that." She caught the ice bag slipping off her forehead and carefully repositioned it.

"Is your name Gail Snow?"

"No."

"What is it?"

She put her hand on my forearm and squeezed it gently. A sad, apologetic frown darkened her face. "Don't be mad at me," she said.

"Why?"

"Promise you won't be mad."

"Okay. I promise I won't be mad."

"I'm Andrew Carlson's daughter—Mara."

I gaped stupidly at her for a long moment, waiting to find out how I felt about it. I decided I was relieved. And happy. Getting Gail Snow back and Carlson's daughter delivered to my door all in one unexpected bundle made me think my luck was beginning to improve.

"I'm sorry for the elaborate subterfuge, Johnny. I did it for my father. I hope you can understand."

"What am I supposed to understand?"

"He was worried about your book, about what you might write about him, so I helped him find out."

"Did he tell you to do it?"

"He asked me to help him. I agreed to do it."

"That's what our brief little affair was all about?"

Mara closed her eyes. "Yes. I didn't count on actually liking you, though. Funny, it made deceiving you easier."

"Why was that?"

"I don't know. I guess because I didn't feel sorry for you. Because I wanted you to be upset that I had run out on you. I wanted you to miss me."

"It worked."

"I'm glad."

"Do you know what your father did to me?"

"Yes. I do now. I didn't know that he was going to force you into actually giving up your book. I was furious with him. I made him promise me that he'd get you out of trouble. No matter what happened."

"Did you love him?"

Mara bit her lip. I thought tears might come, but they didn't. "He was a difficult man," she said. "I sometimes thought I was the only person in the world who ever saw the good side of him. He must have saved all he had just for me. I couldn't help but love him back."

"Was he afraid he might be killed?"

"No. He thought he would live forever. But I was afraid. I persuaded him to tell me what I needed to know to carry things through for you if something should happen. Something did, so here I am."

I was about to ask her about Steckler and the struggle for control of the Night Watch network, when I remembered the possibility of hidden microphones.

I picked up the notepad I kept on the night table, printed out "THIS PLACE IS BUGGED" and held it up in front of her.

She took the pad from me and wrote: "THEN I'LL TELL YOU WHAT WE HAVE TO DO IN THE MORNING—AFTER WE LEAVE THE APARTMENT."

We went straight to bed, too tired for anything more strenuous than a lingering embrace.

As we drifted toward sleep, I found myself wondering why the death of her father, Andrew Carlson, for whom she had professed such great love, seemed to have upset Mara so little.

I wondered about that a lot.

22

FAR ISLAND

Mara and I got up at five-thirty in the morning, packed bags, left the apartment through the basement service entrance and caught a cab a couple of blocks down Central Park West.

By seven A.M. we were at La Guardia Airport.

"Where are we going?" I demanded.

"Bangor, Maine."

"Can't we drive?"

"It takes ten hours to drive. The flight takes less than two."

I had a problem here—an irrational phobia that I didn't want to admit to Mara. I didn't like to fly. It terrified me. I had tried all the standard remedies, and none had worked. As a journalist, I was sometimes forced to take commercial flights, but I always did my best to avoid them. I had worked out a formula: First, I'd do everything I could think of to get the trip canceled. Then, if I absolutely still had to go—and if I couldn't get there by train, car or boat within the day—I'd fly.

By seven-thirty we were on a flight to Bangor, Maine.

The bump on Mara's forehead was the size of a plum and about the same color. She wasn't suffering from double vision or memory loss, so I was consoled: she probably didn't have a concussion. Anyway, she claimed it wasn't bothering her.

Breakfast was served. Cold toast, tepid coffee and rubbery scrambled eggs. I drank orange juice and then, to help insulate myself from my fear of flying, asked the flight attendant for a double scotch. She glanced at her wristwatch disapprovingly—it was just past eight A.M.—but grudgingly produced two tiny bottles of Dewar's and a plastic cup with ice.

I tried to coax Mara to talk about herself. I wanted her to help me take my mind off the stark reality that we were roaring through unbreathable, subzero space, miles above the surface of the earth, wrapped in nothing but a fragile, aging skin of aluminum almost certainly webbed with stress cracks.

Mara felt my hand. It was clammy with perspiration. "I can't believe it," she said. "You're afraid of flying."

I nodded.

"It's the safest form of transportation there is."

"I think walking is considered safer."

Mara laughed. "Airlines average millions of miles without a fatality. You're more likely to die in your bathtub."

I pulled my hand away. "That's fine with me. At least I'd have a clean corpse."

"Really—"

I cut her off. "Don't give me a lecture on airline safety. Regale me with your life story instead. And try to keep it interesting."

Mara slumped back in her seat. "It's not interesting. I don't like to talk about it."

"Talk, or I'll throw up all over you."

Mara talked. She was born in Paris, and grew up on an estate outside the city. Carlson, her father, whom she called "Père," was absent much of the time when she was young—always away on business trips somewhere. Her mother, who died in an automobile accident when Mara was sixteen, was left with the responsibility of raising her. They didn't get along.

"She made me miserable every day of my life," Mara said. "We were rich, had houses all over the place, and she was free to do whatever she wanted. Père was never around, so she spent her time shopping, having affairs and getting drunk."

Mara rested her hand on top of mine and squeezed it gently. "She didn't like me. I know that's a strange thing to say about one's mother, but it was true. She worshiped Claude, my older brother, who was actually quite a dope, I think, but she had nothing but scorn for me. When I was little she used to hit me. All the time. A day never passed without her finding some excuse to inflict some kind of punishment on me—a hairbrush, a belt, a day in my room with no food—whatever she could think of to make life hell for me. Sometimes, when she was drunk, she locked me in the basement. If it wasn't child abuse, it was damned close to it. It would probably have been much worse, but I usually had a nanny to run to, and the other servants sometimes intervened to protect me from her. It cost a few of them their jobs."

Mara asked the flight attendant for another cup of coffee. I asked for another scotch. The attendant refused me.

"When I was older, and stronger, she switched to verbal abuse," Mara continued. "She belittled me, criticized me, undercut me. And she was jealous of the way I looked. She wouldn't let me see boys, and she went out of her way to dress me in the ugliest clothes. We had absolutely nothing in common, and both of us knew it instinctively. I genuinely loathed her. I think now that she was actually a little crazy. I couldn't understand why Père had ever married her. The earliest and most abiding fantasy of my life was that my mother had left us forever and I had taken her place as Père's wife.

"I was so happy when he was home, and so miserable when he wasn't. He doted on me, spoiled me, and my mother was always on her best behavior then. I used to beg him like some pathetic wretch not to go away again and leave me with her. He just never really understood how she treated me. Or he chose not to believe it.

"When I got older I got more daring and rebellious. I really gave her some reasons to hate me. I insulted her, screamed at her, stole things from her, played cruel jokes on her, even began striking her. I was determined to pay her back for everything she had done to me when I was too small and defenseless to protect myself. God, did we have some fights. I stayed away from home for days at a time, started hanging out with creeps, drinking, screwing around. I became a real delinquent."

Mara paused and looked at me. "Are you all right?"

"Fine."

"You look kind of sweaty."

"Don't remind me. You said you became a delinquent. . . ."

"Yeah. Mother helped the process along. I think she hoped I'd get into real trouble and be taken off to prison or something. Once, when I was thirteen she tried to force me into having sex with one of her boyfriends. And it was her idea, not his. She had convinced herself that I was already a slut. In fact, I was still a virgin. She was drunk and she just wanted to see me humiliated and defiled. It didn't work out that way. I was very strong. I bloodied her nose and gave her boyfriend a kick in his crotch he can probably still feel.

"One of the servants told Père about it. It was the only time in my life I can remember him getting violent with her. Most of the time I think he just didn't care what she did. But this time, he beat the hell out of her. I mean he almost killed her—blackened her eyes, broke a rib, put her in the hospital. She pretty much left me alone after that incident."

Mara screwed up her mouth in an expression of disgust and kicked at the bottom of the seatback in front of her. "We were some family. If we'd been poor and living in the States, we'd have been thrown in jail. But in France, anything that happens *en famille*, short of murder, is considered no one's business. And of course if you're rich, you can get away with anything. The only hardships my mother and I had to endure were the ones we inflicted on each other."

Mara excused herself to visit the rest room. I clutched the armrests and listened to the droning of the plane's engines. The slightest change of pitch always made me clench my teeth and stiffen my gut. Here we go, I'd think. This is it. The pilot is about to lose control of the craft and send us plummeting to earth in a fiery ball. We'll all have a couple of minutes of conscious free fall to contemplate the terrible death that awaits us below.

Mara slipped back into the seat beside me and snapped on her seat belt. She had combed her hair and put on a small amount of lipstick. She wet her lips with her tongue and turned a teasing smile on me. "You face has turned a very peculiar shade of green," she said.

"It's a chlorophyll rush," I muttered. "I'm turning into a plant. So what happened to your mother?"

"She was with some degenerate German count she'd been screwing. They were on the autobahn somewhere near Munich, both drunk. It was the middle of the night. He hit another car head-on. The police said they were traveling at well over a hundred miles an hour. I saw pictures of the car. It was crushed flat—I mean it was folded up like an accordion. Grotesque."

Mara shivered. "When I heard about the accident I was sick with guilt. Since I had been praying for years for her to die, I thought *I* had killed her.

"Père came home to stay for a while. Then he packed me off to a girls' school in Switzerland for a year, where I began to straighten out. Then we moved to Washington. I had the chance to start all over again. . . . And I more or less did."

The captain announced that we had begun our approach to Bangor International Airport. I strained my ears to hear the landing gears lock into place. I knew it was only a matter of time before I picked a flight with a faulty landing gear.

"I went to Georgetown for two years," Mara said. "I thought I was interested in government, but I think it was just because of Père. I took a year off and lived in Los Angeles with a friend. I had decided I was going to be an actress. That didn't work out. Then I went to UCLA and got a degree in Romance languages. That was kind of a cheat, because I'd been speaking French, Italian and Spanish since I was a little girl. Then I wanted to be a photographer. There was a brief period when I even wanted to be a journalist. That's the trouble with being a spoiled rich kid—you don't think you should have to work to become something. I didn't want to act, I just wanted to be an actress. The same with photography. I sort of thought that someone would come along and pin a label on my blouse: 'actress,' 'photographer,' 'journalist,' or whatever I wanted. And that would be that. But of course that isn't that. So I've stopped thinking about what I wanted to be, and started thinking about what I wanted to do."

"And?"

Mara snapped her seat belt across her lap. "I'm still thinking."

"You don't do anything?"

"Sure. I'm in the graduate studies program at the University of Maine. Economics. I've been in it three years, and I'm beginning to loathe it. I'm thinking about switching to literature." She laughed self-deprecatingly. "That's what I do, I guess. Study. I've become a sort of professional student."

We landed at Bangor Airport. My pulse and blood pressure began to drop back toward normal. Outside, the weather was overcast and rainy.

I picked up our bags and started toward the car-rental counters. Mara still hadn't told me where we were going, but I assumed that at least we could get the rest of the way by car.

I assumed wrong. She grabbed my sleeve and tugged me down a long corridor to a far wing of the terminal reserved for private planes and charters.

"Jesus—you're not going to charter a plane, are you?"

She shook her head.

"Thank God."

"We already have a plane."

She wasn't kidding.

"Why can't we drive there?"

"Because 'there' is an island twenty miles off the coast."

"Can't we take a boat, then?"

"There are no boats."

"Shit."

I paced nervously around the terminal with my hands in my pockets while Mara filled out some forms and conferred with some airport personnel. She seemed to know everybody by their first names.

Outside on the tarmac half an hour later, I followed her past a line of corporate jets, twin-engine Beechcraft and other assorted small planes to a little high-winged four-seater—a Cessna Skyhawk.

"Whose jalopy is this?"

"Mine."

She helped me climb up into the passenger side, then stowed our bags in the back of the craft. She spent several minutes checking over the airplane. She wheeled a stepladder over and looked into the gas tanks in both wings. She walked around the plane, drawing out small amounts of fuel into a small transparent vial of some kind from several little drain valves under the wings. Each time, she held the vial up to the sky, then, in a wide sweeping motion of her arm, tossed the gasoline out onto the tarmac apron. It looked like some kind of religious ritual, to propitiate the gods of the air. She examined the wing surfaces and peered into the engine compartment. All this made me extremely nervous.

I opened the door and leaned out. "Is something wrong?"

She pulled out the chocks holding the wheels of the landing gear in place. "Relax, Lindbergh. Just a preflight check."

"Where's our pilot?"

"You're looking at her."

Mara pulled herself up into the left-side seat and buckled herself in.

"Well, aren't you impressed?" she asked, displaying a dazzlingly impish grin.

I started to shake. "Impressed? Right out of my wits, I'm impressed."

"Don't *worry*," she said. "I'm a very good pilot. I even have a commercial license." She pulled a clipboard onto her lap. "I can fly anything out there on the field."

There was still enough male chauvinist in me to be briefly infuriated by this cute little boast. It wasn't just that I saw piloting aircraft as a male occupation, but that she could do it and I couldn't. Hell, I was barely able to qualify as a passenger. I watched a Boeing 747 lumber down the runway out in front of us and blast upward into the gray sky on a long dirty tail of black exhaust. With its cockpit's headlike bulge, it reminded me of those giant flying carnivorous reptiles that had been extinct for millions of years.

"How about that 747?"

"Piece of cake."

"Really."

"Well, I could fly it if I had to. They fly themselves, anyway. Onboard computers do everything."

"Mother of God," I mumbled.

Mara detached a microphone from its base down below the instrument panel, pushed it up near her lips and said something into it. The speaker in the cabin's ceiling just above our heads chatted back at her with a garble of exotic numbers and words that meant nothing to me. I marveled at her poise. I even began to feel reasonably calm. I think I had decided that since my death was now inevitable, I was glad that she was going to be the cause of it, and not some unattractive stranger.

Mara flipped some switches and adjusted some knobs. The engine coughed and caught and the plane's propeller started to spin, shaking the little craft violently. Mara taxied the Cessna slowly out of the crowd of parked aircraft and maneuvered it in behind a line of planes waiting to use the runway. She reached across my lap, buckled my seat belt for me, and kissed me hard on the cheek.

In a few minutes we were airborne. I didn't pay close attention to how it happened. I occupied myself reciting some medieval verses memorized in parochial school and trying to keep my toes from curling up inside my shoes.

We were up in the air for one very long hour, pitching and yawing through a bumpy gray day with low visibility. It was damp and chilly, and the purple-black ceiling of clouds we were flying under looked ready to crash down on us at any second. Droplets of rain were already splattering against the windshield. It was a tribute to the magic of Mara's presence that I wasn't babbling incoherently and trying to claw my way under the seat.

Mara dropped an air navigation map onto my lap and pointed to a little apostrophe-shaped green spot circled in red pencil. I pulled the map closer, fighting to hold it steady against the turbulence.

The chart was folded open to the section of the Maine coast that stretched in a northeasterly direction from Vinalhaven to Eastport on the Canadian border. Viewed on a map, the shoreline looked like someone had been at work on it with a hammer and chisel, smashing it up into little pieces. Hundreds of islands of all sizes lay scattered like debris along an impossibly convoluted coast of coves and bays and peninsulas and inlets.

The particular piece of flotsam circled on Mara's map was called Far Island. It was about a mile and a half long, and half a mile wide. It stood well out in the ocean, farther from the mainland than any other islands along the coast. The Bass Harbor Head

Lighthouse, which jutted out from the southernmost tip of the big clawlike piece off the coastline known as Mount Desert Island, was at least fifteen miles distant.

We began to descend. I looked out my side window. Through the beaded drops of rain I could see the ocean barely a hundred feet below. Whitecaps writhed on the dark surface.

Suddenly a rocky, wave-beaten cliff, fringed with a few low pines, slipped by beneath us, giving way to an expanse of bleak, undulating grassland. A big, rambling gray-shingled house swung into view. Flanked by a scattering of outbuildings, it was situated on the crest of a long, sweeping rise of land near the southernmost tip of the island.

Mara circled the Cessna low around it.

"Far Island used to be owned by a millionaire duck hunter," she shouted, over the drone of the engine. "He built the lodge back in the thirties. Then one year the ducks stopped coming. Père bought it from him in 1962."

As we turned I got a view of the entire island. Except for the lodge and its outbuildings, there was nothing. No roads, no other buildings. It was a little piece of wilderness, lost out in the endless folds of the ocean. From up here it looked barren and forbidding. No doubt the foul weather contributed to that impression.

Mara edged the Cessna around in a long shallow turn and touched down roughly across the wind on a tarmac runway laid out at the bottom of a long grassy meadow that sloped down from the lodge.

It was raining lightly, but the wind was picking up fast. It was barreling in from the ocean and breaking across the open fields of the island in powerful gusts. A windsock at the corner of the runway was rigid and snapping loudly. Mara quickly cut the engine and braked the plane to a stop.

We jumped out. Without our weight, the Cessna began dancing and shivering in the wind, like a frightened bird eager to take wing. I helped her roll the craft to a spot at the edge of the landing strip where some tie-downs had been anchored into a cement apron. We hooked down the landing gear, the wings and the tail, unloaded our baggage, and trudged through the snarls of tough, sodden grass up toward the lodge.

By the time we reached the front door, we were thoroughly

soaked. We ducked inside and Mara pushed the door closed against the wind and bolted it.

I looked around. A dank, gloomy, high-ceilinged central hallway engulfed us.

"The bags can stay here for now," Mara said. "We have other things to do." She tugged at my sleeve again. "This way."

We walked through the hallway into a pantry and kitchen. The house smelled musty and damp, but it was in perfect order and appeared to have been cleaned recently.

"Who keeps the place?"

"We used to have a couple who stayed here during the summer. Now there's just a caretaker—Orson Price. He comes out from the mainland twice a month and tidies up and checks on things. He's a dear old man—retired from one of the paper mills up north. Whenever we're coming up, we let him know in advance and he comes out and starts the generator and opens the place up. Today we'll have to do it ourselves."

Mara rolled up a couple of shades to let some light into the kitchen. She found a big flashlight in one of the cupboards and reinserted a pair of batteries stored alongside it.

She opened another door off the kitchen, switched on the flashlight and led me down a flight of steep, narrow steps into a dungeonlike cellar. The floor was dirt, studded at frequent intervals with massive round posts.

"These posts used to be ships' masts," Mara said, slapping one with her hand. "The builder salvaged them from the wrecks of old fishing vessels washed ashore during storms. Or so the story goes."

"They look like plain old telephone poles to me."

"You're so romantic."

"I suppose the house is also haunted by the ghosts of drowned sailors?"

Mara giggled. "Yes, as a matter of fact it is."

"And you can hear them crying out on stormy nights."

"Well, you're in for a surprise. You really can hear them crying out. We'll hear them tonight."

We came to a heavy door with a padlock on it. Mara fished with her hand for the key on the cobwebbed lintel overhead, found it, and opened the door.

On the other side an underground passageway led some fifty feet out from the basement to a sizable subterranean vault. Bolted to a concrete base in the vault was a mammoth old electric generator, sprouting cables and fuel lines and a long length of flexible metal exhaust hose that exited through an opening near the ceiling. There were steps leading up a bulkhead to a surface exit at the back of the vault. It was padlocked from the inside.

I held the flashlight for Mara while she checked the generator's oil and fuel levels and reset the circuit breakers on a big control panel built into the wall behind the generator.

I looked over at the pair of automobile batteries used to start the engine. I was surprised that the cables were already connected to the terminals. I mentioned this to Mara.

"Aren't they supposed to be?"

"Sure. But they ought to be disconnected when no one's here. Otherwise the batteries will run down."

Mara seemed embarrassed by my observation. "Well, whoever was here last forgot to disconnect them."

"Who would that have been?"

"Orson Price, I guess."

"Just hope the batteries aren't dead," I said.

Mara primed the engine, then pressed a red starter button. The massive hunk of machinery growled like a beast disturbed in its lair, belched and spluttered a couple of times, then roared into action, its pair of huge flywheels accelerating until the concrete beneath us began to vibrate.

Mara flicked a light switch on the wall and the bulb in the fixture over our heads began to glow brightly.

We walked back through a passageway now illuminated by a row of incandescent bulbs. In the basement, Mara turned on the water pump and the hot-water heater, then stopped by a long wooden rack and pulled out a bottle of red wine. "A 1982 Château Margaux. Good enough?"

"Good, yes, enough, no. Take two. We deserve it."

She grabbed a second bottle and we climbed back upstairs to the kitchen. From there, the noise of the big generator, closed off in its underground vault, was muffled to a faint, deep, rhythmic pumping sound, like a big heart beating inside the island itself.

Mara opened the freezer. "What would you like for dinner?"

"Won't everything be spoiled?"

"This one doesn't need the generator. It runs on bottled gas. Things keep in here for months."

We settled on something simple: a pair of club steaks, French-cut green beans, and rice.

Mara cooked the dinner on the big black restaurant-sized stove. I set the table.

The dining room, like the rest of the lodge, was oversized, with a row of tall windows that looked out over the ocean. I pulled the sheets off the furniture. The dining-room table was polished mahogany and easily twenty feet long. There were enough high-backed, upholstered chairs to seat eighteen.

"Did your father entertain a lot?" I asked.

"No. The table and chairs were left by the previous owner. He used to bring big parties of duck-hunting pals up here in the thirties and forties. He left a photo album. It's around somewhere."

I found a tablecloth, dishes, linen napkins and silverware in the sideboard and set places for two side-by-side in the middle of the table, with a view of the water. I brought out a pair of candelabra and candles from the pantry and lit them.

It was not a very festive dinner, even so.

As evening fell, a desolate gloom settled with it. It was raining harder. The skies were cold gray, and the ocean surface, half obscured by shredded, curling veils of fog, was agitated. The waves, tips frothed with foam, rolled and heaved and collided in every direction at once, like boiling water.

Looking out the dining-room windows from the table, you could see nothing except the ocean. After a while it was impossible not to fall victim to the disturbing illusion that the whole house was adrift on the angry sea.

And Mara was right about the voices of the drowned sailors. Through some peculiarity in the old building's architecture or its siting, the wind, when it came out of a certain quarter at a certain intensity, created an acute, high-pitched, moaning wail that sounded frighteningly like a man in distress.

Our conversation began to falter in the gathering dark. A gust of wind inspired a particularly heartrending moan from somewhere overhead. I shivered.

"Do you ever come up here alone?" I asked her.

"No. I never have. Père often did, though. He loved the solitude."

I shook my head. "This is a pretty desolate spot."

Mara didn't agree. "It's really quite beautiful when the weather's good."

I glanced sidelong at her. In the candlelight she looked sad and uneasy. She caught my glance and smiled. "We should go to bed early tonight," she said.

"What about the documents? Do you know where they are?"

"We'll get them in the morning."

I was surprised at her firm tone. "We can't have a look at them now?" I prodded. "Where are they?"

"Well hidden. We'll get up early. Dawn, if you can stand it."

"Whatever you say."

"We'll have to leave the island early. Père's funeral is tomorrow. I've got to be in Washington by mid-afternoon."

We cleared the table and washed the dishes.

"Why don't we sleep in the living room," Mara suggested. "You can build a fire in the fireplace. It'll be a little less spooky than the bedrooms upstairs."

I liked the idea. We hauled a mattress downstairs, then Mara went hunting for some linen and blankets while I worked on getting a fire started.

The living room was baronial. Built as a separate wing of the lodge, it was two stories high, with a massive beamed ceiling and facing rows of French doors. You entered from the main hall through a high double doorway onto a stagelike platform a step higher than the rest of the room. The platform contained bookshelves and a grand piano. The walls over the French doors were burdened with dozens of stuffed animal heads—lions, tigers, bears, rhinos, antelope. Hung there years ago by the original owner, they looked dusty, decrepit and grim.

The far end of the big hall, some forty feet from the stage, was taken up almost entirely by a gigantic stone fireplace nearly big enough for me to stand in. A pair of three-foot-high andirons, cast in the shape of owls, with clear agates for eyes, guarded the hearth.

I gathered some paper and kindling from a box nearby, threw on the two smallest logs I could find, and struck a match. The fire flamed quickly, aided by the powerful draft caused by the wind.

I walked over to the French doors and opened one to look outside. It was black, and rain swirled inside the room in gusts. I closed the door. A small blurred flash of light out in the dark caught my attention. I opened the door a crack and peered out through the rain, hooding my eyes under my hands.

Nothing. Palpable darkness.

No, there it was again. I waited. I counted several flashes at regularly spaced intervals. Someone was out there, signaling with a flashlight. The light appeared to be coming from somewhere at the other end of the island.

Mara returned with sheets, pillows and blankets. I described to her what I had just seen. We stood and watched together by the French doors for a few minutes, but the light didn't return.

"A boat on the water," she said.

"It didn't look that far away."

Mara insisted that it must have been a boat. "We see lights here all the time. It's nothing, I'm sure."

We made up the mattress, then sat for a while, finishing off the second bottle of wine and watching the fire. The eyes of the andiron owls flickered and glowed bright orange from the flames behind them, making it appear that they were alive and watching us.

"Tell me about the documents," I said, unable to stay away from the subject. "Do you know what's in them?"

"No. Père never told me. And I was never interested."

"Does anyone else know?"

"I'm not sure. Grayson Steckler must know what's in some of them. But he doesn't know where they are. No one knew except Père. And he only told me their location two days ago."

"How many are there? A dozen? Hundreds?"

Mara shrugged. "A lot."

"How do you know which ones your father meant for me?"

"I don't. He intended to tell me, but he didn't get the chance. You'll just have to sift through them and take what you need."

That suited me. In fact it pleased me enormously.

"How are you going to dispose of the documents? Did your father leave you any directions?"

"I'm going to destroy them."

"Shouldn't we make use of them?"

"To get the charges against you dropped, that's all."

"What about exposing the Night Watch?"

"No."

"You'd let Steckler continue it?"

"I know what you're thinking, Johnny. Forget it. Your part of the bargain was that you would not publish anything about my father."

"Your father also wanted to prevent Steckler from taking over the Night Watch. He died trying to prevent it. But that's exactly what will happen, if Steckler isn't exposed."

"There are other ways to stop him."

"Like what?"

"Like destroying those documents. Without them, Steckler will be nothing. He's not CIA director, after all. He doesn't have the base of power and the access to secrets that Père had. He has no power at all outside the Night Watch."

"No, but he apparently has support from others in the network. It won't just collapse because your father's dead. There're too many besides Steckler who have a vested interest in its success. With their help he'll be able to put things back together, even without the documents. It has to be exposed."

"Well, you can't stop him, for heaven's sake," she snapped.

"Who's going to, then?"

"It's not your concern. Why get in his way? He'll only kill you, too."

"He won't kill anybody if he's in prison."

Mara scoffed at my naiveté. "Men like Steckler don't go to prison. Even if he did, he would just hire someone to get you. Anyway, I can't let you disgrace my father's memory. And profit from it, at that."

I didn't reply. We finished the wine and undressed. Neither of us was in the mood for lovemaking.

Mara picked up the flashlight. "I have to go down and turn off the generator."

The thumping heart ceased beating down below. A minute later Mara returned and crawled under the covers beside me.

It took me a long time to get to sleep. I lay pressed against Mara's back, watching the fire, listening to the old mansion groan and howl under the battering of the wind and rain.

Carlson's cryptic phrase "map of the bunker" came back to me.

Those mysterious pages of Admiral Conover's that I never got to see must have contained the directions to this trove of secret documents Mara was taking me to tomorrow. No wonder Steckler and Westerly and everybody else had wanted those pages so badly. They were the map to the treasure, the keys to the kingdom of the Night Watch.

23

THE BUNKER

I woke to feel warm light on my face. It was coming in the row of French doors on the east side of the living room. The space on the mattress beside me was empty. I could feel the generator thumping underground.

I slipped out from under the blanket and stepped over to the French doors to behold a spectacular sight. The sun was perched exactly on the rim of the ocean. Above it, against a backdrop of intense purple sky, dazzling orange-pink and white clouds hung in tiers, like opera-house balconies, along the horizon. The ocean beneath was blue-green and mirror-calm, its vast dimensions shimmering with the silent explosion of the dawn.

A flock of gulls wheeled far overhead, their raucous cries sweet in the distance.

I unlocked one of the doors and pulled it open. The breeze carried in the smells of the sea.

"I told you it was beautiful when the weather was good."

I turned around to see Mara, dressed in clean, faded blue jeans and a work shirt, bringing in breakfast on a tray.

"Quite a transformation," I admitted.

I grabbed a couple of chairs and a small end table and carried them outside onto the wide stone terrace that flanked the windows.

We sat on the terrace and ate our breakfast in the warm sun. The sense of foreboding that had enveloped the place the night before had so completely evaporated in the glorious view and the bright spring day that it was painful to remember why we were here.

"I'd like to come back here sometime," I said. "When this is all over."

Mara smiled. I hoped she'd extend an invitation, but she didn't. Her forward and playful manner seemed to be hiding someone who was really quite distant and withdrawn. I found it impossible to guess what was on her mind from one minute to the next. I couldn't figure out what motivated her, what was important to her. One minute she was lively and intense, seemingly in tune with my thoughts and emotions—the next minute she was gone, moved to a place where I could not follow. It mystified me, even charmed me, but I feared I would never get close to her, no matter how hard I worked at it, no matter how much I yearned for it.

We walked from the house down a rough stone path to one of the outbuildings, a weathered barn with a large cupola perched astride the ridgepole.

"The stables," Mara said. "The original owner kept horses here during the summers. I would have loved to have one here myself, but it wouldn't have been very practical. Anyway, Père didn't like horses. He was allergic to them."

I followed Mara into what had once been the tack room. It was small and dusty and devoid of furniture. The walls were paneled in varnished wood that had darkened and peeled over the years. Four saddle brackets protruded from the near wall. One still had a saddle on it—an old English one, its leather cracked and blackened with age. On the back wall a couple of bridles still hung from a long row of tarnished brass hooks. Two faded and dusty yellow ribbons from some long-forgotten horse show were pinned to the wall near one of the bridles, along with several browned photographs.

Mara reached up, grasped the last brass hook on the right and twisted it clockwise a full turn. I waited to see a secret panel flip open, or a wall slide back, but nothing happened.

She grinned, watching my puzzled reaction. "This way," she said, pointing out the door.

We walked a short distance to another outbuilding behind the stables. It was a small, windowless wood structure, about eight feet wide and twelve feet deep.

"This used to be an icehouse, in the days before the generator was installed."

My jaw fell open like a child watching a magic show. I was witnessing an extraordinary feat of levitation. The icehouse was slowly rising from the ground. About three feet of air already separated it from the concrete slab that served as its foundation, and it was still inching upward. Six feet from terra firma, it quivered slightly and stopped. It hung there in midair, balanced on a single smooth steel cylinder, like an enormous square flower on a stem.

Mara pointed to the cylinder holding it aloft. "Nothing high-tech about it. It's just an old hydraulic lift—the kind they hoist your car up on at Midas to install a new muffler. Père had the lift platform altered a bit and then just bolted the icehouse to it."

I looked down at the concrete slab where the icehouse had been. A trapdoor was cut into it. Mara knelt down, grabbed the iron ring that served as the door's handle and tugged on it. The door swung up to reveal a long, narrow flight of metal stairs beneath.

"Père brought some construction workers down from Quebec," she said. "They put in the landing strip and this bunker, both. That was about twelve years ago. Père told them they were building a bomb shelter. None of them spoke English. I remember because I was here part of that summer and the workmen used to tease me about my Parisian French."

Mara led the way down with her flashlight. I counted twenty-six steps—double the length of an ordinary flight of stairs in a house. At the bottom, Mara punched a series of numbers into a combination lock, pushed open a steel door and switched on an overhead light fixture.

We were in a long, low corridor with cement-block walls. The air was dank and stagnant, like a cellar that had been closed up all year. Mara led the way down the corridor. We passed a door on our right.

"What's in there?"

"Supplies," Mara said, blandly. "All the files are in this room."

We came to a second door. Mara produced a key from her jeans pocket and opened it.

On the other side was a low-ceilinged underground vault about twenty feet square. The middle of the chamber was dominated by a long, sturdy oak table with several swivel chairs pushed against it. Two fluorescent light fixtures hung down from the ceiling. Against the wall immediately to our right was an old green metal office desk on which sat a great deal of sophisticated-looking radio equipment. The remaining three walls were solidly lined with six-foot-high gray metal filing cabinets. I pulled open the first drawer I came to. It was jammed tight with documents. I opened the drawer below it. The same. I tried a second filing cabinet, then a third. Every drawer I opened was full.

"This is incredible," I whispered. "There are thousands of documents here."

Mara was standing in the door, one hand on the lintel over her head, the other on her hip. She looked impatient.

"What's the matter?" I asked.

"Don't think you're going to go through all of them. It would take days."

"I can see that. I'll try to make a rough inventory of the contents first. Then I can pick out what I need from that."

"You've got about two hours. That's it. It's seven now. We have to leave here at nine-thirty for me to make all my connections to Washington. I have things to do at the house. I'll come back here for you at nine-fifteen."

Mara switched on a fan behind a grille in the wall. "It's an air-circulating system." She pointed to a small panel on the wall by the door. "Those switches let you raise and lower the icehouse from in here."

"Don't lower it on me. The generator might conk out and leave me buried alive."

"And happy."

"Happy?"

"Happy."

"What's that mean?"

"Look at you. You're all sweaty and excited. The way you look when we're about to fuck."

Before I could produce a snappy rejoinder, Mara had retreated up the steps and out of earshot.

I turned to the cabinet nearest me, opened it and pulled out a thick file at random. It was labeled IRAN, 1980–1984. Under that was a list of subheads: "I.P. (Indigenous Personnel); Intelligence Sources; Backgrounds; Military; Op. Greenback; Op. Red Letter." The file contained about a hundred loose pages. Some were long lists of names grouped alphabetically by categories like "Trusted Sources," "Suppliers," "Activists," "Liberals," "Soviet Sympathizers," "Khomeini Followers," "Rafsanjani Loyalists,""Bani-Sadr Loyalists," "Military Sources," "Dual-Nationalities," "Pahlevi Family," "Shah Supporters," "SAVAK," and so on. I skimmed the remaining pages. Other pages contained intelligence information on Iran gathered from a number of sources—NSA, CIA, SAVAK, Eastern Bloc, NW (for Night Watch, I guessed) and other abbreviated sources I couldn't decipher. And there were detailed summaries of two separate operations, one aimed at freeing the American embassy hostages in Iran in 1980, the other at destabilizing the regime in 1984.

The first, Operation Greenback, involved a team of retired American and French military officers acting as intermediaries in the paying of a $20 million ransom to a group of Iranian Shiite clerics close to Khomeini. According to the documents, it was a miserable failure. The Iranians swindled them, taking the money and doing nothing in return. The money appeared to have come from some unidentified source inside the Pentagon. It looked as if the U.S. government, using the Night Watch as a third party, had tried to buy the release of the embassy hostages. Several of the clerics involved were later assassinated.

The second, Operation Red Letter, was a complicated and bloody attempt to overthrow Khomeini's regime by organizing a group of former SAVAK spies and saboteurs to mount an attack on Khomeini's residence in Qum. It cost $3.5 million and failed. Forty-three people died.

I could recall nothing about either of these affairs ever surfacing in the Western press. I had not even picked up rumors about them. That in itself was extraordinary. When huge sums of money change hands—or when men die—word about it usually gets out.

Both operations were Night Watch specials. And both had been fiascos. I wondered if this was typical of the quality of Night Watch work.

The answer, I quickly discovered, was no. The next file I plucked from the same drawer, dubbed Operation Dracula, detailed a four-year-long Night Watch campaign of sabotage against Romania's Ceauşescu regime, including the assassinations of several Securitate officials and the head of an unpopular rural relocation program.

Another file described a successful plot to overthrow the dictator of a small African nation. He was more than overthrown. His family and closest advisors were slaughtered, and his head was cut off, placed on a pole and exhibited in the central square of the capital.

I tucked these files back in place, walked back to the first file cabinet in the row, and began an orderly survey of the contents of everything in the room.

By the time the two hours had passed, I had managed, working flat out, to glance at only about a third of the documents in the files.

The picture that was emerging from them left me numb. It was the journalistic equivalent of King Solomon's mines. Or King Tut's tomb. There was enough here for a hundred books—enough to topple many governments, enough to alter the fortunes of thousands of individuals.

The documents divided themselves into two main categories. One category covered the Night Watch network in all its various aspects. One whole drawer contained files of the active members of the network, complete with biographies, recent photos, professional skills, past record of activities and so on. Other drawers contained detailed descriptions of different kinds of contacts, sources and safe houses in different countries. There were pages and pages of lists of suppliers of all kinds—drugs, prostitutes, illegal weapons, false documents and on and on. There were ledgers detailing receipts and expenditures.

There were bank statements from dozens of banks in Zurich,

Panama, Liechtenstein, Geneva, the Bahamas and other countries. There were files listing such mundane matters as the best hotels to patronize in various cities, the best cab services, the best air rentals and so on.

There were long inventories of weapons and other hardware. There were maps showing locations of various weapons and explosives dumps and secret training bases. There were documents detailing plans for operations not yet initiated.

And there were the reports on what were euphemistically referred to as "actions." These included those operations in Iran, Romania and Africa whose files I had looked at earlier.

Yet, as mind-boggling as all this was, the documents devoted to the Night Watch accounted for only a fraction of the total. As far as I could tell from my hurried inspection, three or four file cabinets contained it all. No doubt Carlson had preferred that the records involving this shadowy enterprise be kept to an absolute minimum. The fewer potentially incriminating paper trails the better, even inside the rarefied secret world of the Night Watch.

The second category of document, occupying the drawers of twenty file cabinets, consisted of highly sensitive intelligence. It was broad and deep and unbelievable. Beyond anything I could ever have imagined. The files were maintained alphabetically by country, starting with Albania and ending with Zimbabwe/Rhodesia. There were data on each country's economic, financial, social, political and military situation. There was intelligence on each country's leaders, on important figures in the sciences, the military establishment, the various branches of the government, the political opposition, the police and criminal elements. The information went well beyond what their subjects would include on their résumés.

For example, the file on Gunther Holzmann, the leader of a right-wing political party in Germany, contained this little snippet: "GH has close ties with some criminal elements, as well as former SS members. Families of once prominent Nazis, including Goebbels, Goering and Himmler families, secretly donate large amounts to his political campaigns."

Or this, from the file on the president of Mexico: "Millaflores is married, but secretly homosexual. One former boyfriend tried to blackmail him during last election, threatening public exposure. Millaflores had him killed."

Or this, from the file of the senior senator from the State of New Jersey: "Sen. Quinn is secretly backed by the Mafia, through NJ labor unions. He has also taken bribes from the following sources: A&B Construction, Freid Drug Laboratories, Ancom Oil Refineries, Zucco Hazardous Waste Disposal."

A few of these secret reports originated with the Night Watch, but the bulk of them came from elsewhere—from American sources like the CIA, the NSA, the DIA, the FBI, and from dozens of other intelligence and police establishments in various countries.

Carlson had clearly been very selective. The entire library of restricted documents of the CIA and other U.S. intelligence-gathering agencies would certainly number in the millions of pages. But much of it was bureaucratic junk—outdated, erroneous, misleading, exaggerated, contradictory and confusing. I knew this from personal experience. But everything here seemed of considerable value. There was no junk. It was all choice stuff. Carlson had assembled a connoisseur's selection of the world's best secrets.

How had he done it? I could understand the presence of so many files from the American intelligence agencies—Carlson had direct access to all of it. He had obviously worked out a safe and efficient way to make copies of what he wanted and move them up here.

The material from sources outside the United States required more sophisticated strategies. Much of it would have had to have been bought, stolen or traded.

His hoard of secrets had put Carlson in a position to coerce or blackmail an extraordinarily large number of people and governments. Did Steckler or Westerly—or any of the other members of the Night Watch—know the extent of this?

How Carlson must have reveled in the unique power he possessed. And it had finally cost him his life. His greed for control was his vulnerability. He had simply gone too far.

I shivered. I was appalled by what the man had done. It was arrogance on a breathtaking scale—a folly of grandeur, of moral certitude—a self-righteous absolutism one associated only with the monarchs and dictators of the past.

Carlson had used his unique position to aggrandize a rare and unlimited form of raw power—power unshackled from the web of debilitating relationships, dependencies and debts that those who ruled the world faced every day. It was the power to determine the course of great events, the power to reward and enrich loyal allies and friends and bring ruin down on one's enemies. The power to influence, to shape, to prevail. And with that extraordinary power was attached absolutely no corresponding accountability or responsibility. As long as the world remained ignorant, only he alone was judge of the moral rightness of his actions. Carlson had taken on the power of a god.

Despite my shock, I also felt a morbid kind of kinship with the dead director. My own greed, my own compulsion, differed from his in many ways, but I coveted the same secrets, after all, and sought to put them to use to bring down those I had decided were worthy targets of my mistrust or moral outrage. Carlson had destroyed his villains in the dark of the night. I preferred to drag mine out in the sunlight and inflame the mob against them.

I heard Mara's footsteps on the metal stairs. She stopped inside the doorway. "Find what you need?"

I threw up my hands in a gesture of helplessness. "I haven't had time to go through even half of the drawers."

"Is it necessary?"

"The stuff here is unbelievable."

Mara affected not to be interested. "We have to leave. It's after nine."

"Who did all the clerical work?" I asked.

Mara's brows furrowed in impatient annoyance. "What clerical work?"

"These files are meticulously maintained and pretty up-to-date. And there are thousands of them. Somebody has been pretty busy."

"My father."

"How could he have found the time?"

"He brought assistants with him sometimes."

"No, he didn't. You said—and I believe you—that you and he were the only ones who even knew this bunker was here. If you don't count the French Canadians who built it and went back to Quebec thinking they'd just installed a bomb shelter for a wacky American millionaire."

Mara glanced at her watch. "Can we talk about this on the way?"

"Was it you?"

Mara heaved an enormous sigh of resignation. "Yes, damn it, it was me."

"You lied to me, then."

"Yes, I lied to you. Again. I'm sorry."

"Then you know everything that's here. You're in this business up to your eyeballs."

"I just filed the stuff. I didn't use it."

If it hadn't been for the almost giddy euphoria I felt from wallowing in the forbidden secrets of Carlson's files, I would have been furious at her deceptions. Instead, I just laid out the rest of my accusations in the matter-of-fact voice of someone reviewing the obvious:

"You've been living and working here for years, then, haven't you? That's why no one knows about you. And that's why you have your own plane. So you can commute back and forth to the University of Maine. Orono's just a short ride from the Bangor airport."

Mara ignored my words and changed the subject. "I've got an idea," she said, her tone suddenly blithe and cheerful. "Why don't you just stay here. I'll come back tomorrow. By then you'll have had a chance to go through everything. When I get back you can help me destroy the files."

Her suggestion caught me off guard. "All right," I said. "That's a good idea. . . ."

"Can I trust you not to sneak off with anything?"

"Where can I sneak off to?"

"True." Mara checked her watch again. "I can't wait another minute. Can you turn the generator on and off all right?"

"I'll manage."

"There's no telephone here, you know. If something happens, the only way you can get to the mainland is by boat. There's one down at the dock. Could you operate it in an emergency?"

"If necessary."

"Good. Okay, then. I'm sorry, Johnny. I really do want to be honest with you."

"We'll straighten it out when you get back."

"Okay." She started toward the door.

"Wait a minute."

She turned.

I pointed at the file cabinets. "Steckler wants all this, right? This is what he's after."

"I suppose."

"But he doesn't know where it is?"

"No."

"Don't you think he'll be after you, then?"

She laughed. "He doesn't even know what I look like. He thinks I'm living in Switzerland somewhere. He hardly knows I exist."

"You don't think he might expect to find you at the funeral?"

"I'm a big girl, Johnny. I can take care of myself."

"Why don't you just stay here with me?"

"I'd sort of like to make my father's funeral."

"Of course. I'm sorry."

"I'll be staying at our house in Georgetown."

"Alone?"

"There's a live-in couple—George and his wife, Tessa. They'll be there."

"And tomorrow?"

"I'll fly back to Boston in the morning. I'll be in Bangor by noon. Back out here by one. That okay?"

"I guess."

"Don't worry about me."

"If you say so."

Mara laughed. "You're not worried about me a bit. All you can think about is these files. You're addicted to secrets, Johnny. Be careful. I don't want you to O.D. on them."

Mara clutched my shirt in her fist and pulled me to her. She flicked her tongue mischievously across my ear and then turned and disappeared out the door. I listened to her footfalls down the corridor and up the steel rungs of the stairway.

There goes the world's least grief-stricken daughter, I thought. Grief-stricken: hell, she wasn't even depressed. Why was she bothering to attend the funeral? Appearances, I supposed.

Andrew Carlson must have been even more of a bastard than Tracy had made him out to be. And yet Mara had spoken so lovingly of him.

You just couldn't trust people these days.

24

THE SHOWROOM

I climbed the steps from the bunker and stood in the shade under the raised floor of the icehouse to watch Mara take off.

She gunned the little Cessna down the strip and into the air with the insolent casualness of a teenager burning rubber out of a parking lot. Low out over the ocean she banked, gained altitude and flew back over the island, headed north toward the mainland. She waggled her wings a few times in a little good-bye wave. I smiled, then bit my lip to hold back an emotional rush. She was a big girl, as she had said. She could take care of herself at least as well as I could take care of myself. Probably better.

The morning sun flashed off the plane's windows. In a couple of minutes the Cessna became a fading silver speck in a brilliant blue sky, and I could no longer follow it with my eye.

I went back down into the bunker.

On my way back along the corridor I paused by the mysterious closed door. The lock was a modern tumbler affair—nothing esoteric, but nothing I could break into, either.

I had seen a set of keys on the desk in the file room. I retrieved them and tried them in the lock. They didn't fit. I remembered that there was a board with keys on it hanging at the top of the cellar stairs back at the lodge.

I bent down for a closer look at the lock. It was a Yale. I went back to the lodge, took the board of keys out and sifted through them. One Yale key.

I rushed back to the bunker with the Yale key hot in my hand and pushed it into the lock. It slid in halfway and then stuck. I fiddled with it for several minutes, twisting the knob furiously with one hand while trying to jam the key home with the other. I couldn't force it into the lock.

Patience, I whispered. Maybe the key that fit was not a Yale, but a duplicate cut from a blank.

I trudged back to the house a second time and returned with the entire board of keys. I worked up a sweat trying all twenty-five of them. None fit the door.

In frustration, I pounded on the door with the bottom of my fist. It popped open.

My jaw dropped.

The lock had been set, but whoever had done it had not pulled the door tightly closed. The spring bolt had not clicked into place. I flipped the bolt to its unlocked position, found a light switch just inside the door on my right and turned it on.

Two bright banks of fluorescents flickered on to reveal another subterranean chamber about the size of the file room. But instead of file cabinets these walls were lined with open shelves extending to the ceiling. A long workbench ran down the center. A couple of adjustable stools were pushed against the work table just in front of me. Screwdrivers, pliers, hammers and other common shop tools littered the bench.

It looked like a stockroom—shelves crammed with parts, and a workbench to make minor repairs.

I walked down along one side to see what kind of stock was on the shelves. The first item I encountered was a hand grenade. Under it a small printed card provided some details:

M-57 fragmentation hand grenade. In current service, US Army, Marines. Similar type: M-26A2.
Body: sheet steel with a notched fragmentation coil.
Charge: 5.5 oz. Composition B, tetryl pellets.
Fuze: M-217 electrical impact, with one-second delay.
Weight: 1 lb.
Kill range: 18 yards.
Packed 30 to a box.
Delivery: three wks.
Price: $6.50 ea. $180 per box.

The M-57 was the first in a whole shelf of various models of grenades, all lined in a neat row—the M-34, the M-61, the M-67, the M-68, the Mk-2, the Mk3A2, the AN/M-8, the ABC/M-25A1 and something called a ring aerofoil grenade. Some were fragmentation, some smoke, some gas, some concussion. Under each was a descriptive card, with the price.

The shelf immediately under the grenades contained three styles of grenade launchers—the M-79, M-203, and Xm-174—along with a sampling of the 40mm grenades they fired. Under each was a descriptive card with specs and prices.

Every shelf in the room was similarly stacked with sample weapons of the widest variety—antitank and antipersonnel mines, revolvers, automatic pistols, rifles, assault guns, machine guns, submachine guns, mortars and recoilless rifles.

One shelf contained displays of color photographs of some of the items too large to fit on the shelves—or indeed to fit in the room. These included a variety of items from bombs and guided missiles to aircraft armament systems to helicopters and fighter planes.

In one corner, propped on top of a large suitcase-sized crate, was a device that looked like a cross between a bazooka and a recoilless rifle. I bent down to read the card Scotch-taped to the crate:

FIM-92A Stinger missile (alternate).
Shoulder-fired from its own sealed disposable transport container and launch tube.
Dual stage solid-propellant motor.
Maximum range: 6,000 yards.

Guidance: optical tracking sight with laser designator. Resistant to
ECM jamming.
Weight: 34.5 lb.
Delivery: 3–4 wks.
Price: $75,000 ea.

I shook my head in astonishment. The one-man portable Stinger
was one of the most sophisticated—and potent—weapons in the
U.S. arsenal. The missile was so deadly, in fact, that the United
States supposedly restricted its availability to NATO and other
allies. The Stinger was an extraordinary equalizer, giving the individual foot soldier or terrorist the edge against a multimillion-
dollar fighter-bomber aircraft. It was a Sword Excalibur, a David's
slingshot, a true giant-killer. And here was a floor sample, fresh
from its packing crate, available for the price of a luxury car.

In the drawers of a small desk in the back I found price lists,
mailing lists, currency conversion charts, shipping information, and
stacks of blank documents and forms, like end-user certificates,
necessary for the purchase and international shipment of any U.S.
military ordnance.

There were also several loose-leaf binders containing a listing
of other armaments available for purchase, complete with photos,
specs, performance characteristics, prices in different currencies,
current availability and shipping time.

For example, a single Hughes AH-64 advanced attack helicopter, loaded with dozens of advanced electronic systems and a choice
of three armament configurations—either a 30mm chain gun and
four M-200 rocket pods with seventy-six 2.75″ rockets; or sixteen
Hellfire laser-seeking antitank missiles and two M-158 rocket pods
with fourteen 2.75″ rockets; or sixteen TOW antitank missiles—
would set the buyer back a stiff $7 million and change. Supplies
were very limited and delivery time was six months to a year.

M-113A1 armored personnel carriers were available for just over
a hundred thousand dollars apiece.

An XM-1 Abrams tank could be had for $2.6 million.

M-19 60mm mortars were $18,000 apiece.

About the only things not listed were large navy vessels and
nuclear weapons.

All the ordnance was of U.S. manufacture. And beyond the

single samples of smaller items like pistols and hand grenades, none of them was stocked in this room. The supplies were warehoused and shipped from other locations. The billing and bookkeeping was also done at other locations. This was just a showroom—a place to bring a prospective buyer who wanted a safe and private place to look at some sample merchandise. It was a very specialized catalogue store for a very select clientele.

Now I understood the full purpose and meaning of the landing strip out in the field above me, with its unusually long and well-maintained runway and night landing lights. Large private jets could fly in and out freely, day or night. And since the island was well off the U.S. coast, it was even possible that planes could come from abroad without being picked up by U.S. coastal radar and without having to submit to U.S. customs and immigration.

The island was a perfect spot from which to operate any number of clandestine activities, when you thought about it. And if the weather was bad, the house had many bedrooms. Guests could be accommodated for days—weeks—in complete isolation and privacy.

Carlson had been an arms merchant for years, long before he became head of the CIA. So this storeroom just represented a continuation of an old line of trade. And since the weapons were all American-made, his access to them, through government and Pentagon channels, would be easy and well protected. The small items he probably bought outright and retailed at a high markup. For the big-ticket purchases, he simply acted as an independent agent for the U.S. government, taking a commission on each sale.

I lingered in the room a while longer, picking up weapons at random and putting them back. The convenience of this arrangement was obvious. By being able to obtain and sell such a staggering array of ordnance, Carlson could not only make great amounts of money, he could wield strong influence among the many groups and nations seeking them—particularly those forbidden by U.S. government law to purchase them. For the government, Carlson served as a cutout, a middleman who provided a convenient way for it to get around its own laws and sell more weapons.

I turned out the light, closed the door and returned to the file room, my admiration for Andrew Carlson's extraordinary achievement still growing.

I paced around, trying to decide on a sensible plan of attack. I felt an odd tension in the presence of all this material. I was jittery, pumped full of adrenaline. This was a forbidden zone. Most of the material in these files was highly classified. Only a handful of people in high government positions would ever have been permitted to see it. And none of it, of course, was supposed to be here, hidden underground in an island off the Maine coast.

And what was I going to do with it? I felt like a grave robber who had broken into the tomb of an Egyptian king. I was surrounded with wealth beyond my dreams, but it was also beyond my ability to cope with it in any practical manner. I could not possibly remove it all. Or even a fraction of it. And why was I even thinking of doing such a thing? Especially in the face of my promise to Mara that I would help her destroy the material. And indeed, what use did I have for it if I intended to keep my promise to the late Andrew Carlson?

All I needed, after all, was just a handful of bargaining chips—a few documents whose publication would acutely embarrass the present administration or so threaten to compromise its clandestine activities somewhere that the new DCI at Langley would race to the phone to tell the Justice Department to drop its case. I had already seen any number of files that would suffice.

Despite Carlson's assurances, going to the CIA with these so-called bargaining chips would be an extremely dangerous maneuver. If I produced authentic secret documents, I would be incriminating myself utterly—waving before one branch of the government the very evidence another branch could use to clinch an espionage case against me. I would have to hit them hard—threaten to wreak utter havoc. I would have to convince them they had no option but to back off. And I would have to do it in such a way that they would not be able to double-cross me. The thought of that eventual confrontation made me shiver.

But could I let all the rest of this treasure just go to waste? The opportunities represented here for a journalist were colossal, mind-boggling. The information in the files was priceless, unique, beyond wealth.

No wonder Steckler coveted them. The files represented extraordinary leverage over leaders and nations. The ability to shape events on a worldwide scale. The power to change things. I certainly didn't want Steckler to get them. But I didn't want to see them destroyed, either.

The more I thought about it, the more paralyzed I was to act. I just kept circling the room, working myself into a frenzy of frustration and indecision.

I left the bunker and roamed around the island for a while, trying to decide what to do.

Walking near the shoreline, I came to the dock down below the lodge. It was a substantial pier, about ten feet wide and thirty feet long, built in a protected cove of deep water. It offered space to berth four boats. There was only one tied up there at the moment: a fairly weathered twenty-seven-foot cabin cruiser.

How many file cabinets' worth could be crammed aboard the boat? Six? ten? How many trips would it take to remove all the files and relocate them elsewhere—say in a bank vault?

Four or five? A dozen?

Not very practical. There was, in truth, no easy or fast way to remove the documents and hide them somewhere else. The obstacles were formidable, and time was far too short.

If only I could persuade Mara to leave them right where they were. That seemed like the only workable possibility for saving them. At the moment, we were the only two people alive who knew the documents were here.

But Mara probably wouldn't cooperate.

The most realistic alternative for me was to grab an armful of the most useful ones and run with them. Say the hell with the rest. Let Mara destroy them. Let Steckler have them. Let whatever happens happen. Devil take the hindmost.

That's what I should do. But I couldn't persuade myself. To take a few papers from this incredible hoard was to risk missing the most important. It would be like grabbing a handful of gold coins from a sunken treasure while overlooking the jewel-studded bishop's crosses or Aztec sun wheels.

What the hell could I do? Sit down there in the bunker for the rest of the day taking notes?

It was maddening. What I needed was a way to transfer the whole library of secret documents onto microfilm. I actually spent about fifteen minutes wondering if there were some way to do this. I fantasized bringing in a planeload of technicians and equipment and working them around the clock until they had reduced the entire pile of papers to a couple of rolls of microfilm.

All problems have solutions. That's what a math professor in college used to tell us.

But I was one man, alone, and I had only a few hours. I had to accept the inevitable. There was no way. I got up and started back toward the bunker.

And then I thought of a way.

25

UNEXPECTED COMPANY

I returned to the dock and climbed aboard the cabin cruiser. The water was calm and the air clear. No bad weather in sight. I could easily make out the low outline of distant hills on the mainland to the north.

I found the map locker inside the cabin, and the map for this section of the Maine coastline. The nearest populated area appeared to be a little hamlet called Seawall, not far from the Bass Harbor Head lighthouse, about fifteen miles across the water. I should be able to get over there, find a phone, make the call, do my errands and be back in a couple of hours.

I went back to the tack room in the stable and twisted the brass hook counterclockwise a full turn. From the doorway I watched the icehouse settle back onto its cement foundation with a barely audible rumble.

Back at the boat I quickly went through the cabin and all the compartments, fore and aft. Everything necessary was on board: two anchors, flares, life jackets, a fire extinguisher, an emergency flag, a box of tools, a flashlight, a depth finder and all the needed charts.

A folded-up newspaper lay on one of the bunks. I picked it up and opened it. It was *The Wall Street Journal*. The date on it was May 18—the day before yesterday.

Someone had used the boat only two days ago. I puzzled over this. Mara had mentioned a caretaker, Orson Price, who regularly came out to check on the place. But if he had brought the boat out, how did he get back?

I supposed the boat might have been on the mainland for repairs, and Price might have towed it back out behind his own boat. I doubted that Orson Price read *The Wall Street Journal*, though. Maybe he had company. Maybe he had a stockbroker son paying him a visit.

The hell with it. I wasn't going to get paranoid about it. I had too much to do.

The cruiser was a twin engine, and the fuel tanks were three-quarters full. I found the switch on the control console for the blower and flipped it on. The exhaust fans in the engine compartment immediately started whirring, sucking any gasoline fumes out of the hold.

I started the engines, cast off the lines and eased the twin screws into forward gear. I cleared the dock and headed out into the open water, holding my breath. I was familiar with this kind of craft from the summers during college I had spent working at a boatyard on the New Jersey shore. But that was quite a few years ago, and every boat had its own personality. I was also venturing out into unfamiliar waters. I proceeded cautiously.

Too cautiously. I followed the compass on a north-northeast heading at so slow a crawl that it wasn't until I had been out in the water for twenty minutes that I noticed that the currents had actually carried me farther away from the mainland. I wasn't even making headway. I was drifting out to sea.

I gave the engines some throttle.

It took me about thirty minutes to reach the mainland. I hovered about two hundred feet offshore, dodging sailboats and other craft, looking for something resembling the town of Seawall—or any town.

I hailed a fisherman checking his lobster pots from a Boston Whaler. He pulled alongside and gave me directions. Two miles farther along the shore I found a cluster of buildings high up on a bluff, and a substantial boat landing down on the water.

Fortunately only one old man was at the landing to witness my incompetent maneuverings around the dock. He sat on a canvas folding chair watching me as I backed and turned and bucked and stalled, several times barely avoiding a head-on collision with the pilings.

Finally, growing bored with the embarrassing spectacle I was making, he ambled down to the edge of the dock, caught the line I threw him, secured it and helped me pull the boat alongside and secure the other lines.

I locked the console and the cabin and stuck the keys in my pocket.

"You're from away, ain't ya?" he said, in a rich Down East accent.

I jumped down onto the dock. "Yeah. Away."

"I could tell," he said.

"I guess you could."

He nodded. "I'd a helped you soonah. But you didn't ahhsk."

"Well, let me ask you this. Where's the nearest phone?"

"Where you callin'?"

"New York. What difference does that make?"

"Well, Arnie Toyvo—he's the nearest—but he won't let any-body make long-distance calls."

"I'll call collect. Or pay him."

"Won't make any difference to Arnie. He thinks long-distance calls wear the phone out."

"Where's the next nearest phone, then?"

"That'd be Mrs. Husey's. She lives in that gray cottage over theyah." The old-timer pointed at a tiny house up the hill behind the dock.

"Thanks," I said. I started toward it.

"She's not home," he said.

"Where is she?"

"She's down to Augusta. Vis'tin' her daughtah."

I regarded the old man through narrowed eyes. He was getting a little too much mileage out of this encounter.

"Where's the nearest phone where I can make a long-distance call to New York?" I asked carefully. "Right now?"

The old man scratched his neck. "I guess your best bet would be down to Earl's Cash 'n' Carry. It's hahhf a mile. Turn right at the top of the rise heah. He's got a pay phone."

I started up the hill again.

"Might be out of order," I heard the old man say behind me. "Was last week. . . . Don't say I didn't warn you."

The phone at Earl's Cash 'n' Carry was not out of order. I got Frank Chin on the third ring.

"Where are you, Johnny?"

"Never mind. I have a question for you. Imagine a room full of documents. Thousands of them. If you piled them in one pile it'd probably be thirty feet high. I don't have the time or the means to remove them. But I need the information on them in some form I can take with me. I've got only about a day to get it. Here's what I have in mind. . . ."

I outlined my plan and asked if he thought it would work. He said it would.

"Will the stuff be legible?" I asked.

"Sure. No problem." He gave me a few technical suggestions. "Colonel Zimmer asked about you," he said.

"What did he want to know?"

"I guess he was wondering if you were still alive. You know— after what happened to Carlson. Can I tell him you're okay?"

"Sure."

"You have his number?"

"I guess so, why?"

"He was afraid you'd lost his number."

"Tell him I don't need his help, thank God. At least not yet."

"I'll tell him."

"See you, Frank."

A young kid with yellow hair pulled a beat-up old Chevy pickup in to Earl's Cash 'n' Carry for gas. I asked him if he'd drive me to Bar Harbor, the nearest town of any size.

He looked at me with an expression of openmouthed astonishment. "That's twenty miles away," he said.

I wondered if he was related to the old man on the dock. "Would fifty bucks cover it? Round trip?"

The kid smiled like it was Christmas morning. "Cover it? Hell yes. I'll take you all the way to Portland for that."

"Bar Harbor is far enough."

He reached across and unlatched the passenger-side door. It shuddered open with a jarring, rust-bound squeal. "Hop in."

I arrived back at the island by two-thirty that afternoon, carrying a big cardboard box of supplies under my arms and a big new dent in my Visa card credit line.

I started the underground generator up again, opened a bottle of beer, and unpacked my box in the kitchen: two days' copies of the *New York Times*, three large bottles of Diet Coke, three bags of Cape Cod potato chips, a floodlight with a collapsible stand, four high-resolution videotapes, a camera tripod, and a $1,200 camcorder, complete with case, rechargeable battery and close-up lens.

After unpacking the camcorder I spent about half an hour familiarizing myself with its operation. Then I fetched another beer and thumbed through the newspapers.

There was a long article about Andrew Carlson. The official word, completely accepted by the press and the government, was that he had died of natural causes. The president was quoted as saying that he had narrowed down his potential choices of a successor to head the CIA, and would announce his nomination sometime in the next few days. The article named three people believed to be under consideration. One was a Midwestern businessman, one was a former division head at the National Security Agency, the other a retired Army intelligence officer. I had never heard of any of them.

I closed the paper, packed all the gear back in the cardboard box and took it down into the bunker and set it up. I anchored the camera on the tripod and adjusted it so it was aimed directly down toward the surface of the big table in the center of the room. I set up the floodlight beside it, and placed a file open on the table beneath it.

With the close-up lens, the camera was able to focus on the page with surprising sharpness. I could even read the print through the tiny built-in monitor viewfinder.

I adjusted the camcorder to record at its slowest speed, then sat down and started turning the pages of the file rapidly. Frank Chin had assured me that all I needed was a split-second steady exposure for each page—just enough to capture it on at least one frame. That frame could later be frozen on a viewer and copied, using special equipment.

Since one tape would record for six hours, I could copy all the documents I was physically able to place in front of the camcorder in that time. I estimated I could do at least one every two seconds. That was thirty a minute, eighteen hundred an hour. A six-hour tape, therefore, would hold 10,800 documents. Two tapes, 21,600 documents. Allowing some time for moving and stacking documents, and for taking short breaks, I estimated I could copy twenty thousand documents in twelve hours. If I had the time—and the stamina—I would start a third tape. Somewhere between twenty thousand and thirty thousand I guessed I would probably exhaust the supply of documents.

It was six P.M. now. Mara would return in about nineteen hours. If I worked through the night I could do it—I could copy everything.

I opened a bag of potato chips and a bottle of Diet Coke. I removed the contents of the top drawer of the first file cabinet and stacked them neatly on one side of the table. I took a folder from the top of the stack, opened it and slid it under the lens, checked that the camcorder was registering it in focus, and started recording.

The taping went slowly at first. I spent too much time pulling stacks of documents from the file cabinets, arranging them in neat piles on the table before I put them under the camcorder lens, and returning the stacks of videotaped documents to the file cabinets when there was no more space on the table.

It wasn't really necessary to refile the documents, I decided. So I began dumping the taped files in hasty piles on the floor. That speeded things up. I also became more adept at turning pages.

Gradually, I fell into a rhythm. Stack after stack of documents I pulled from the file cabinets, slapped on the table, and fed, page by page, under the camcorder lens. The machine whirred quietly. It was the only sound in the bunker. The air felt stale and humid. I was quickly covered with sweat from the exertion. I stripped down to my undershirt and used my shirt to mop the sweat out of my eyes.

Sometimes something caught my attention on a page I was copying and I would pause to take a closer look. The material continued to stun me. I kept getting these tremendous surges of adrenaline every time I thought about what I was doing. My hands sometimes trembled so much I was forced to stop and take a few minutes to settle myself down.

At midnight I stopped the camcorder to change tapes. I had videotaped the contents of just over twelve full file drawers. Thirty-two drawers remained. I opened the second bottle of Diet Coke and another bag of potato chips. I was sorry I had bought the chips. They were greasy and I had to wipe my fingers frequently to avoid smearing the documents.

The contents of one cabinet I didn't have to copy. All four drawers were stuffed with cash. The top two were filled with dollars—neat stacks of wrapped and tallied bills in denominations of tens, twenties and hundreds. The third drawer down contained varying amounts of mixed currencies—Japanese yen, English pounds sterling, German marks, French francs, Swiss francs, Spanish pesetas, Italian lire, Austrian schillings, Greek drachmas, Portuguese escudos, Pakistani and Indian rupees, Finnish markkaa, Lebanese pounds, Jordanian and Kuwaiti dinars, Saudi Arabian riyals, Swedish kronor, Israeli shekels, Turkish liras—a little bit of everything.

The bottom drawer of the cabinet contained dozens of forged passports, visas and other ID materials in many nationalities. There were also folders containing entire false identities, from birth certificate, passport, driver's license and credit cards to family photographs and personal letters.

I brought the camcorder over to the file cabinet and videotaped the stacks of currencies in the opened drawers and a sampling of some of the forged materials.

By six in the morning I had filled the second videotape. I stopped the camcorder and removed the cassette. The effects of twelve straight hours of shifting documents and turning pages were beginning to tell on me. My eyes were swimming, my head ached, my hands were sore and the muscles in my forearms were beginning to cramp.

I counted the file drawers remaining: Sixteen. At the rate I was covering them, the third tape would get twelve, leaving four undone. I had a fourth tape. If I could stretch myself to go another eight hours, I could get everything. Or damned close. It would probably take me until two in the afternoon. Mara was due in at one, but there was certainly a chance she would be late.

I needed fresh air. I climbed out of the bunker and took a walk back to the lodge to stretch my legs.

I walked around to the stone terrace off the living room to admire the view. The sky was clear, soft. On the mainland, tiny points of light still winked in the hazy predawn shadows. A warm breeze, heady with the briny smells of the sea, was whispering in from the south. Several miles out, in the broad swath of pale light cast across the water by the fading moon, I could see the running lights of a ship—a fishing trawler or a pleasure yacht—moving down the coast. The eastern horizon glowed red with the new day.

I felt a strong desire to stretch out on one of the terrace chaises with a vodka and tonic, watch the sun rise and then sleep for twenty hours.

Someone laughed.

The sound was distant, but loud and sharp. It seemed to have come from out on the meadows beyond the landing strip.

Goose bumps popped out on my flesh. I held my breath and listened, but I didn't hear the sound again. I was sure it was a human laugh I had heard, but I also had to accept that my overwrought and overworked senses might well be playing tricks on me.

There was an owl whose hoot sounded quite a bit like a laugh. Perhaps that was all it was. I listened a few minutes more. I heard only the breeze ruffling the tall grasses.

I returned to the bunker for the final push. I opened the last bottle of Diet Coke and took a long drink, counting on the caffeine to give me a lift. I turned the camcorder back on, slid a file under it and started turning pages.

By noontime I had filled a third videotape.

One cabinet remained to be copied. I popped my last tape into the camera. I felt utterly punch-drunk. My fingers were numb and I was having a hard time coordinating them. I kept fumbling the documents and knocking folders onto the floor.

I videotaped the last document in the last folder at exactly 12:53 P.M. I turned off the camcorder and extracted the fourth cassette. The equipment had performed flawlessly for over eighteen hours of nearly continuous operation. That was more than I could say for myself. I was ready to drop.

The bunker was hot, even with the exhaust fan going. It reeked of paper chemicals, sweat and potato chips and looked like the collection point for a Boy Scout paper drive. The floor was buried under dozens of haphazardly stacked and toppling piles of documents.

All that remained was to put the whole mess to the torch. For that pleasure, I would await the return of Mara Carlson.

I placed my four videocassettes in a clear plastic freezer container I had purchased for the purpose and secured the airtight lid. I wrapped the container six times around with packing tape, pushed it into a waterproof bag, and sealed the bag shut.

I hefted the resulting package in my hand. It weighed a couple of pounds and was about the size of a clunky clock radio.

Even through my fatigue I felt a giddy thrill of satisfaction. No one, I thought, not even the world's most advanced nuclear scientists, had ever compressed so much explosive power into so compact a space. All that remained was to get it off the island and into a safe place before anyone knew I had it.

I staggered up the steps and stood under the shadow of the icehouse, blinking in the glare of the midday sun. Mara's Cessna was not on the landing strip. I dragged myself to the stable to lower the icehouse back into place over the concrete foundation, then plodded back to the lodge, the plastic freezer container squeezed tightly under my arm.

In the kitchen I mixed myself that long-awaited vodka and tonic, took it out on the terrace and settled into a chaise to wait for Mara.

By one-thirty I had consumed two vodka and tonics. Mara's plane had yet to appear. I wasn't especially worried. Under the circumstances, I would have been surprised if she had returned exactly when she had promised.

Still, I kept looking north, across the island, hoping to catch sight of her little Skyhawk winging in from Bangor. I stared at the empty sky for minutes at a stretch. My heart speeded up once when I caught a glint of sunlight off some wings. But the plane circled back north and quickly disappeared.

It required great concentration to keep my eyes open. I knew I should lug myself upstairs and go to sleep, but I didn't want to miss her.

Predictably, I fell asleep on the chaise.

When I woke the sun was low in the sky. I sat up, groggy and stiff, and stretched my arms. My glasses had fallen off. I fumbled around underneath the chaise with one hand until I found them. I slipped them on and looked at my watch: five-thirty in the afternoon.

Still no plane on the landing strip. She was four hours overdue. Not serious, I told myself. But I was beginning to feel uneasy.

I swung around and pushed myself to my feet. I picked up my empty glass and the plastic container of videotapes from the glass table next to the chaise and went inside.

In the kitchen I removed a frozen dinner from the refrigerator freezer and set it out on the counter to thaw. I thought better of it, went back to the refrigerator and withdrew a second frozen dinner.

It would be dark in an hour. If Mara wasn't here by then, I wouldn't see her until the morning. The landing strip had lights, but she knew I wouldn't know how to turn them on, and I doubted that she'd fly after dark anyway.

I didn't like the idea of spending the night here alone. Now that I had videotaped the documents, I wanted to get away.

I thought of leaving in the boat. I could make the mainland before dark. Why shouldn't I? I had absolutely no reason to hang around. From the mainland I could call the Carlson house in Georgetown and find out if Mara was all right. If she was still there, I could meet her in Bangor. Or New York. And I could get my videotapes stored in a secure place. That was what mattered most.

I heard a sharp scraping noise followed by a solid thud. It came from the dining room. It sounded as if something soft and heavy had hit the floor.

Pulse racing, I dashed through the pantry and into the dining room. I stopped abruptly in the doorway and tried to come to terms with what I saw in front of me.

The room was occupied.

Men were sitting around the table. Five of them.

Two were leaning back in their chairs; one was slumped forward, his head resting in his arms.

And one man had fallen from his chair. He was lying on the floor in a twisted position. He made no effort to get up.

The man at the head of the table was older than the others. He sat with one arm hooked over the back of his chair, the other resting on the tabletop. His head lolled to the side, as if he were either very drunk or too tired to hold it upright. His eyes were focused directly at me. He looked terrifyingly familiar.

I felt unable to move or breathe.

It was Andrew Carlson.

26

ESCAPE

I thought I was hallucinating.

It was the only way I could at first accept the incredible tableau assaulting my eyes.

Fatigue, stress, fear. They had finally compromised my senses. I was seeing things.

I remained in the doorway, my hands braced hard against the jambs, opening and shutting my eyes, waiting for the images of the five men at the dining-room table to fade.

They didn't fade. And they didn't move, either.

Except for Carlson, the men were wearing military-style combat fatigues with a camouflage design. There were powerful smells of cordite and blood in the room.

I walked slowly around the table, stepping over the man on the floor. I was trembling violently. My pulse hammered in my ears so hard it hurt.

At the back of Carlson's chair I paused. I examined his hand, stretched out, palm down, on the table. His fingernails were purplish-black and swollen. That didn't seem possible. I bent closer. The fingernails were gone. I was looking at pulpy flesh. The back of the hand was covered with round, cratered black marks, like cigarette burns. They were on his face as well—around his eyes and his mouth.

He had been tortured.

It didn't make any sense. None of it made any sense at all.

I looked down the table. Two of the faces I recognized. There was Carlson's driver, Tony, who had maneuvered us out of trouble so brilliantly in Central Park; and there was the man who had ridden up front with him, the one with the Uzi. Squint, they called him.

The other two I thought were probably the ones I had encountered guarding Carlson's room in the hospital when I went to see him.

Carlson's personal bodyguards.

I walked around the table again. Each man had a bullet hole in the back of his neck. The man on the floor lay twisted over on his back. I guessed that if I turned him over I would find he also had a bullet hole in his neck.

There was blood on the floor. A couple of thin trails of it led across the rug and out the door. It appeared that they had been shot and then dragged in here.

When?

When I was down in the bunker? I wouldn't have heard the shots from there. Or it could have been earlier, when I was off the island buying the camcorder.

When had I last looked in the dining room? Not since Mara and I ate our dinner here during the storm.

I went back into the kitchen. The house was still. The generator below made the only sound, throbbing in the earth like Poe's telltale heart.

I ran out onto the terrace. I stood and listened. A breeze was stirring the needles in the big pine tree that shaded the north end of the terrace.

Whoever had done this must still be here.

I had to get off the island.

I had to warn Mara.

In the living room I grabbed my overnight bag, shoved the container with the videotapes inside with my clothes, zipped it up and slung it over my shoulder and headed out the front door.

The possibility of ending up trapped inside the lodge with those five corpses was too nightmarish to contemplate. I felt better out in the open, exposed as I knew I was.

I ran along by the stables, then dashed out onto the long, sloping field that led down to the icehouse and to the boat dock beyond. I ducked into the stand of evergreen bushes by the icehouse to catch my breath. The evergreens, mostly pines, were dense and low-growing, and offered a good hiding place. And from this vantage point I had a view of the front door of the lodge, part of the stables, the landing strip and the long meadow to the north. I could also see the shoreline by the boat dock about a hundred feet down to my left.

The sun was just touching the rim of the ocean. The wind was picking up. It would be dark in half an hour. I should wait right here until then. I crouched down in the bushes, my eyes scanning back and forth from the landing strip to the lodge to the dock.

The shoreline around the dock was rough and uneven. A steep sloping jumble of kelp-covered rocks bumped down to the water. Foot-high waves slapped gently in among the rocks and slowly retreated, trailing a froth of white foam across a short beach of sand exposed by the low tide. A large gull was perched on one of the dock pilings, looking out to sea.

The gull spread its wings and lifted off suddenly, its shrill cry piercing the afternoon dusk.

That was when I saw him.

He was walking south along the water's edge, about three hundred feet away, headed toward the dock.

He was outfitted in black—black knit cap, black pants and sneakers, and a black sweater with leather patches over the elbows and shoulders. A short-barreled automatic weapon hung from his shoulder on a long strap. His face was painted with cork or something similar. The effect was to exaggerate the size of his eyes and lips, like those of an old-time vaudevillian in blackface.

He moved quickly along the shore, threading his way among the rocks and debris with an agile, effortless stride.

I watched him, too paralyzed with terror to draw a breath.

When he was about fifty feet from the dock, he stopped, waded out a few feet into the water and knelt down.

He seemed to be lifting stones from the bottom and tossing them aside. An inflated rubber raft, about eight feet long and four feet wide, popped out of the water. He hauled it back in among the rocks, and from some compartment in the raft withdrew a couple of containers and rested them on a flat boulder.

I crouched there by the icehouse for what seemed like a very long time, inhaling and exhaling with measured effort, my hands pouring sweat onto the strap of my overnight bag, while the figure in black collected more containers from the raft.

He hauled the raft back out into the water and weighted it down with stones again. When he was satisfied with its placement, he picked up the containers and set off along the shore, back in the direction he had come.

Was he alone? I doubted it. The massacre of Carlson and his men must have required a team. The raft looked big enough for four. And there could be other rafts.

I followed him with my eyes as he retreated north along the shore. About a hundred yards up, there was a small cove, and he disappeared from sight. A few seconds later he reappeared, hopping from rock to rock near the water's edge.

After another fifty yards, he turned in from the shore and disappeared again behind a broad, grass-covered hillock. I waited for him to emerge on the other side, but he didn't. A while later I thought I heard voices from behind the rise.

I waited until dark. Or as dark as it was going to get. The sky was cloudless and a full moon was rising off the water to the east.

I crawled out of my hiding place and worked my way slowly toward the hillock, jogging in a crouch, hugging the shadows of the big rocks along the shoreline. The voices grew louder. I could hear them easily over the hissing surf and the dead grass stalks agitated by the wind.

Near the top of the small hill I lowered myself into the grass and crawled the last twenty feet to the crest.

Directly below and in front of me I counted four men. All were clad in black, like ninja. One was opening the containers from the raft. I caught a flash of aluminum foil. Freeze-dried rations. Another was building a fire. He had arranged a little pile of sticks on top of some dried grass, and was in the process of lighting it. It smoked briefly, then caught. The other two were sitting against the rocks. One was sifting sand lazily through his fingers, the other had pulled a cap over his face and seemed to be napping.

Behind them, partly hidden by a stand of scrub brush, was a tent they had fashioned by draping a square of canvas over a low branch of a small tree and pegging the corners into the ground. In the bright moonlight I could make out a groundsheet inside, and sleeping bags.

I watched them fix their rations and eat in silence. Occasionally they passed a water canteen around. I saw two automatic rifles propped against the tree that supported the tent canopy.

They were relaxed and unhurried. If they thought that anybody else was alive on the island with them, they didn't seem concerned about it.

I crawled back down from the top of the rise and hurried across the meadow to the boat dock.

The moon was bright on the water now, and I could see the cabin cruiser easily. I advanced slowly toward it, trying to avoid making any sounds. If anyone was waiting for me, I knew that I wouldn't have much warning.

The cabin cruiser was unoccupied. I got down on my hands and knees and pulled the side of the boat tight against the dock. I tossed my overnight bag on board, then rolled up onto the deck after it.

I put the key in the ignition and started the blower to clear the fumes out of the hold.

I had to get away quietly. I remembered that I had seen an oar stowed in an aft compartment, under the seats. I retrieved it, then unhooked the lines, fore and aft, from the cleats on the dock, and pulled them into the boat.

Standing in the well at the aft end, I braced the oar against one of the pilings and gave it as hard a shove as I could, then ran to the helm.

The launch drifted soundlessly from the dock. I steered the craft toward the wide mouth of the cove, holding her straight as I could against the slight wash of the waves. About thirty feet from the dock, she lost headway and started to drift backwards.

I bent over the side, plunged the oar in the water and pulled as hard as I could, twisting the oar like a canoe paddle to keep the boat on a straight course.

Gasping from the effort, I cleared her out past the mouth of the small cove into the open water, where she was immediately caught in a strong current.

I dropped the oar, jumped to the helm, pulled the throttle out and turned the ignition key.

This far from shore, the noise of the engines wouldn't matter. I was already well away. And in a minute or two I'd be completely out of reach. They wouldn't be able to shoot at me, and they certainly wouldn't be able to catch up with me in their damned rubber dinghy.

The ignition fired, the engines turned over, spluttered and stalled. I tried again. They fired, caught and stalled again. I pumped the choke and twisted the key again. Same result. They fired several times, then died. I pushed the choke off, thinking I had flooded both engines, then let the ignition crank for a good thirty seconds. The sound seemed to boom across the water. The engines weren't flooded.

I fumbled in the dark for the big flashlight in the cabin, found it and pulled up the floorboards over the engine compartment. I knew the batteries were okay, because the engines were firing.

What was wrong? I couldn't see anything amiss below.

With the flashlight trained on the engines, I cranked the ignition over and over. They still spluttered and died.

I looked at the fuel gauges. Both needles rested dead on empty.

I had drained the tanks on my trip to the mainland and back the day before. So caught up had I been in my videotaping scheme, I hadn't even thought about refueling.

The boat was now well out in the open water beyond the edge of the protected cove. It was caught in the current and drifting rapidly south, away from shore. I remembered from my trip to the mainland how strong the movement of the water was out here. The oar would do me no good.

I could see the silhouettes of the high bluffs against the moonlit sky on the south end of the island. They were now at my stern and rapidly receding. In a few more minutes I would be swept out to sea.

I had no choice. I had to jump.

I started to pull on an inflatable life vest, but then thought better of it. It would only slow me down. My survival would depend not on a life vest, but on reaching shore as fast as I possibly could, before the icy water numbed me and I fell victim to hypothermia.

I grabbed my overnight bag, emptied it of everything but the sealed plastic container with the videotapes, swung the strap over my head and across my chest and pulled the buckle up as tight as it would go. This would slow me down, too, but I was not leaving the tapes behind.

I climbed up on the gunwale, took a deep breath and dove as hard as I could toward the shore.

The waters seized me in a frigid embrace, crushing the wind out of me. My muscles started burning from the terrible spasms shooting through them. It was impossible not to panic. I was at least a hundred yards from shore. I flailed my arms and legs uselessly for several seconds before I got myself into anything resembling a rhythm.

I gasped and kicked and tried to keep myself in a crawl, slicing through the water with as powerful a stroke as my arms could manage. I quickly began to lose the sensation in my fingers. Instead of cutting through the water and propelling myself forward, I felt as if I was punching it with my fists and going nowhere.

In less than a minute I felt exhaustion closing in. I began to give in to the possibility that I might not make it.

Twice I actually stopped and floated for a few seconds, trying to get air in my lungs. The water no longer felt cold. It felt hot against my chest, as if it were burning me. Then it felt pleasantly warm. The shore seemed hardly any closer at all. I feared that the current might have turned me so that instead of swimming toward the shore, I was actually swimming parallel to it.

As my strength ebbed, my panic grew.

I couldn't feel my arms or legs anymore. I knew they were moving in the water, because they were splashing around me.

Something struck me in the side.

It was a rock outcropping. I grabbed for it. It was slippery. I lost it and drifted on past.

I hit another rock. This time I managed to clutch something solid and hold on. My feet drifted down and touched the bottom.

The current had carried me sideways to brush against the tip of a narrow peninsula that in the dark I had not even seen.

I crawled up between two big rocks onto a small patch of sandy beach and rolled myself up into a ball, shivering so hard it felt like convulsions.

I had lost all sense of where I was or what I was doing. I kept blacking out, only to be brought momentarily back to consciousness by painful spasms in my muscles. I couldn't get up. I couldn't move. All I could do was shake.

Eventually I passed out for good.

27

INDECISION

I don't know how long I lay there between the rocks. It may have been an hour. It may have been longer. The moment I regained consciousness I started to shiver again. I couldn't stop. My teeth chattered continuously. I tried covering myself with sand, hoping to extract some warmth from the insulation. But the sand was as wet as my clothes. Instead of trapping my body heat, it seemed to leach it from me.

I knew I had to do something to get warm.

I uncoiled myself and struggled back up on my feet. Stumbling and gasping, I eventually worked my way back up from the shore, across the stretch of meadow near the landing strip and up the path to the lodge.

The moon was high now. It seemed almost as bright as daylight as I pushed my way through the heavy clumps of grass, still shaking violently. My sneakers squished loudly and my clothes, caked with cold wet sand and soaked with icy salt water, clung to me, tugging at elbows and ankles and knees, weighing me down. The slightest breeze battered against my skin like an Arctic blizzard.

But I was alive.

And I still had the videotapes.

The growing apprehension and dread of the past few days seemed burned out of me. Gone. Evaporated. I was standing on rock bottom, with no adrenaline left in me to send flutters to my stomach or chills to the back of my neck.

The house was dark. The generator, with no demands on it, thumped away lazily in its subterranean vault.

I realized there was a risk that some of the gang that had murdered Carlson and the others might be inside, but I was no longer capable of worrying about it. Getting warm and dry was all that mattered.

I groped through the dark to the kitchen and found the other flashlight I had seen in the drawer near the sink. Cupping my hand over the beam to keep the light as restricted and dim as possible, I climbed upstairs.

In what appeared to be Carlson's bedroom I changed out of my wet clothes and toweled myself dry.

There were clothes in a closet and a dresser, and they fit me reasonably well. I found fresh underwear and wool socks, and chose a wool shirt, a pair of lined canvas duck-hunting pants, and a heavy sweater. I was still shivering, but I felt immensely better.

Carlson's shoes were too small. I squeezed my sneakers back on over the wool socks. They would dry out eventually.

My overnight bag was full of sand. I removed the plastic box with the four videotapes inside and checked their condition. Thank God I had taken the precaution of sealing them in a watertight container.

It would have made sense to hide them somewhere, but I couldn't bear the idea of parting with them, even temporarily.

Downstairs in the back hall I found a well-worn L. L. Bean duck-hunting jacket with expandable rubber-lined pockets for holding game. I put the jacket on, squeezed the container into a pocket and zipped it shut. Bulky, but bearable. I grabbed a pair of binoculars hanging on an adjacent hook and hung them around my neck.

My stomach had been growling with hunger for hours. I had to get something in it. Standing at the kitchen sink, with the flashlight lying on its side on the counter and casting its beam across in front of me, I drank the remaining orange juice from the container we had brought out, consumed half a loaf of bread, a glass of milk, several handfuls of potato chips, a chunk of cheddar cheese and the last piece of a coffee cake. I found four slices of ham left in the refrigerator and wrapped them, along with two hard rolls and a package of processed cheese, in a plastic bag and tucked it into another one of my rubber-lined pockets.

I climbed the two flights up to the lodge's attic and looked out the small window on the north gable with the binoculars. Their campfire was visible—a dim orange glow, with an occasional spark floating skyward. The moon was bright enough so that I could pick out the silhouettes of the four men, sitting against the rocks, eating or talking.

I thought about Carlson and the macabre tableau in the living room below. I was finally beginning to make some sense of it.

The director must have staged his own death. I remembered that when I had returned to New York Hospital his body was simply gone. Nobody on the floor knew where. The nurse caring for him, I remembered, was not on the hospital staff. And the men guarding the room were his own. Getting whatever cooperation was necessary from the hospital to carry out the deception had probably not been difficult. Carlson was head of the CIA, after all.

Then he had come up here, bringing his team with him. That explained the copy of *The Wall Street Journal* in the boat. His purpose must have been to set a trap for Steckler. He no doubt expected that Steckler would rush up here looking for the documents the minute he believed Carlson was dead.

Mara's unpersuasive display of grief over her father now made sense. And so did her failure to return. She knew the whole plan. She knew he and the other men were here when we arrived. They had come out on the boat the day before. It was probably her father she had waggled the plane's wings at when she flew off yesterday, not me.

Having baited his trap, Carlson then sat back and waited for Steckler to walk into it. No doubt he planned to kill Steckler as soon as he landed on the island.

But Steckler, cagey as a Mafia don, was not so easily fooled. He sent his own advance team to the island as a precaution against surprise. They found Carlson and his men, ambushed them and killed them.

The grisly scene they had arranged in the dining room was probably just Steckler's boys having a little fun after a hard day's work. A little joke for their boss when he arrived to collect the files in the bunker.

I went back downstairs and out to the stables. I turned the brass hook to activate the hoist under the icehouse.

Down in the room in the bunker where the weapons were displayed, I examined the hand grenades, lifting each sample and reading the card underneath. There were essentially two types—those that detonated five seconds after pulling the pin and releasing the detonator, and those that exploded on impact. I picked the M-57 and the M-68—the two with electrical impact fuzes—and left the others alone. That meant I would only have two grenades, but I couldn't afford to take both kinds and risk confusing them. The impact fuzes seemed safer. I didn't have to count. All I had to do was throw.

I tucked the two grenades into another of the hunting jacket's capacious pockets. Laden with grenades, binoculars, food, a flashlight and the box of videotapes, I was beginning to feel like the Michelin tire man.

I inspected the machine guns and rifles again, but they were of no use. I couldn't find a single bullet for any of them. This was a catalogue store, not an arsenal. Customers selected their bullets from a printed price list and received them in the mail, or by UPS or Federal Express, or however the Night Watch shipped them. I was lucky that the grenades came already armed.

I looked at the Stinger missile, sitting by itself on its packing crate in the corner. I hefted it. According to the instruction booklet that came with it, it weighed 34.5 pounds. It was portable, but far too cumbersome and inappropriate a cannon for my purposes.

I climbed the steps back up to the surface and looked around. The moonlight washed the entire island, fields and buildings alike, in strong silver light. I stood there under the icehouse for several minutes, making careful three-hundred-sixty-degree sweeps with the binoculars. I picked up no movement.

I walked across to the stables, found my way to the tack room with the flashlight and lowered the icehouse back onto its foundation.

What I didn't understand was my own presence here.

Why did Carlson want me on the island? He obviously hadn't intended for me to come up here to pick up those documents he had promised me in the hospital: he had fully expected to be alive. If his trap had sprung the way he intended, I would just have been in the way. Worse, I would have been a potential witness against him.

But clearly he had arranged that I be here. Mara had at first tried to hustle me off the island, but then she had actually suggested I stay, so I'd have the time I wanted to look through the documents. Carlson must have approved of that. But why?

By the time I had worked my way across the open meadows to the top of the rise overlooking the spot where the men in black had pitched their camp, the moon was darting in and out of fast-moving clouds.

I trained the binoculars on their camp. The fire had died into a small pile of embers. I could make out two men sitting by the fire, and a third on his knees in front of the sheet of plastic they had fashioned into a tent. He was packing up the radio I had noticed earlier.

I couldn't locate the fourth man at all.

On my hands and knees I moved in closer, until I was crouched behind the last big rock between us. I estimated I was within a hundred feet of their fire.

I pulled out the two grenades. I put one on the ground and squeezed the other one in my hand. I slipped a finger through the loop attached to the pin and tugged at it gently, but didn't pull it out.

A hundred feet was an easy lob. I had been a good-field, no-hit third baseman on my high-school team. I would have no trouble with a hundred feet. A simple toss. That was all it was. From third to first. A snot-nosed tot could make that throw, Coach Shaughnessy would have said.

I decided I would throw the second grenade immediately after the first. Just to be sure. I had to kill all four. No margin for error on that. I looked through the binoculars again. The one who had been packing up the radio had joined the two by the fire.

Where was the fourth?

I spotted him finally. He was under the improvised tent, lying in a sleeping bag.

Problem. I didn't know much about hand grenades, but I knew that a man lying down inside a sleeping bag forty or more feet from the point of detonation would not be killed. The blast would blow right over him. His ears might ring, but otherwise it was likely he wouldn't be hurt.

To kill three and leave one alive would be to guarantee my own demise. It had to be all four.

I waited. The grenade began to feel warm in my palm.

"We'll be here a friggin' week," one of them said. His voice sounded alarmingly close. Instinctively I lowered my head against the rock.

"Why?"

"Looking for those documents."

"I told you. Steckler knows where they are."

"Why'd we try to squeeze it out of Carlson, then?"

"He told us to."

"And then he tells you he already knows?"

"He told me it was okay. So he must know."

"He told you it was okay because what the fuck else was he gonna say?"

"He coulda said 'I'll ream your ass.' "

Somebody laughed.

"You think somebody else told him?"

"Nah. He doesn't know. We'll have to look for them."

"I don't think they're here. I don't think there's a friggin' thing here. Carlson woulda told us."

"Steckler says they're here."

"Let *him* find them, then."

They all laughed.

"Carlson's daughter could've told him."

"I didn't know he had a daughter."

"Somebody told him."

"Bullshit. He doesn't know. We'll be here a friggin' week, looking under every friggin' rock on the island."

There was a long silence. One of the men lit a cigarette.

I waited.

An owl glided past overhead on soundless wings, then dipped down into the grass in front of me. A small squeak, and the owl reappeared, its wide wings fluttering, and sailed off again, a small bundle of fur just visible in its talons.

"You didn't tell us when he was coming."

"I did tell you, fuckhead. Tomorrow morning."

Another silence.

"We oughta move 'em out of the dining room," someone said. "It's real unprofessional, doin' that."

"What do you know about professional?"

"I know what's sick. And what's sick ain't professional."

A raised voice: "You callin' me sick?"

"Knock it off, assholes."

Silence. I could hear the wind slipping through the grass with a reedy, whistling hum.

"Time to turn in, anyway," someone said.

One man stood up and stretched. The others sat for a few seconds longer, then they got up, too. One prodded the fire with his boot, covering the glowing coals with dead ashes.

I had to throw now, before they moved to their sleeping bags. My hands were soaked with sweat and shaking as if I had palsy. I worried that the grenade would slip prematurely from my grip when I threw it.

The moment was on me, and I was immobilized by indecision. If I threw now, I would only kill three. But if I didn't throw now, what other chance would I ever get?

Then why kill them?

There was an alternative.

Sneak off and hide.

Just wait them out. Wait until they had all left, and then find some way off the island. I had the videotapes, after all. That's what counted. And that's all I wanted. I didn't want to kill anybody—even these despicable bastards.

But I couldn't hide for days. And Steckler was coming.

I put down the grenade I had been holding and wiped my palms against the sides of my pants until they were dry. I looked through the binoculars. They were moving toward the tent.

Maybe this was better. At least all four would now be in the same spot, under the tent. I picked the grenade up again and waited.

I watched the three pull off their sneakers and sweaters and climb into the sleeping bags.

The throw was now longer—between 120 and 150 feet. From deep behind third base across the diamond to first. And I had to be right on target. I had only two chances and at night it was hard to judge distances.

The odds were no longer so good.

There was something else. The sheer pitiless brutality of killing someone—blowing him apart—while he lay asleep was beyond what I was capable of doing, no matter the justification.

I knew that by now I had hesitated too long and thought too much. I set the grenade back down on the grass and buried my face in my hands.

The moment defined me. I was not just indecisive. I was a coward. No matter what moral excuses I made to myself, I had lacked the courage to go through with something I knew I should have done. These men were killers. They deserved to die. And letting them live was just putting my own life at risk.

It wasn't really a moral choice. I had no feeling for these men. It was fear of the violence itself that prevented me from acting. I knew that if they had been attacking me I would have answered back, I would have fought for my life. But I was incapable of killing them in cold blood.

That should have made me feel good about myself. But it didn't. It made me wonder if I were capable of acting in my own best interest in a crisis.

I picked the grenades up, tucked them in a pocket and slipped backward down the rise until I was far enough away to risk standing up. I tried to run. Halfway across the meadow I stumbled on a rock and fell on my face. I stayed there.

No sounds came from the vicinity of the campfire.

I crept back to the house and let myself in. I locked the door, then fumbled around in the dark with my flashlight, checking and locking all the other doors and windows on the ground floor, thinking even as I did it what a futile gesture it was.

I played the flashlight around the dining-room table. The grim spectacle remained. Carlson and his elite bodyguards had proved no match for Steckler's men. What chance did I have? Visions of rifle butts smashing through the French doors in the middle of the night flitted through my mind. The only thing I had going for me at this moment was one extraordinary piece of luck. Steckler's men didn't know I was on the island.

In the kitchen I poured vodka in a tumbler until it was half full, threw in a few ice cubes from the gas refrigerator, sat down at the kitchen table and took a long drink of the stuff.

The vodka calmed me down. I finished the glass off, then went upstairs. I found Carlson's bedroom and lay down on his bed. I fell asleep fully clothed. I didn't even bother to remove the hunting jacket, bulging as it was with ham, rolls, cheese, videotapes and hand grenades.

28

THE SWORD EXCALIBUR

I woke up around dawn with a headache and the tight flutter of fear in my gut. I rolled off the bed and lifted the corner of a shade to see out the window. The island was shrouded in a deep blanket of white mist. From the second floor I could barely see the ground below.

I slipped out of the house and followed the stone path down toward the stables. The mist was so heavy that walking through it felt like wading through a rain cloud. It swirled visibly around me, its damp tendrils wetting my hair and face. The stones on the path and the tufts of wiry grass around them glistened in the fog with a lacquered sheen.

The silence was eerie, broken only by the occasional muffled clang of a buoy over in the direction of Great Duck Island. Even the gulls, whose raucous cries had wakened me the day before, were still.

I climbed up into the empty hayloft, pulled the ladder up after me and propped it against the opening in the floor of the cupola that straddled the ridge of the stable roof. The ladder was old and brittle, with loose rungs that strained and creaked under my weight.

One of the cupola's four windows was broken and the flat surfaces inside were predictably coated with several inches of bird droppings. But there was adequate space. And when the mist cleared I would have a view in all directions. If I had to, I could hole up here for several days. And I knew I might have to.

I cleared a place to sit under one of the windows, leaned back against the wall and caught my breath. The smell of damp, rotted hay and the acrid ammonia stench of the bird droppings assaulted my nose. I pulled out a hard roll and a slice of ham from my pocket and ate my breakfast.

The fog began to dissipate toward midmorning. It thinned out gradually from the top down, revealing glimpses of clear blue sky while the earth below remained shrouded in white.

Just about the time the island began at last to materialize through the gauze of mist, I heard the drone of an airplane engine.

The plane passed low overhead, barely fifty feet above the stable. I reached for the binoculars.

By the time I was able to focus them, the plane had circled around and vanished inside the curtains of fog still hanging over the water. I didn't see it again until it was actually touching down on the far end of the landing strip. I tried to hold the glasses steady on it as it rolled along, but all I could distinguish inside the cockpit was a dark blur.

At the near end of the runway it swung around and taxied to a stop. It was Mara's Cessna four-seater.

The door on the pilot's side opened. Through the binoculars I saw white sneakers and tight blue jeans as Mara stepped onto the footrest on the landing gear strut and let herself down.

She hopped to the ground with an energetic bounce, pulled a bag out after her, and slung it over her shoulder. She slammed the door of the Cessna shut with a nonchalant shove of the elbow, and started off at a fast walk toward the lodge, swinging her bag back and forth. She looked like a kid coming home from school.

She was alone.

Why had she come back?

I scanned the meadow north of the landing strip where the four men were camped. I saw no sign of anyone. But I knew they were out there.

The impulse to shout, to warn her, to run out after her, was powerful.

I resisted it.

I watched her open the lodge's front door and go inside. About ten minutes passed. I pictured her standing in the dining room, discovering her father. My stomach bunched up tight as a fist. I kept the binoculars on the field to the north, dreading the appearance of Steckler's men.

I heard the generator start up.

A few minutes later Mara appeared on the terrace. She stood there, nervously fidgeting with her hands, looking up and down the island. She appeared dazed and confused.

She now knew that her father's plot to trap Steckler had failed.

She paced back and forth across the terrace, beating her fists against the sides of her legs in agitation. She jumped off the terrace suddenly and ran down toward the dock. She disappeared from my sight over the steep rocky slope near the shoreline.

She would see that the cabin cruiser was missing. What would she make of that? That I had taken it and fled the island? Possibly. I had certainly tried.

Mara popped back into view and dashed across the field toward the house.

I scanned the field again. No sign of anyone. I trained the glasses on the Cessna and was hit with a sudden and obvious inspiration: get Mara, get us on the plane and get out.

I put the binoculars down. I might not have much time.

I got down from the cupola as fast as my bulging coat would let me, moved the ladder across the hayloft and slid it down to the ground floor. On the last rung I lost my footing and fell hard on my side. The hand grenades in the coat pocket slammed against the floor. I closed my eyes and gasped. A pin had to be pulled to release the safety catch before they could detonate, but I was still momentarily terrified.

I picked myself up, limped to the stable door and flung it open.

The fog had lifted completely now. I stopped just inside the door.

Steckler's men—all four of them—were standing around the Cessna. I ducked back inside, cursing violently under my breath. Jesus, Mary and Joseph, why hadn't I seen them?

I went into a stall that had a high barred window and peeked out. The men were waiting for someone. They were completely at ease. Two were leaning against the side of the plane, a third had a hand on the wing, and the fourth was doing some kind of isometric exercises with his arms and upper body.

It struck me that they must think the Cessna was Steckler's plane. They're standing around waiting for him to come back out of the lodge.

No chance now. I couldn't cross the open space to the lodge without being seen. I climbed back up to my cupola.

The men were getting impatient. One of them shouted something in the direction of the lodge. I prayed that Mara had seen them and hidden herself somewhere.

A low rumble vibrated faintly in my ear. The sound faded, then deepened and gradually grew louder. I searched the sky to the north with the binoculars and found it, a black speck two inches above the horizon.

I watched it grow nearer.

Flights south out of Bangor occasionally passed overhead, but this one was low. About a mile out it dropped down even lower, dipped into a shallow turn and began a three-hundred-sixty-degree circuit of the island. It was a twin-engine. I scanned the flank and the vertical stabilizer for a company logo or an airline name. Nothing. Just the plane's ID number.

I counted the windows aft of the cockpit. Four. It probably seated a dozen.

Was this Steckler?

Off the eastern side of the island the twin-engine pulled out of its turn and headed north, back in the direction from which it had come.

Or just a sightseeing charter?

Out over the water it made a sharp bank to the left, leveled out, then banked left again to bring it around in line with the landing strip.

It was Steckler.

Instinctively I shrank back from the edge of the window as the plane rumbled in on its approach. It touched down at the edge of the landing strip and rolled out. It used the whole runway.

It taxied up alongside Mara's Cessna and stopped. The door opened and a retractable set of stairs swung out and down and bumped onto the ground.

The pilot stepped out, carrying a flight bag. Two other men followed him. One, a young blond man in a windbreaker, had an Uzi slung under his arm. The third man's exaggeratedly erect posture and stiff gesturing were instantly familiar. I trained the binoculars on him. Colonel Westerly.

I looked back at the plane's open doorway. Steckler finally appeared. He ducked forward slightly, his hands on the side of the frame, and stepped down onto the ground. He said something to Westerly, and the colonel said something to the men by the Cessna. They came over and shook hands with Steckler. They talked for some time. Explaining recent events, no doubt. Westerly strutted around the Cessna, peering inside.

If they were wondering who had landed in the Cessna, they didn't seem especially concerned about it.

The pilot went back into his plane. Steckler led the rest of the group up the path toward the house.

I couldn't decide what to do. I couldn't imagine that there was anything I could do. Except wait.

The day got warm. I removed the cumbersome hunting jacket. I checked the sealed container with the tapes, to reassure myself that something worthwhile was yet going to come out of this nightmare.

After about an hour, Steckler's men emerged from the house, each dragging one of the corpses from the dining-room table. They had removed the dead men's belts and tied their ankles together with them, leaving enough slack to provide a grip for their hands. The corpses' heads bounced in the dirt and against the rocks, and their arms trailed out behind them. Carlson's body was dragged out last.

They loaded the five bodies onto the twin-engine and climbed aboard. The pilot took off.

The plane headed directly south, out over the ocean, and leveled off low over the water. Several miles out the craft banked around in a long, shallow turn. I followed it with the binoculars. I saw the cabin door open. I watched the four bodies tumble out, one by one, and splash into the sea below.

The twin-engine returned to the island, landed and taxied back to its original position.

Steckler and Westerly emerged from the lodge, paused outside the door and turned and looked back inside. Westerly arched his back and pulled in his chin in that particularly cocky manner of his.

Mara walked out.

The binoculars slipped from my hands. I scrambled for them on the floor and got them back to my eyes.

Behind Mara was Steckler's bodyguard, the young blond man in the windbreaker. His Uzi was pressed against the base of Mara's neck. She walked on ahead as if she hardly noticed. The expression on her face was vacant, dazed. There were gashes on her forehead and under one eye. She walked with her arms dangling at her sides, ignoring the blood running across her mouth and onto her chin.

They came down the path to the stables. I heard their feet on the floorboards below. Westerly was saying something, but I couldn't make out the words. They went into the tack room.

I trained the binoculars on the icehouse. After a few moments it started to rise off its foundation.

The three men led Mara out of the stables and down into the bunker. The other four, having fed the bodies of their victims to the sharks, followed behind them. The pilot busied himself checking over his twin-engine. He also performed a detailed inspection of Mara's Cessna, and topped up the Cessna's two wing tanks with gasoline from the pump nearby.

For an hour and a half I watched them bring up file cabinets from the bunker and load them onto the twin-engine. They had patiently restacked all the documents in the file drawers. At some point the pilot must have complained that the aircraft was overloaded, because they brought all the file cabinets back out of the plane, minus their file drawers, and piled them in a big, disordered heap near the runway.

Grayson Steckler was going to get those priceless files after all. And the hundreds of millions of dollars in all the numbered bank accounts as well. The Night Watch would be his—lock, stock and document.

With the files finally loaded, everyone collected on the airstrip, next to the twin-engine. Their mood was upbeat. Two of Steckler's goons started horsing around, taking turns seeing who could punch the other the hardest on the arm.

Mara stood zombielike in front of the man in the windbreaker, her head down, her hands hanging lifeless at her sides. I was surprised that they still hadn't taken the trouble to at least bind her wrists together. They seemed to dismiss her as a threat. They had apparently beaten her. Had they also drugged her? She appeared completely cowed and submissive, as if she were in shock. The blond in the windbreaker was still holding the Uzi on her, but not very carefully. The gun's muzzle kept drifting away from her neck.

The pilot stepped down out of the plane, carrying a clipboard and a worried frown. He still seemed disturbed about the aircraft's weight. He talked to Steckler, then Steckler and Westerly conferred at some length. The others stood around. Westerly went aboard the plane and reemerged with a pair of overnight bags. He carried them over to the Cessna and shoved them into the small cargo area behind the backseat.

So some of the passenger load was going to be shifted to Mara's Cessna. What did they intend to do with Mara?

I climbed down a second time from the cupola and the hayloft. Earlier I had noticed a small door near the back of the stables, facing east, away from the lodge and the landing strip. I pushed it open and slipped outside. I hurried down toward the shore, then worked my way around the shoreline until I had put the icehouse between me and the party out on the landing strip.

I crawled on all fours up the slope to the icehouse. I could see the men and the two planes framed between the bottom of the raised icehouse and the top surface of the cement foundation that covered the bunker. There were enough tall weeds growing around the foundation to keep me out of sight.

When I reached the edge of the cement, I hesitated. To reach the stairs to the bunker I had to duck under the icehouse and take about six steps across the foundation to the steps, on the side farthest from me. There would be nothing to hide behind. If anyone looked this way during the few seconds it took, he would see me.

The four men and the bodyguard in the windbreaker were boarding the twin-engine. Steckler and Westerly stood apart,

watching them. Westerly had taken over Windbreaker's responsibility. He was holding his pistol to Mara's neck. Her hands were
still untied. She was cradling one arm, as if it hurt.

Were they going to take her in the Cessna with them? Maybe
they needed her to fly it.

I dashed across the cement and down the steps.

I bolted through the door into the room with the weapons,
flicked on the light and stood there, gazing blankly at the rows of
shelves as the precious seconds ticked by. I felt paralyzed with
indecision and panic, like a man whose house is on fire and can't
decide what to take with him before making a run for his life.

I needed something better than grenades. I needed the modern
equivalent of King Arthur's sword.

My eyes fell on the Stinger missile, sitting on its crate in the
corner. Was it live? Or just a display model?

I decided I would have to find out. I lifted the missile onto my
shoulder and ran back up the steps. I paused just below the opening. I could hear the airplane's engines revving.

I bolted up the remaining steps, across the cement top and down
into the grass behind the icehouse. The wind was blowing out of
the south, so the plane would taxi up the field and pass directly
overhead as it took off.

I crawled through the grass until I was out in the open between
the stables and the icehouse. Steckler and Westerly were still standing on the edge of the landing strip, Mara in front of them. The
plane taxied down the strip, turned at the extreme far end and
lined itself up with the runway.

The pilot applied throttle to the engines and the plane began
moving. I was going to have to stand up to fire the Stinger, so I
retreated down the slope toward the shore until I was at least ten
feet below the level of the landing strip.

I had browsed briefly through the Stinger's operations manual
two days ago, but instructions were hardly necessary. The weapon
was elegantly simple. Basically you just pointed the thing toward
the sky and pulled the trigger. A two-stage rocket would launch
the missile. Then, to score a hit, all you had to do was hold the
bright white spot of the laser homing device on the target. The
missile would do the rest.

I swung the hinged telescopic sight up and locked it into position, flicked one switch to activate the laser and released the safety catch to arm the missile.

From my position down on the slope I could no longer see the airstrip or the plane, but I could hear the engines roaring as the craft approached takeoff speed.

Visions of my wretched inability to throw the hand grenade the night before filled my head. Now I was getting a second chance. It was still cold blood, but this time the stakes were compelling. I felt no moral qualms.

I must be calm and deliberate, I lectured myself. Calm and deliberate and determined. The missile had a range of 3.5 miles, and I needed the twin-engine to be out over the ocean before I fired. There should be plenty of time. I feared only that I would hesitate again until it was too late.

I wiped the sweat out of my eyes with the back of my coat sleeve and steadied the Stinger on my shoulder, its muzzle pointed skyward.

29

DILEMMA

The afternoon was warm and humid, and the twin-engine, burdened with five passengers and probably a ton of documents, strained mightily to get airborne.

It came thundering off the end of the runway so low that the wheels of the landing gear were plowing through stalks of dead weeds, barely more than a foot off the ground.

It roared directly toward me, like a hawk closing on its prey. I fell to the ground in a hot blast of wind and kerosene fumes. One of the landing gear's tires missed my head by inches. The Stinger missile spun off my shoulder, cartwheeled across the ground and crashed into a rock outcropping twenty feet away.

I pulled myself back on my feet and stumbled over to rescue the missile. I dropped down on my knees and examined it. It wasn't damaged in any way that I could see. I hoisted the launch tube back onto my shoulder and struggled to stand up again. I was disoriented and dizzy, and had completely lost sight of the airplane.

By the time I found it, it was well out over the water, and still very low. It was having trouble gaining altitude. I pushed the missile's sight against my eye. I couldn't seem to adjust the optical tracking system. The telescopic sight was more powerful than my binoculars, and it had a very narrow field of view. All I could see was a meaningless blur of clouds and sky. I fumbled frantically for a knob or ring or button to focus the lens.

I took my eye from the sight again and scanned the horizon.

The aircraft, about a mile away to the south, was banking in a shallow left turn. It looked to be scarcely a hundred feet over the water.

I located the focus adjustment and tried the Stinger's sight again, but I still couldn't find the plane. I was shaking so hard I couldn't hold my eye steady in the sight.

I sat down, propped my back against a rock, rested an elbow against my knee and tried again. I managed finally to get the aircraft centered in the sight. The plane had leveled out of its turn and onto a heading that was bringing it back over the east side of the island. It was still climbing slowly.

Now that the craft was coming almost directly toward me, it seemed to hang stationary in the sky. I heard myself breathing very rapidly. I hated the waiting. I hated having so much time to think of all the things that could go wrong. Whether the missile would fire. Whether I would hit the plane if it did. What I was going to do about Westerly and Steckler. If there was any way to stop them taking Mara off in the Cessna. Whether they would shoot her and drop her into the ocean as they had her father.

The twin-engine loomed huge in the telescopic sight, overwhelming its narrow field of view. It seemed on top of me. I took my eye away. The plane was close enough—maybe five hundred feet up and a couple of thousand feet away.

I pressed my eye against the sight and squeezed the trigger.

I felt a sharp bang, like a rifle report. The impact against my shoulder was negligible. I took my eye from the sight. The missile had left the launch tube, but with hardly any force. It was floating upward barely twenty feet over my head and looked about to drop to earth.

Jesus, my luck, I thought. A seventy-five-thousand-dollar dud.
A man's voice behind me was shouting something.

I heard a sharp sizzle, like the burning of a firecracker fuse, then
another, much deeper concussion. I had forgotten about the second stage. The missile, which had seemed momentarily suspended
in midair, took off skyward with an angry, roaring *whoosh*.

Mesmerized by the Stinger's performance, I almost forgot the
follow-through. I jammed the sight back against my eye and frantically sought to bring the spot of white light from the laser tracking
device to bear on the aircraft. The missile was designed to home
in on the laser beam. I had to get the beam centered on the target
so the missile could lock onto it. If I didn't find the plane with it
immediately, the missile and its warhead would shoot harmlessly
on past.

I found the aircraft, but I couldn't keep the scope on it. The
plane danced wildly up and down in the sight. I held my breath
and willed my hands to steady it on the side of the plane, just aft
of the cockpit, and hold it there.

The twin-engine suddenly disappeared from the scope. I flinched
in surprise.

The explosion reached me a split second later. I dropped the
launch tube. Where the plane had been, an enormous flower was
blossoming against the sky, intense red at the center, with hundreds
of long black petals and puffy white blooms fanning out over the
ocean in a dazzling pyrotechnic display.

The flower wilted and faded, its cottony petals quickly shredded
and deformed by the winds aloft. The waves below hissed and
erupted as burning fragments of the aircraft splashed into the sea.

And thousands of sheets of white paper drifted down through
the bright afternoon like falling leaves. Caught by the breezes, they
swirled and skidded and spiraled in an ever-widening fan, until
finally, lazily, page by page, they settled onto the ocean. The waves
turned momentarily white with floating paper.

I jumped to my feet, shoved my fists into the air and let out a
long, lung-bursting whoop of triumph. A wave of savage delight
swept through me, more intoxicating than anything I had ever
experienced. It was some time before I realized that a man's voice
behind me was bellowing in rage.

I jerked my head around.

They were standing at the end of the landing strip—Mara in front, Westerly and Steckler behind her.

Steckler looked as if he had been transformed into a marble statue. He stood motionless, mouth slightly ajar, arms out, eyes gazing blankly at the wisps of white smoke where his aircraft had been.

Westerly reacted like a mad bull, bellowing and snorting and waving his arms in red-eyed fury.

Mara came to life. With blazing suddenness, she spun around and kicked Westerly in the groin so hard he doubled up in mid-bellow and toppled to the ground.

Before either man could react, she was sprinting madly toward the stables, her body bent forward and zigzagging, her arms clasped oddly together in front of her, and pumping from side to side to gain speed.

Steckler stood watching her. He was still in shock. Westerly recovered and, with a loud groan of agony, pulled himself unsteadily up on his knees. He was still clutching the pistol.

The colonel braced the pistol on his knee, took aim at Mara's retreating form and fired several times. Plumes of dust blossomed up around Mara's feet as she ran.

Operating on some new level of brute instinct, I snatched a grenade out of my coat's side pocket and heaved it at Westerly.

It bounced on the grass ten feet past him. Steckler came out of his trance, saw the grenade, and dropped flat to the ground. Westerly continued firing at Mara.

The grenade didn't explode. I had forgotten to pull the pin to arm it. I yanked the second one out and jerked the pin free with a forefinger. Westerly's kneeling form gave me just the frame of reference I needed—I was throwing in from left field to home plate and I wanted it to bounce in front of the catcher.

I hurled it hard. It struck the ground five feet in front of him and exploded. The blast lifted him off his knees and blew him backward a good ten feet, where he collapsed to the earth like a discarded string puppet.

I looked for Mara. She was moving slowly up the path toward the lodge, weaving drunkenly from side to side.

I looked around for Steckler. I didn't see him.

Mara reached the front door of the lodge and fell down. I ran up the path after her.

She was on her back on the stone floor of the entranceway, gasping for breath, her face contorted with pain. When she saw me, she erupted in tears.

I knelt down. The left leg of her blue jeans was streaked with blood from the knee to the ankle.

"He hit you," I said.

She nodded.

"Hold on."

I ran inside, found a bottle of antiseptic in a medicine chest, grabbed some sheets and towels from the linen closet and a knife from the kitchen, and ran back out to her. She was still lying flat, arms at her sides, her chest heaving rapidly.

I slit the left leg of the blue jeans up to the thigh and folded the cloth up past the knee. The bullet had entered the back of her leg, just above the knee and a little to one side. The wound was large and jagged and blood was flowing from it at a heavy rate. I couldn't find an exit wound.

I grabbed a small chair from the front hallway and propped her leg up on it. I splashed antiseptic on a towel and pressed it hard over the wound. Mara tensed and groaned from the sting. I tore several strips from a sheet and fashioned as tight a bandage as I could. I was no expert at first aid, but I assumed the point was to arrest the bleeding as fast as possible. That meant elevating the wound and applying pressure to it. "Keep your leg up on the chair," I said. "And don't move it."

"Where are they?" she gasped.

"Westerly's dead, I think. Steckler must have run off. Does he have a gun with him?"

Mara craned her face around toward the landing strip. "I don't know. But you'd better get Westerly's."

That made sense. I ran down to the landing strip. The pistol was lying in the grass about five feet from Westerly's blasted corpse. I managed to retrieve it without looking directly at the body. The weapon was still warm to the touch and surprisingly heavy. It was an automatic of some kind.

Back by the front door of the lodge I showed it to her.

"The son of a bitch," she whispered. "It's a .357 Magnum. See what's left in the clip."

"I don't know how to open it."

"Give it to me."

I handed her the pistol. She laid it on her stomach and with one hand snapped the clip out of the bottom of the hand grip and counted the bullets left in it. "Four rounds," she said. She slid the magazine back into place. "Do you know how to use it?"

"Not really."

"I'll hold it, then."

"Like hell you will." I took the pistol from her and dropped it into one of my pockets.

"What in God's name are you carrying in that coat?" she asked.

I glanced down at the jacket, bulging around me like a clown's costume. "A little bit of everything."

Blood was soaking through the sheet on her leg. I removed the bandage, made a thicker one out of more folded bedsheet and wrapped it around her leg as tightly as I could. She closed her eyes and clenched her teeth from the pain, but didn't protest.

"That's the best I can do," I said. "We've got to get you out of here."

Mara opened her eyes but didn't reply.

"Can you fly the plane?" I asked.

"Don't think so."

"You sure?"

She reached with her right arm across her middle and touched her left forearm delicately with her fingers. "Arm's broken," she said. "Here."

For the first time I noticed that the arm was red and swollen all the way from the wrist to the elbow. "What happened?"

"They grabbed me. Steckler broke it."

"On purpose?"

"Yeah. With the fireplace poker."

"So you'd tell him where the documents were?"

Mara nodded. "I fought. But the bastards held the broken arm . . . and they twisted it. I couldn't stand it."

I swallowed. The thought of it made me quiver with disgust and fury. "Why the hell didn't you hide?"

"I did hide. They found me."

I went back inside, tore apart an old venetian blind and carried a couple of the wooden slats back to the front entrance. I broke them up into four foot-long pieces and tied them to the arm with strips of bedsheet to make a splint. I tore two more strips of sheet to make a sling and to lash the arm tightly against her side.

I lifted her up, helped her drape her good arm around my neck, and started down the path toward the landing strip.

"It's no use," she said. "I can't fly it."

"The plane has a radio," I said. "We'll call for help."

Mara pulled her head against my neck and kissed me. We made it all the way to the Cessna without falling down. I lowered her carefully onto the ground. "You'll have to tell me what to do," I said.

"Help me into the plane. It'll be faster."

I lifted her up again.

"The passenger side," she said. "It'll be easier. The seat slides farther back."

It was still not easy. With her one usable arm pulling and me pushing from underneath, we finally managed. I went around and climbed in on the pilot's side. Mara's face was ghostly white and damp with sweat.

"You okay?"

She nodded. "Feel a little weak."

Moving her had increased the bleeding. The dressing on her leg was showing red again.

"The master switch," she said, pointing across my lap. "Turn it on." I scanned the instrument panel, shaking my head in confusion.

"Way over—lower left."

I found it and flipped it on. Mara pulled out the microphone and started working the radio dials. She sent out distress calls on every frequency and waited for replies. Finally she dropped the microphone back into its sleeve under the instrument panel and sank back against the seat with an exhausted sigh. "I can't raise anyone. The voice frequencies are all line of sight. If we were up in the air it'd be easy. But we're too low and too far away."

"What about the radios in the bunker?"

Mara shook her head. "Steckler had them all removed and loaded on the plane you shot down."

"Anything in the lodge?"

"No. Nothing. All the communications stuff was in the bunker. There was a radio on the boat, but the boat's gone. . . ."

"I know. Thank me for that."

"Company," Mara said.

I looked up and saw Steckler walking toward us. He was holding both hands in the air.

"Get the pistol," Mara warned. "Quick."

I fished in the coat pocket and pulled it out.

Steckler walked to the wing on my side and stopped, about ten feet away from the open cockpit door. I pointed the pistol at him. Steckler looked at it suspiciously, as if he questioned its authenticity. I felt Mara's hand come around and push the safety off. Steckler grinned.

"It's Westerly's," I said. "And there are four rounds left."

"No need for that," Steckler replied. "I'm unarmed." He rested his hands against the edge of the wing.

"Don't trust him," Mara whispered. "Not for an instant."

Steckler appeared in full control of his emotions. To look at him one would have guessed he was just a motorist who had run out of gas.

I, on the other hand, was wound up as tight as an eight-day clock. It was a little bit ridiculous. I had just destroyed his plane, killed his crew and sunk a ton of priceless documents with a Stinger missile, blown Colonel Westerly all to hell with a grenade, and was now aiming a .357 Magnum at Steckler's stomach at point-blank range. Yet I was the one who felt threatened.

He seemed to sense instinctively that I wouldn't use it on him. He certainly didn't appear worried about it.

"What do you want?" I demanded.

"I want to make a deal with you," he replied.

"I'm listening."

"Shoot him," Mara whispered.

He heard her. His eyes registered a brief flicker of alarm, but that was all. "I can fly us all out of here," he said.

"Why would you want to?"

"I have no other way to get off the island."

He had put it all together very quickly, I thought. He knew Mara was wounded and in no condition to fly, and guessed I didn't know how.

"You want to save her life," he said. "You'll have to get her to a hospital."

"No," Mara said, her voice harsh. "Shoot him."

Steckler pointed to the rear of the cabin. "You can get in the backseat," he said. "Hold the pistol on my neck all the way. What can I do to you?"

"Then what?"

Steckler shrugged. "Then we land at Bangor. You call an ambulance, I go on my way."

"You killed Carlson," I said. "And the others."

"No, I didn't," he replied in a matter-of-fact tone. "But I did see you kill a few people."

"In self-defense."

Steckler tilted his head to the side in an attitude of regretful disagreement. "That airplane didn't pose any danger to you. You shot down innocent men."

It wasn't a good time or place for a debate. "And I should kill you, too, Steckler. You know I should."

Steckler nodded, as if to say he understood. "Just think it through first, Brady. You're an intelligent man. Killing me will only put her life in danger."

"Mara's all for it," I said, reminding myself what he and Westerly had just done to her. "And I don't blame her."

"Of course," Steckler countered. "She wants revenge. That's understandable. But let's face it, Brady. If you want her to live, you'll need my help."

His argument was compelling. I glanced back at Mara. She was resting her head against the seat back. Her jaw was clenched tight.

"What else can we do?" I said. I turned my eyes back on Steckler. He hadn't moved. His own eyes kept shifting back and forth between Mara and myself, appraising, calculating.

"We'll stay here," Mara replied. "I won't die."

I wanted to believe her, but I didn't think the odds were in our favor. The broken arm might be okay for a day or two, but the gunshot wound was an emergency. "The bullet's still in your leg," I said. "And you're losing a lot of blood."

"We'll cut the bullet out. The bleeding will stop with a tight bandage." She was doing her best to sound matter-of-fact, but her voice was shaky and weak, her mind preoccupied by the pain.

I thought of Mara dying on this island, with me unable to save her. "If we stay here, what'll we do about Steckler?"

Mara just shook her head. "We'll kill him," she said flatly. "It's the only solution."

"She'll die, Brady," Steckler said. His self-assured tone was fading. He was beginning to press.

"Take my word for it, Brady," he went on. "Gunshot wounds are messy. Even if you stop the bleeding, the wound will get septic. Bullets are dirty. She'll get a hell of an infection. And if her arm isn't set in a few days it'll never heal properly. She could lose it, in fact."

"He's trying to scare you, Johnny. He's desperate. All he's thinking about is how to save his own life. That's all that concerns him. . . . Don't worry about me. We'll be okay here for a few days. We have food at the house. I can rest. With the cast and bandages I'll do fine. In a day I should be strong enough to fly. I'll be all right. We'll make it."

"Don't believe her, Brady," Steckler said. "She won't be better in a day or two. She'll be much worse. And no one knows you're out here. How long will it be before someone rescues you? A week? A month? There's no communication with the mainland. There's no boat, no other way to get off the island except with this plane. You want to stay here and watch her die by inches and not be able to do anything about it?"

"I filed a flight plan," Mara said. "Bangor knows I'm here."

"But they also know she comes out here for weeks at a time. They aren't going to come looking for her for a hell of a long time."

"He'll trick us," Mara warned me. "I promise you. He'll trick us and he'll kill us both."

Steckler took a step closer. I aimed the pistol toward his head. He raised his hand. "Listen to me, Brady," he said. His tone was insistent, pleading. "I'm your only chance. What do you have to lose? I'll fly you back. All I want is to get off this island. We'll be quits. I don't want to kill you. Carlson is gone. That was all that mattered. And you don't have to kill me. You've destroyed the documents. We're even. But you don't have much time. She's dying while you sit there trying to make up your mind. Look at her, Brady. She's white as chalk and getting weaker by the minute."

Mara leaned her head against my back. I felt her hand tighten on my arm. "Shoot him, Johnny," she whispered. "For God's sake, please shoot him."

30

DECISION

The alternatives were bleak ones.

Letting Steckler fly us out seemed our only chance, whether Mara liked it or not. The problem was, it wouldn't work. Sitting in the back of this little plane, holding a pistol to Steckler's head, just wasn't credible. It would be a joke, a completely hollow threat. Once we were in the air, he could radio ahead to an airport, explain that he was being held at gunpoint and request assistance. When we landed, I would be arrested and Steckler would go free. And there wouldn't be a damned thing I could do about it. I certainly couldn't shoot him when we were in midair just to show him I meant business.

I was willing to risk that much if I could be reasonably sure that Mara would be saved. But Steckler, who had every reason to want Mara dead, could decide to make the flight a lot longer than necessary. A couple of hours in the air would be more than Mara could take. And again, what could I do about it?

Mara was right. We should kill him. He had already killed her father, and as long as he remained alive and free, he would continue to be a mortal threat to both of us, no matter what he said.

But after I killed him? Then what?

I saw myself stranded out here with Mara on this godforsaken island, standing by helplessly, watching her slowly die.

I had to decide.

The longer I just sat here, paralyzed by indecision, the worse the situation would get.

I steadied the pistol on Steckler's chest and glanced sidelong at Mara. She was sitting very still. "Are you sure you can't fly?" I asked.

"I'm sure."

"What if I help you?"

"What do you mean?"

"You tell me what to do. I'll do it."

There was a long silence. Mara thought about it. I watched Steckler's face. He was thinking about it, too.

"That's suicide, Brady," he said. "It takes hours to learn how to fly. Even if you got it into the air, you'd sure as hell never land it in one piece."

I glanced at Mara. "Why can't we do it? You can see, you can talk, you can use the radio. One arm and one leg are okay. If I make a mistake you should be able to correct it."

"I might not."

"I still like our chances better than the alternative. How long a flight is it to Bangor?"

"About forty-five minutes."

"Isn't there anything closer? How about Bar Harbor? They must have an airport. And a hospital."

"They do."

Steckler, still leaning on the edge of the wing, dropped his head and shook it sadly. "You'd be a fool, Brady, even to attempt it. She's weak and disoriented. She won't be able to fly the plane at all, and you won't have the faintest idea of what you're doing up there. And all it takes is one little mistake, one error of judgment, one failure to do the right thing at the right time, and you crash to your death. And you'll be so panic-stricken you'll be making mistakes all over the place. Think about it. It takes fifty hours of flying to get a pilot's license—and you're going to fly with no experience? Suicide, Brady. Plain and simple suicide. And you take her down with you."

I knew that if I allowed Steckler to persist, he'd scare me out of it. What the hell, flying terrified me as a passenger.

I looked at Mara. "Let's do it," I said.

Steckler's composure abruptly evaporated. "You're a god-damned fool, Brady!"

"Shoot him now," Mara said. Her voice was impatient. As if to say, Okay, we've decided on a course of action, let's hurry up and get it over with.

"She's probably going to die, anyway, Brady," Steckler warned, his voice shaking. "But you don't have to. Don't listen to her. She's too disabled to think clearly. Don't kill yourself in a stupid attempt at heroism."

I reached back for Mara's good hand and placed the pistol in it. "You kill him," I said.

Later, I wondered why I did that. It seemed both perverse and cowardly. But what went through my mind was simple enough. I thought I had already slaughtered enough people that day. And I knew I couldn't kill a defenseless human being standing in front of me, no matter how justified it seemed. But I thought Mara probably would. She had all the justification anyone needed.

Of course Steckler saw me hand her the weapon. And he certainly believed she'd kill him.

He must have been thinking about it, in fact, because he reacted instantly and with considerable ingenuity. Instead of running off as fast as he could, he dropped to the ground, crawled under my opened door, then back along the plane's fuselage and out from under the tail. Once back on his feet, he trotted off at an almost insolently slow pace, certain that Mara would not have a shot at him. In seconds he was effectively out of range.

Mara fell across my lap, pointing the pistol out the doorway. "We've got to kill him!" she cried.

"It's too late. Let him go."

Mara straightened herself in her seat, kicked open the door on her side and twisted herself around to see behind the plane. Steckler was a hundred yards away, disappearing down the slope where earlier I had unleashed my Stinger missile. Mara fell back against the seat with a deep shudder. I didn't know if the tears in her eyes were from the pain or the disappointment.

"Don't waste energy on him, Mara. Maybe he'll starve to death out here before anybody finds him. We've got to get you help."

She didn't reply.

I glanced down at her knee. The dressing was solid red and blood was dripping off the bottom of her pants leg. I was appalled to see that a small puddle had already formed on the floor.

"How far is Bar Harbor?" I asked.

"Half an hour."

"Let's go, then," I said. "Right now. Before I lose my courage. Skip everything but the essentials. If we get there fast enough I won't need to know anything."

Mara nodded. She pulled herself upright. I buckled our seat belts and checked that both doors were closed and latched.

Mara leaned forward, set the fuel-tank switch on the panel between our seats to BOTH, then pointed to the red knob in the center of the instrument panel. "This adjusts the fuel mixture. All the way in is rich. We'll leave it there. If you pull it all the way out, like this, you'll kill the engine." She pushed the knob back in.

She put her hand on a black knob next to the red one. "This is the throttle. All the way out is idle, all the way in is full power. To start, I pull it all the way out and push it back a quarter of an inch, like this."

"This is taking too long, Mara."

"Okay. You're going to have to control the brakes and the rudder pedals. Put your feet on them."

I found the two pedals, positioned like the brake and clutch in a car, and planted my feet on them.

"The tops of the pedals are brakes," Mara said. "Separate for each wheel. The bottoms of the pedals control the rudder and steer the front wheel. You're going to have to steer the plane down the runway with them. I'll direct you. Keep your movements smooth and steady. Don't overreact."

She pointed to the ignition key next to the master switch on my side of the panel. "We'll skip the mag tests. Press both feet against the tops of the pedals. Brakes. Keep them there. Now turn the key all the way to the right."

I turned the key. The propeller sputtered, then spun, the engine kicked to life. Mara gave it some throttle, vibrating the plane and filling the cockpit with a loud roar. After a few seconds, she eased the throttle back to idle.

"Now take your feet off the tops of the pedals."

I did. The plane started rolling forward.

"Press down slowly on the right pedal. Just your toe against the bottom."

The plane swung slowly around toward the right, facing down the runway.

"Now the left pedal. That's it. Perfect. Now brakes!"

I jammed both feet down hard on the top half of the pedals. The plane shuddered to an abrupt stop.

"That's okay. No more brakes now. Just steer with the bottoms of the pedals and try to keep us straight on the runway. The plane will tend to veer left, so favor the right pedal a little. I'll get us in the air."

I took a deep breath. My mouth was dry. "Okay."

The Cessna started moving forward. I found the pedals awkward and imprecise, and we were quickly zigzagging all over the runway as I tried to compensate to keep us going straight.

"Not so much," Mara shouted, over the engine noise. "You're jumping on them."

We zigzagged the entire length of the strip. Near the very end I was finally able to hold the plane straight.

"Brakes!" Mara called.

I hit the brakes. We jerked to a halt near a tall patch of weeds at the edge of the tarmac.

"Sorry," I muttered.

Mara managed a smile. "We'll call that one practice. There's no wind. We'll take off in the other direction. Steer us around to the left."

I pushed down on the left pedal. Mara inched forward on the throttle and we swung around until we were facing back down the landing strip.

Mara opened the throttle further. The plane started forward and instantly began to veer left. I corrected quickly, got us straight.

Mara increased throttle. I corrected some more. The pedals became noticeably more responsive. It was easier now to hold us on course.

Mara pushed the throttle to full. The Cessna was eating up the runway with alarming rapidity.

"When we lift off, press a little on the right pedal," Mara cried.

She pulled back on the wheel and the Cessna rose smoothly off the ground and pulled to the left. "Now," she said. "Easy."

I increased my foot pressure on the right pedal. The plane yawed back to the right. Mara cranked the wheel left and inched it forward as we gained speed. She clenched her teeth with pain. We straightened out.

"Too much pedal! Ease off!"

I swallowed hard and let my right foot come back slightly.

"Okay!" Mara straightened the wheel and then eased it back toward her, bringing us into a climb.

In seconds we were up and out over the water.

After a short climb Mara eased the wheel forward and the throttle back.

"We did it!" I cried. I felt close to bursting with euphoria. I had expected it to be so difficult—to be nearly impossible. But here we were, up in the air and on our way.

Mara smiled, but her face glistened with a pallid sheen of perspiration.

"Hang on. We're halfway home," I said. "We're going to make it."

She nodded. "The pain alone should keep me awake."

Mara reached down low on the panel between us and rotated a wheellike device a few notches. I felt the airplane's nose drop slightly.

"Trimming the plane," she explained. "For level flight."

Near the top center of the instrument panel several radios were banked. Mara dialed up a frequency on one of them and played with some knobs. "I'm setting the automatic direction finder to home in on Bar Harbor's radio beacon," she explained. "Now all we have to do is get there."

"And land," I added.

"And land," she repeated, mouthing the words softly.

Mara pulled the microphone out of its sleeve and keyed it. "Bar Harbor, Bar Harbor Unicom, Skyhawk eight-zero seven-two Charlie. Do you read?"

There was a brief silence, then a strong male voice boomed in over the cabin speaker: "Skyhawk seven-two Charlie, this is Bar Harbor."

Mara answered: "Bar Harbor, this is seven-two Charlie, two-five south. I have an emergency."

"Seven-two Charlie, this is Bar Harbor. Your transmission is weak. Say again, please. Over."

Mara repeated her message.

"Seven-two Charlie. We copy. What's your problem?"

I looked down at the ocean below us. Three big sailboats trailed long wakes across the barely ruffled surface. I took a deep breath and let it out slowly, willing my body to relax. So caught up had I been in the drama of the last hour that I had forgotten completely about my abject fear of flying.

"Seven-two Charlie. This is Bar Harbor. What is your emergency? Over."

I pressed a hand against my bulging coat pocket of videotapes. Carlson's entire secret library, a distillation of the best of Western intelligence—exclusively mine. And no one in the world knew I had it. What an incredible coup I had pulled off.

"Skyhawk eight-zero seven-two Charlie. This is Bar Harbor Unicom. What is your emergency?"

A slight bump distracted me from my thoughts. The wheel in front of me rotated a little to the right and I felt the airplane begin to lean into a turn. I glanced across at Mara.

She had dropped the microphone. Her head was hard against the side window and her eyes were shut.

"Ahhh, Skyhawk eight-zero seven-two Charlie. Bar Harbor Unicom, do you read? . . . What is your emergency? . . ."

31

GRANDMOTHER

I screamed Mara's name.

Her eyes flickered open for a second, then closed again.

The terror that seized me was profound and shattering. I didn't think it was possible to be so frightened. My insides seemed suddenly to be under a pressure so great that I thought I might literally explode. My nightmare was made real. There was no waking from it.

Had I thought that Mara was dead, I probably would have lost the struggle right there. But my mind fastened on the idea that since I had put her in this situation, I had an obligation to do everything in my power to ensure that she survived. Dedicating myself to that obligation helped fight off the weight of stark, mindscrambling panic that coursed through me like an electric current.

The pressure of that terrible current of fear reached an unbearable intensity and then abruptly peaked. My emotional circuits finally just overloaded and switched off. I slipped into a state of mental numbness bordering on shock.

My perceptions and senses seemed altered, muffled. I was still aware of our hopeless predicament, but I had somehow managed to shut the likely consequences out of my mind. Part of me had already surrendered to the probability that I was going to die, while another part of me was willing to go on and play out the string just in case there was a chance of pulling through.

I yelled at Mara until my voice grew hoarse. With my fear I felt a helpless fury. If she didn't come to, we were lost.

Desperate to do something, I grabbed the pilot's wheel in front of me, and with the same instinct that would make one turn a car's steering wheel before it went off the road, I swung the wheel back from its rightward tilt over to the left.

The plane instantly straightened out of its right turn and started banking steeply to the left.

I jerked the wheel from right to left and back several times until the plane seemed to be flying straight ahead. But by the time I had managed that, we were descending into a dive and gaining speed rapidly. I pulled back on the wheel and the Cessna's nose popped up and the air speed dropped so sharply I thought for a second we had stopped flying.

The wings began to shudder and buffet. A horn started blaring a high-pitched whine somewhere over my head. The whole plane began to vibrate.

I pushed forward on the wheel. I desperately wanted to do something with the throttle, but my fingers were locked, white-knuckled, so tightly around the wheel that I couldn't have let go anyway.

The Cessna's nose sank sickeningly and the plane's speed increased. The damned horn stopped, but now the wind screamed in my ears as the plane dove again.

The blue sky out the windscreen in front of me had vanished, replaced by the darker ocean. We seemed headed straight toward it.

Over the roar of the wind I could hear myself wailing and babbling incoherently. The sounds were involuntary—the cries of a terrified human being.

I pulled back on the wheel, fighting the impulse to jerk it back sharply.

I stared, mesmerized, at the sea, rising toward me with an awful finality. The patterns of waves that wrinkled the surface grew steadily larger.

At the top of the windscreen the horizon miraculously reappeared—a widening band of bright blue pushing down on the darker ocean.

The plane slowed. The sea had now vanished below the windscreen. I pushed forward on the wheel, but too late. The plane was climbing again. I dreaded hearing the scream of that damned horn again. I nudged the wheel forward a fraction more. The climb became less steep, and I felt the craft picking up speed again. The horn stayed silent.

The horizon came back. It was slanting uphill to the right. I cranked the wheel left. For a few precious seconds I seemed to be flying level, then the sea came charging up the windscreen again. In my panic to stabilize the plane, I was still overcorrecting.

I don't know how long the roller-coaster ride lasted. It seemed endless, but it was probably no more than a minute or two. Gradually, agonizingly, as I got better control of the wheel, the climbs became less steep and the dives less precipitous. Finally I had the plane in approximately level flight.

Every nerve was still trembling with terror, but I felt a small thrill of triumph. I had somehow gained control of the wild beast of an aircraft before disaster overtook us. I sat motionless, clutching the wheel and fighting to steady my breath, unable to think what to do next. I stared at the instrument panel. A dozen round, black, meaningless gauges stared back at me.

I didn't know where we were headed, how fast we were flying, how high we were, or how long we could continue on like this before something happened.

Mara had slid farther down against the window. The strips of sheet wrapped around her leg were solid red and wet. Blood continued to drip slowly from the bottom of her pants leg onto the floor. I uncramped my right hand from the wheel, reached across and pulled her back up in her seat. I felt for the carotid artery in her neck. She still had plenty of pulse.

I thought she might lose less blood if I could get her legs up. She might even regain consciousness.

I unsnapped my shoulder harness and seat belt, leaned across, and with my right hand tried to pull her legs up on top of the instrument panel. In the process, I banged one of her knees against the control wheel in front of her.

The Cessna plunged into another diving turn.

I grabbed the wheel with both hands, bellowing curses at the top of my voice, and struggled to right the craft again. We bounced around the sky again for a while, but this time I got us out of the turn and back into level flight with fewer mistakes and over-corrections.

The wheel was slick with blood from my hands. I wiped my palms dry against the hunting jacket.

All through this—from the moment I first realized that Mara had passed out, to my mistaken attempts to prop her legs over the instrument panel—I had remained totally oblivious of the voice in the cabin speaker over my head.

"Skyhawk eight-zero seven-two Charlie, this is Bar Harbor. Do you read? . . ."

I recovered the microphone from the floor on Mara's side, pressed it to my lips and shouted some kind of an acknowledgment. The voice at the other end didn't hear me. I yelled louder. Nothing.

The same monotonous message came back at me over the speaker: "Skyhawk seven-two Charlie. This is Bar Harbor. Do you read? Over . . ."

I looked at the microphone in my shaking hand. There was a big button on the side. I pressed it and tried again: "Hello! Bar Harbor? Can you hear me? Hello!"

There was a pause. I listened to my own panting breath against the mike.

Then this: "This is Bar Harbor. Go ahead."

I swallowed, pressed the mike button again and answered in a quavering voice: "Thank God. Listen, we've got problems. Can you still hear me?"

"This is Bar Harbor. We copy you fine. Go ahead."

"The pilot is badly wounded," I said, fighting to keep my voice steady. "She's passed out. Lost a lot of blood. I'm flying the plane. That's an exaggeration. I don't know a goddamned thing about it. I need all the help you can give me."

There was a long pause, then this incredible response:

"Roger, seven-two Charlie. Suggest you contact Bangor approach control on one-twenty-five point three for radar assistance. Over."

I squeezed the microphone so hard it almost slipped from my grip. "I can't contact anyone! I don't even know how to operate the goddamned radio! All I know is you're the closest airport. The pilot needs medical help immediately. You've got to get us down!"

"Stand by, seven-two Charlie. . . ."

I glanced at Mara. Her head moved and she groaned slightly. For a brief few seconds I entertained the hope that she might be regaining consciousness. But she wasn't.

At least the bleeding seemed to have abated. The pants leg was already saturated from the knee to the ankle, but I saw no fresh blood.

I looked out the side window. There was a large sailboat in the water below us, her bright red, white and blue spinnaker bellied full of wind over her bow. The boat looked to be scarcely a couple of hundred feet away. I could make out individual members of the crew.

What had happened to Bar Harbor? A new terror swept through me: I had lost radio contact. I keyed the mike. "Hello, Bar Harbor? We need help here. Fast. Can you hear me?"

"We copy. Stand by, seven-two Charlie."

We copy. Jesus Christ. I had the feeling those would be the last words I would hear just before we plunged into the North Atlantic.

I decided I had better try to decipher some of the instruments in front of me.

Mounted on top of the panel at the center was a magnetic compass. That, at least, I thought, I would have no trouble understanding. I was wrong. The instrument was swinging wildly back and forth, spinning a series of numbers and letters past me that were meaningless.

My feeling of helplessness intensified.

What the hell were they doing at Bar Harbor? Were they too scared to take on the responsibility of trying to bring down out of the sky some jerk who had no right being there? Were they drawing straws on who would get the shit detail?

I wished I were still a practicing Catholic and believed in God. If we survived this, I *would* believe in God.

Two of the dials in front of me I was able to decipher. I could read our air speed: ninety miles an hour. Or was it knots? Probably knots. What was the difference? Fifteen percent stuck in my head. But which was greater? Bar Harbor would know. If Bar Harbor cared. Why the hell was it taking them so long?

I was also able to decipher the altimeter. At least I thought I could. The long needle was on zero, the short needle on the 2. It must mean we were two thousand feet above sea level. The long needle was dropping slowly toward the 9. I edged the control wheel toward my chest. The needle stopped.

As a reluctant passenger on commercial flights, I had always felt an atavistic conviction that the closer we got to the earth, the safer we were. Now my fears were reversed. I wanted to get up higher, to put more distance between me and the cold, deep ocean below.

A couple of centuries passed.

The speaker over my head crackled. I heard the voice of an elderly woman:

"Skyhawk seven-two Charlie, this is Bar Harbor Unicom. I'm Grace Winterthur. Everyone calls me Grandmother. What's your name, dear?"

God in Heaven. They had turned me over to a little old lady.

"What's your name, dear?"

"My name? Uh. John. John Brady. Jesus, listen. We need some serious help here. In a hurry."

"I understand. You've got every right to be scared half out of your wits, but try to relax. Between the two of us we're going to get you safely back down to earth. Right now it's important for you to stay calm." The woman's voice was a mixture of maternal kindliness and no-nonsense.

"I'm not the calm type," I replied. "But I'll try."

"That's the spirit, dear. The first things we need are your position and your heading."

"I don't know. We're out over the ocean somewhere. We were headed toward Bar Harbor. I don't know where the hell we're headed now."

I heard Grandmother clear her throat. "Can you be a bit more precise?"

I swallowed hard. "No. That's the best I can tell you."

Grandmother didn't let herself sound overly concerned. "Do you know your altitude?" she tried.

"About two thousand feet—I think."

"That's good. Is your plane in stable flight?"

"I guess so . . . the altimeter is pretty steady."

"That's excellent, dear. Are you in the right-hand seat?"

"No. Left. Pilot's side."

If that information surprised her, she didn't say so.

"All right, dear, now find the dial on the top row in front of you," she directed. "The one farthest to your left. That's the plane's air-speed indicator. Can you read it to me?"

"Ninety miles an hour. Or is it knots?"

"Knots," she replied. "Now look at that little glass bulb sitting right on top of the instrument panel. That's the compass. Can you read it?"

I squinted at it and sighed. It was a blur. "Sorry. The damned thing is dancing all over the place. All I can see are the numbers three and six shooting back and forth behind the needle—or whatever the line on the glass is called."

"That's okay. Where did your flight originate?"

"I'm sorry . . . ?"

"Where are you coming from?"

"Oh. Far Island. About twenty miles off the coast."

"I see. . . ."

Grandmother fell silent. I guess she was digesting all this, but the sudden awful void created by the absence of her voice in the cockpit caused the choking panic to flood my chest again. I feared she was gone forever. I keyed the microphone anxiously: "Grandmother?" Christ, how plaintive and pathetic I sounded.

"I'm right here, dear. I'm raising Bangor DF, so we can get a fix on your position. Now when I tell you to, key your microphone and just keep talking into it for a few seconds. Bangor will do the rest. Hold on, now. . . . Okay. Go ahead."

I found myself tongue-tied.

Grandmother came back on: "Just key the mike and say anything, dear. Just say 'ahhhh.' "

I pressed the button on the mike: "Our father who art in Heaven hallow'd be thy name thy kingdom come thy will be done on earth as it is in Heaven . . ."

"That's enough, dear."

After a few more exercises like this, Grandmother gave me the bad news:

"You're heading due east, John—away from the coast. The best thing for us to do is try to set you down on the water as gently as possible. If you can keep the plane airborne, we can get an air-sea rescue team out there in about fifteen minutes."

"Then what?"

"They'll pull you out of the water."

I might survive a plunge into the Atlantic, but Mara never would.

"No," I said. "We can't do that. You have to get us to the airport. Mara—the pilot—she's badly injured."

"What's her condition?"

"A broken right arm and a bullet wound in her leg. She's got a pulse, but she's unconscious. She's lost a lot of blood."

"Do you think you can maneuver the plane yourself?"

"If I have to, I'll do it. Just tell me what to do."

There was a slight pause. Grandmother was no doubt weighing the odds. She didn't weigh them long.

"Okay, dear. We'll bring you down at Bar Harbor. Let's get right to business, then. First, I want you to look out your side window and tell me if the wing is parallel to the horizon."

"Looks parallel. . . ."

"Good. Now look out the windshield in front of you. Is the horizon level out there?"

"Yes."

"Above the nose of the plane?"

"Yes."

"How high above?"

"It's bobbing up and down. I don't know. Six inches maybe."

"That's good. Now find the dial between the air speed and altitude dials—the one with the little airplane wings. Can you find it?"

"Okay. I see it."

"That's the attitude indicator. That line represents the horizon. When you bank left or right, you'll see the wings on the dial bank with you. When you climb or descend, the wings will move above or below the horizon line. If you're in level flight the wings should be sitting exactly on top of the horizon line. Are they?"

"Yeah. More or less."

"Good. Now remember what that looks like, because you're going to have to bring that plane back into level flight after you turn it. Between checking the horizon out the windows and looking at that gauge, you should be able to do it. Okay so far?"

I licked my dry lips. "Yeah. Okay."

"We'll forget about the rudder pedals and just steer with the control wheel. When I tell you to, crank the wheel slowly a little to the left—just two or three inches—until you feel the plane begin to bank. Don't make any sudden movements. Do everything gradually and smoothly. Go ahead and do that now. . . ."

I began cranking the wheel slowly leftward. My hands were squeezing it so tightly I had trouble at first even moving it. "We're turning. . . ."

"Now bring the wheel slowly back level."

"The plane's still turning! . . ."

"That's right. It should be. Let it turn. . . . We need to get you around about fifty degrees from your present heading. Now ease the wheel right just a little. The plane should start leveling out. Watch the horizon. Just before you come up level, start easing the wheel back straight again. . . ."

"The plane's turning the other way! . . ."

"Okay, turn the wheel left . . . *slowly* now. . . . Don't over-correct. . . ."

After a few more alternating yaws to the left and right, I got the plane fairly steady. "Okay. . . ."

"How are the wings? Level with the horizon?"

"Yes."

"The nose?"

"It's level."

"Altitude?"

"I think it dropped."

"That's okay. Pull the wheel back straight toward you about an inch. And hold it there. You should feel the nose lift up."

"Yes."

"What is the altimeter doing?"

"Ahhh, nothing. . . . Yeah, now it's going up. . . ."

"Good. Let the plane climb for a bit. . . . What's the altimeter say now?"

I squinted at it. "Ninety-two hundred feet."

"Look at it again, dear. What number is the short needle on? Read the dial as if it were a clock."

It did look like a clock, with the minute hand moving clockwise past the nine toward the zero, at the top. The hour hand was nearly dead on the two. "Five minutes to two. Now it's two o'clock."

"You're back to two thousand feet."

I had reversed things, reading the 9 under the long needle and the 2 under the short needle as ninety-two hundred. How had I managed to read it right earlier? Dumb luck?

"Now, dear, ease the wheel forward, bring the plane back into level flight. Watch the altimeter."

"Okay. It's steady on two thousand."

"Now let go of the stick for a few seconds and tell me what the altimeter does."

Reluctantly I removed both hands from the wheel. "It's starting to drop. The long needle's going back toward the nine."

"Okay, dear. Now we're going to trim the aircraft for level flight. You see that small wheel down low on the panel beside your seat?"

It took me a few moments to find it. "Okay, I see it."

"That adjusts the trim tab. Rotate the wheel downward about an inch."

I remembered seeing Mara adjusting it. I pressed a thumb against the edge and rotated it. "Okay."

"How's the altimeter doing now?"

"Still dropping."

"Rotate it back some more."

"We're climbing now."

"Rotate it forward."

I finally got the wheel adjusted so that the plane would fly level without any pressure on the wheel, forward or back.

"Now look out the windscreen. What do you see?"

The horizon was no longer perfectly flat. There were bumps. Hills. I was looking at land.

"I see coastline."

"You're heading back toward the mainland. You did it! You turned the plane. How do you feel, dear?"

"Okay." I felt like crying.

Even in my distress I had to admire Grandmother's handholding. It was perfect. She was an extraordinarily soothing pres-

ence, exuding complete, matter-of-fact confidence. I felt pathetically grateful to her.

She was also keeping me so busy that I no longer had the time
to contemplate the appalling danger of the situation.

The compass had settled down. With her help, I was finally able
to read it. I had the plane pointed roughly north.

She explained to me how to set the heading indicator, a dial
that rotated around the nose of a pointer shaped like an airplane.
Once the number matching the magnetic compass reading was
centered over the pointer on the dial, the heading indicator then
operated just like the compass, but more quickly and accurately,
allowing for more precise course corrections.

As soon as she was convinced I had the indicator set properly,
she took me through a series of very small, shallow left turns, until
the number 30 had rotated around over the nose of the indicator.
This put us on a heading of 300 degrees—roughly west-northwest.

These turns came easier. I was able to straighten back into level
flight without staggering all over the sky the way I had earlier. I
was beginning to get some feeling for flying the plane.

I was even beginning to believe we might make it.

I reached across and pressed my fingers against Mara's throat.
Her pulse seemed weaker. The blood on her jeans was beginning
to dry. She looked pale as tissue paper.

Grandmother was talking to me: "John, you're about twenty
miles out, and roughly on course to the airport. At your present
speed you'll be here in less than fifteen minutes. We have to slow
down the plane and decrease your altitude. I want you to get down
to seventy knots and seven hundred feet. We'll do it gradually.
When you get within three miles of the airport, I'll be able to see
you, and you'll be able to see the runway. When we've got you
lined up, we'll bring you right on in."

The imminent prospect of having to land the plane brought
back spasms of the gut-twisting fear I had felt earlier. Landing
would be the crunch. Literally. Grandmother sensed my sudden
anxiety.

"Nothing to be afraid of, dear. Absolutely nothing. It's a beautiful, clear day and you'll be flying straight into a slight head wind.
Basically all that the landing means is gliding down until you touch
the runway. Your air speed will be very slow, and the Cessna has

a lot of stability and forgiveness. The airport will be clear of traffic, and an ambulance is here waiting for your friend. I'll be out on the runway myself with a portable radio, telling you exactly what to do. So far you've done just great. I know you're going to come through this just fine."

I felt like crying again.

A sudden shadow disturbed my peripheral vision.

I looked out the left side window and was astonished to see a helicopter hovering near my left wing. Three men were inside. One of them was pointing a TV camera at me.

A loud male voice suddenly vibrated in the cabin speaker over my head: "Skyhawk seven-two Charlie, this is Pete Robichard, Channel Five Eye-in-the-Sky for Eyewitness News. We picked up your situation a few minutes ago. You're quite a story, pal! I'm going to go on the air with you now, live."

32

DESCENT

I didn't want to believe it.

"Grandmother. I've got company. A press helicopter. He's right beside me."

"I hear him," she said. "Please get off this frequency immediately, young man," she snarled. "You're endangering lives."

The TV newsman protested in a hurt voice: "We're here to help you, Bar Harbor. We can give you accurate readings on Seventwo Charlie's position."

Grandmother was obliged to welcome the help. So was I. The pilot of the helicopter broke in and rattled off some letters and numbers that meant little or nothing to me. Grandmother thanked him.

"We'll stay with him," the pilot offered.

"Okay, but stay well clear of the plane," she warned.

The pilot promised he would. Then Robichard, the Channel Five reporter, took over again. Helping me was fine, but he also had a story to cover. A damned good story, by the standards of TV journalism. Great visuals, great human interest. And in plenty of time for the evening news. At that moment I both despised and envied him.

Robichard held the chopper's mike open, so that his lead-in, fed back to his studio on a satellite uplink, was also monopolizing our frequency:

"This is Pete Robichard, reporting to you live from the Channel Five Eyewitness News Eye-in-the-Sky Telecopter. We have a real drama unfolding here, high in the air over the famous resort town of Bar Harbor. Seems the pilot of a private plane has either passed out or died—we'll find out in a minute—and the plane you now see in your picture is being flown by someone who's never flown before. I've got that brave—and very frightened—individual on the line right now. . . . Sir, can you hear me? Can you tell me what's going through your head as you face this life-threatening situation? How confident are you that you'll actually be able to land the plane?"

Jesus Christ, was the man serious? Of course he was. I took a deep, ragged breath.

"Sir, we're live on Channel Five," Robichard repeated, the impatience in his tone suggesting that he was extending me a privilege I was showing signs of not deserving. "Could you give us your name, please?"

Grandmother was trying to say something, but the reporter's voice kept drowning her out.

I keyed the mike and tried to contain the homicidal fury welling up alongside my fear. "Listen, Pete. I'm kind of busy right now. Would you please get your 'telecopter' the fuck out of my face?"

"Well, you heard him," Robichard said. "That's one terrified human being up there, hanging on with grim determination in the face of what would seem to be insuperable odds. The only thing standing between him and sudden death at this moment is a seventy-year-old grandmother, who's trying to talk him down. She's quite a story in herself. As soon as we have a chance, we'll go back to the Cessna and talk to the man who, as you can see on your screen right now, is very busy at the controls. . . ."

Grandmother's voice cut in. It was heavy with menace: "Mr. Robichard! You're flirting with serious felony charges. You must get off this frequency immediately and stand clear of that plane!"

I never heard Robichard's voice again, but his helicopter stayed right on me. I knew what he was going to do. He would stay patched in to our frequency and feed my conversation with Grandmother back to the studio, along with a live picture of me struggling with the plane. If the station was an independent, then the networks and CNN would pick up tape of our adventure and run it on the evening news. If it was an affiliate, they would probably feed the story live to New York. If the network news executives thought it was diverting enough, they'd break into the afternoon soaps and broadcast it nationwide.

What a way to die: live on national television.

Grandmother was talking to me again. She guided me through another course correction, and started me on a slow descent, cramming every second with detailed instruction. She had me bring the Cessna down from two thousand feet to about seven hundred by throttling the engine down very gradually. This made the plane's nose want to dip. To counter it, I had to hold the wheel back against considerable pressure to keep the plane flying level. Now, instead of diving, we were more or less floating down.

Grandmother rehearsed the landing procedure with me, indicating the controls involved, how I was going to use them, and what the landing was going to look and feel like. She kept me busy reading back the numbers on the tachometer and the air-speed indicator until I had lowered our speed to about sixty knots— barely fast enough to get a ticket on the throughway.

I was sweating furiously from the effort, and the muscles in my hands were cramping from holding the wheel back, but I was getting it done. And Mara still had a pulse.

The helicopter pilot was now communicating with Grandmother on another frequency, updating her on my position and progress. I caught glimpses of the cameraman behind his lens, and Robichard beside him, talking into a mike. The chopper had backed away a little, but it still hung near me, like a vulture patiently watching for its prey to expire.

"Tell me what you see below, dear."

I wiped the perspiration out of my eyes with a coat sleeve. "On the left, coastline, mostly land. On the right, water, islands—looks like a bay."

"That's Frenchman Bay. You're just over the eastern edge of Mount Desert Island. The town of Bar Harbor is right ahead of you. You're about seven miles from the airport and doing fine."

The broad clusters of buildings looming ahead of me looked to be right in my path. I glanced anxiously at the altimeter, fearing I had made another mistake. The long needle was on zero, the short needle halfway between zero and one. One was one thousand, so I was at five hundred feet. Was that high enough to clear everything? The helicopter apparently thought so. It was flying at the same altitude.

"What do you see now, dear?"

"A wide swath of water ahead of me, like a river. I see a bridge over on my left."

"Good. Now look across the water. . . ."

A mixture of relief and dread swept over me. There, ahead and a little to the left, a huge gray-black cross appeared, looking like some gigantic ceremonial megalith laid out on the surface of the earth by a prehistoric tribe. The airport runways.

"I see the airport."

"Good! I'm out on the field now, with radio and binoculars. I can see you quite clearly, dear. Hold your present course, and hold your altitude. The runway you're going to use is the one perpendicular to your present heading. It's ahead of you and to your left. Can you see it?"

"Yes."

"Good. When I tell you, make a very shallow, very gradual turn, to line up with that runway. After you've done that, things will happen fairly fast. Stay calm and alert. As soon as we both think you're in position, I'll tell you to start your descent. Okay?"

"Okay."

I watched the airport start to slide past me. Trees, buildings and field appeared as close as if I were standing looking at them from a nearby hill. I saw three fire engines. And two ambulances. One for Mara, I thought. And one for me.

"Now, dear: Crank the wheel left. Slowly. That's it. . . . Bring it back straight now. Let the turn continue. That's it. . . . You're coming around nicely. Keep turning. That's it. Now start cranking the wheel right to bring it out of the turn. Don't worry about losing altitude. Crank right a little more. . . . That's enough turn. Get your wings level. Your left wing's dragging. Get your wings level. . . ."

I couldn't do it.

By the time I had managed to level out I was parallel to the runway, but well past it, flying along the right side of it.

"You turned a little late, dear. Don't worry. You've still got time to get back over it. Crank the wheel a little left. . . ."

I froze.

Holding the wheel dead level, I watched the broad swath of field that bordered the runway slide away beneath me. I was aware of Grandmother's voice, but I could no longer make out what she was saying.

The plane seemed dangerously close to the ground. I was still, in fact, several hundred feet up, but I felt much lower. I doubted I could clear a two-story building. I wanted to get out. I looked across at Mara. Was she still alive? *Please God, let somebody rescue us.*

I had to climb, to get away. I pulled the wheel back toward me. The Cessna's nose pitched upward and shuddered. I felt the plane falter, like a car running out of gas. I needed more power, but I couldn't unclasp a hand from the wheel to open the throttle.

"DO NOT CLIMB! REPEAT, DO NOT CLIMB! KEEP THE WINGS LEVEL WITH THE HORIZON!"

It was Grandmother, bawling at me in a tone that demanded to be obeyed.

I eased the wheel back forward. The Cessna's laboring engine smoothed out, and the vibrations stopped. I looked for the altimeter, but couldn't remember where it was. I felt my chest heaving and my pulse pounding in my ears.

"Are you trying to ruin my day?"

It took me a while to compose myself enough to answer. When I did, she immediately resumed her directions, as if nothing had gone wrong.

The next minutes are vague in my memory.

Somehow Grandmother got me turned around and headed back

toward the airport. It was a sloppy, hair-raising turn, with me regressing back to my first tendencies to overreact with the controls. The Cessna staggered and lurched this way and that, sideways, up and down and all over the place. What remained of my self-confidence was shattered. A dozen times I expected the plane to just nose over into the ground and put us out of our misery.

Grandmother, meanwhile, had returned to her old patient self, brimming once more with can-do optimism despite my falling apart right in front of her. What she was telling me, and what she was trying to bring about, weren't quite the same in any case. She wanted me to believe I could actually bring the plane down in one piece. But she was aiming for a controlled crash.

More by miracle than design, I got the runway just about dead in my sights coming back.

"You're right on the money, now, dear. I knew you could do it. Now let's bring it down."

Now I was ready. Anything to end the nightmare.

Her words flowed through me like a voice in the back of my head: "Ease the throttle back. . . . Come back on the wheel at the same time. . . . Keep the nose up level. . . . That's it. Back on the throttle some more. . . . Back on the wheel, nice even pressure, let the nose drop just a little now. . . . That's it, she's coming down fine. . . . Close the throttle right down to idle. . . . Don't let the nose drop so much. . . . Pull back on the wheel. . . . You're just about right. You're going to glide in like this all the way."

"What about flaps?" I said. I remembered Mara lowering the flaps when we had landed at Far Island. She had pushed that flat black lever on the center of the instrument panel, next to the mixture control. I remembered it distinctly because I had been alarmed by the abrupt slowing of the plane's speed.

"Never mind flaps," Grandmother replied. "We're keeping it simple. . . . What I want you to do now is locate the red knob next to the throttle. See it?"

"Yes."

"That's the lean mixture. When I tell you to, pull it back toward you all the way. Do it quick. I want you to touch down with the engine off. That's very important. Okay?"

"Okay."

"You're drifting a little right. Get the nose back near the center line of the runway. Keep the runway straight ahead of you. . . .

You're about a mile out, now, and doing nicely. . . . Don't let that left wing drop down. . . . Easy, now. No quick motions. More back pressure on the wheel now—hold the nose up. . . . Too much. Ease forward on the wheel, let the nose come back down a bit That's it. . . . You're drifting left. Keep the nose straight."

The airport was now directly under me. I held my breath. The broad tarmac path I had been zeroing in on was now slipping beneath me. I felt another roaring surge of panic.

Grandmother was still talking: "You're about fifty feet up. Almost home. Stay in the air as long as you can. You have plenty of room to roll out. . . . When the wheels touch, try to keep the plane straight, wings level. . . . Now, pull the wheel back, that's it, dear. Ease it back some more. You're coming down beautifully. . . . Keep holding back, holding back. Hold the plane off the ground a little bit longer. . . . That's it, dear. . . . You're at ten feet, five feet. . . . Keep holding back. . . ."

I felt that I should have hit the runway by now, but the plane was still flying. I had the illusion, from the nose-up attitude of the craft, that I was climbing.

"Pull the red knob! NOW!"

I reached forward, grabbed the red knob with sweat-soaked fingers and yanked it.

The engine died.

Grandmother said no more.

The craft struck the runway with a jarring thud and bounced sickeningly up into the air again.

The left wing swung down. I cranked the wheel right. The plane soared about thirty feet, then dropped back to the tarmac. The nose wheel hit first. The Cessna lurched to one side, and the right wing scraped the runway, throwing up a shower of sparks.

It was an accident in slow motion, drawn out in separate stages of destruction by the doomed craft's long, soaring leaps between its collisions with the ground.

The next crunch collapsed the nose wheel and spun the Cessna sideways. The left wheel lifted off the ground and the plane lurched over on its side, dragging a wing along the runway with a loud, rending shriek of metal. The whole airport was spinning around me, trees and hangars and parked airplanes whipping past my eyes with the dizzying speed of a carnival ride.

Mara's left arm flew out and slapped against my chest.

I closed my eyes and threw my arms up over my face.

The roaring, crashing, careening came finally, mercifully, to an end.

I felt light-headed and short of breath, as if someone had punched me in the stomach. I bent forward, groaning for air. Over the ringing in my ears I heard the wail of sirens. When I caught my breath, I collapsed back against the seat and let my head fall against the side window.

Someone was opening the passenger-side door. A man and a woman lifted Mara out of the seat and laid her on a stretcher. The wallet from the back pocket of her jeans fell out onto the seat.

My door opened. Two medics were there. I let one of them reach in and undo my shoulder harness and seat belt. They started to lift me from the seat, but I pushed their hands away. I was okay, I said. I picked up Mara's wallet from the passenger seat and tucked it into my jacket pocket, along with my precious videotapes.

I crawled out the door and onto the ground. I felt warm blood trickling down my forehead. The medics helped me get up and put me in a wheelchair. A fire truck pulled up beside us. I saw Robichard's helicopter landing nearby.

They rushed me across to the ambulance and lifted me into the back. I settled on a jump seat next to Mara's stretcher. A medic climbed in on the other side, slammed the back door, and the ambulance was in gear and racing out of the airport, its siren blaring.

A crowd ten deep had already congregated behind the tall storm fence separating the field from the public parking lot. A traffic jam was developing on the access road. Three police cruisers, Mars lights flashing, rolled up in front of the ambulance and moved out, clearing a path for us.

I looked back at the airport. The Cessna lay out in the middle of the runway, resting on its belly. Its undercarriage had collapsed and one wing was bent back at a sharp angle. The plane looked like a dead bird. A crowd had already begun to collect around it.

I caught a fleeting glimpse of a solitary figure some distance from the crash. It was an elderly lady in a windbreaker with a portable radio in her hand and a pair of binoculars draped around her neck. She was standing in the grass by the edge of the runway, her free hand resting on a hip, surveying the wreckage.

Grandmother.

*   *   *

They checked me over in the emergency ward, put a bandage on my forehead and let me go. I lay down on a sofa in a small waiting room outside the operating room and waited to hear about Mara.

I watched myself flying an airplane on Channel 5 news. They had shown Robichard's film four times so far since five o'clock. The crash landing at the airport looked quite spectacular, but I was beginning to get bored with it.

At seven that evening the doctor walked in, still in his green surgical gown and cap. He was short, bald and dark-skinned. His name was Madani. He was Iranian.

"She's in the recovery room," he said. "She'll be okay. We gave her a transfusion, set the arm and removed the bullet. The leg will take time to heal. The slug damaged some cartilage. She'll need physical therapy. The knee itself is fine."

"When can I see her?"

"She's been through a lot. Let her sleep. See her in the morning."

I nodded. Been through a lot, indeed.

Madani opened his palm and showed me the bullet he had removed. "I have to report this to the police, you know. Stab wounds, bullet wounds, that kind of thing. You understand."

"Sure. I've already explained to the police what happened."

"What *did* happen?" he asked, enveloping me with a look of wide-eyed curiosity.

I yawned. "We were doing some target practice out on her father's estate on Far Island. She shot herself in the leg."

"How did she break her arm?"

I coughed into my fist. "Well, she fell on it after she shot herself. She was a little panicked, you can imagine."

Madani's eyes narrowed. He smirked. He tossed the bullet up in the air and caught it. "She was using a pretty big weapon for target shooting. This looks like a .357 Magnum."

I shrugged. He didn't believe me, but it was the best I could come up with. I made a mental note to be sure I told Mara how her accidents had occurred before she had a chance to talk to anybody.

I had already sold a longer version of the same story to Captain Boudreau of the Bar Harbor police—and to Pete Robichard, the intrepid Channel 5 reporter who had followed me in the helicopter.

He beat the ambulance to the hospital and managed to corner me almost as soon as we hit the emergency room. It was a toss-up whether to give him an interview or just break his nose. I decided what the hell—I was alive. I felt expansive. Also, I realized that if I didn't talk to him, he was just enterprising enough to try to find out what had happened on his own. That would not be good.

I told Robichard I'd give him my story exclusively if, in return, he'd help hide me from the rest of the press. He eagerly agreed. We found a vacant room and locked the door. Once comfortably inside, I proceeded to bury the only fact about me that he had— my real name—under a deep pile of lies. I told him I was Mara's fiancé. I was an American, but lived abroad. We had flown up to the house on Far Island to put family things in order following her father's death at New York Hospital last week. After our honeymoon, we planned to move to New Zealand, where my uncle's family owned a large sheep ranch.

I sneaked out of the hospital after dark, rented a car and drove to a shopping center. At a big discount store I bought a cotton shirt, underwear, socks, a pile of toiletries, a nylon windbreaker, a cheap canvas suitcase and a blue plastic flight bag.

I ate a pizza and drank three bottles of beer at a nearby Pizza Hut, then booked a room at a Holiday Inn. I stuffed the container with the videotapes into the plastic flight bag and asked the desk clerk to store it for me in the office safe.

A good view of myself in the full-length bathroom mirror made me understand why people had been edging away from me. I looked like an ax murderer. My hair was wild, I had two days' stubble, my face was streaked with dirt and my eyes were red and puffy. The old hunting jacket I was wearing was four sizes too large and bulged obscenely from its side pockets. The sleeves and the front of it were smeared with dried blood.

I also smelled like the Tet Offensive. Pungent waves of sweat, blood, gunpowder and solid-state rocket propellant from the Stinger rolled off me and hung in the room.

After a long shower and shave I felt marginally restored. I opened the windows to air the place out, stuffed the clothes I had been wearing, along with the extra underwear and socks I had just bought, in the canvas suitcase and parked it on a chair.

I turned on the television set, but couldn't watch it. I read the newspapers I had picked up. There was one item of interest. The president planned to announce his choice of a new Director of Central Intelligence tomorrow.

This was tomorrow. I stayed up to watch the eleven o'clock news. The president had not yet made his announcement. There was no explanation for the delay, but a spokesman promised it would be made shortly.

I watched myself land the Cessna again. The station followed the footage with Robichard's interview of me at the hospital. I had removed the hunting jacket during the interview, but I was still dirty, tired and disheveled. On camera, I looked furtive and peculiar, like an escapee from a maximum-security prison trying to pass for an ordinary citizen. I was sure that anybody watching could tell that everything I said was a lie. I prayed that the interview was not picked up by the network. If anyone in New York saw this, I would be in trouble.

How much trouble was I really in? I wondered.

If Steckler eventually made it back to the mainland, how much would he dare reveal? Hardly anything, I thought. And except for Colonel Westerly's, all the bodies were deep in the sea. Maybe Steckler would even bury Westerly, with all the time he had on his hands.

I was too exhausted to consider all the ramifications. I got ready for bed.

Mara's wallet lay on the dresser where I had deposited it when I emptied out the hunting jacket. I picked it up and looked at it again. I had gone through its contents thoroughly back at the hospital, hunting for her medical insurance card and something with her blood type on it.

I pulled out her driver's license and studied it. Something about it had disturbed me earlier, and I couldn't figure out what it was. I felt an odd sensation every time I looked at it. Very peculiar. It was as if something on the card had a meaning that wasn't quite registering.

Her photograph was a couple of years old, and like most ID photos it wasn't especially flattering. But there was something else in the photo, something familiar beyond the fact of Mara's face. It was reaching out to me. I was getting the feeling of the message, but not the content. Maybe it was no more than the effect of all the stress. A form of hallucination. A temporary derangement of the senses. In the morning the feeling would be gone.

I slipped the license back into the wallet and placed it back on the dresser. Tomorrow I would take it to the hospital and leave it with Mara.

I climbed into bed and turned out the light.

Despite my fatigue, I couldn't sleep. The events of the day kept rushing back, replaying themselves in my head: I saw the bodies falling into the sea from Steckler's plane; I saw the plane exploding in midair, I saw Mara running; Westerly shooting; Westerly dying. I saw Steckler, leaning on the Cessna's wing, staring at me; and Mara trying to shoot him; and Steckler running. I saw myself in the Cessna, Mara unconscious beside me. I twisted and turned and opened my eyes and stared at the dull glow of blue light coming through the room's curtains. The instant I closed my eyes again, the images came flooding back. I wondered if I would ever sleep again.

I got up, went to the bathroom and swallowed an antihistamine tablet. Besides stopping a runny nose, an antihistamine made a reliable sleeping pill.

I looked for something to read.

I picked up Mara's wallet from the dresser again, removed the license and looked at it under the light of the bedside lamp. The sensation of something familiar was so intense that I could feel it crawling up my insides. What on earth was it?

I stared at the license for a long time.

When the realization finally dawned, I laughed out loud. Then I walked around and around the room, holding the ID in my hand and saying no to myself out loud over and over again.

I sat down on the bed, lost in thought. I convinced myself that I must be mistaken. But the idea wouldn't go away. I was onto something.

Too worked up to sit still, I got dressed and went out. For over an hour I walked around the town of Bar Harbor and along the water's edge. It was a warm night and the moon was bright over the harbor.

The more I thought about it, the less incredible it became. It even started to become plausible. I decided that my suspicions were justified.

I went back to my motel room and telephoned Tracy Anderson.

SECRETS

I was in Mara's room by eight A.M., the earliest the hospital would allow me through the door.

She was propped up in bed on a pile of pillows, her left forearm in a cast. An IV tube was taped to her wrist. She looked pale, but otherwise healthy. She was holding a hairbrush in her right hand, trying to comb out her hair.

Her head fell back on the pillows when I walked in. "Thank God," she murmured. "Nobody here would tell me what had happened to you."

The other bed in the room was empty. I sat down, overwhelmed by a flood of conflicting emotions. I wanted to run to her side and put my arms around her and hold her hard, but I held back. There was too much on my mind.

She looked at me with an expression of alarm. "You *are* okay, aren't you, Johnny?"

"Yeah, I'm okay. What about you?"

She rested the brush on the bedclothes. "God, I hurt all over. What happened? Tell me. I passed out in the plane, didn't I?"

I described the whole adventure, from the moment she passed out and a rescuing angel known to me only as Grandmother took over, until the hospital finished patching up her wounds. I also told her the story I had concocted to explain what we were doing out on Far Island.

"You think they believe you?" she asked.

"Sure. It's more plausible than what actually happened, don't you think?"

"Almost anything would be."

"I wonder how Steckler's doing out there?"

Mara looked out the window, biting her lip thoughtfully. "I've been thinking about that, too. I bet he's found a way off by now."

"How could he?"

"I remember his goons mentioned something to him about the raft they came out on. He's probably found it by now."

I had forgotten all about the raft. "Even so, you think he's strong enough to row twenty miles to shore—against that current?"

"He only has to get to Great Duck Island. That's five miles away. There's a lighthouse there. They have a radio."

"Well, maybe the current would pull him out to sea."

Mara fell silent. I thought I knew what was on her mind. "You still think we should have shot him, don't you?"

Mara let her head sink back against the pillows. "Yes. It sounds outrageously criminal, doesn't it? But he's much too dangerous alive."

Somewhere in the back of my mind I had the idea that I was going to ruin him with the material on the videotapes, and that would be so much better than killing him. But I hadn't thought out exactly how it could be done. It was just a promise I had made to myself. "I'm sorry about your father," I said.

She turned her face to me. I studied it in a way I had never studied it before, noting the precise shape of her features—eyes, ears, nose, forehead, chin, lips, cheekbones.

"He brought it on himself," she said.

"It was a damned clever plan," I replied. "Faking his death and then setting that trap for Steckler. It should have worked."

Mara shook her head. "Steckler knew Père too well."

We looked at each other. Mara's expression was solemn. She knew I had questions to ask.

"Why did you come back to the island when you did?"

Mara gazed down at the hairbrush. "It was supposed to be all over by then—Steckler dead, Père back in control and on top of things. I was going to help him tidy up—get rid of the documents, and so on. He really did intend to close down the Night Watch. He knew it was getting out of hand. Even if he got Steckler, he knew it was only a matter of time before somebody else tried to grab it—somebody like Westerly. Père believed he was the only man in the world who could exercise that much power in a responsible way."

"You think he did?"

"I think he did at first. But I'm not the person to ask."

"He should never have had that kind of power," I said. "Ever. He had elevated himself to a place where he could crush anyone who got in his way, or anyone who just annoyed him—like me. And he could do it invisibly, with no concern for the consequences. He was playing God, visiting his wrath on anyone he chose, without reason or justification."

Mara patted the hairbrush against the mattress. She didn't seem to want to look at me.

"You don't agree?"

"Oh, yes, I know you're right, Johnny. Père had an obsession about controlling everything. It started with those around him and eventually came to include the whole damned world. If he hadn't been so good at it, he'd have failed a long time ago. But eventually everyone betrayed him."

"And why not? He never trusted anybody. He lived in a world of naked power plays. There was nothing else. Everything he accomplished he did by force or blackmail. People can't tolerate that indefinitely. He invited them to turn on him."

"They betrayed him because he had something they wanted."

"And he wouldn't give it to them," I added.

Mara shrugged. "Are you going to betray Père, too?" she asked, confronting me with those transparent blue-gray eyes.

"What do you mean?"

"Steckler saw the files strewn all around the bunker. He assumed someone had already pillaged it and removed important documents. Now he knows who did it—you."

I could not tell her about the videotapes. "You saw what happened to the documents. They went into the drink, along with the plane and Steckler's goon squad."

"You didn't remove any? Before Steckler got there?"

"No."

It was a politician's truth—technically accurate but completely false. Strictly speaking, I hadn't taken any. But on the other hand, I had also taken everything. I wished I could admit to her what I had done. I would someday. But not now. It was too dangerous. Until I decided myself what I was going to do with the videotapes, I couldn't risk telling anyone. Especially Mara. What she didn't know wouldn't hurt her, as the old saw had it. And knowing I was in possession of the Night Watch's entire secret library could certainly get one hurt.

Mara's eyes narrowed in suspicion. "How come? Didn't you stay to find what you needed to beat your spy charges?"

There are few things more hateful than having to expand on a lie you wished you didn't have to tell in the first place. "I didn't get the chance," I replied. "I took the cabin cruiser to escape from Steckler's men. It ran out of gas, I had to swim back."

Mara poked the bed with the hairbrush. Neither of us spoke. "Tell me something," I said, breaking the tense silence. "What was I doing there?"

Mara wrinkled her brow. "What do you mean?"

"It obviously wasn't to salvage some documents for my legal defense. Carlson was alive. He and his men were already there, in place, waiting to ambush Steckler. He had no reason to let me come up and nose around through his secret files. It would be just about the last thing he'd want me to do. As long as he was alive, he was still in a position to honor our original agreement. He didn't need to compromise himself by letting me see all that incredible material down in the bunker. So what did he want me there for?"

Mara ran the brush nervously back and forth across the sheet. "I don't know," she replied, with a strong catch in her throat.

"He didn't tell you?"

"Yes. He told me. He said that bringing you out there was just following through on the whole deception. He said we had to be certain to act exactly as if he had really died. Steckler would be suspicious, alert for the slightest indication of a trick. But if he knew that I was taking you up there, letting you into the bunker, then Steckler would swallow the bait and rush right after the documents himself. Père underestimated him, that's all."

"How did Steckler know I was going up there with you?"

"That was the easiest part of the whole deception. His people were following both of us like a pack of beagles. They saw us leave La Guardia for Bangor, and they saw us leave Bangor in the Cessna."

"You noticed all this?"

"Yes."

"Well, thanks for letting me in on it."

Mara shrugged. "I was worried that if I told you, you might do something rash and upset the whole plan."

"Okay. Then what? After he had used me as bait to lure Steckler to the island—what was supposed to happen to me after that?"

"If Père had been able to get rid of Steckler, he would have gotten the charges against you dropped, just as he promised."

"After I'd seen what was in the bunker?"

"Père would still have expected you to honor your part of the bargain."

"Did you really believe all that?"

Mara didn't answer immediately. She started brushing her hair again, working on a snarl that had developed in a long lock over her left ear. With only one usable hand, it was difficult, and she winced as she tried to pull the brush through. "Not entirely," she admitted.

I pushed myself off the bed, walked over to the window and looked out. "You know what I think?"

Mara didn't ask. She just kept brushing her hair.

"I think that Carlson intended to kill me. That's the only explanation that makes sense. He would never have allowed me to see all those documents in the bunker otherwise. I had become an irritant to him, after all—a dangerous nuisance. He was tired of fending me off. So in his paranoid cleverness, he decided that while getting rid of Steckler, he could get rid of me, too." I turned from the window and faced her. She stopped brushing. "And it's damned hard for me to believe that you didn't know that."

"I worried that that was what he might be thinking, Johnny," she said.

"But you went along with it, anyway?"

"No. I made sure that it couldn't happen."

"How did you do that?"

A nurse came in to change the IV and the dressing on her leg. I left the room. I walked aimlessly around the hospital, feeling miserable. Our entire relationship—if you could dignify it with that appellation—seemed constructed of subterfuge and deception. Why were we lying to each other so much? After all we had been through, there was still no trust between us.

I returned to Mara's room. She was sitting up, looking bored, snapping through the pages of a magazine. "I thought you'd run off," she said. Her voice was angry. She kept her eyes on the pages.

I sat back down on the adjacent bed. "How did you make sure that Père wouldn't kill me?" I asked her.

She sighed and slipped a little farther down in the bed. She didn't want to tell me.

"Don't leave me wondering about it," I said.

"It was very simple. I told him that you were somebody very important to me. That was all I had to say. Père hated to hear me say it, but he loved me. I knew that if I told him that, he wouldn't harm you."

"When did you tell him?"

"The day on the island—just before I flew off and left you in the bunker." She grinned. "I know. You think that was cutting it pretty close. But I honestly don't believe he really ever intended to kill you, anyway. If he had, he wouldn't have bothered with that whole elaborate espionage frame-up. He'd have simply hired somebody to bump you off."

Mara reached a hand out toward me. The gesture brought a lump to my throat. I wanted so much to love her, and I kept wondering if she was ever going to give me the chance. I moved across and sat down on the bed beside her. We kissed. She ran her hand gently through my hair and stroked the back of my neck.

"In his own peculiar way I think he admired you," she said.

"You scared him, Johnny. Your book threatened more than just to uncover his Night Watch network. It forced Père to begin to look at himself differently, to think about what a biography of him might say. He started to worry about his epitaph, his place in history. That was your doing. That was also part of the reason he wanted you at Far Island. He would never have admitted it, but he wanted to take you into his confidence. He wanted you to see those files, he wanted to impress you with what he had done. Père was bothered terribly by the anonymity of his power. He saw himself as a selfless patriot, a soldier keeping guard on the barricades, a man doing great things that the country could never know or appreciate. He coveted the chance to show off his accomplishments to someone on the outside. That turned out to be you."

"But once I saw the files, I would have been twice as dangerous to him."

Mara agreed. "He was willing to risk that, I guess. If his plan succeeded, he expected he could keep you to your part of the bargain by holding the threat of those spy charges over you. I guess he thought he could do that indefinitely. That would have been part of his triumph, too, you see. He would have shown you how big and important the story was that you had been trying to get, and still have prevented you from revealing it. That was Père— he always had to have everything both ways."

"Did you really have a funeral in Washington?"

"Yes. A cremation. Then a memorial at St. John's Cathedral. About a thousand people were there. Including the president. It was very impressive. I cried a lot. Mostly from guilt. The eulogies seemed so naive and ironic. I began to wonder how Père would ever recover from playing such a cruel hoax on everyone. I thought that when he finally did die, no one would come to his real funeral except me. Well, it really was his funeral, after all, wasn't it?" Mara started crying softly. "I guess I was the only one who didn't know it."

She found some tissues on the bedside table and dabbed her eyes. "Christ, Johnny, I should be so happy. You saved my life. Twice. And we're both alive, and together. I should be so happy, but I feel so miserable. The whole world has just come apart. Père is gone. And I can't even think about him anymore without feeling ashamed of the things he's done."

The door opened and a nurse stuck her head in. "Excuse me, there's somebody here to see you."

Mara looked at me questioningly. I got up off the bed. My knees felt wobbly and my insides shaky with anticipation.

Tracy Anderson walked in.

Mara recognized her instantly. Her eyes widened in awe, then switched quickly over to me for an explanation.

My eyes were on Tracy. I saw immediately that she had gone to a lot of effort for this particular entrance. And it was one of her best. She looked radiant, splendid. Beautiful and mature at the same time. She had studied her part and got it just right. No jewelry, no furs, no sunglasses, no entourage. Hardly any makeup. Her clothes and manner suggested an amiable, well-heeled suburban matron with good taste, charming manners and a sense of social responsibility. She was playing the role of someone whom you would be expected immediately to love, trust and respect. And what struck me especially was the powerful sense I got that Tracy felt perfectly at home in the part.

I turned to Mara. "This is a friend of mine," I said. "Tracy Anderson. She's just flown up from New York. Tracy, this is Mara Carlson."

Mara's face was beaming. "Miss Anderson? Oh my God. The movie star. Père—my father—used to talk about you all the time. What are you doing here? I mean—I love your films—God, I feel so embarrassed!"

Tracy stood for a moment between the beds. She seemed ready to say something, but she just kept looking at Mara. The smile she wore when she had entered faded to something like an expression of acute heartbreak. I looked from Tracy's face to Mara's and then back again. I felt almost unbearably choked up inside.

They shook hands. Tracy cleared her throat, sat down on the bed opposite and then completely fell apart. She didn't burst into tears—she exploded.

Mara glanced up at me, alarmed. "What's the matter?" she whispered. "What's the matter with her?"

I had tears in my own eyes now. "She's just a little overwhelmed," I said, straining to talk past the lump in my throat. "Seeing her daughter for the first time."

34

THE FATHER

Was Mara really Tracy's daughter?

The evidence was circumstantial, but persuasive. It was the date and place of birth on Mara's driver's license: April 4, 1963. Paris, France. The same date and the same place where Tracy had given birth to her daughter. That was all the evidence I had when I called Tracy and asked her to fly to Bar Harbor. For Tracy, it was certainly enough.

Beyond that? Well, Tracy and Mara looked alike. That was apparent as soon as you saw them together. And of course there was Andrew Carlson's role in the matter. It was he who had taken Tracy's baby girl when she was a week old, and he would never later admit to Tracy what had become of her.

Obviously, Mara wasn't the only child born in Paris on that

date. But the odds that both Tracy and Carlson's wife had given birth to baby girls there on the same day were astronomical. And even though Carlson appeared to have kept his family life secret and apart from his professional life, wouldn't he at least have mentioned such a coincidence to Tracy at the time?

I had intended to look into it further. That's what I was supposed to be good at, after all—getting at the truth, digging up the secrets and bringing them out into the daylight.

I was going to start by finding out whether Mara and Tracy's daughter had been born in the same hospital. A simple and obvious thing to check. But I never did even that much. I decided that it didn't matter.

Tracy wanted Mara to be her daughter, and Mara wanted Tracy to be the mother she felt she never had. There was no one around interested in a different outcome, so why should I risk ruining everything for everybody, myself included?

That's not the way John Brady, investigative journalist, used to think. But times were changing.

The first few hours Tracy and Mara spent together were a little difficult.

It was mostly my fault. I had tried to prepare Tracy over the phone, but she had been too excited to listen to me. And I hadn't prepared Mara for it at all. I had wanted to surprise her, but there are surprises and there are surprises. This was a little more than she was ready to handle.

From the moment it first dawned on me—staring at Mara's driver's license late at night in my motel room—that they were probably mother and daughter, I had worried about how they would get along. I suspected Tracy would be jealous of her beautiful daughter, and that Mara wouldn't fit the image, burned into Tracy's imagination over many years, of what her daughter was supposed to be like. And I feared Mara would find her mother impossibly trivial and self-centered.

When I returned to the hospital later that morning, the new relationship already seemed to have bogged down seriously. They both wore the look of strangers stuck in an elevator and forced to make conversation. Neither knew what to say to the other, or even how to behave in the other's presence.

I intervened as forcefully as I could. I spent the next couple of hours putting on a show, pacing the small hospital room and talking nonstop about almost anything that came into my head, drawing all the attention to me and giving them both a chance to overcome their self-consciousness.

I regaled Mara with anecdotes from my long and bumpy friendship with Tracy, then in turn regaled Tracy with an account of what had happened between Mara and myself, from her tying me to the bedpost, to me hitting her over the head with a saucepan, to our escape together from Far Island. I left the sex out of the stories on both sides, of course, but I realized as I was talking that it was obvious to each that I had slept with both of them.

At one point I left the room to run an errand. When I returned I realized that they had been talking about me. They looked at me and smiled in a peculiar, knowing way. I guess I turned red, because they both burst out laughing. It was a profoundly intimate moment, and from that point on, the two women began to accept each other.

I hadn't intended it that way, but their mutual knowledge of me became the bridge over which they finally established a rapport.

A few hours later, in fact, they were in giddy spirits, talking and laughing and joking like a couple of teenage roommates. They discovered they had a thousand things to talk about, a thousand feelings to share.

I was just in their way, so I bowed out of the conversation and spent the rest of the afternoon wandering aimlessly about.

I was drunk with joy and pride at having brought them together. I felt as if I had found the missing piece to the world's rarest, most perfect treasure. And in the process I had rewarded all three of us immeasurably. All that, on top of the triumph of having just snatched Mara and the four videotapes from the jaws of defeat and death. Enough bliss for a lifetime. I really felt good about myself for a few hours.

After leaving Mara behind at the hospital in a shower of hugs and kisses, Tracy and I went out to dinner. She was full of ambitious plans. I had never seen her so excited. She said she felt her life was complete and whole for the first time. She spent four hundred dollars on dinner for the two of us at the most expensive restaurant in Bar Harbor, much of it going for the vintage champagnes, the only beverage Tracy was willing to drink to excess. Several times we phoned Mara at the hospital, waking her up to tell her how sorry we were she couldn't enjoy the revelry with us.

Shadows hung over our celebration, even so. The biggest was that of Andrew Carlson.

Tracy was sorry about his death, but she could not understand the depths of his cruelty—to have actually stolen her daughter from her.

I found myself taking Carlson's side. "It was complicated," I argued. "Twenty-seven years ago you were a poor teenager, unmarried and pregnant. You didn't want a child, you wanted a career. Carlson helped you solve your problem."

I told Tracy that I thought Carlson was probably in love with her, but because of his marriage, his age, his vulnerability to blackmail and his fear of her rejection, it was a love he dared neither declare nor pursue.

So he kept her daughter instead. And he loved her fiercely, doted on her. She became the central passion of his existence, the focus of all his love for the rest of his life.

"There was no chance," I said, "that when you decided you wanted to find her, Carlson would let either you or Mara know the truth. He couldn't undo the past, but he could bury it. And that's what he wanted to do."

Over a third bottle of champagne, we eventually agreed to forgive Carlson for his sins. Especially since he was no longer around to create any further complications.

I asked Tracy if she had told Mara who her real father was.

Tracy admitted she hadn't. "Mara has enough to cope with for one day," she said. "My God, imagine what must be going through her head? When we're a little more familiar and comfortable with one another, I'll tell her the rest."

"Who was her father?" I asked. "You never told me, either."

Tracy flung her fingers out in a gesture of dismissal. "It's not important."

"Not important?"

Tracy studied me across the white linen and the candles. Our waiter hovered nearby. He had made a big fuss over Tracy as soon as we sat down, and as a gesture of his continued devotion he seemed to have assigned himself exclusively to our table for the evening. He topped up our champagne glasses after every sip. I noticed that he had big ears.

Tracy picked up a napkin and dabbed some imaginary tears from her eyes. "It's been such an emotional day," she said, trying to divert me from the subject.

"Don't I deserve to know?" I persisted.

"Yes, I suppose you do."

I knew by the distressed expression on Tracy's face that the evening was about to be ruined.

"Grayson Steckler is her father."

I slumped in my chair and shut my eyes.

"The senator I told you about was real enough. We did have an affair. He just wasn't Mara's father. Over the years I had begun to pretend to myself that he was. It was so much more romantic that way. But the unfortunate truth is that Grayson is her father. He was a business associate of Andrew's then. I used to see him around a lot. Whenever he was in Paris, he stayed at Andrew's house. I never liked him much. I was afraid of him."

"How did he become her father, then?"

"He came to Paris once when Andrew was out of town. He had keys to the mansion, and he arrived unannounced one weekend when I was there alone. . . ." Tracy broke off the story and turned to her champagne. The waiter oozed over to fill her glass and gush over her role as Clavdia Chauchat in *The Magic Mountain*. This waiter was a real film buff.

Tracy thanked him with one of her seventy-millimeter smiles and sent him away for more champagne. "Isn't it nice he remembered that? I made that movie in Germany when I was twenty-four. *Der Zauberberg*, it was called in German."

"What did Steckler do? Rape you?"

Tracy settled her glass on the table and looked away. "They didn't call it that then."

"What did you call it?"

"He forced himself on me, put it that way. I could have screamed and fought, I suppose, but the end result would have been the same. It was easier—and safer—to give in and get it over with. I complained to Andrew later. He was upset. He promised me he would warn Grayson to stay away from me, but I don't know if he did or not. Anyway, at my insistence, he changed the locks. A few months later I moved into my own place."

"It was just that one time? You're sure it really was Steckler?"

"It was him. I wasn't sleeping with anyone else at the time. I never told him, of course. I didn't want any further involvement with him. Maybe that's another reason I was willing to give the baby up—give Mara up. God, she actually has a name of her own now, doesn't she? My Juliette."

There were times when Tracy infuriated me so deeply it was all I could do to keep from grabbing her by the neck and banging her head on the floor. This was one of those times.

"For Christ's sake, Tracy," I began, keeping my voice to a harsh whisper so the waiter couldn't hear, "you were in bed with Steckler just a few days ago! The same bastard who raped you and knocked you up years ago! If you didn't like him then, why the hell are you fucking him now? There's something missing from this picture."

Tracy met my furious stare with cool, resigned eyes. "Someday, Johnny darling, you're going to realize that there are some secrets you don't want to know."

"That's it? That's all you're going to tell me?"

"That's right."

"You intend to go on sleeping with him? Assuming the son of a bitch ever gets off that island?"

"Of course not."

" 'Of course not,' " I mimicked angrily. "Why not?"

"I don't need to anymore."

Tracy refused to say anything further on the subject. She insisted it was no longer important. I finally gave up.

"I'm tired, Johnny. It's been a long day."

The waiter brought the check to me. Tracy took it, and paid with a credit card.

The waiter gave me a knowing little smirk.

35

DETOUR

The next morning Mara was released from the hospital. She wasn't able to support herself on crutches because of her broken arm, so we had to rent a wheelchair for her.

We located Grandmother at the Bar Harbor airport, where she ran an air charter service. She was about five feet tall, tanned, trim and ebullient, with a bone-crunching handshake. The web of fine lines around her bright blue eyes lent her the look of a woman in her early fifties who had spent too much time in the sun. In fact, she was seventy-two. She was known locally as Grandmother, she explained, because she had three daughters who had given birth to a total of fifteen children. She exuded an upbeat, straightforward charm that was totally disarming and captivating. She was the sort of individual who instantly made you feel happy to be alive and in her company.

Mara kissed her and thanked her profusely for saving our lives. As for me, I was reduced to a quivering emotional wreck for the second time in twenty-four hours. I hugged Grandmother hard, and blabbered out an incoherent stream of praise and thank-yous, while tears poured down my cheeks so copiously that I felt as if I had sprung a leak.

Grandmother patted me gently on the back. "My goodness, dear," she said in a worried voice. "Get a grip on yourself."

We chartered a plane from her on the spot, and insisted she fly us to Bangor in person.

We needed a twin-engine to accommodate the four of us, the wheelchair and our luggage. Grandmother, convinced that I had the makings of a first-rate pilot, persuaded me to sit up front with her for some further training. I humored her, but assured her that I was retired from flying forever.

The four of us had an emotional time. In Bangor we hugged and kissed Grandmother some more in farewell, and then, swearing we'd keep in touch on a regular basis, we left her and flew on to New York City.

We went first class, at Tracy's insistence. Mara sat on the aisle because of her leg, with Tracy beside her. They did all the talking. Some remembered excerpts:

Tracy, in her best bossy inflection: "You're moving in with me until your leg's better. Don't argue. I have a big, empty apartment. In fact, you ought to just move in permanently."

Mara, reasonable, but insistent: "I'm twenty-seven years old, Mother. I have my own apartment. I can take care of myself. Really."

Tracy, impatient: "I know how old you are, darling. That has nothing to do with it. I'm hiring a nurse and a physical therapist for you, and you're staying with me until your arm and leg are completely healed."

Mara, exasperated: "My God. I'll be fine in a week or two. Don't start running my life for me."

Tracy, hurt: "I'm just trying to be a responsible parent."

Mara: "I know. But you're babying me."

Tracy: "Don't be so cruel. Indulge me a little. I've missed out on twenty-seven years of babying."

Mara, brightly: "Okay. I'll make a deal with you. The first baby I have, I'll dump it in your lap and let you raise it."

Tracy, alarmed: "You're not pregnant, are you?"

Mara: "Mother! I'm making a joke."

Tracy, scolding: "Well, don't you dare. You're not going to make a grandmother out of me!"

Mara, amused: "Why not?"

Tracy, shocked: "Why not? My God, what would people say?"

Mara: "What people?"

Tracy: "What people? Who do you think? My public. Fans . . . people who see me all the time in the movies and on television."

Mara, innocent, deadpan: "Oh, those people. They'll say 'Doesn't Tracy Anderson look wonderfully young for a grandmother?' "

Then this, later:

Tracy: "As soon as we get to the city, we're going to do some serious clothes shopping. You're a beautiful girl and you need a much more sophisticated wardrobe. You look so common in those blue jeans. . . ."

Mara: "Woman, Mother. I'm a woman, not a girl. . . ."

And this:

Tracy: "I want you to see my dentist and hairstylist. You've got a front tooth that needs bonding immediately, and your hair has been seriously neglected. . . ."

Mara: "As soon as I can walk again, I'm going to run away."

In a single day they had progressed from uneasy strangers to bickering family. It was inevitable that they would butt heads, considering how strong-willed they both were. But I wasn't worried about that. Their relationship would be volatile, but it would endure. They wanted each other.

I was more worried about Steckler. I didn't think Mara should ever know that he was her father. She would resent Tracy deeply. I had already told Tracy as much. "Tell her she's Carlson's daughter," I said. "She'd appreciate that. That's what she grew up believing, so why change it? She loved him—and obviously he loved her. Nobody could have been more of a father to her than he was."

Tracy observed that my repeatedly articulated respect for the truth seemed to be wearing thin, but she promised to consider the idea seriously.

At La Guardia Airport Tracy wanted to call Oscar to come collect us in her limousine. Tracy hated taxis, particularly New

York City taxis, but I didn't think we should sit around the airport lounge for several hours, waiting for Oscar to find his way out to us. I persuaded her that we could take two taxis, one for the two of them, our luggage and Mara's wheelchair, and one for me. I had an extra stop to make, anyway, I said.

I wanted to get the blue flight bag with its precious cargo of videotapes safely tucked away in the safety deposit box of a midtown bank.

We made our way out to the cab stand. There was the usual rude bustle and shouting. I rolled Mara's wheelchair down the line away from the dispatcher, found a reasonably clean and new-looking cab and got Mara and Tracy into it. The driver not only spoke understandable English, he recognized Tracy. He immediately began knocking himself out to make them comfortable. Celebrityhood sometimes had its advantages.

"We're having dinner together," Tracy reminded me, standing at the back door. "We'll get Juanita to make her Guatemalan specialty."

"What the hell is that?" I asked.

"Darling, she's becoming a wonderful cook," Tracy insisted.

I leaned in and kissed Mara.

"And after dinner," Tracy said, very pointedly, "you're going straight home." She kissed me on the cheek, poked me hard in the stomach and then slid into the backseat beside Mara. I caught Mara's impish grin and winked at her. I closed the door and waved, and off they went.

I looked at the long line waiting at the cab stand and decided to go back inside the terminal and telephone Sam Marks for a situation report on my case. I found a bank of public telephones—one of those free-standing stalks with phones sprouting from its sides, separated by small panels arranged at shoulder height. You could get more privacy out of an opened newspaper. I grabbed a handset and fished in my pocket for a quarter.

Between the moment I released the coin into the slot and reached a finger up to begin dialing Sam's number, I became aware of a woman in a white kerchief.

She was standing out in the middle of the concourse, clutching two big suitcases, and looking around. She seemed uncertain of her destination. She was in her late thirties, and appeared, under her dowdy spring coat, to be thickset and muscular, like a female wrestler. She glanced over in my direction and then immediately looked away.

I felt as if every hair on my body had become a porcupine quill. Was it Helga?

What should I do?

She cast her eyes in my direction again, hesitated for a few seconds, then started walking toward me.

It required all my self-control to remain calm. I told myself that I could easily outrun her as long as she insisted on carrying those bulky suitcases. And if she intended to kill me in the same manner in which she had murdered Conover, she would need them. She depended on anonymity and surprise, not speed. I looked at them—a pair of depressingly innocent Samsonite-style green cases. Concealed in the bottom front edge of at least one of them was a spring-loaded needle, dipped in a fast-acting, fatal poison.

As long as I didn't let her get close to me, I told myself, I would be okay. My adrenal glands paid no attention to me. They were pumping full blast.

She was still headed straight toward me, still looking directly at me. I glanced around, and my panic intensified. I was trapped in a dead end. Behind me stood a concession stand; on my right, thick floor-to-ceiling plate-glass windows; on my left, a blank concrete-block wall. She had cornered me.

She was near enough now so that in order to get away from her I would have to risk dodging right past her.

I clutched the phone in my hand and stared at her, completely transfixed. I knew I should run, but I was afraid to move.

What would she do? Just brush past me, as she had done with Conover? Clip me in the leg with the front edge of one of those suitcases? I hung up the handset and turned so that I was facing her. I had some desperate idea of fending her off, kicking at the suitcases if she swung them too close, knocking them out of her hands.

She was barely ten feet away. She slowed her pace somewhat, but she was still barging directly at me. There was no possibility of getting past her now. I contemplated just lunging at her, bowling her over with a sudden push and running like hell.

Why was she looking at me like that?

She slowed to a gradual stop directly in front of me, blocking my path, the suitcases firmly in her hands. I raised my own hands instinctively, ready to ward off a blow. I had ceased breathing about a minute before.

"Excuse me, mister, do you know where the airport buses are?"

I gasped, then swallowed some air: "What?"

"I'm looking for the buses into the city. I just got here from Milwaukee. I've never been in New York before. My son was going to pick me up, but he got an emergency call. He's a resident. At Roosevelt Hospital. Have you heard of it? He told me to take a Carey bus. But all I see are taxis. They cost too much. Aren't there some buses here somewhere? My son said there were."

I let my hands fall to my sides. I felt faint. I leaned against the phone bank for support and nodded.

"Are you all right?" she inquired.

"I'm fine. Thanks."

She wrinkled her brow in concern. "You look a little peaked."

"No, I'm fine. Really. The buses are right over there. Go straight on past that newsstand and then bear to your right. You'll see the sign."

"Oh, thank you so much. I hope everybody in New York is as polite and helpful as you, young man."

"I'm sure they will be."

"Well, I've heard terrible stories," she said, shaking her head.

"Just rumors, madam. Have a nice stay."

I walked back out to the taxi stand, forgetting all about my phone call. I felt silly, but my knees were shaking with relief. What the hell, I thought, it *could* have been Helga.

The line at the cab stand was longer than ever. I didn't care. Chuckling to myself over my paranoia, I walked along the loading platform, looking to snare a cab that hadn't yet pulled into the pickup line.

A pair of hands grabbed me from behind, twisted my arms into a full nelson and pushed me quickly off the curb. Before I could yell, another pair of hands clapped over my mouth.

I was dragged and shoved between two parked taxis and into the opened rear doorway of a black limousine, double-parked alongside the cab line.

The hands released me and the door slammed closed. I pulled

myself up off the floor and onto the backseat, still clutching my blue flight bag. The heavily tinted windows cast the compartment in a kind of brown twilight. The visibility was further reduced by the asphyxiating haze of rough Balkan or Turkish tobacco. I blinked and coughed.

He was sitting on one of the jump seats, smoking a cigarette and studying me with a dispassionate gaze. He rapped his knuckles on the glass partition and the limousine surged forward.

"I apologize for the rude treatment," he said. "But since you never bothered to call me for help, I have been forced to volunteer it. Again, I apologize."

It was Colonel Zimmer.

36

THE COLONEL'S OFFER

"What the hell do you think you're doing?" I yelled at the Israeli. "Stop the car and let me out."

Zimmer shook his head morosely. "Don't complain so much. I'm saving your life. Just sit still and be quiet for a moment. I'll explain."

"Where are we going?"

Zimmer didn't reply.

"Take me into Manhattan," I demanded. "Park Avenue and Forty-sixth Street. I'm going to my bank. You can explain everything on the way."

The colonel sighed and crushed out his cigarette in the ashtray by his arm with a vigorous twist. Some of the still-burning ashes fell on the limo's carpet. He opened the window and threw the butt out.

"Leave the window down," I pleaded. "I'm choking in here."

Zimmer pressed the control and raised the window back to within an inch of the top.

"What makes you think you're saving my life?"

The Mossad agent picked up a folded copy of *The New York Times* from the floor beside him and handed it to me. "Have you seen today's paper?"

I opened the *Times* and scanned the headlines. It was in a single column, top left—the second lead:

PRESIDENT PICKS NEW CIA DIRECTOR

Grayson Steckler Succeeds Carlson As Agency's Head

WASHINGTON, May 23 — President Bland today announced his choice to replace the former Director of the CIA, Andrew Carlson, who died of a heart attack last week in Manhattan's New York Hospital. Bland's new appointee, Grayson Steckler, a partner in the New York firm of Steckler and Wycoff, is well known in Republican circles, where . . .

I didn't bother to read the rest. I folded the paper and placed it on the seat beside me. Zimmer was examining me in that peculiarly familiar manner of his, trying to read the thoughts behind my eyes. It was hard to disguise the shock I felt. Steckler had not only gotten off that damned island in record time, he had succeeded to the last job on earth I wanted him to have.

I affected as much lack of interest as my modest acting talents permitted. "So?" I said.

The colonel laughed. "So? So he will kill you. What do you think?"

"Why?"

"You know the answer."

"I do?"

"Of course. You have important documents that he believes belong exclusively to him."

"All I have is what I need to get the government off my ass. That's not very much. It's certainly no threat to him."

"He feels differently. He has already sent out assassins to kill you."

I thought of the lady from Milwaukee I had just mistaken for the infamous Helga. "I don't believe it."

"If I let you off in Manhattan right now, you wouldn't survive until morning. I promise you. Do you want to test me, or will you take my word for it?"

"What the hell am I supposed to do?"

"Leave the country. Now."

I took a deep breath of the smoke-filled air. "I don't want to leave the country." I coughed.

Zimmer's expression remained grim. "You have no choice."

"I can't leave," I countered. "The government's holding my passport."

"A minor technicality. We can get you out. Tonight. On an El Al flight."

"To where?"

"Flight Zero-zero-two departs at four P.M. for Tel Aviv. I can arrange it. We will go together. You'll have protection all the way. At the other end, in Tel Aviv, we can also arrange a passport for you. And papers. ID. A whole new identity."

"That's crazy. Then what am I supposed to do?"

"Where you go and what you do will be your business."

"Why are you doing this big favor for me?"

"You remember that I told you you might someday be in a position to help us."

"I remember. So what?"

"So you are now in that position."

"How can I be?"

Zimmer lit another of his foul-smelling cigarettes and looked out the window. We were not heading into Manhattan. We were on the Grand Central Parkway, on the way to JFK.

"I haven't agreed to anything," I warned him. "Take me into Manhattan."

The colonel leaned toward me. "Listen, Brady. This is serious. I'm serious. If you need time to think about it, okay. We have some time. The flight doesn't leave for three hours. We'll talk in the El Al terminal. There's an office there we can use. It'll be secure."

"What are you trying to do? Turn me into a fugitive for the rest of my life? I'm facing a criminal trial. I'm out on half a million dollars' bond. I *can't* leave the country, even if I wanted to. The government would issue a fugitive warrant for my arrest."

Zimmer shook his head. "You don't see the big picture, Brady. It's life or death. Steckler is determined to kill you. Why don't you believe me?"

I didn't say anything. Zimmer was trying to stampede me into something. The Israeli smoked his cigarette. We sat in silence the rest of the way to the El Al terminal at JFK. I honestly didn't know whether to believe him or not. Steckler had everything he wanted. He wouldn't really even miss the documents from Carlson's bunker all that much, since he was now in a position to replace most of them. As long as he didn't know that I had those videotapes, what threat could he think I posed? Wouldn't he get enough satisfaction just out of letting me go to trial on espionage charges?

I didn't understand why Zimmer was so insistent on getting me out of the country. Was he helping me, or kidnaping me?

We went into the El Al section of the international building, the colonel leading the way, his two tough-looking associates behind me.

They took me behind the reservation desks into a little lounge reserved for pilots and flight attendants waiting to go on duty. A couple of people were in the room. Zimmer politely asked them to leave.

"Let's come to the point, Brady," he said, gesturing toward a chair. "Steckler knows you have Carlson's files. He can't tolerate that."

"I don't have his files," I lied.

"He thinks you do."

"How do you know what Steckler thinks?"

"I have talked to him. He told me."

"You talked to him?"

"He is now head of the CIA. I am a high-ranking officer in the Mossad. Our two agencies have been collaborating for a long time. Given the state of the world, we will no doubt continue to collaborate for a long time to come. I have to do business with him, don't you understand?"

"How does that apply to me? Did he send you to twist my arm?"

"No. Of course not. He knows nothing of this. I want to make a separate arrangement with you."

"What do you have in mind?"

"In exchange for our assistance, I ask you for Carlson's files. Let me alter that. I ask you only for a copy. You can keep a set for yourself."

"I don't have Carlson's files," I repeated.

Colonel Zimmer laughed good-naturedly. "But you do have the files. On videotapes. Probably in that flight bag you've been holding on to so tightly."

Zimmer enjoyed watching my face as I groped in my head for some explanation for his seemingly telepathic powers. Then it came to me. I had made one small slip, one seemingly insignificant indiscretion that was now going to become a terrible mistake.

"Frank Chin told you?"

"Yes. He was completely innocent of the value of what he was saying, of course. He told me only that you had asked him about using videotape to copy documents. He thought it was a novel idea. That's why he told me. But I knew immediately what you planned to do. And I see now that you have done it. Congratulations. It was novel indeed. Really quite ingenious. I think we might make use of the technique ourselves, in fact."

"I can't give you the documents, Colonel. It's completely out of the question."

"We will make copies of the tapes. That will be easy to do. Then you can have the originals back."

"First you want to turn me into a fugitive. Now you want me to commit treason against my country."

"Israel would never use the files against the United States. We may withhold information from each other, but we don't betray each other. We are allies, after all. We do have basic interests in common."

"You haven't seen the files," I said, and then I wished I hadn't. No point whetting his appetite further.

I was beginning to sweat. Zimmer had me captive. If I didn't agree to his plan, there wasn't much to prevent him from simply taking the tapes from me by force.

"Did you tell Steckler about the videotapes? Is that how he knows I have the files?"

Zimmer nodded somberly.

"Jesus Christ. Why did you tell him?"

Zimmer shrugged and looked out the window.

I found myself staring at the mass of scar tissue that used to be his right ear. Zimmer had sealed my fate. Of course Steckler would want to kill me now. And with Steckler after me, there was only one place I could go to for help: "You told him so he would stampede me in your direction?"

Zimmer displayed his gold molars in a broad grin. "I told you you'd make a good spy, Brady. You understand how people think. That's a valuable talent."

"Then I guess you'll make a duplicate set of tapes for Steckler, too."

Zimmer shrugged. "I promise you we won't do that."

"Why should I believe you?"

The colonel crushed out another cigarette in a nearby ashtray. "I may have to withdraw my compliment on your powers of understanding. Because we obviously would not want Steckler or the CIA or anybody else to know we have them."

"So you'd screw Steckler out of the tapes?"

"You can call it that. And get you away alive. Don't forget that."

"Won't he know what you've done?"

"I don't think so. We'll deal with it if we have to. Steckler understands the game."

I groped for some kind of compromise that might spring me from the colonel's trap. "I'll go this far," I offered. "I'll give you everything relevant to Israel's legitimate concerns. All the Arab stuff, all the Iranian stuff . . ."

Zimmer raised a hand to cut me off. "That doesn't work, Brady. It would take us too long to collect the material from you. And the results would be uncertain. You're going to have technical problems recovering readable documents from the tapes. You'll have to isolate and copy each frame. It will take time and sophisticated equipment. We can't wait for that. Besides, Israel's legitimate concerns, as you put it, can only be decided by Israel, not by you. Sorry. We need the whole thing."

"What if I refuse?"

Zimmer avoided a direct answer. "When I say we'll help you," he replied, "I want you to understand that we're prepared to go beyond just a passport and a new identity. We'll pay you money."

I pretended to be interested. "How much money?"

Zimmer pretended to think about it. "A million dollars."

"What if I ask for two million?"

Zimmer said nothing.

"How high will you go?"

"As high as you want . . . within reason."

"How about ten million?" I tried.

The colonel hesitated for a few moments. "That's pretty high. But I would say that it might be possible."

"Let me tell you something, Zimmer. The files are worth a hell of a lot more than ten million. Aside from the extraordinary information in them, they contain the numbers and passwords for dozens of blind bank accounts all over the place—Switzerland, Panama, the Bahamas—anywhere the banking laws are favorable. The totals are in the hundreds of millions of dollars."

Zimmer's brows shot up in surprise. "Well . . . if the money can be gotten out, we can make a deal to split it in some fashion."

"Split it?"

"Yes. So much for Israel. So much for you."

"And what if I still say no?"

With a low groan Zimmer stood up from the chair he had been sitting in, and began to pace the small room. "Brady. Listen to me. Whatever happens, you can't go back home. Not for a long time. It will not be safe for you. You must believe that. I know what you think. You think you're going to play hardball with your government—wave some files under their noses and say 'If you don't drop the spy charges against me and leave me alone I'll expose this, and this, and this . . .' "

The colonel lit a cigarette and threw the match on the floor. "It won't work that way," he continued. "Because Steckler will never let you get that far. He'll go to the president if he has to, tell him the kind of national-security risk you really pose. If you had just a few sensitive secrets that could embarrass them, then yes, you might be able to make a deal. But you have everything. Everything! You have the king's gold. You have his crown and scepter—the artifacts with which he governs, the symbols of his authority, of his power. From their point of view you put the sovereignty of the government of the United States in jeopardy. They can't permit that. It's a matter of national self-defense. You may have intended only to get back at Steckler, to expose the existence of the Night Watch, but now you possess the potential for far more destructive acts. You are now as big a threat to the country's stability as Carlson ever was. They won't let you live. Whether they recover the tapes from you is secondary. What they must stop you from doing is ever making use of them. Or even being in the position to threaten using them. Which is what you have in mind to do, of course."

Zimmer inhaled deeply from his cigarette and let the smoke trickle out the corners of his mouth in thin plumes. "You have the treasure, but ironically you will find that it is of absolutely no use to you. Because unlike Carlson, unlike Steckler—unlike a sovereign nation-state—you have no means for protecting yourself. You don't have an army, you don't have national borders behind which you can defend yourself from attack. You don't even have a personal bodyguard or a base of political power, like Carlson. Let's face it, if you stay, your position is hopeless. I'm your only way out of this. I don't care myself what you do with the tapes— I'll leave that to you. I'll be satisfied simply to have the copies. But I must have that much. I have a responsibility to my own government. The tapes contain material vital to our national security. You can understand that that must take precedence over any personal dealings with you."

"In other words, if I don't give you the tapes, you'll take them."

Zimmer shrugged. "I'm offering you a way out, Brady. A way to stay alive and also to keep the tapes. I'm offering to hide you, to give you reasonable security. That's the best I can do. And that's better than anyone else can do. But I can't make things perfect for you. Refuse it if you want, but if you do, I leave you to your fate. I won't take any responsibility—and I won't feel any responsibility—for what happens to you."

The colonel got up to leave. "So. Think it over. If you go with us, we'll have to put you through El Al security about an hour before the flight departs. That leaves you about an hour. Go take a walk, think about it. Just don't leave the terminal area. Steckler's hounds are waiting for you outside. Stay inside and we'll keep an eye on you—protect you. If you want to accept the offer, be back here in an hour."

With that ultimatum, Zimmer departed the room.

I walked down the long corridor from the El Al desks to the big, echoing lobby of the International Departures Building. It was thick with travelers and charged with the peculiar tense, subdued excitement that usually infests a busy international-airport lounge, a crucible of emotional stress if there ever was one.

Amid the rush of feet and the stationary islands of embracing couples and chattering relatives, I scanned the wide arena for evidence of Zimmer's "protection." I immediately spotted two of his men, one on each side of me, keeping a discreet distance, but hanging close enough to tackle me if I tried to make a run for it. The colonel's warning about Steckler's "hounds" was likely no more than bluff—a polite way of telling me not to try to get away. Zimmer was just trying to stay on the good side of me, so convinced was he that he had made me an offer I couldn't refuse.

What would Zimmer do if I gave him the tapes? Betray me, most likely. His loyalty was to Israel, not me. He had made that clear. And he and his government would have much more to gain by pointing Steckler in my direction than by protecting me. But first, of course, he had to separate me from the tapes.

I stopped at a pay phone and called Tracy's apartment. Tracy and Mara had come in and gone out again to do some shopping, her secretary, Dolores, said. I told her to tell them I had been delayed, and not to worry. I would see them shortly.

For a brief moment I considered calling Steckler. I would offer him a deal—the videotapes in exchange for dropping the charges against me. Then we would promise to leave each other alone. Forever.

I laughed out loud at my own lapse of common sense. Steckler would certainly agree. And then squash me like one of Zimmer's foul cigarette butts.

I had a lot to do in the next hour, I realized, if I was going to survive to anything approaching old age.

37

RUN TO NOWHERE

I stopped in a gift shop and bought four paperback books and a copy of *The New York Times*. One of Zimmer's men loitered in the mall just outside the store, watching me. At the cash register I asked the clerk if she stocked any blue plastic flight bags like the one I was carrying.

"Sure," she said. She pulled one out of a cabinet behind her and laid it on the counter. "It's got a slight tear," she said, holding up a corner of the strap to reveal the damaged area. "But it's the only blue one we have left. If you'd rather have a white one . . . ?"

I quickly put my hand on hers and pushed the strap back down on the counter. I didn't want Zimmer's men to see it. "No. This one is fine. Just put it in a shopping bag for me, would you?"

She gave me an odd, sidelong glance, then packed the case in a shopping bag and handed it to me. I slipped the books and the newspaper in with it, paid for everything with cash and went off to find a men's room. Zimmer's men followed.

Two of the stalls in the rest room were occupied. I locked myself in the empty stall between them, removed the flight bag I had just purchased from the shopping bag, opened it, and dumped the four paperback books inside. I heard someone come in. I zipped up the flight bag, wrote out my name and address on the tag, and draped the strap over my shoulder. The flight bag with the video-tapes inside I slipped into the shopping bag, which I tucked under my shoulder.

When I went out, one of Zimmer's men was combing his hair at a sink. He quickly shoved the comb back in his pocket and followed me out.

I walked down the concourse, studying the departure schedules of all the foreign airlines. Zimmer's man fell in about fifty feet behind me. I couldn't locate his partner.

I covered the full length of the concourse three times, window-shopping like a tourist with time to kill, then stopped at the Qantas ticket counter. Qantas had a flight for Sydney departing in three hours. And they had room. I charged a ticket on my Visa card. Economy class, one way.

"Luggage?" the ticket clerk asked. She was a thin blonde with a rich Aussie accent.

"Just this," I said, sliding the blue flight bag with the books in it up onto the counter.

She looked at it and then at me. "You can carry it aboard with you, sir, if you like."

"No thanks, I'd really rather check it."

Her forehead creased momentarily in puzzlement. "As you like, sir."

She ticketed the bag, dropped it onto the conveyor belt behind her and wished me a "g'day" and a pleasant flight.

I walked across the mall to a bar, sat down and ordered a beer. Zimmer's man took a seat at the far end.

His partner materialized almost instantly at the Qantas counter, and started grilling the blonde who had just sold me the ticket. I could see her shaking her head, indicating that whatever he was requesting, she wasn't going to go along with it. The Israeli began to get agitated. He ran off for reinforcements. A few minutes later he returned with a small delegation, including several airport officials and a policeman. I could guess what he had told them. He had reason to believe there might be a bomb in that blue flight bag. That would get their cooperation.

Several other ticket agents appeared from behind the counter. Someone stopped the luggage conveyor belt. There was a heated discussion. The senior ticket agent swung open a panel in the counter and let the Israeli, the policeman and the officials in behind the counter.

Afraid he was missing all the action, the colonel's man at the bar deserted me and dashed across the mall to join the scene behind the Qantas counter.

I gulped down the beer and returned to the gift shop. This time I bought a canvas suitcase more or less similar to the one I had purchased in Bar Harbor; Tracy had taken that one home in her limousine. Further down the mall, I went into the small drugstore I had noticed earlier. It sold new videocassettes. I bought four.

Back in the men's room again, I transferred my precious videocassettes to the suitcase, bulked the rest of the interior out with crumpled pages from the *Times*, zipped it up and filled out my name and address on the tag. I unwrapped the four blank cassettes, dumped them into my blue flight bag and slung it back on my shoulder.

Out in the concourse this time, no one was following me. I stopped at the Aeroméxico counter and purchased a ticket on a flight to Mexico City scheduled to depart in one hour. I checked the canvas suitcase with my videotapes onto the flight.

The clerk ticketed it. I made her show me the stub, to be absolutely certain the numbers matched the one in my hand. I watched as the suitcase rode the conveyor belt through the little opening with the strips of rubber hanging down and disappeared from my sight. God forgive them—and me—if they misplaced that bag, I thought.

I shouldered my blue flight bag, now containing four blank videocassettes, and headed back to the El Al crew's waiting lounge.

The colonel burst into the lounge a few minutes behind me. "What are you trying to do?" he demanded. He was red-faced and furious. It was the first time I had seen him lose his composure. "Your idea of a practical joke?"

"Just testing your intentions," I said. "Now I know what they are. No matter what I do, you're going to take those tapes."

Zimmer nodded. "Good. Then you are smart enough to accept my offer."

"I want a different deal."

"What are you talking about?"

"Asylum and money won't do me any good. I'm an American. My life is here. I don't intend to spend the rest of it on a remote ranch in Paraguay, like some Nazi fugitive, waiting for Steckler's men to find me."

"What do you want, then?"

"Kill Steckler. Kill him and then you get the tapes."

Zimmer laughed.

"The tapes are worth it," I persisted. "You know they are. And it's the only deal that will do me any good."

"You aren't really serious."

"I am serious."

"We can't do it."

"Why not? Moral scruples? Faintheartedness? You kidnapped Eichmann, you rescued a planeload of people at Entebbe airport, you tracked down and killed the terrorists of the Munich Olympics. You stole enough enriched uranium from the U.S. to start your own nuclear-weapons program. I could go on. The Mossad can do it if it's worth it. And this is worth it."

Zimmer shook his head.

"There's more than me at stake here," I said. "You're forgetting Mara Carlson. Her life is not safe either, as long as Steckler's in a position of power."

"He won't bother with her."

"Of course he will. He's already bothered with her. She'll be the first one he'll go to when he can't find me."

The colonel gave me his long, appraising stare again.

"I mean it," I said.

"You just thought of it," he replied. "A spur-of-the-moment thought. It's no good."

"It's damned good. It's excellent, in fact. The more I think about it, the better I like it: Steckler for the videotapes."

"Suppose I have to turn you down?" Zimmer said. "Then what will you do?"

"Not your concern. I'll take my chances playing hardball with the U.S. government. If you won't get rid of Steckler for the tapes, maybe they will."

"I want the tapes first," he demanded. He no longer pretended to be friendly.

"Fuck you," I replied genially. "I'll get on the plane, but you don't get the tapes until Steckler is dead—and you can prove it to me."

"Even if we were to agree, it would take weeks to mount such an operation."

"I can wait."

"Excuse me," Zimmer said. He turned and left the room.

I sat down, feeling more pleased with myself every second.

Zimmer returned in a few minutes. Too few, I thought, to have conferred seriously with any superiors. "Very well," he said. "We've decided it's worth it. You have a deal. No money, no passport, no papers. Just Steckler in exchange for all the video-tapes. For us to keep. No copies for you."

I refused. "No. I keep the originals. You get a copy."

Zimmer considered this. "Okay. Let me see them, then."

"What do you mean?"

"Open the bag and let me see them. I don't trust you. Let me see that you actually have the videotapes."

I opened the bag and held up the cassettes. "One, two, three, four. That's all there are. Satisfied?"

Zimmer nodded curtly. I stacked the cassettes back inside the bag, zipped it up and followed him to the departure lounge.

El Al is famous for its boarding security checks. No terrorist has ever hijacked one of their planes, because the airline scrutinizes every individual and piece of luggage with great care. And does it several times.

Two airline security agents opened my flight bag and examined the videocassettes carefully. A long interrogation ensued. What was on these tapes? they demanded. Why did I not have any other luggage? The whole thing seemed ridiculous to me. If Zimmer was pulling strings to get me on the flight, why the hell were they subjecting me to this? Was it a matter of rigid adherence to their security regulations? Or was there a communication breakdown? It even looked for a while as if they weren't going to let me on board. One official kept telling me—and everyone else within earshot—that any of the cassettes could easily be a bomb.

Finally Zimmer intervened. He identified himself to the chief security agent and told him to just put the bag through the X-ray machine and let me go. He'd take full responsibility for any rules that were broken in the process.

I put the flight bag on the little moving belt and watched it disappear into the X-ray device. Five seconds later it trundled out the other end. I picked it up and slung the strap back over my shoulder.

We still had half an hour to go before we would be allowed aboard the plane, so all passengers were sent back to wait in the departure lounge.

As I walked back, with the colonel breathing on my neck behind me, I noticed that the strap of my flight bag no longer had that little tear in it.

There were two possibilities: Either the strap had miraculously mended itself or I was carrying a different flight bag from the one I had put into the X-ray machine.

I had to admire Zimmer. The son of a bitch was really very clever. He had arranged his own switch. He had somehow rigged the machine to stop my bag and disgorge a look-alike he had had made up and stuck in there in advance, after getting a good look at my bag and the number of videotapes inside.

It was very hard to keep a step ahead of this guy. And if I hung around very much longer, I would soon be one step behind. I sat down in the lounge. Zimmer sat beside me. We weren't talking to each other anymore.

I unzipped the bag and looked inside. Zimmer watched me out of the corners of his eyes. There were four videocassettes—the same brand as the ones I had just purchased.

I began to wonder. Should I accuse him of the switch or pretend to be taken in? Did they have a VCR somewhere nearby with a freeze-frame control on it? Were they slipping in the first of the blank cassettes at this very moment? I had to assume they were.

I checked my watch. The minutes crept by with glacial slowness.

One of the colonel's men appeared and said something to him

in a low voice. It was in Hebrew, so I didn't understand it, but I didn't need to. I could read his expression. He was telling him that the four cassettes were blanks. Zimmer said something in a sharp tone of voice. The aide shook his head. Zimmer barked at him, reprimanding him for something.

Zimmer turned and glared at me with a ferociously accusing frown. It began to dawn on me what was going on. They were wondering whether they had fucked up or whether I had somehow tricked them again and reswitched the bags.

They were thinking that the tapes were blank because they had taken back their own planted bag by mistake, instead of mine. The bags were identical, after all, except for the tiny tear in the strap, and they had obviously not noticed that. There was no way they could know that the cassettes in both of them were blank.

So they thought I still had the genuine cassettes.

"You don't intend to honor your part of this deal," I said.

Zimmer didn't reply. He didn't even look at me. For the first time, he was beginning to get rattled. He now knew I wasn't going to cooperate. That left him one option. He was going to take the tapes from me by force. And probably very soon.

"I'm going to the bathroom," I said.

The colonel glanced over at me, then pointed to a rest room across the lounge area. I nodded.

I walked over to the rest room, followed by his same two agents, shut myself in a stall and waited. I let ten minutes pass.

The announcement came over the speaker in the rest-room ceiling. "All passengers on El Al Flight Zero-zero-two, please proceed to the boarding area." I stayed put. Zimmer came in.

"Brady," he called. "It's time to go."

"Give me another minute," I said.

"What's the problem?"

"Upset stomach."

"The plane is boarding. Hurry up."

I waited another five minutes, then came out of the rest room. Zimmer was pacing back and forth in front of the door. His two men were standing nearby.

"Let's go," he barked.

We walked across the lounge to the boarding gate. The airline personnel were checking boarding passes and putting each passenger through yet another time-consuming security check. The colonel was burning with impatience. He took me directly to the front of the line, shoved his credentials in front of one of the security people and demanded that we be let on board at once.

The security guard had a little problem with this and called the chief of security over to ask his advice.

I turned and ran.

I waited until I was well out on the main concourse before I looked back. Four men, including Zimmer, were chasing me.

I dashed up the steps and ran along the mezzanine level. My pursuers were obviously fit. They were gaining on me rapidly, except for Zimmer, who smoked too much.

I ducked into a restaurant, burst past the maître d' and headed toward a door at the back, next to the bar.

I pushed through the door and found myself standing in a small kitchen. Two cooks were talking. It was mid-afternoon, and the kitchen wasn't busy. One cook was leaning against a counter, the other was standing by a stove, lazily stirring a big pot of spaghetti sauce.

This was far enough, I decided. I ran to a corner by the glass-washing machine and stopped. They looked up.

The swinging door whooshed open and three Israelis came storming through.

I raised my hands in surrender. The three crowded around me. Zimmer came puffing along behind. I was sure now that I had removed any doubt from their minds that I was carrying the genuine tapes.

"Okay," I said. "Just don't try to take this bag from me again. We made a deal."

"Okay, okay," Zimmer rasped. He was badly out of breath and in a furious mood.

I stepped out from the corner by the racks of glasses. The two cooks were still standing by the stove, mouths open, watching the drama. The colonel waved his hands to indicate to them that nothing was wrong. He apologized for the intrusion. They continued to stare.

Now was better than never. I zipped open the bag, tipped it upside-down over the boiling pot of spaghetti sauce and gave it a hard shake. The four cassettes tumbled into the sauce.

The cooks bellowed in unison.

One of the Israelis grabbed the empty flight bag and wrenched it from my hands. Another one plunged a hand into the pot and then withdrew it, screaming.

Zimmer had the most presence of mind. He grabbed the pot by its two side handles and tipped it onto the floor.

Twenty gallons of boiling red spaghetti sauce hissed across the kitchen tiles. The four videocassettes floated along in it like little houses swept away in a lava flow.

Zimmer grabbed a towel, scooped the cassettes from the sauce and threw them up on the counter.

One of the Israelis shoved me against a wall, pushed his forearm against my throat and punched me in the stomach. I groaned and slid onto the floor, gasping for air.

A violent fracas erupted. The cooks went running out into the restaurant, screaming at about five octaves above middle C. A manager appeared seconds later at the door with a couple of waiters, but none of them dared come inside. I heard a female voice out in the restaurant yelling for someone to call the police.

The colonel took one look at the melted plastic covers of the cassettes and unleashed a volley of harsh syllables in Hebrew. It didn't take a biblical scholar to guess at their general meaning. Then, just as quickly as his fury had flared, he smothered it and turned his attention to the next problem—placating the outraged restaurant staff.

I pulled myself to my feet and started toward the door. I caught one last glimpse of him as I sneaked out. In the middle of the yelling voices and the mess and confusion, he gave me one last fleeting sample of that distant, hard look of his. I had beaten him, and he wasn't going to lose any sleep over it. He had done his best; now he'd cut his losses and go on to the next thing.

Zimmer would have no hard feelings. That was a luxury for the careless and the self-pitying. The colonel would simply put the matter behind him—and after a few days he would probably have no feelings about it at all.

I missed the flight to Mexico City.

I caught the next one, a few hours later, and arrived at Benito Juárez International Airport in the Mexican capital at one A.M. The terminal was almost empty.

I found my canvas suitcase very quickly. It was riding around and around all by itself on one of the baggage carousels, where it had been unloaded hours before.

I pulled the suitcase off, opened it, and felt the hard plastic cases of the four videotapes still safely tucked in among the crumpled pages of newspaper. I zipped it back up and took a taxi into the city.

I spent the night in the Del Prado Hotel, getting drunk on Mexican beer and watching the traffic on the Paseo de la Reforma from my sixth-floor window.

38

TRACY'S LAST FAVOR

Late the next evening I was back in my apartment in Manhattan. No one had broken in. Everything looked innocent, normal. I had unplugged my phone and answering machine, so there were no messages, good or bad, waiting for me. I showered and changed my clothes, feeling a humble pleasure at wearing my own again.

I called Tracy Anderson. I started to explain my disappearance, but Tracy immediately cut me off. "Darling," she cried, with an almost manic cheerfulness. "You really must come over at once."

She was using the voice that meant she was trying to conceal something from me. "What's the matter?" I demanded.

"Nothing's the *matter*, Johnny. But we have something very important to discuss. You must come over immediately."

I started to ask her about Mara, but she hung up.

It was just past eleven P.M. I hurried down the three blocks of Central Park West to her apartment in the Dakota, wondering what the hell she could be so exercised about that she didn't even care to hear what had happened to me during the past twenty-four hours.

I was afraid it concerned Mara.

Tracy greeted me at the door. She was wearing a black floor-length evening gown and pearls, and was heavily made up. A fragrant cloud of perfume and champagne enveloped me.

She grabbed my hand, kissed me quickly on the cheek and pulled me down the foyer toward the living room. She was holding me by the wrist, and squeezing it very hard, as if she were afraid I might try to get away.

I expected to see Mara come rolling out in her wheelchair. I saw something else instead. In the center of the living-room rug, in black tie and tuxedo, stood Grayson Steckler.

He had his hands in his pockets and was nonchalantly shifting his weight from sole to heel in his patent-leather pumps. Rarely had I seen a human being look more pleased with himself than Steckler did at that moment. He stuck his chin forward a bit and regarded me with a condescending grin.

"Well, well, Brady. How are you?"

Tracy released my wrist. I glared at her, astonished. "What the hell are you doing?"

Tracy wore a tight, enigmatic smile. She flashed her eyes brightly in my direction, but they focused on my forehead, not on me. She chose not to hear me. She fluffed her platinum tresses with the back of her hand. "Grayson took me to the opera," she said, airily. "*La Bohème*. My favorite."

Tracy hated the opera.

"We were having some champagne," Steckler said. "Join us, why don't you?"

I finally managed to get my mouth closed and the expression of abject confusion off my face. Tracy brought me a glass of champagne. I took it from her and stood there, holding it uncertainly. I felt as if I had been dropped into the middle of a drama without knowing my lines—or even what the play was about.

"Sit down," Steckler said. "Relax." He waved toward a sofa near him.

I walked over to a chair some distance from the sofa and sat in that. Steckler made himself comfortable on the sofa. His champagne glass was on the side table. He leaned over and recovered it.

Tracy had disappeared.

She would not have have betrayed me, I thought. Not intentionally. I had told her everything that happened on Far Island. She knew that Steckler had tortured Mara to get information from her. She knew I had destroyed the plane and killed Westerly. She knew we had left Steckler behind on the island after Mara had tried to shoot him. She knew everything except that I had copied all of Carlson's documents on videotapes.

So Steckler had lied to her, had persuaded or pressured her into this, just as Carlson had talked her into inviting me here before. Did she know that she had lured me into a trap? Or was I missing something?

"I must congratulate you," Steckler said, twisting the stem of his glass playfully between his fingers. "I understand you actually landed the plane at Bar Harbor yourself. As a pilot I can appreciate what was involved. Really an astonishing performance. You have every right to be quite proud of yourself."

There was no hint of irony in his tone. Unlike Carlson, Steckler was at home with small talk. I remembered our first meeting, and his long monologue on court tennis. He used small talk as a weapon, to put his quarry off guard, to lull him into a state of inattention.

Carlson had been a bull. He attacked you head-on. Nothing fancy, just an all-out charge. But Steckler was a cat, a tiger. He stalked you, played with you. Then ambushed you.

"I had almost as much of an adventure myself," he said, patting his bow tie with his fingers. "There was a rubber dinghy, left by my men. Took me hours to find the damned thing. Anyway, I rowed it over to Great Duck Island. Hell of a time I had. The seas got rough, and there was a nasty five-knot current I had to fight. Took me six hours of paddling. I made it, though." He flexed a forearm. "All that tennis paid off."

He grinned at his little joke, then became serious again. "I took Colonel Westerly with me, by the way. Gruesome business, hauling his carcass into that little rubber raft. But I thought he should get some kind of burial, even if it was only at sea."

Carlson had claimed Steckler was crazy. A psychopath, he had called him. Was he right? I began to suspect so. How could Steckler manage to be so convivial, so matter-of-fact? It chilled me. I kept swallowing, trying to catch my breath. I wondered if he had men outside in the hallway to cut off any possibility of my getting away. I hadn't noticed any, but if it was a trap, I wouldn't have.

Steckler watched me. I watched back. The expression on my face must have amused him, because he grinned.

"Well, enough about all that," he said. "Have you heard my good news? The president has appointed me to succeed Carlson at the CIA."

I nodded.

"And I'd like your help," he said.

I didn't reply. I heard the toilet flush in the bathroom off Tracy's bedroom.

"You really have a talent for this business, Brady," he said. "I'm very impressed with your resourcefulness. I mean that quite sincerely. Copying those documents on videotape was an inspired idea."

Steckler yawned. Was he tired, or just bored? People also yawn from tension. But Steckler didn't seem tense at all. He seemed smug. He was enjoying the role of magnanimous victor.

"You do realize, however, that you'll have to surrender them."

"I don't intend to." The words came out in a hoarse whisper. I coughed to clear my throat.

Steckler managed a gentle chuckle. "It's simply not possible for you to keep them. You should know that."

"I don't know that."

"You're an incredible security risk with those documents, Brady. You must know that."

"Does that make you uncomfortable?"

Steckler laughed. "No, not really. You see, I have the president on my side in this matter. He knows all about Carlson and the Night Watch."

"How did he find out?"

"I told him. I convinced him that Carlson had become a dangerous menace to his administration. Well, he didn't need much persuasion on that front. He already knew that. He realized that Carlson had to be quietly gotten out of the way."

"So you offered to do the job?"

"You're exactly right. I offered to do it."

"And as a reward you got Carlson's job."

"I suppose that's right, too. But it was the president's idea. I never pushed for it."

"And you'll continue the Night Watch."

Steckler ran a finger around inside his collar, as if suddenly uncomfortable. The statement seemed to have caught him by surprise. "Well, as a matter of fact, yes," he said. "The world being the sort of place it is these days, the Night Watch has become an indispensable secret arm of the national defense. It has to go on. The president understands this. He wants it to continue."

"If I give you the tapes, what do I get in return?"

Steckler was amused. "Get? You don't get anything."

"You won't drop the espionage charges against me?"

"That's a matter for the Justice Department to settle. It's not my affair."

"So there's no reason for me to give them up, then, is there?"

Steckler leaned forward, holding his glass between his hands and resting his elbows on his knees. "Oh, there certainly is. If you don't, you see, we'll kill you."

My throat felt tight and dry. I moistened it with some champagne. I tried to meet his gaze, but it was difficult. I heard the antique clock on the mantel ticking. The room seemed unusually stuffy. All the windows were closed. What the hell was Tracy doing?

Steckler leaned back. "Where are the tapes, by the way?"

"In a safety deposit box in a midtown bank."

Steckler nodded approvingly. "Very wise. You and I will go down there in the morning when the bank opens and retrieve them."

"How do you know I didn't make copies of those tapes? It's pretty easy to do."

Steckler's eyebrows rose. "Did you?"

I had said this only to defy Steckler, to show him that he couldn't intimidate me so easily. But of course he had already assumed I might make copies. And that meant it didn't really matter whether I gave him the tapes or not. My fate was preordained.

"No," I said. "There are no copies."

Steckler laughed easily. "How the hell will I be able to trust you on that, Brady?"

"I don't know."

"You ought to think of some way," Steckler replied.

"I'll try."

He looked away. "Your future could depend on it," he said.

At last Tracy came into the room. She walked up to the back of the sofa where Steckler was sitting and embraced him from behind, slipping her arms lovingly around his neck and stroking his chest with her hands. She avoided looking in my direction.

He craned his head around to gaze up at her, his rugged face creased in a foolishly pleased grin. He placed a hand over hers.

I was sick with despair. If Steckler were manipulating her, or forcing her to do something against her will, would she be acting like this?

She had told me that she despised him. Had she meant it? She had admitted he was Mara's father. And she had admitted sleeping with him lately. What did all that mean? Did she actually love the son-of-a-bitch? She was unpredictable, but she wasn't stupid.

I had known Tracy for a long time. I had always trusted my instincts about her. But if I were to trust them now, I would have to conclude that Tracy was manipulating Steckler.

How could that be?

Tracy leaned over him and whispered something in his ear. Her gown hung open to reveal her famous breasts, shaded provocatively by the long, perfect sweep of her blond hair. I actually felt aroused and jealous.

Tracy straightened up, tugged playfully at Steckler's earlobe and glanced across the room at me. I couldn't read her expression. She seemed to be smiling, but with her lips only. Her eyes were conveying something else.

She stepped back a short distance from the sofa, watching Steckler, as if she expected him to do something.

He did.

He dropped his glass of champagne and scrambled suddenly to his feet. He started toward me, his hand reaching inside his tuxedo for something—a gun, I thought. I tightened my grip on the arms of my chair, too terrified to move.

Steckler's face was congested with rage. His eyes looked on fire. He opened his mouth as if to bellow some awful curse.

No sound emerged. Instead he stuck his tongue out partway, like a panting dog.

He lunged toward me. I started to rise. I threw up an arm to ward him off. I expected his head to slam into my chest. Instead he stopped, clasped both hands to his stomach and slumped forward at the waist, as if someone had just punched him in the solar plexus.

Crouched apelike, he whirled around and staggered toward Tracy, who stood frozen by the entrance to the front hall, her hands raised protectively over her breasts. She jumped to one side to avoid him. He stumbled past her and lurched through the doorway into the hall.

I jumped up from my chair, wondering what the hell to do. Tracy stepped out into the hallway behind Steckler, so I followed her.

Steckler careened across the carpet like a clown on ice and lost the final vestiges of his balance in front of Jan Vaček's big, gloomy masterpiece, *Prussian Blue*. One hand shot out toward the canvas, searching in panic for something to break his fall.

Steckler's fist punched right through the painting.

Tracy gasped.

As he fell, his fingers caught the jagged edges around the hole he had made and tore the painting wide open from the center all the way to the bottom edge of the frame. The canvas parted with the comic sound of ripping pants.

Steckler landed hard on his side, rolled over onto his back and lay motionless, his hand sticking through the canvas and resting on the painting's frame at the bottom.

I looked at Tracy. Her face radiated an expression of thrilled triumph, like that of someone who has just dived off a hundred-foot cliff and emerged from the water unscathed.

She held her right hand toward me, palm inward. An antique gold ring with a large stone set in it glittered on her index finger.

"My last favor for Andrew," she said, catching her breath. Her voice was loud, amplified by adrenaline. "I was supposed to do it before. Days ago. *Weeks ago.* I needed courage. I couldn't find it."

"Jesus. He asked you to do this?"

Tracy clasped her hands together. They were trembling violently. "We had an agreement. Grayson for my daughter."

I glanced down at Steckler. His eyes were open and his wrist remained hooked through the painting. He seemed to be staring up at the destruction he had inflicted on the work, his features frozen in a permanent look of embarrassed astonishment.

"What was the stuff that killed him?"

Tracy shivered with disgust. "Something of Andrew's. I don't know the name of it. It stops the heart."

"So Carlson beat him, after all."

Tracy put her arms on my shoulders and pressed her head against my chest. I felt her fingers dig into me. "No. You did. You found Mara for me. I did it for you. *You* beat him."

"What do we do now?"

Tracy pulled her head back and smiled up at me. I saw tears in the corners of her eyes. "Call the police, darling. And act very surprised."

I slipped my arms around her and held her. She wept for a long time.

39

THE FINAL DISPOSITION
OF THE TAPES

During the summer I come to this park every day. I bring my lunch from a delicatessen on First Avenue and sit here on a bench overlooking the East River. It's a beautiful couple of acres of greenery on the north side of the U.N.'s General Secretariat building. The United Nations tends it and polices it vigorously. It's the only piece of nature left in Manhattan where you can sit or stroll without being pestered by bums and drug pushers or menaced by vandals and muggers.

I got into the habit of coming here during the weeks I spent in my attorney's office, answering questions put by the New York Police Department in its investigation into the death of Grayson Steckler, and helping Sam grapple with the problems of mounting a defense for my espionage trial.

That's all behind me now. The police are satisfied that Steckler died of a heart attack. Tracy's superb acting helped overcome the ambiguous results of an autopsy. As for the mysterious disappearance of Colonel Westerly, the attorney general's office of the State of Maine determined that he most likely died with six others in a plane crash off the Maine coast during May of last year.

The grand jury indicted me on three of the four espionage counts, but Sam was able to cast so much doubt on the authenticity of the classified documents forming the basis of El Cardozo's case against me that the U.S. Attorney's Office finally decided not to prosecute.

Andrew Carlson is still believed to have died at New York Hospital. In fact, Mara recently received an urn from the funeral home in Washington, D.C., that supposedly contains his ashes. The disappearance of Carlson's driver, Tony, and Squint and the other two men who acted as his personal bodyguards remains an unsolved mystery.

Tracy got her bail money back, and I had to shell out fifty thousand dollars to Sam's law firm. It wasn't my own money. It turns out that Mara was able to gain access to several of the Night Watch's foreign bank accounts and empty them out. Some had been set up under her signature, so it proved relatively easy. I think she came away with three and a half million dollars, altogether. She's still working on getting out more—there's something like half a billion squirreled away in dozens of banks—but there are difficulties.

She wanted to give me a million. I agreed to take only enough to cover my legal expenses. Since Andrew Carlson was the cause of them, that seemed fair. The rest of the money, as far as I'm concerned, belongs to her.

Mara and I are not lovers anymore. We're just friends now. Our relationship quickly became a harder struggle to maintain than either of us was willing to endure. The details aren't particularly interesting. We soon realized we just didn't have enough in common to survive the excitements of our first days together.

And there was the not insignificant matter of her mother, Tracy Anderson. Although neither of them ever raised the subject with me directly, it was clear that they were unhappy with the fact that I had slept with both of them. Mara was jealous of the past, Tracy of the future. Not much I could do about it.

So we all remain friends. Mara has dropped her graduate studies and become a militant environmentalist. Far Island, which she inherited from Andrew Carlson (who she still believes was her father), she's turned into a center for the study of environmental problems. The last time I saw her, she was dating an impossibly homely but brilliant young biologist involved in genetic research.

Tracy's new TV sitcom is an unexpected hit, and she's back in the limelight bigger and bolder—and more beautiful—than ever. She's been seeing this country gentleman lawyer who owns a horse farm outside Leesburg, Virginia. He plans to run for the U.S. Senate next year and wants to marry Tracy. Tracy hasn't made up her mind yet. I get a call from her every other night for my latest thinking on the subject. I'm advising her to stay single.

Meanwhile, Shelly Wells—she of the callipygian posterior and the tendency to go narcoleptic when excited—has admitted to the enjoyment of my company. We've been living together since last fall. I've been helping her finish up Tracy's long-delayed autobiography, and she's been helping me research my book. Tracy's advice to both of us is to get married, and since Shelly just discovered she's pregnant, we probably will.

My book is that same old book—a biography of the late director of the CIA, Andrew Carlson. With the director dead and the Night Watch out of business, it's become a much easier book to research. People are willing to talk again. And even if they weren't, I know far more now than I did when I first embarked on the project some two years ago.

The book will clear up a lot of mysteries, but I still haven't figured out how I'm going to describe in print Carlson's death and the related events that took place on Far Island and in Tracy's apartment.

I can't be completely truthful without exposing myself and Tracy Anderson to charges of murder. The only solution I can think of is to postpone publication until Tracy and I have both died. That may be a while. And I'll never get to read all the great reviews or spend the sub-rights income. So be it. I can't censor the most vital part of the story just because it happens to involve me. I didn't hold back anything the first time I wrote about Tracy and me, all those years ago in that infamous magazine article. And look what that did for me.

In a few minutes I expect to be joined by Colonel Wolf Zimmer.

He's retired from an active role in the Mossad (or so he claims) and is now part of the Israeli U.N. delegation. He's promised to let bygones be bygones and allow me to interview him for my book.

Along with my own lunch, I've brought the colonel a roast-beef sandwich with Russian dressing, an orange, and a bottle of seltzer water. My treat, I told him over the phone.

I've brought something else, too. I stopped off at the Bank of New York on Park and Forty-seventh and picked up the four videotapes I keep in a safety deposit box there.

I have them in the attaché case beside me.

Colonel Zimmer was right about them. No individual neither protected by a government nor in charge of his own standing army can possibly risk keeping them in his possession. They are lethal documents. I can't use them without exposing myself to arrest or assassination. Or both.

And ironically, the longer I risk holding them without using them, the less valuable they become. Secrets are not like gold. They're alive—organic. And with time they decay, rot, spoil, turn rancid.

I reproduced and transcribed a section of one tape just to test this. In the course of a year, I discovered, half the subjects in a dozen of the files had either lost their positions of power or been exposed for the very crimes and shortcomings detailed in the secret documents or they had died, naturally or otherwise. The documents containing their secrets had now, in effect, lost about fifty percent of their value.

In another ten years almost everything on the tapes will be worthless, reduced to warmed-over scandals and footnotes for historians. *Sic transit . . .*

There's another problem with the tapes. If the section I transcribed is representative, then the files are shot through with serious errors and contradictions. Classifying material as secret doesn't make it more reliable, but less, because the stuff rarely gets verified. This has always been the problem with secret files anywhere—whether in police states or in democracies. The files become accepted as fact by those few who have access to them, and the subjects of those files suffer—sometimes fatally.

"Facts," by themselves, are meaningless, in secret files or anywhere else. There are eyewitness accounts; there are documents, sworn statements, tape recordings, hearsay, rumors, assumptions, deductions, opinions and many other things. But there are no facts. There are just versions of events—pieces of evidence that can be analyzed, corroborated, pondered over, sifted through and finally assembled to provide some rough, provisional approximation of the truth.

Unreliable secret documents are like cheap pistols—they can hurt both the user and the victim. The rich possibilities they would seem to present to a muckraking journalist are largely an illusion. They are not the privileged inside view of the truth they at first appear to be. They're just another source, and, in many instances, not a very good one. If I were to pursue some potentially important story uncovered in these files, I would still have to do all the legwork I've always had to do. There are no shortcuts to getting at the truth.

Of course the files still have enormous potential for damage. But damage isn't what I want to do anymore.

Still, it will painful for me to part with them. Making off with them represents an achievement of which I remain very proud.

Since Colonel Zimmer is the only person alive who knows about the tapes, I've decided I can't resist telling him about the triple switch I pulled on him and his men last year. It's just been frustrating as hell not to be able to brag about it to anyone.

After we've talked and finished our sandwiches, I intend to show Zimmer the tapes, then walk up to the railing in front of our bench and toss them into the East River—just to see the expression on his face.

It's all the mileage I'm ever going to get out of them, I'm afraid. Here comes the colonel now. . . .